MW01173362

THE THIEF

AND THE

Painter

CANDICE CLARK

Content Warning

THIS BOOK CONTAINS DARK SUBJECT
MATTER THAT MAY BE TRIGGERING TO
SOME. IT IS INTENDED FOR MATURE
READERS ONLY. PLEASE REVIEW THE
LIST BELOW AND CONSIDER THESE
CAREFULLY BEFORE CONTINUING.
YOUR MENTAL HEALTH MATTERS.

MURDER (ON PAGE)
SEXUAL ASSAULT (ON PAGE) (NOT BETWEEN MC's)
CHILD ABUSE (ON PAGE)
DOMESTIC ABUSE (MENTIONED) (NOT BETWEEN MC's)
SOMNOPHILIA/DUB CON
STALKING
ANXIETY
DEPRESSION/THOUGHTS OF SUICIDE
ALCOHOL/PRESCRIPTION DRUG USE

Spotify Playlist

SLEEP TOKEN - ALKALINE
LOSTBOYCROW - POWERS
MOVEMENT - US
SLEEP TOKEN - GRANITE
MAX - LIGHTS DOWN LOW
SAM HUNT - MAKE YOU MISS ME
BAD OMENS - JUST PRETEND
KEVIN GARRETT - PULLING ME UNDER
BANKS - THIS IS WHAT IT FEELS LIKE
HAYDEN JAMES, FARR - LOST TO YOU
BAD OMENS - THE DEATH OF PEACE OF MIND
EDWIN MCCAIN - GHOSTS OF JACKSON SQUARE
BLACK ATASS - NIGHT AFTER NIGHT
SLEEP TOKEN - THE LOVE YOU WANT
YEARS & YEARS - WORSHIP
MILCK - DEVIL DEVIL
SLEEP TOKEN - SUGAR
WILLOW - WAIT A MINUTE
SLEEP TOKEN - GIVE
SLEEP TOKEN - JAWS
RED - LOST

https://spotify.link/mFmMoZlpGDb

"Fate lines are twisted with surprises."

There is a critical moment in this book when the main male character hears those words. Like him, I have to believe that it was fate that led me to the indie book community. Fate that led me to the many wonderful friends that believed in my ability to do this, even when I couldn't even fathom it myself. This book is for them as much as it is for me. Without them, these characters and the world they live in wouldn't exist. They would never have become real people to me, as I hope they'll become real people to you. So, thank you.

Thank you, Yvette.
Thank you, Lindy.
Thank you, Bridget.
Thank you, Paula.
Thank you, Julia.
Thank you, Ari.

And thank you to everyone else who boosted me up and supported me during this process. A process that's burned a good number of brain cells, but that's okay. I didn't have that many to begin with.

xoxo
Candice

"ART IS TO CONSOLE THOSE
WHO ARE BROKEN BY LIFE."

— Vincent van Gogh

"EVERYTHING HAS CHANGED
AND YET, I AM MORE ME
THAN I'VE EVER BEEN."

— Iain Thomas

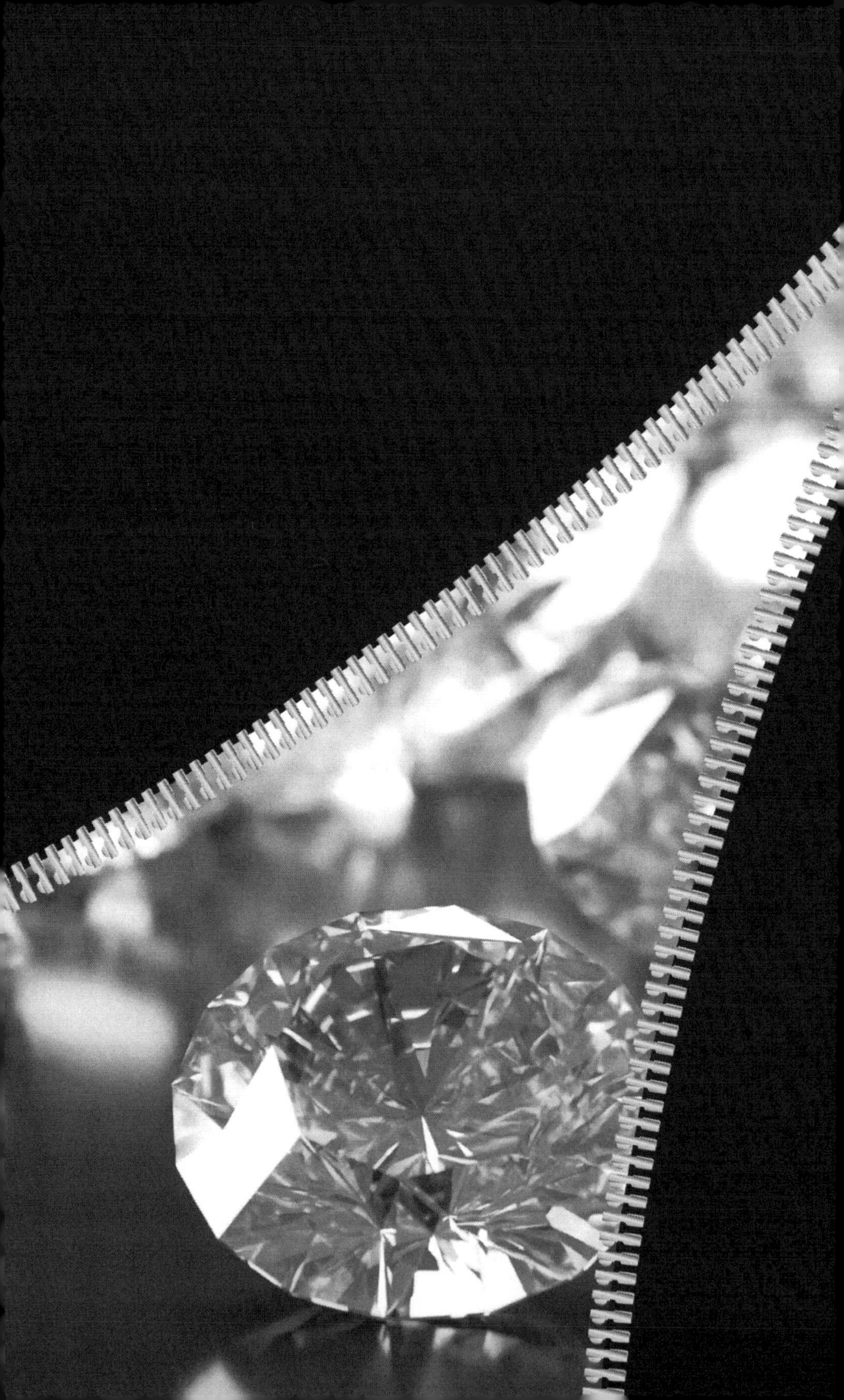

PROLOGUE

Merrick

13 YEARS OLD

People were so fucking gullible. A little bump, a slight graze, or an innocently distracting smile was all it took. In the hour I'd been wandering around The Battery, I'd already lifted three wallets. The sum total of cash I'd collected didn't amount to much; did no one carry cash anymore? All I'd gotten was a measly $27, but that was three or four meals for me, which was more than I'd had in the last week. It's not like I could count on my father to provide me with basic necessities like food, shelter, and clothing. Peter Stratford didn't do anything for anyone unless there was some benefit in it for him. Not even for his own son. The truth was, my father was a bum. And worse than that, a drunk. And when he drank, he got mean. Hell, he wasn't the nicest guy when he was sober, come to think of it. But at least when he was sober, I didn't have to choose between finding a place to hide out or becoming his punching bag for the night.

In my short 13 years of life, I'd had more injuries than I could count. What started as pushing and the occasional backhand had become bruises that could no longer be covered and repeated trips to the ER. Dad always had a cover story ready for the doctors, though. If there was one thing my father was good at, it was bullshitting people. He'd turn on the charm and showcase his smarmy grin, and they'd eat his shit up and probably ask for seconds. At least it worked with most people, especially the ladies. Unfortunately for the both of us, it hadn't worked so well with the teachers at my last school. After noticing a pattern of injuries, the teachers notified the district, who then contacted social services. Faster than it took to blink, I was pulled from public school, and he began "homeschooling". I use that term as loosely as possible. He'd basically found a homeschooling association that allowed him to pay a fee, turn in quarterly "reports" on my progress and call it a day. In actuality, he wasn't teaching me squat. And since I was no longer in school and getting free lunch, I got one meal a day, at best. Many days, I just went hungry.

At first, I hadn't been keen on turning to a life of petty theft. But considering, when not drunk off his ass, my father was the very definition of a smooth criminal, I guess it ran in the blood. God, I hoped that was all I'd inherited from the man. Well, that and my dark hair. With the inky black strands, I was a miniature version of my father. I'd once heard a woman compare him to a fallen angel. What a joke. More like the devil. Either way, considering my genetics, I guess it made perfect sense for me to be out here robbing people blind.

I'd been picking pockets and running petty scams since I was 10. Having smaller hands and nimble fingers often came in handy. Whether it was switching cards during a game of three-card monty or swiping a wallet from a loose back pocket, I had always had a penchant for taking things that didn't belong to me. Whenever I had the occasional flare-up of conscience, I just reminded myself that no money equaled no food. I did what I had to do to survive. Most of the time, I didn't feel guilty about it. My marks were almost always walking around in designer clothes, name-brand shoes, and flashing expensive-looking jewelry. So no, I didn't often feel bad. What I did feel was envy. Here I was, risking life and limb for scraps, and they were walking around with Rolexes on their wrists. I wasn't stupid enough to believe that running away from home would solve my problems, though. As much as I'd like to be free of my sorry excuse for a father, I knew I'd be worse off on the streets. There were far scarier things out there. A punch I could take, but some of the other things I'd witnessed in the darker alleyways of downtown Charleston, I couldn't. So, for now, I did the best I could to get by. But I swore to myself that one day, I'd have everything I deserved and more. Always more. Because once you'd had a taste of nothing, you could never accept less.

One day, I'd be someone to be envied, someone important. The minute I turned legal, I'd get as far away from Peter Stratford as possible, and I'd never look back. No ties, no emotional attachments. I'd be my own man, and I'd make a name for myself. As I watch a couple walk by, obviously coming from some glitzy event, the woman decked out in diamonds—a thought occurs to me. Yeah, I'd make a name for myself. Hell, maybe I'd make several.

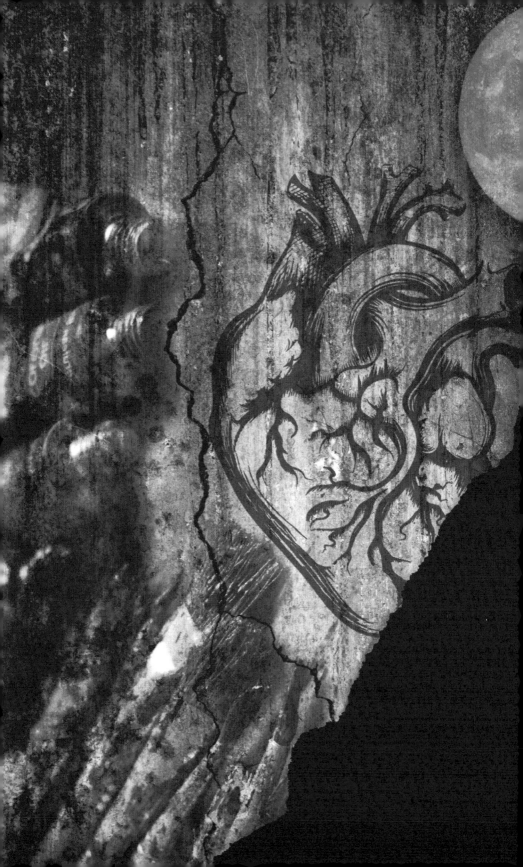

CHAPTER 1

Amelia

If rumors were to be believed, this entire city was haunted. That was typical of Southern towns as steeped in rich history and as covered in blood as Charleston, South Carolina. I didn't mind the ghosts, though. Over the years, they'd become companions to the shadows that followed me everywhere I went. From a young age, I'd heard and seen more than the average child, even when compared to other children raised within the upper crust of Charleston society. Having a mother with the reputation of being a black widow will do that to a kid. But, now, it seemed, as an adult, the sins of the mother were fated to become muses for the daughter.

My ghosts manifested themselves in the form of art. The sketches and paintings hung and stacked upon themselves within my studio, wouldn't be out of place on the walls of some dreary gothic castle. In reality, they most likely ended up the conversation piece of some stuffy party, where high-priced champagne and trysts in shadowy corners went hand in hand with cigar smoke and the trading of stock tips. I knew my paintings had been purchased by buyers from all over the world, but the darkness splashed across my canvases still lent to a reputation as somewhat of an oddball, even in the eccentric circles of the Southern upper class. While I could put on a ball gown and mingle with the best of society when the occasion called for it, I was honestly more at home in a cemetery or wandering around downtown Charleston long after the partygoers that usually littered the streets had gone to bed. For them, sunset was when the city really came alive. For me, I'd take those few precious hours after all the fun but before the sun came up, when everything settled to an eerie silence.

In truth, I'd spent most of my life in the dark. I knew that embracing the nightmares that flashed behind my eyes, then releasing them onto a tightly pulled piece of cloth, wasn't a healthy coping mechanism. My best friend, Siren, often told me that I needed therapy … or Jesus. I suppose I better start praying because my mother would never allow a shrink to get up close and personal with my demons, and it wasn't for fear of me saying something that might incriminate her. She just wouldn't be able to handle the embarrassment. The shame of having a daughter whose issues couldn't be quelled by several glasses of wine and a Xanax. You just didn't *do* therapy when your peers spent their days sipping sweet tea and blessing people's hearts and their nights sleeping with each other's husbands. This lifestyle often led to the complete and total nervous breakdown of what was once a belle with a life to be envied. One whose existence was now reduced to long "vacations" at the old family plantation in the country and whispers behind delicate hands that sported manicures to rival even the deadliest of monsters.

To avoid suffering a similar fate, I chose to channel my childhood traumas in a way that kept my mother placated and money in my pocket. My money. Not family money. I didn't want a dime of the fortune my mother had spent a lifetime amassing, first on her back, then on the dotted line of a life insurance policy. Or should she say *policies*? In my short 24 years, I'd been a Carrow, a Winston, a Prescott, a Michaelson, and a Stratford. Each stepfather came and went in the blink of an eye. Not via a divorce attorney, but in a very tasteful casket. Appearances had to be maintained, after all.

Husband number five seemed to be sticking, however. I wasn't sure if it was because he and my mother were a perfect match in both tastes and temperament, or if it was due to the fact that Peter Stratford had turned out to be a con artist of the highest caliber. I was sure my mother would rather be stuck in an unwanted marriage than admit that the man that she herself had conned into holy matrimony shortly into my teenage years had been conning her right back. Peter and my mother seemed to have been cut from the same cloth, albeit cloth with two very different price tags. My mother was a killer, dressed in silk and pearls. Peter was a con man and a violent drunk. But only behind closed doors, where he always made sure the bruises and scars could be easily hidden from the world, beneath the designer clothing my mother so preferred. Luckily for Suzanne Stratford, she had still been riding on the coattails of her last husband's will when she found out that her new husband was flat broke.

They were a match made in Hell. In fact, the only good thing that seemed to accompany stepfather number 5 was Merrick. *Merrick.* Just thinking about him made my heart stutter a little. When my mother took the plunge again shortly after my 15th birthday, I had expected to have to feign love for another aloof father figure. What I hadn't anticipated was for that father figure to be accompanied by a freshly turned 17-year-old son. I'd like to say that, at 17, Merrick had been your typical rebellious youth with more mouth than sense. But, even then, there were shadows in his eyes that told of dark deeds and barely healed wounds. It wasn't long before I learned the hard way that his stoic demeanor and tightly leashed rage were simply byproducts of his environment. At 17, Merrick had seemed to be on the cusp of something, whether great or terrible, I hadn't been sure. Now, at 26, he was one of Charleston's youngest entrepreneurs and philanthropists, though I believed that most of our social circle considered him a trust fund baby. To the outside world, a sophisticated and charismatic bachelor. They had no idea that his father had entered the marriage to my mother as part of a scam because he was broke. Even now, I had no idea how Merrick made his money. To me, he was a fountain of secrets and cold indifference. Which I guessed was only fair, considering I did my best to keep the terror that made up the darkest parts of my soul hidden from prying eyes. Even his.

Which explained why I was currently sitting alone in a cemetery at midnight. While that in itself wouldn't be out of the norm for me, the surrounding streets seemed unusually quiet tonight. It was a Friday after all, and Friday nights in Charleston, even at midnight, would usually be filled with raucous barely-legals stumbling down the streets after exiting some bar they'd managed to con their way into with a fake ID. Or I'd be hearing the crackling of a loudspeaker for one of the guided ghost tours coming to an end. But not tonight.

The weather was already sweltering, and it was only late April. But that too wasn't unusual for the South. I liked to make jokes that we lived in the prettiest part of the "armpit of the United States". My mother, however, didn't find that amusing. She would attempt to lecture me on "being a proper young lady". I was anything but proper. My outward appearance was a direct contrast to the trauma in my past and the art I created. Maybe it was *because* of those things that my wardrobe looked like a color factory explosion. I loved tie dye, neons, and jewel tones, the latter of which was my favorite because they tended to compliment my deep green eyes. My hair was a mass of auburn curls that leaned more towards strawberry blonde than the true copper red I wished I'd been born with. Nine times out of ten, you'd find them tossed up into a messy bun at the top of my head. Natural curls and Southern humidity did *not* mix. I also had a bad habit of accidentally painting my long locks when I wasn't paying attention. When I felt the urge to paint, nothing else around me existed. It was almost as if I'd entered a trance of sorts. All of my inner turmoil, stress, anxiety, and fear would pour out of me and onto the canvas. Whenever I finished a painting session, I almost felt ... purged. My soul, a tiny bit lighter and a little less black. When I wasn't actively painting, I was sketching. Siren often likened me to a monster, having crawled my way out of the muddy swamps because my fingertips were constantly stained black from the charcoal I favored. I'd usually just laugh those jokes off, though. It was easier than dredging up the fact that both Siren and I knew that monsters were real. We'd lived with them for years. I was probably one of the only people on the planet who knew that Siren had a shaded past all her own, and knew what lay underneath all those pretty tattoos on her back. Scars of the physical, mental, and emotional variety.

A text chime suddenly jolts me out of my inner musings, the noise ridiculously loud in the too-quiet night. I usually put my phone on silent when I visited the cemetery. I didn't like to disturb the dead, and while I didn't mind the ghosts, I also didn't need any more than the ones I carried with me every day.

Just as I reach into the pocket of my oversized linen overalls, the text sound chimes again. Cringing inwardly, I quickly silence the phone before looking down at the display. Speak of the devil, and she shall appear. At least electronically.

> Bitch, are you asleep?
Siren

> I know you're not asleep. I'm watching you right now. Jk. But seriously, I bet you're out, lurking around town. If you are, text me! I'm so bored!
Siren

Smiling, I shake my head ruefully. Siren was always bored. Of the two of us, she was definitely the more outgoing one. The extrovert to my introvert. While I was perfectly content to hole up in my studio, elbow-deep in paint, Siren was forever thinking about her next set of plans. I was sure it was a form of rebellion to combat years of suppression and abuse. How she'd kept that abuse hidden for so long, I still didn't know. We'd been best friends since childhood, from the day we'd met in second grade, when I'd been getting teased for my frizzy hair and in retaliation she'd convinced Tiffany Wilson that she was adopted, we'd been inseparable. Tiffany wasn't adopted, as far as I knew, but it didn't

11

take much to make an eight-year-old cry. Siren probably knew more about me than anyone. She knew the ins and outs of my personality, my favorite foods, my favorite hobbies. But she didn't know what made me tick. Because, despite how close we were, I feared that if I was to let her into my brain, she'd never make it out again. So, over the years, I'd told her the bare minimum. For her own protection and because she was already dealing with enough shit of her own. It was the parts of me she did know that made her able to predict that I wasn't currently in bed.

Hello opposite me. You're right, I'm not asleep. I'm at St. Philip's.

Me

Omfg, you're in the graveyard at night again? I swear, you're a member of the undead.

Siren

Sometimes it feels like it. Lol. And stop ragging me! It's peaceful here.

Me

You can't even sketch at this time of night! Come out with me. We can hit up Prohibition. Find some hotties and let them convince us to go back to their place. ;)

Siren

Prohibition will be closing in two hours. Besides, I'm getting ready to head home. I've got an early meeting with my agent.

Me

That wasn't a lie. I did, in fact, have a meeting with my agent. He'd called me to let me know that there was some issue with my latest painting. The majority of my art was held in a gallery in Downtown

Charleston. It was showcased there, available for sale to anyone who happened to wander into the gallery, but most of the pieces were also listed on my website. The gallery sales were handled by the broker there, and the website sales were handled by my agent. I would normally put him off. I wasn't big on the business end of the art world. If I was honest with myself, I hated selling my work. Nearly everything I painted felt like an extension of me, so when it came time to sell, it was almost as if I was giving away a part of myself. Buyers could speculate all they wanted as to the inspiration for my art, but only I knew the truth, and that was that the darkness that bled onto the canvas most of the time I sat down to paint were scenes from my nightmares. Except a lot of those nightmares weren't actually nightmares but memories pulled from the deep recesses of my mind. And almost all of those bad memories could be traced back to my mother. Even thinking about her now causes a knot of anxiety to form in the pit of my stomach. Despite the rumors surrounding my mother's previous marriages, some of which I had a disturbing amount of insight into, our relationship had always straddled the fine line between life and death without actually tipping over. Any time we were together, a threat hung heavy in the air. I wasn't sure what stopped her, especially knowing that I was privy to some of the darkest parts of her. I knew it wasn't love or even affection. My mother had always been detached and cold. How I turned out to have any semblance of empathy for others, I had no idea.

> Fiiiiine. Go make your millions. Just don't forget us little people when you move out of this shit hole town and become famous. 😵

Siren

> First of all, I'm sure I'll never be famous. Secondly, I don't wanna move out of this "shit hole" town, as you say. I like it here. It has...character.

Me

> You'll never be famous? Remind me again how much your last painting sold for?

Siren

She was goading me. I knew she was. This was a common bit between the two of us. I'd downplay my accomplishments, and she'd remind me how much talent I had and what I could do with it. Siren was the ultimate hype person. Which came in handy when you had a family that was constantly talking down their noses or shitting all over you. Outside of my mother, my stepfather was, well ... he was a bastard. Plain and simple. Then there was Merrick. Despite his demeanor of general irritation whenever I was around, he was still the closest thing I had to family. Which made the crush I'd harbored for him since I was 15 very inconvenient. In my mind, I knew we weren't related by blood, so the idea of something happening between us didn't skeeve me out. I may have, in fact, entertained a fantasy ... or 500 ... about what it might be like if Merrick ever let his iron control slip and saw me as a woman, not just his annoying little stepsister. But I wasn't a fool. Even without the barrier of our de facto familial relationship, Merrick absolutely refused to recognize the possibility that there was a single sexual bone in my body. If by some miracle of God, he ever did, the gossip mongers of the city would have a field day with two step-siblings fooling around with each other. I had a feeling a scandal like that would finally push my mother over that fine line. Bringing myself back to the present, I realize I haven't responded to Siren's last text.

> I don't know darling, I haven't a head for numbers. *imagine me saying that in the most posh British accent I can muster and waving my hand in the air like a Queen*
>
> **Me**

> A likely excuse! Although, that visual will stay with me for a long time. Imagine you, my little tie dyed corpse bride, being a member of the British upper class? God, I'm so glad you're not like one of those vapid airheads your Mother runs around with.
>
> **Siren**

The very idea of my mother "running around" with anyone was laughable. My mother and Siren had a love/hate relationship. As in, Siren loved to hate my mother. I was positive my mother returned the sentiment. Of course, she would never say it outright. She'd just make it glaringly obvious by her resting bitch face and the thinly veiled snide remarks that she wielded like daggers. Suzanne was anything, if not civilized, even with people she disliked. It made it easier for her to wield the knife if you trusted her enough to give her your back. Siren and I exchange a few more texts, not regarding my mother thank God, and then end our conversation with the promise of a girls night tomorrow night.

Exiting the cemetery, I walk the short distance back to my townhouse. I lived in downtown Charleston, and anyone would tell you that everything within downtown Charleston was within walking distance of everything else. Besides being a city full of rich history, it was also a college town. At any given moment, the streets were littered with students walking from here to there. Of course, I did have my own car, but there was just something about wandering the cobblestone streets, especially at night, that helped clear my head.

At 24, I lived on my own, so I wasn't beholden to anyone else's schedule. I ate when I wanted, slept when I wanted, and painted when I wanted. More often than not, the latter would have me neglecting the former. But that was the life of an artist. When the muses struck, you were compelled to see it through. Or, in my case, to purge. It was the selling of that art that allowed me to be able to afford my own home, car, and the lifestyle to come and go as I pleased. I was an independent woman. Despite the horrors I'd seen growing up, I tried my best not to let it affect my day to day. I tried to keep a positive outlook on life. Maybe that was because I'd seen firsthand how fragile that life was, or maybe, it was because I was determined to rebel against the idea that I'd inherited my mothers penchant for being a bitter old shrew. Whatever it was, it spurred me to be kind to everyone I met, regardless of social status.

Just as I begin dipping my toe into the pool of introspection, I realize I'm already standing in front of the wrought iron gate that surrounds my home. My townhouse sat smack dab in the middle of historical downtown. With its black fence wrapping all the way around the property and the landscaped yard full of greenery and flowers that seemed to have burst free overnight, my home was pretty enough to be featured on a postcard. In fact... it probably was. Every weekend, The Market would be teeming, with booths full of art and photography featuring picturesque Charleston homes just like mine. With its traditional white-painted siding and tall staircase leading up the front door, it was definitely worthy of being the focus of any tourist's camera. I took pride in my home, and I loved every square foot of space because it was *my space*. But nearly every one of my waking hours was spent in the little outbuilding adjacent to the house. My studio. My little jaunt in the cemetery, combined with the unexpected impending sense of doom that had set in at the call from my agent earlier, had me going straight inside and changing into an old t-shirt and shorts and heading right back out again. Regardless of what time I had to be up in the morning, I knew I'd spend the next several hours in my studio, releasing all the pent-up tension and nerves swirling inside me.

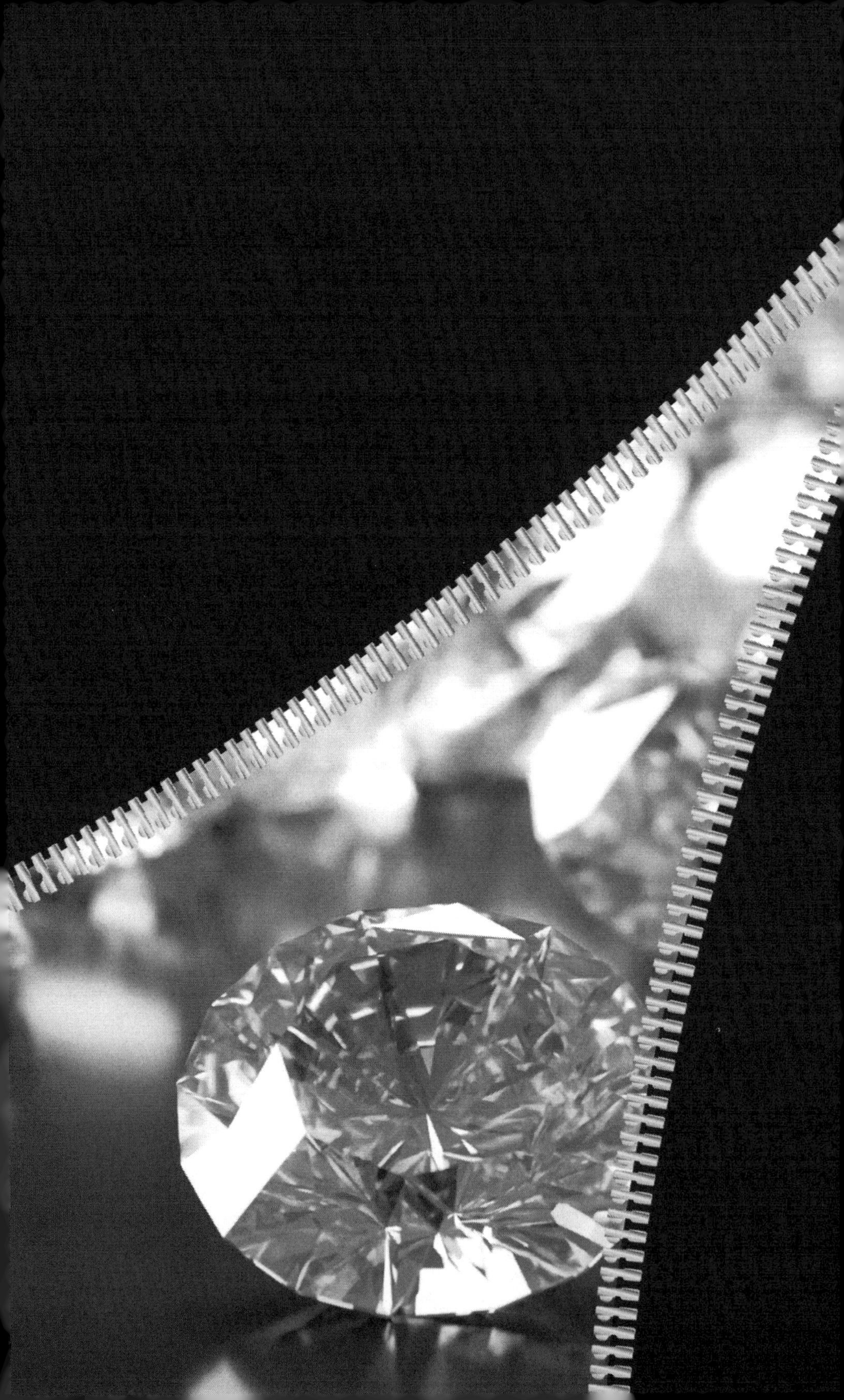

CHAPTER 2

Merrick

There was a fine sheen of sweat dotting my forehead, and I prayed that I'd be out of here before that sheen had the chance to turn into drops. The last thing I needed was to start sweating my ass off and leave behind forensic evidence that would allow the FBI to finally put a face to the name, *The Black Knight*. A moniker that had become synonymous with a number of high-profile thefts. Everything from priceless jewels to million-dollar paintings. According to reputation, there was nothing The Black Knight couldn't steal. *Oh how wrong they were.*

While it was true that almost any material possession, regardless of protection or security, could be mine, there was one thing that I'd *desperately* wanted for years that I'd yet to acquire. My own version of the Hope Diamond, or in this case, maybe emerald would be more accurate. Unfortunately, it wasn't so easy to steal something that lived and breathed. It was true that I frequently operated within the space of "morally gray", but what I craved was something that I knew I couldn't just take. I had to earn it.

Growing up, I'd spent countless days worrying about when I'd get my next meal. As a kid, out of necessity, I'd turned to petty crimes to sustain the pesky habit of wanting to eat three meals a day. Within a year, picking pockets had evolved into lifting watches and jewelry. I was good at it. It

19

only made sense, considering it was in my blood. You see, living under the thumb of a man like Peter Stratford, I'd never had anything of my own. Nothing that was really mine. Then, one day, right after my 17th birthday, I had an epiphany. I realized that in order to have the life I truly wanted, I would need to make myself into someone better. Someone with money, influence, and power. Because it was on that fateful day that I saw something that I knew I *had* to call my own. Something that I didn't wanna have to share with anyone. Something that was *mine*. That was the day I met Amelia Carrow.

At 15, she'd been a gangly teen with frizzy hair, a smile that was a little too bright, and eyes that held an ocean of secrets. Looking into those eyes had felt like drowning, and it was then that I'd realized air was overrated. In the beginning, it had been obsession at first sight. But over the years, when other emotions, volatile emotions, came into play, I finally got a true grasp on what I was feeling. Love. It had always been love; I just didn't recognize it for what it was. To mask my shock at having been struck dumb by a girl for the first time in my life, I'd come across a little too cold. A little too uninviting. Her too-bright smile had dimmed a fraction, and I'd felt like the biggest shit on the planet. I mean, it wasn't her fault that every time she looked at me, I felt like I'd been punched in the gut. Well, maybe it was, but I knew it wasn't intentional. Over time, I'd come to learn that Amelia was the most kindhearted person I'd ever met. Something else I wasn't used to.

Given her young age and the fact that I knew both of our parents would try to use the information of my infatuation as leverage in their own sick games, I vowed to myself then and there that I'd keep a tight leash on my emotions until I could figure out a way to get our parents out of the picture. Over the years, God knew I'd tried to contain my feelings. There may have been a time or two when the line I'd drawn in the sand had blurred a little, but I always found a way to talk myself back from it.

In the meantime, I'd honed my skills as a thief and amassed the wealth, power, and respect that I not only thought would make me worthy of her but that would allow me to protect her. Over the years, the jobs I'd taken on had become more dangerous and highly publicized, but with great risk came great reward. I was now a self-made millionaire. Most of the things I stole, I sold through my long-time fence, Deacon. Being similar in age, we'd developed a friendship. He was the only person who knew both my moniker and real name. Coming from his own humble beginnings and with a past riddled with tragedy, we'd bonded in a way that I didn't think was standard practice for a thief and their fence. Somehow, he'd become my best friend, and a lifeline I'd held onto more than once to keep myself afloat. However, at this present moment, I was contemplating Deacon's murder.

If it wasn't for a tip from one of his "sources", I wouldn't be in this Manhattan highrise, sweating my ass off, trying to crack this Gardall safe. It wasn't the safe itself that was causing my current level of perspiration, though. It was the fact that there was no fucking air conditioning in this apartment. In researching this job, I found out that the owners of this loft were what's referred to as "snowbirds". Meaning they spent half the year here and half the year somewhere else, depending on the weather in each location. And, of course, when they weren't staying here, the utilities were shut off, a fact that Deacon's source had conveniently forgotten to mention. So here I was, in a black turtleneck, ski cap, leather gloves, and pants, sweating my balls off. I swore, when I got out of here, I was gonna choke Deacon to death with my garrote. Well ... after he fenced what was inside this safe.

Three agonizing minutes that felt like hours later, and I was in. Opening the safe, I did a quick sweep of the contents. Lots of cash, several leather-bound books that appeared to be ledgers of some kind, and four red leather boxes. I wouldn't be touching the cash or the books. My sights were set on what was inside those boxes. Gently removing the first, I quickly opened it to reveal a stunning diamond choker with a massive teardrop ruby in the center. The second, third, and fourth boxes confirm that the entire Cartier set was present and accounted for. Slipping them into the sling bag attached to my back, I quietly close the safe before making my way out of the condo via a flight of service stairs at the end of the building's hallway. There were cameras in the hallway and stairwell, but Deacon had already hacked into the system and overridden them so that Rodney, the overnight security guard at the front desk, would see nothing out of the ordinary. The video would play on a loop until shift change in the morning. By the time they realized there was something wrong with the feed, I'd be long gone, and the jewels would be on the other side of the globe, in the hands of their new owner.

Contrary to popular belief, I hadn't chosen the moniker of The Black Knight. In fact, despite my younger self's plans, I made absolutely sure that no calling card of any kind was left behind when I targeted a mark. It made it harder to compile a list of charges if the police couldn't link any of your crimes together. Regardless, I'd been given the nickname, and a fair number of notorious thefts had been laid at my doorstep, garnering me a reputation in both the underworld of criminals I had the misfortune of dealing with as well as in the eyes of the law. It didn't bother me. I was sure there were far worse things the media could've dubbed me. At least this name lent to an air of mystery and danger, which, of course, just ratcheted up my ego.

As a kid, I'd been a bruised, half-starved, miserable little prick. As a teenager, I'd been quick to temper and rebellious to a fault. Now, as an adult, I was alternating ice and fire, encased in armor. Dual sides of my personality, both of which I needed in order to run in the higher circles of Charleston society. As much as I hated having to fake civility and rub shoulders with the same snobs that had once turned their backs on the kid version of me begging on the streets, I couldn't wait to get back to the city. I wanted to see Amelia. I might be in a different state, but I always knew what she was up to at any given time. I had eyes and ears everywhere. Thanks to those eyes and ears, I knew Amelia had an early morning meeting with her agent tomorrow. There was no way I'd be missing that. The guy was a sleaze. Oh sure, to outward appearances, he seemed to be the epitome of sophistication. Smooth and charming. But on the few occasions I'd had the misfortune of being in the same room with him, I didn't miss how his eyes roved over Amelia's form despite the fact that the man was married with two kids. Knowing that, it wouldn't surprise Deacon one bit to find out that I'd opted to fly back home tonight instead of tomorrow, as originally planned. Don't get me wrong, Amelia could handle herself. She was strong. Stronger than any other woman I'd ever met. But from the first moment I'd laid eyes on her, her demons had become my demons, even if she didn't know it. And while I'd never be of the white variety, this knight wouldn't let her fight all her battles alone.

After exiting the building and blending in with the pedestrians littering the busy New York streets, I pull out my phone and hit Deacon's name in my contact list. He answers on the 4th ring. Because he's busy? No. Because he knows I hate waiting, and he wants to be an asshole. So, of course, I tell him that the moment he picks up.

"Yo bro, any hitches in the program?" Deacon says by way of greeting.

"You're an asshole," I reply without preamble.

I can hear the smile tugging at his lips when he answers. "Now, is that any way to talk to your bestie? I thought we were still in the honeymoon phase of our relationship, and you were supposed to be kissing my ass?"

"I've known you for 11 years. The magic is gone. In fact, I'm seriously considering filing for a divorce. Whether I take you for alimony is gonna hinge on your answer to my next question", I say in a biting tone.

The silence hangs heavy in the air, and I give him a minute to squirm before I continue.

Deadly as a rattlesnake, I ask, "Did you or did you not know that there was no fucking air conditioning in that apartment?"

Deacon bursts out laughing, breaking the tension I'd worked so hard to build. "Sorry, dude! I just assumed that since you almost always have boiling lava simmering in your veins, you wouldn't notice if the room was a little warm."

"Oh, don't worry. I'm gonna have an outlet to spew all that boiling lava onto in about an hour," I reply through clenched teeth.

"I don't know why you're so upset. I've seen you work in far less comfortable situations. Remember the time you had to break into that palace vault owned by the Sheik of … fuck, I can't even remember … and steal that ring he'd given his late wife when they got married? You know, before she realized that he was a piece of shit."

I did remember that job. That was one of my most publicized heists. The wife that Deacon was referencing had been one of Hollywood's top leading ladies at the time. The Sheik had come in, swept her off her feet, and she'd basically given up everything to be with him. Then he'd made her life a living Hell. The ring in question had been her engagement ring, which had been splashed on the cover of every magazine and newspaper in the world at the time. It had all been for show, of course. Behind closed doors, he was evil incarnate. She'd later committed suicide. I wasn't sad to see the piece go when Deacon had sold it off. Jewels like that had a way of carrying ghosts with them.

Totally changing the subject without answering, I say, "I'll meet you at the designated location for the handoff in one hour."

Agreeing, we disconnect. An hour later, I make the drop, handing the jewels over to Deacon while making sure to give him an in-person ass-chewing over the air conditioning situation. During the time that all this is taking place, my private jet is being fueled up and ready for take-off, with me having called ahead to tell them to be ready within the hour. I'd need to shower and get a few hours of sleep before showing up unexpectedly at the gallery where the majority of Amelia's work was showcased and where she'd most likely be meeting Mr. I'm Eyefucking You At All Times. She wouldn't thank me for the unexpected appearance, but I didn't give a shit. Someone had to look out for her, and I'd be damned if I let that someone be anyone other than me.

During the roughly two-hour flight back to Charleston, I couldn't keep my mind from wandering back to the day my life was changed irrevocably and the world had tipped on its axis. To this day, and to my constant surprise, it still hasn't righted itself. It didn't bother me, though. I just learned to look at everything from a different perspective.

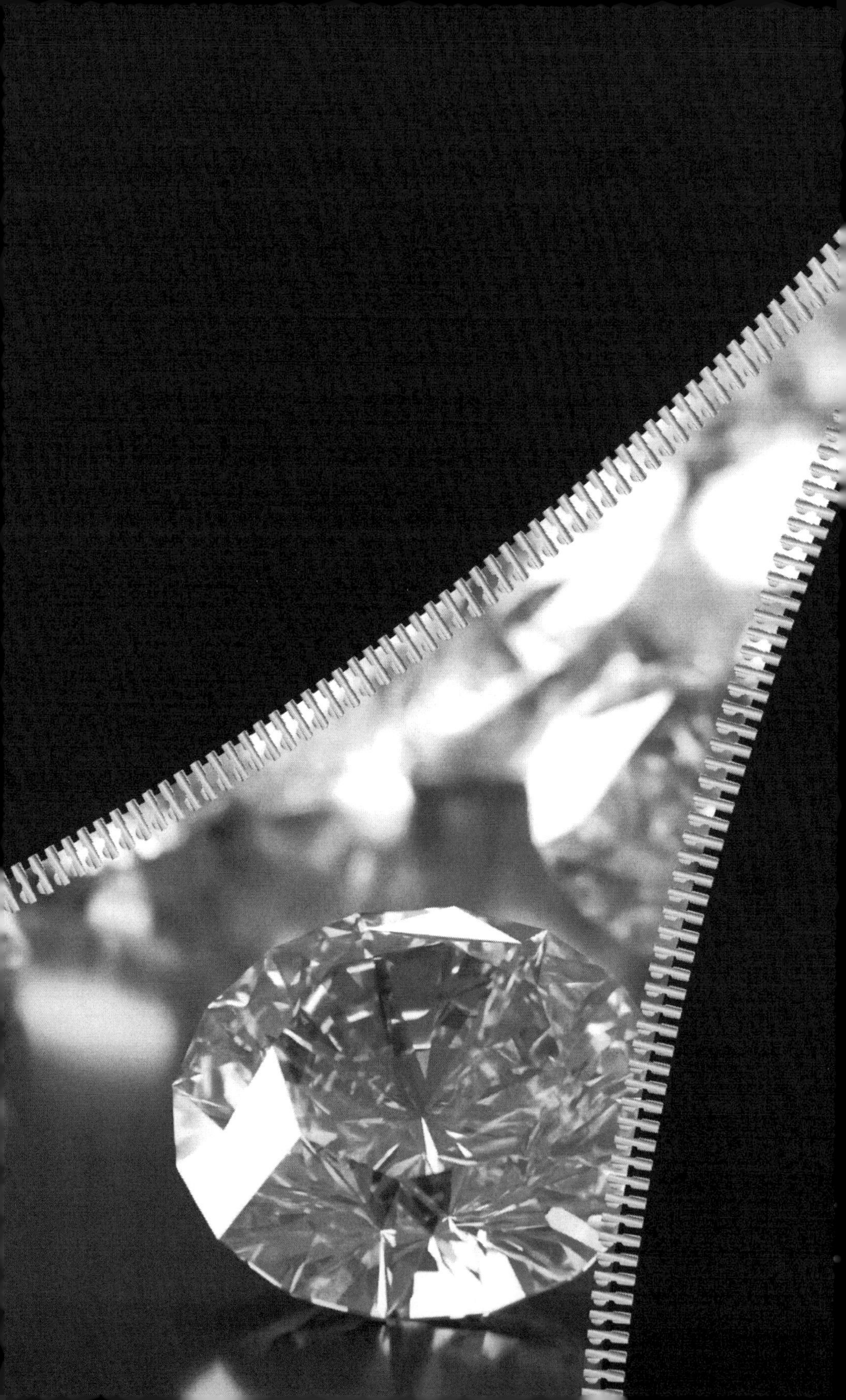

CHAPTER 3

Merrick

17 YEARS OLD

The Devil was alive and well, and he lived in Charleston, South Carolina. I'd been crashing on my friend Deacon's couch for the last week. Being two years older than me, he lived alone in a house on the outskirts of Savannah, Georgia. The old-man and I had gotten into it again a few nights ago, and even though I already topped him in height by a good two inches and had about 20 pounds on him, he still held his own during a fight, especially when he was drunk. And he was usually drunk. I'd gotten in a few punches, but still left the rundown two bedroom house we were currently squatting in with a black eye, dislocated shoulder, and with what I was pretty sure was a broken rib, if the persistent agony in my side was any indication.

I was no stranger to pain. In fact, I'd commemorated the last toe to toe with the mean shit by getting my first tattoo. The brass knuckles inked onto the side opposite my broken rib had hurt like hell, but the pain of the needle had distracted me from all the other parts of my body that were screaming for attention. Depending on how life went for the remaining year that I was required to live under my father's roof, I may develop a new addiction, and it wouldn't be long before I ran out of canvas to cover. I would make sure to get the ink in places not visible to the naked eye. In my fledgling line of work, I didn't need any distinguishing marks to show up on someone's camera.

One more year. That was it. One year, and I'd be free of that SOB. I wanted to leave sooner, but my father had told me point blank that I wasn't going anywhere. He just kept repeating that I needed him to survive. I scoff inwardly at the notion. I didn't need him for shit. I had my own money. A nice little nest egg saved up so that when I was free from the chains that bound me to Peter Stratford, I could finally live the life I knew I deserved. For years, I'd watched people around me take and take, living in the lap of luxury, while I had spent years crying out for help and surviving on scraps. Nobody ever came to save me, so I'd saved myself. I'd done what I needed to do to survive. Okay, sure, maybe I'd done a little more than was absolutely necessary, but it had been years since I'd taken from someone who couldn't afford it.

I'd come a long way from that 13-year-old boy picking pockets on The Battery. Shortly after my 15th birthday, I met Deacon. He'd been an up-and-coming fence with more connections in the criminal underworld than any 17-year-old should have. I'd found out later that his father was a politician and about as crooked as they came, which explained how he managed to get his foot in the door to so many places. Even so, Senator Hawkins refused to recognize his bastard son. So Deacon had been raised by a single Mother who'd done the best she could, even if her best wasn't always good enough. I'd never pressed him for more details about his early years because I knew it was painful for him to talk about. I just knew his Mom had died when he was 10, and because his father wouldn't acknowledge his existence, he'd gone into the Foster Care system. Naturally, I'd been wary the first time we met. The phrase "honor amongst thieves" was horseshit. Already, I'd learned that honor only extended to certain people, and everyone had a price. So far, Deacon was the only exception.

Graduating from picking pockets and petty scams hadn't been easy, but I seemed to have a natural talent for taking what didn't belong to me. I also had a good eye for recognizing things worth stealing. Over the years, I'd done my research. Studied the masters of art, the different grades of gems, how they were cut and learned to recognize valuable antiques and what period they were from. Soon after I started to form a reputation, I needed a fence to broker the items through. That's how I'd met Deacon. He'd taken one look at me and proclaimed me to be his "young protege", which I'd laughed off at the time, but it had turned out to be true. He'd taught me a lot, and in return, I'd made him a lot of money. Over the last two years, we'd become more than just business acquaintances doing shady deals in back alleys. As cheesy as it sounded, we'd seemed to connect on a level that went beyond friendship, and he'd now become the first member of my "found family". He'd also been the only person I'd ever confided in when it came to my home life. Which was why, when I needed a place to lay low for a few days, I could always come here.

Looked like I'd be heading back to Charleston soon, though. I'd gotten a call a few hours ago from the old-man that something big had developed, and I better get my ass back home ASAP. Whenever my father said *something big* was happening, it either meant he'd been arrested or scored big with whatever scam he'd cooked up most recently. It obviously wasn't the former; otherwise, he'd have called his lawyer instead of his son. I knew he'd been working on something before I left. He'd just kept referring to it as "paydirt". He said that about a lot of things. So I could only imagine what kind of shit storm I'd be walking into when I got back. Shooting Deacon—who wasn't home at the moment—a text to let him know I was leaving, I pack my single duffle bag and head out to my Chevy Impala that's currently sitting in the driveway. I said I had money, not that I was stupid with it. First of all, growing up with nothing made me appreciate the value of a dollar. I also knew that within the blink of an eye, I could be right back at the bottom. Secondly, I would never let my father know just how much money I had saved or where it came from. The minute he found out that his son had a knack for more than just nickel-and-dime cons, he'd attempt to use me for everything he could get. I wasn't an idiot. I was careful with what I spent and where I spent it.

Tossing my duffle into the passenger seat, I get in my car and head toward the Savannah Highway. A little under 2 hours later, I'm back in Charleston. Pulling up in front of the address my father had listed in his voicemail, I feel my eyebrows becoming one with my hairline. The townhouse is an ostentatious white-washed monstrosity. With its big white columns, it's the picture of wealth and screams, "I donate to charity but only for the tax write-off". It's surrounded by wrought iron, and there's a massive gate and intercom set up, blocking a driveway that disappears around the back of the house. What the fuck is my Dad doing *here*?

Pulling up to the intercom, I press the button warily. A low, polite voice comes on, and I identify myself as Peter's son. Almost immediately, the gate just beyond the hood of my car opens. Looking ahead, I debate the merits of driving in versus making a run for it. Being an untrusting person by nature, this feels like some sort of trap. Wondering what the fuck my father is up to, I tentatively pull in and follow the driveway to the back of the house, where there are several other very expensive cars parked. Getting out slowly, I feel like at any minute, someone's gonna jump out from behind a tree to tell me I'm the sucker for some television prank show. With a house like this, I can only imagine the deteriorating flesh bag that my father must be swindling. He's obviously told her he has a son, though; otherwise, he wouldn't have called me to come straight here. Walking back around to the front of the house, I stare at the huge brass knocker on the front door. What overkill. Hadn't they heard of that modern invention called "the doorbell"? Just then, I look to my left to see what looks like a large old-fashioned bell hanging off the side of the house. *You've gotta be freaking kidding me.* Deciding not to look like a total fool by ringing this miniature version of a fucking church bell, I opt for the knocker. After only about 30 seconds, the heavy door opens to reveal an elderly woman dressed in a classy but cheap housekeeper's uniform. Wow, Peter Stratford meant it when he said, "something big was happening,"

The woman looks down her nose at me, at once appearing suspicious and subservient.

"May I help you, sir?" she asks politely.

"Uhhh, yeah, I was given this address by my father, Peter Stratford. I was told to meet him here?"

The look of suspicion intensifies, but still, she bows slightly and ushers me inside. "Ah, yes, sir, right this way. Your father and Mrs. Stratford are in the parlor."

My feet falter a step. "I'm sorry, did you say *Mrs.* Stratford?" I say, doing my best to hide the incredulity in my voice.

The housekeeper doesn't miss a beat but continues through the entry-way. "Yes, sir. They've been awaiting your arrival. If you'll follow me."

In a state of total bemusement, I follow behind the old woman—through an entryway the size of our current house—into what I'm guessing is the parlor she spoke of. What I find inside stops me in my tracks. My father is standing at a sidebar in a three-piece suit, mixing a drink while a woman, who can't be more than 35, sits on a chaise lounge that I know costs more than my car. The housekeeper, whose name tag reads "Gloria", announces me, then leaves without another word. The younger woman stands up and makes her way over to me, extending a manicured hand that clearly has never seen a hard day's labor.

"Ahh, you must be Merrick. I'm so pleased to finally meet you. Your father has told me so much about you. I'm Suzanne, your father's new bride. Don't feel you have to call me mom, though. Suzanne is fine."

The woman's posture is still, and her words seem cold and have a ring of untruth to them, that immediately puts me on guard. Still, I shake her hand gingerly before turning to my father.

"Well, I see you've been busy," I say it in a joking manner for the woman's benefit, though if the narrowing of my father's eyes is any indication, he realizes I'm being a smartass, and he's not amused. I read his silent message loud and clear. *Don't you dare fuck this up.*

31

"Welcome home, Merrick," my father says by way of greeting. "Shame you had to miss the wedding, but you going out of town to spend time with your sick friend was commendable. Regardless, you're here now. You should go up and make yourself presentable for dinner. Gloria can show you to your room."

What the actual fuck is he talking about? Home? Wedding? Sick friend? I really wanna call him out, but I've been an unwilling sidekick in enough of my father's schemes to know by now that it's better to just play along. I'm sure he'll reveal everything I need to know about this latest scam in time.

Suzanne pipes up just then, saying, "Oh no, wait, Peter. He needs to meet Amelia first." She glances at her watch with an irritable expression. "I called her down twice already, so she should've already been here. I may just have to send Gloria to fetch her."

I raise an eyebrow at her use of the word "fetch". Just as she's opening her mouth to call out for the housekeeper, a scuffing sound comes from the direction of the entryway. I'm assuming this Amelia person is another servant? I inwardly roll my eyes, wondering what exactly my father's endgame is here and how he thinks he's going to pull off some type of con on this lady who's clearly gullible but has so many eyes and ears around. I wait, hearing the scuffing sound get louder and already counting the seconds until I can get the Hell out of this house. I look down at my phone, and shoot a text to Deacon to let him know he may be seeing me again sooner rather than later. Soon, the scuffing sound stops and with it comes a wave of something that smells like … flowers? Roses, maybe. The smell is so out of place in the room that it forces me to look up.

If it were possible for a heart to stop beating while still allowing the person to remain upright, I'd be a medical marvel … or a zombie. As it is, I have to remind myself to breathe after a few seconds or risk passing out right here in the middle of this giant marble crypt. What I assumed to be a servant is most definitely not. It's a girl, yes. A young girl, maybe a year or two younger than me. Taking a quick perusal without being too obvious, my brain catalogs several things right away. The scuffing sounds must've been coming from the well-worn pair of Chucks on her feet. Her hair is a giant mass of frizzy curls, the color of the sun just as it begins to set. Mostly blonde but with hints of red that even I, as a man, can tell are natural and not from a box or salon. Her skin is creamy and pale, with a dusting of freckles across her nose, cheeks, and the top of her forehead. She's also got, if I'm not mistaken, a smudge of dirt on her face. But her eyes. It's her eyes that hold me immobilized. They're large and green like emeralds, and I suddenly have the unbidden thought that I've never wanted to steal something so badly in my life.

So transfixed am I by her eyes it takes me a minute for my brain to catch up and realize she's staring right back at me. Her head cocked to the side a little like a puppy does when it's curious about something. Suzanne suddenly steps between us, breaking the intense eye contact as she walks up to the girl to whisper under her breath what I'm assuming she thinks I can't hear. I'm thankful for the reprieve because it allows me to pull much-needed air into my lungs.

"Amelia!" she hisses. "There was a dress laid out on your bed for you to change into. That aside, you couldn't even bother to run a brush through your hair? And you've got a streak of paint on your cheek, for God sake."

The girl, Amelia, gives a small shrug, then peers around Suzanne at me again. Turning back to me with a small shake of her head, as if she's dismissing the girl's small acts of rebellion, Suzanne gestures towards her and says, "Merrick, this is my daughter Amelia. Amelia, this is Peter's son, Merrick."

I watch the girl's eyes go wide, which just makes them impossibly larger. Appearing as though she wants to get a better look at me but doesn't want to enter the room, I see her feet hesitate just at the threshold to the parlor. Seeming to make a split-second decision, she waltzes up to me with a goofy grin on her face. She doesn't hold out her hand or make any move to hug me or anything, but instead, she looks me square in the eye before saying, "So you're my new brother, huh?"

I have a moment where my brain flatlines, but when it finally comes back online and processes the word "brother", I have the immediate urge to throw up. Okay, throwing up is an exaggeration, but it definitely leaves a bad taste in my mouth where this girl is concerned. Whatever that feeling was, that put a vice around my heart when she walked into the room, was definitely not brotherly. I glance over at my father, who's eyeing me suspiciously, then at Suzanne, who's looking at once, embarrassed and annoyed. I can't even begin to process or identify all the emotions swirling inside me at this moment, but I know, after years of practice, not to let any of them show on my face. Pasting on a bored expression, I look back to the girl before replying with a shrug of my own, "I guess."

Her nose scrunches like she doesn't care for my answer. Not sure what she expected from me, but clearly, she didn't get it. Was she looking for a reaction? Was it excitement or disgust? Either way, she gives me one final look before effectively dismissing me, then exiting the room the same way she came. Suzanne calls out after her to change before dinner, but the girl gives no reply. I have a feeling she'll show up to dinner in the same pair of jean overalls she just had on. The idea makes me wanna laugh. A small smile starts to form on my face at the same time that I glance back at my father to see him watching me closely. The smile immediately falls away, leaving behind the blank mask of boredom that's my usual MO.

Peter Stratford may not be the smartest when it comes to a lot of things, but he's a master manipulator and a world-class bullshitter, which means he can recognize bullshit from others just as easily. I realize I have to be careful around this girl, especially where my father is concerned. If he ever got wind that I had any feelings towards her, aside from what's in line with the con, he'd use her to hurt me. He'll use any means at his disposal to hurt me. He always has. But not this. I won't let her become a pawn in the deadly game of chess my father and I are playing. Not when I intend to eventually take him off the board.

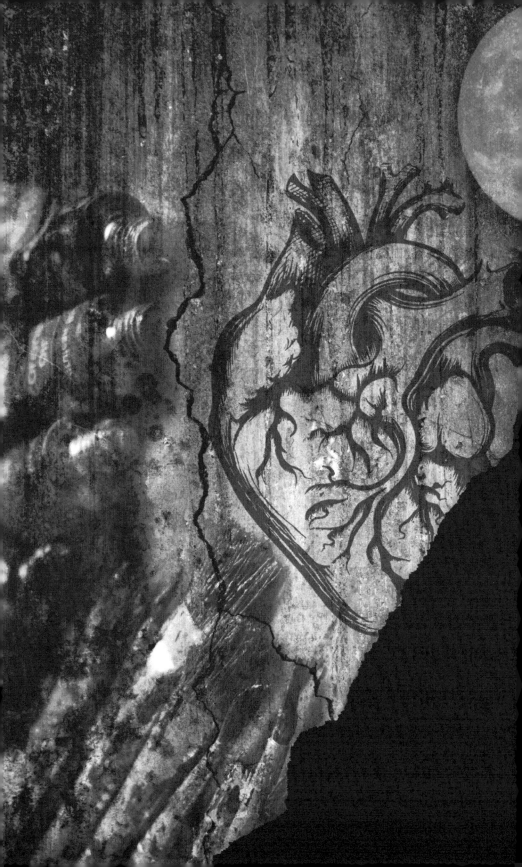

CHAPTER 4

Amelia

It's the scream that wakes me. Who's screaming? It's a woman, but I don't recognize the voice, and she seems so far away. My heart breaks for her, though. The sound is one of absolute terror. I feel like my brain is stuck in a fog.

I sit bolt upright in bed, it takes me a minute to realize the screams are coming ... from me. The last dying echoes reverberate around the dark bedroom, bouncing off the surrounding walls before finding their way back to me like a punch in the chest. I can't breathe. Gasping for air, I fumble in my nightstand drawer, for my prescription bottle of little blue pills. The nightmares don't come every night. Sometimes I'll go weeks without having one, but when they do come, I wake up already in the throes of a panic attack. Fumbling with the top, I pop a pill into my mouth, making sure to quickly follow it with a drink of water from the cup on the bedside table. They're fucking disgusting if they start to dissolve on your tongue before you have a chance to swallow them down. Throwing my legs over the side of the bed, I put my head between my knees. The urge to throw up is nearly overwhelming. Attempting to steady my breathing, I squeeze my eyes shut, hoping that if I squeeze tight enough, the last vestiges of the dream will disappear. But they don't. Like pictures being scrolled through on someone's cell phone, they flash inside my mind, one by one, in quick succession. Dark blood soaking into cream-colored carpet. White foam oozing from an open mouth. My mother, standing stoic, staring at me with cold, dead eyes.

Shaking my head, I force myself to a standing position and into the bathroom. Looking at myself in the mirror above the sink, the girl staring back at me is more familiar than the woman I've tricked the rest of the world into believing I am. I've lived with these demons for so long that I'm more used to this face than the made-up one I present to everyone else. Assessing my reflection, I see pale skin, bedraggled hair, and bloodshot eyes that still hold remnants of the horrors within. Tearing my gaze from the mirror, I quickly strip off my sweat-soaked pajamas and climb into the shower, where I crank the knob to nearly scalding. As I stand under the spray, I breathe deep. Feeling my medication start to kick in, my heart rate slows to a speed that doesn't feel like horses galloping in my chest. I'm not sure how long I stand under the water but when I come out, wrapping myself in a thick white towel, I feel nearly human again. Exiting the bathroom, I head straight to the bed and strip all the linens away. Glancing at the clock on the nightstand, I see that it reads 5 a.m. There's no point in trying to go back to sleep, and I'm not sure I'd even want to, even if I could. I have to meet with my agent in a few hours, so after putting the sweaty sheets in the washer and then quickly throwing on a loose-fitting t-shirt and pair of shorts, I head downstairs for a cup of much-needed coffee. After that, I'll go into the studio for a few hours and attempt to purge the demons still clawing at my bare heels.

Stepping out of my car, I double-check the time on my watch. I'm actually a few minutes early. I probably could've walked here, but the tone of my agent's voice over the phone last night had me a little on edge, so I decided to drive instead, wanting to get here as soon as possible. God, I hope there's actually a reason for this meeting, and it's not just gonna turn out to be an attempt to rush me into creating more work. He has a bad habit of doing that. Despite the majority of the gallery patrons being tourists and foot traffic that just wanders in off the streets, there's still a small parking area in the back, and today, I'm thankful for it. Not that I mind parking on the street. I love my little Audi, but I'm not quite as over protective of her as Merrick is with his Bentley. I would've been fine parking at a meter, but I would've had a hell of a time finding an empty one. Even on an early morning like this, there are already tons of tourists meandering up and down the sidewalks, and I know I'd have wasted way more time trying to find street parking.

Entering the gallery through a side door, I take a moment to wander around, looking at not only my own work but the work of several other local artists. This gallery showcases not only oil paintings such as my own but those done in other mediums as well, including acrylics, sculptures, and modern art. Although, mine does seem to be the darkest by far. Strolling up just behind a snobby-looking couple dressed all in black, I stand quietly and eavesdrop on their conversation. The male is telling, who I assume is his wife, all about the uses of shadows in the painting and how the artist had clearly been inferring their own feelings on the current climate of today's political state. I nearly gag. I want so badly to speak up and tell him just how far off the mark he is, but my agent, Adam, takes that moment to catch my attention, entering the front door of the gallery. Leaving the couple to debate over completely ridiculous theories, I make my way over, taking in the ever-present three-piece suit and slicked-back hair. For a man in his early 50s, he isn't too bad to look at. In fact, a lot of women would probably find him attractive. Knowing what I do about his personal life, including the fact that he's married with kids, immediately puts him in the "no" category. Adding to that, there's been plenty of times that I've caught him checking out my cleavage or ass when he thought I wasn't looking. The man stood so close to me that I could smell the infidelity on his breath. The combination was enough to make me involuntarily cringe whenever he got too near. But he was the best art agent in town, and so I tolerated the lingering stares and the occasional boob graze with gritted teeth and as little face-to-face interaction as possible.

Stopping myself before I can mentally compile an entire list of the qualities that make my agent such a scumbag, I relax my face into passively polite as I meet him halfway across the room. Seeing that he's about to move in for a hug, I quickly stick out my hand to shake, hoping it will dissuade him from attempting to touch me. It doesn't. The hand I'd extended ends up being crushed between our bodies as he envelopes me in what I'm sure he thinks looks like a friendly gesture, but what I know is just an excuse to feel me up. Just as I'm about to pull away, the contact having lasted slightly longer than was appropriate, the bell over the front door chimes, and I glance over, my gaze colliding with the cold, penetrating eyes of my stepbrother. I'm not sure why I feel guilty, as I haven't done anything wrong after all. Still, I break the embrace with Adam as quickly as possible, turning to face Merrick with a questioning look. His gaze moves from me to Adam before darkening significantly. As he shoots a death glare at my agent with those eyes of his, I take the opportunity to steal a quick glance at the rest of him. While Adam looks nice in a three-piece suit, he has nothing on Merrick, even dressed as he is now in a pair of black slacks and a deep green button-down with the top few buttons undone. Like Adam's, Merrick's dark hair is expertly styled, but unlike Adam's slicked-back look that lends to his image as a greasy rat, the natural waves of Merrick's hair are slightly longer on top and faded on the sides. He obviously uses some kind of product, but whatever it is must be expensive because, even though not a hair is out of place, it still looks soft, and I can't help but indulge in a quick fantasy of what it would feel like running through my fingers. As I stand there, lost in the daydream, I must miss Merrick moving because when my eyes come back into focus, he's standing directly in front of me. Realizing I've likely been caught gawking at him, what first comes out of my mouth has a biting edge to it.

"Merrick. What are you doing here?" I ask, my tone suspicious.

"Well, this is an art gallery. The most likely scenario would be to purchase some art," he replies with a bored expression.

Narrowing my gaze on him, I open my mouth to reply, but before I can say anything, I'm cut off by Adam's voice.

"Mr. Stratford, so nice to see you. I'd be happy to show you some excellent pieces by some very talented artists in the area."

Rolling my eyes behind Adam's back, I cross my arms over my chest, knowing that there's a pitch coming. Adam knows all the influential parties in town, and I know he would consider it a coup if he was to become the personal art buyer for Merrick Stratford, one of the richest men in the city. However, I'm taken slightly off guard when Merrick, his eyes still boring holes into me, dismisses Adam without even looking at him.

"I don't need help deciding what type of art I like, Templeton. I can recognize value when I see it."

His use of only Adam's last name, combined with his clearly annoyed tone and the fact that he hasn't looked at the man more than once since he entered, would be enough to insult or piss anyone else off. Clearly, Adam doesn't get subtlety, though, because his slick smile never falters as he tells Merrick not to hesitate to call him if he changes his mind. Turning back to me, his expression morphing from "used car salesman" to "concerned friend", he gently grasps my elbow and attempts to guide me slightly away from Merrick as he says, "Amelia, let's go to the office in the back so we can speak privately."

Looking back to Merrick, who still hasn't moved away to look at any of the art, I reply, "It's fine. We can talk here. What's going on?"

Glancing between me and my stepbrother, Adam says in a hushed tone, "Well ... I don't know if you've heard, but one of your paintings was recently stolen."

Startled, I quickly look around the gallery, checking for anything missing on the walls. None of the slots for my work are empty. Confused, I look back to Adam, saying, "I don't see anything missing."

Before I can even finish my sentence, he's already shaking his head at me. "No, not from here. The last painting you sold. The one titled *Her Eyes Were Wild*. It was stolen from the new owner's loft in Manhattan."

Confused, I say, "Who on earth would want to steal one of my paintings? I'm nobody. It's not like my art is worth anything on the black market."

Hearing a snort behind me, I turn to find Merrick looking back at me, expression morphing from amusement to condescension in the blink of an eye. Already on edge over the news I've just been given, and, if I'm being honest, simply because Merrick always seems to know how to rile me up, I ask, "You think this is funny?"

"What's funny is you using a term like "the black market" as if you have any idea what that is."

"Hey! I'm sure that's a real thing. Besides, what other reason would someone have to steal one of my paintings if not to resell it?"

"Three," Adam pipes up. "They've actually stolen three."

Gawking, I swing my head back in Adam's direction, my eyes so wide I'm sure they'll fall out of their sockets and roll across the hardwood floors any minute now. My voice nearing whatever note it is that opera singers use to break glass, I demand, "What do you mean three?! You said *a* painting!"

Making the universal symbol for "quiet" with his hands, Adam replies, "Well, it wasn't until I found out about this most recent theft and started calling around for information that I learned that two others had also gone missing. Turns out the owners of those paintings just filed claims with the insurance companies, which is why the news didn't get back to us."

Even though I'm dreading the answer, I ask it anyway, "What were the other two paintings that were taken?"

"*The Stars Never Rise* and *Of Crimson Joy*," Adam replies with a slight wince.

I can feel a pit developing in my stomach. Those were the two paintings I sold right before *Her Eyes Were Wild*. They were also two of my favorites, and even though it nearly kills me every time I have to sell one of my paintings, I know they're going to homes that will display them with the respect they deserve. Most people don't know it, but my art is deeply personal to me, each one revealing more of the darkness that lurks inside. And as much as it hurts to part with them, I'd do just about anything to keep from having to rely on my mother's money to survive. Not when I know that that money is coated in blood.

Suddenly, Merrick's voice interrupts the turmoil roiling inside me, "Do they think the same person took all three?"

I know he's speaking to Adam, but again, his eyes are on me when he asks the question. He doesn't look overly concerned, but he's watching me as if waiting for ... something. Some particular reaction from me? Maybe he thinks I'm a ticking time bomb, and at any moment, I'm going to dissolve into hysterics. He should know me better than that.

Squaring my shoulders, I look back at Adam as I wait for him to answer Merrick's question. Turning back to him, Adam replies in a nervous tone, "The police aren't sure. They think so, but they wouldn't say with any certainty, and they wouldn't tell me much else. Only that the work was done by a professional. They have no idea how the thief got into, much less out of each location. Because Amelia is no longer considered the owner of those pieces, I don't think they thought it was any of my business, so they were pretty tight-lipped."

Merrick nods slowly before turning and walking over to one of the sculptures in the center of the room, but I don't miss what appears to be a small smirk at the corner of his mouth. I can't believe he thinks this is funny. Nothing about this situation is amusing. Three of my paintings are out there ... God knows where and with God knows who. Paintings that I poured my blood, sweat, and tears into. Every piece has a small nugget of tragedy hidden within its strokes. Despite critical acclaim, I've always been hard on my work, and I have no idea what I could've painted that was so captivating that someone would risk prison to steal not one but three of them. Which begs the question, would they stop at three? Or would they want more? My eyes make another sweep of the gallery, slower this time, taking in the faces of those loitering around the open space. Could one of them possibly be the thief? Is he or she hiding in plain sight? The endless questions have my gut churning to the point that I worry I'm going to be sick.

Thanking Adam and making him promise to update me with any new information, I go to step away, but before I can, he moves into me for another hug. With my arms plastered to my sides, my gaze clashes with Merrick's over the top of Adam's shoulder. He's back to looking at us now, his stance rigid, fists balled at his sides. Just as I put my hands on either side of Adam's waist to push him away, I see Merrick take one menacing step in our direction. Before he can move further, however, Adam moves back, and I'm blessedly free. Making my way to the front door of the gallery, I exit out into the late Spring heat that's way too hot and sunshine that's way too bright, breathing a grateful breath of fresh air, even if it is already stagnant with humidity.

I feel him before I see him. He doesn't even need to speak for me to know he's there. He stands quietly behind me for a moment. I know it sounds crazy, but I feel like he's always there, always watching, even when I'm not aware of him. And most days it's very hard to be unaware of him. He exudes such power but with a grace that makes me think of a panther stalking its prey.

"This isn't your fault, you know. You shouldn't feel responsible."

Scoffing, I tilt my head to the side to look up at him. Way up at him. In proximity this close, the height difference between us is much more noticeable. It makes me feel like a small child, which is why my words come out a little snarkier than I intend. "I don't. I just feel bad. It's a normal human emotion. You know, empathy? I know you've probably never felt it, but surely you've heard of it. And I don't like not knowing where my work is."

Scratching his chin, which was probably clean-shaven when he got up this morning but that's already showing hints of a 5 o'clock shadow, he mutters sarcastically, "You know, I have heard of it. But you're right, I don't feel it. At least not for those people. They were probably money-hungry bastards who only bought your work so they'd have something to talk about over a boring dinner. They could never fully appreciate what it is you give them."

Squinting my eyes against the midday sun, I try to get a better look at his face. I can't tell if he's complimenting me or insulting me. Maybe he's doing both. When I sit back and think about it, he does this all the time. One minute he's putting me down, the next, he's picking me up off the floor. It's actually quite infuriating. "And what, exactly, is it that you think I give them?"

Looking down, I see his eyes flit quickly to my mouth before coming back to meet my gaze. It's quick, so quick that I almost wonder if I imagined it. "A piece of your soul," he says. Bringing his arm up, he puts on a pair of sunglasses and stares straight ahead, effectively dismissing me. But before he walks away, I hear him mutter under his breath, "Save some for the rest of us." Now I *know* I didn't imagine that. But before I can comment, he steps off the curb and makes his way across the street towards a parking garage. It doesn't escape me that he didn't actually buy anything from the gallery. Hell, he didn't even really look around. What was he even doing here? I'll add that question to the top of the laundry basket full of others and worry about that later. I can only handle one mystery at a time, and right now, the location of my missing paintings is all my brain is capable of.

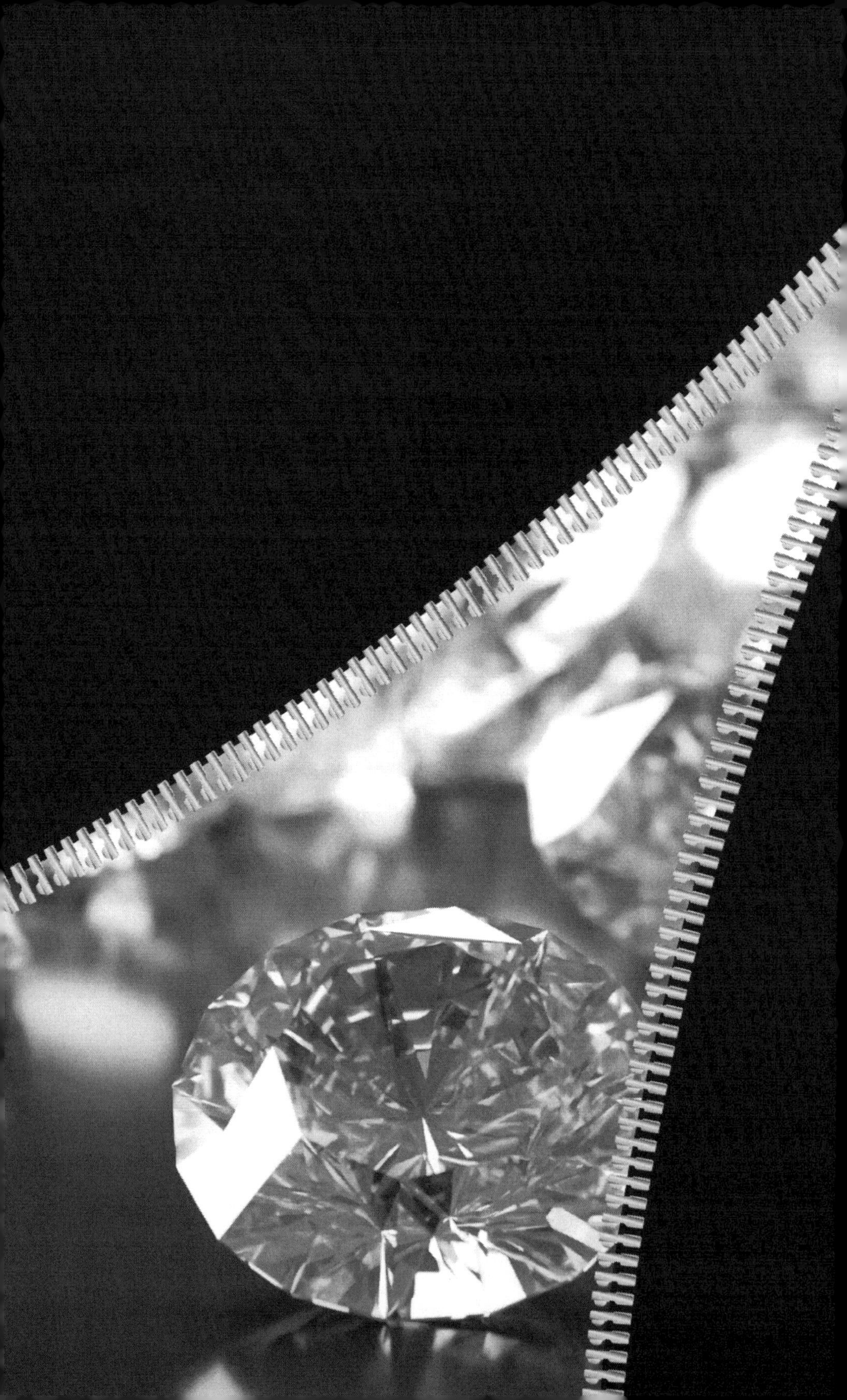

CHAPTER 5

Merrick

That motherfucker. Sitting outside of a very nice two story brick home on the outskirts of the city, I watch as the front porch light turns on and Adam Templeton steps outside, followed closely by a scantily clad woman who most definitely isn't his wife. I happen to know that Mr. and Mrs. Templeton have a fully restored and very ostentatious plantation home halfway between Charleston and Edisto Beach. That's not all I know about Mr. Templeton, though. I also know that his wife isn't the only one he's cheating on. He also cheats on his taxes and at cards. He's in debt to the tune of around $45k to a local loan shark, and don't even get me started on how much he owes the IRS. In fact, the amount of knowledge I have about Amelia's handsy little agent would probably make him shit his pants. Which is exactly why I'm currently lurking at the curb two houses down from where he is right now.

You would think that even with as much time as I've spent sitting in my car, watching Amelia and being just a general creep, that doing something like this would have me questioning my life choices. It doesn't. He touched her. Hugged her ... *twice*. Grinding my molars, I remind myself to stay calm. That after tonight, the number of unwanted hugs will be dropping to *zero*. Looking on, I watch as Mr. Agent leans in to press what appears to be a very sloppy kiss on the woman's mouth. Smooshing her back into the door jam, he looks like he's trying to swallow her entire face, and for what feels like the millionth time, I would love to know how this man could possibly have roped not one but two women into having sex with him. The visuals that pop, uninvited, into my head make me wanna vomit. However, this little disgusting display of PDA is exactly the ammunition I was hoping to get tonight. Don't get me wrong, I wouldn't have been above sneaking up to the windows or even breaking into the house to get what I need, but it seems that Adam's libido is doing all the heavy lifting for me.

Pulling out my phone, I not only snap a handful of pics but take as much video as I can with the limited amount of light in the area. When it seems as though Adam is done mauling her face, the woman begins to make her way back into the house. Quietly slipping out of my car, I head down the sidewalk in his general direction, meandering like I haven't a care in the world. Like I'm not walking down a dark street at nearly 11pm, about to accost one of Charleston's prominent citizens. Ok, maybe "accost" is a little dramatic. In actuality, I only plan to scare him a little. Just so he knows that he isn't to come within perfume smelling distance of Amelia ever again.

Leaning against the trunk of a tree under the cover of shadows, I wait until he's almost upon me before stepping out from the darkness and making my presence known. As I expected, the little bastard jumps a mile into the air, and I'm sure he's probably just pissed himself. What a pussy. I stand in the middle of the sidewalk, blocking his path, making sure I've stepped far enough into the light of the nearby streetlamp, so that he can make out my face. The recognition is almost immediate. So is the fear. I can practically see it leaching out of every pore as he stutters out, "Mr. Stratford ... you ... you scared me." Pressing his hand over his chest, he asks, "What are you doing here?"

"I should think that would be obvious, Templeton. I've been following you," I reply, not bothering to suppress the devious smile that breaks out onto my face.

I watch as confusing mares his features, followed quickly by wariness. If I'm not mistaken, the little man is beginning to sweat. The idea that I've caused such a visceral reaction sends a little jolt of adrenaline through me. What can I say? I'm a sick fuck.

Schooling his features, he straightens to his full height, which is still about 3 inches shorter than my 6'3" frame. He squares his chest, which I'm not sure if he's doing to make himself appear larger or if he's attempting to give himself a confidence boost because it's starting to dawn on him what's going on here. He doesn't know the half of it. If he did, he'd be running down the street, screaming in terror. As it is, he tries his best to play it off by smoothing his palm down the front of his shirt where his tie would normally be. I'm sure it's a subconscious gesture because it takes him a second to remember that he isn't wearing one. Even in the low street lights, I can see that he's wearing the same dress shirt he had on under his suit this morning, which has been haphazardly buttoned, and his hair is disheveled. It doesn't take a genius to figure out what he's been doing tonight. Still, he attempts to play it off with a saccharin smile as he asks, "Why on earth would you be following *me*?"

Prowling towards him, I move until I'm clearly invading his personal space. To his credit, he stands his ground and doesn't attempt to back away from me, even as he has to look up slightly to meet my eyes. Ensuring that eye contact stays unbroken, I say in a menacing tone, "I think you know exactly why I've been following you Adam. You touched something that doesn't belong to you this morning, and I know that wasn't the first time either. I'm here to ensure that it doesn't happen again."

The look of confusion returns with a vengeance before his eyes go wide, and he bursts out with, "You mean the paintings? You think I stole them? I didn't! I swear!"

Scoffing, I shake my head slightly. Jesus, this man is thick. Knowing that I'm going to end up having to spell it out for him like he's a fucking preschooler, I say, "No, no, no, Adam. What you put your hands on is far more valuable than any piece of art you'd ever get the privilege of selling.

49

You touched *her*. Put your arms around her as if you had the right. Let me ask you something Adam. When you forced your body against hers, did you enjoy the feeling of her soft breasts pressed against your chest? Could you feel her nipples through the fabric of your shirt? I want you think long and hard before you answer those questions Adam, because if I don't like what you have to say, you'll be taking a long walk off a very short pier, but not before I cut off what I'm sure is the smallest part of you, to send to your mistress in a FedEx box."

Vigorously shaking his head before I've even finished the last sentence, his face a mask of terror, he wisely says, "I swear I didn't feel anything! It was just a friendly hug. It meant nothing!"

Leaning down so we're nearly nose to nose, I inhale deeply. The scents of expensive cologne, sex, and pure unadulterated fear fill my nostrils. The first two do nothing for me, but the third brings out a side of me that I thought I had repressed a long time ago. Staring into his eyes, I say, "It meant something to me, Adam. I didn't like it. So I'm gonna give you one more chance to prove to me that you know how to keep your fucking hands to yourself. Amelia Carrow is off limits to you from this day forward. You don't touch her again. If you so much as make eye contact with her, I'll send these cute little pictures I've taken," I gesture to the phone, showing him one of the photos on the screen before continuing, "not only to your wife, but all of her brunch friends, the administrators at your kid's prep schools, and the CEO of every business and charity board you sit on. You may sell the art, but the artist herself already belongs to someone and that someone would sooner cut off your hands than allow you to depreciate the value of his most prized possession. Are we clear?"

Reminiscent of one of those dashboard bobble heads, he nods frantically and says, "Yes, okay. I'm sorry. It won't happen again, I swear."

"Good. Now, run along home. You won't wanna miss out on that dinner your wife left warming for you in the oven. I think it's pot roast night, isn't it?"

My comment has the desired effect. Even in the dim light from the street lamp located halfway down the block, I can see the color drain from his face. Nodding again, he backs away before crossing the street and walking down to where his car is parked on a shadowy corner. Putting my hands into the pockets of my slacks, I turn slowly and stroll back down the sidewalk to my own car. I have no way of knowing if he'll say anything about this little encounter to Amelia, but if I was a betting man, and I am, I don't think he will. The fear on his face, the sweat dripping down his temple, and the speed in which he ran to his car are pretty clear indicators that I got my point across and that he'll be too afraid to mention this to anyone.

Climbing back into my car, I sit for a moment before starting the engine, letting the quiet from the night surround me. Heaving a sigh, I lean my forehead against the steering wheel. How did I get here? How did I become this person? Stealing? Stalking? Threatening prominent members of society? I take a minute to ponder what brought me to this point, and if I'm honest with myself, I know exactly how it began.

CHAPTER 6

Merrick

8 YEARS OLD

The crawlspace in the cellar was my current hiding place, at least for the last week. Before that, my go-to spot had been my closet, but he'd found me there easily enough. Even when he was so drunk that he wouldn't be able to tie his own shoelaces, it was almost as if he kept just enough working brain cells to allow him to track me down, wherever I was. He wasn't quiet about it either. I always knew when he was close because his weapon of choice was an old, worn leather belt that he'd tauntingly snap as he worked his way throughout the house looking for me.

I knew what would happen if he found me. The same thing that always happened. He'd grab me by my hair and drag me through the house to my room before throwing me down. Wherever I happened to land is where I'd received the first lash. The next would usually follow if I had the nerve to try to stand. Sometimes I made it to my feet, sometimes I didn't. Not that it made much difference. I'd end up covered in welts and bruises and confined to my room for the next several days, barely able to get out of bed to even use the bathroom. Seeing as I was only eight years old and he was a grown man in his prime, I didn't have any hopes of fighting back, but someday I would. Someday, I'd be big and strong, maybe even stronger than him, and I'd make him pay for every single mark he'd ever put on me. Until then, though, I was stuck with the next best option, and that was to run and find a spot where I could hide until he'd burned off most of the booze.

This explained why I was currently sitting with my back pressed to a concrete wall, knees pulled up to my chest and attempting to breathe as quietly as possible. Why was it that whenever you really needed to make as little noise as possible, your breath always seemed to blast out of you like a symphony?

He wasn't like this before Mama died. Or maybe he was, and I just didn't remember. She'd been gone for a few years, and I couldn't really remember what her face looked like anymore. What her voice sounded like. All I remembered about her was the way she smelled. Like Springtime. Fresh wildflowers and ripe fruit. I'd come across a trunk full of her things a few months ago, and they'd still smelled just like her. I wasn't sure why my father hadn't thrown them out or given them away to Goodwill, but whatever the reason, I was grateful because sometimes, when things got really bad in the house when I was laying in bed too sore to move, I'd snuggle up with one of her old dresses and just inhale the scent and try to remember a life that wasn't so shitty.

Sometimes, I thought that maybe the reason Dad hated me so much was because I reminded him of Mama. I knew I got the majority of my looks from him; everyone said so. But my eyes were all her. Chocolate brown and warm. I wondered if maybe he couldn't stand to look into my eyes when he was sober, and that's why he drank so much. I just wished we could go back to a time when my entire world didn't center around pain.

Just as the thought occurs to me, I hear the sound of the cellar door opening, and fear suddenly has me in a chokehold. I can hear the incoherent mumblings of a man so miserable with his own life that he hoped to find a better one at the bottom of a bottle. I sit, stock still in the crawl space, waiting to hear the telltale sounds of the belt snapping, but it never comes. It's so quiet, in fact, that I wonder if maybe he decided against coming downstairs and has gone off to search another part of the house. No sooner do I have that hopeful thought than I hear heavy footfalls coming down the stairs above me. Pausing about halfway down, I hear his voice for the first time since I took up residence in my hidey-hole for the night. When he speaks, it's no longer a mumble but clear enough that I can hear the distinct slur at the end of words.

"I know you're down here, you little shit. I've looked everywhere else, and I know you're not stupid enough to try running away. You'd never survive without me. If I've told you once, I've told you a million times, you'll die out there on those streets alone. Just come out from wherever you're hiding, and I promise you won't get the belt."

He was lying; I knew he was. He'd said similar things before, and in the beginning, I'd actually been naive enough to believe him. I'd come out of hiding in the hopes that he'd be lenient or that we'd be able to just be miserable together. He was unhappy. I was unhappy. Why couldn't we just be unhappy together? But I knew better now. I knew that showing myself would only make the pain come that much faster. So here I stayed, crouched low, trying to be as still as possible. Even in his drunken state, I knew he'd hear any movement that was out of place.

"Come on now, boy. You can't hide forever. You've gotta come out sometime. It'll only be worse for you if you keep makin' me hunt you."

The malice in his tone was crystal clear. He enjoyed the things he did to me. It wasn't just that he hated me. I'd come to the realization a long time ago that he just liked to hurt people. He hurt them, stole from them, lied to them, conned them. And he liked it. He was the very definition of evil.

Sudden steps snap me out of my reverie. He was coming down to the base of the stairwell. Reaching the bottom, I could hear him walking around the dark space, occasionally tripping over things and cursing up a storm. I squeeze in tighter, trying to make myself as small as possible. If he finds me now, when he's already worked up, he'll just hurt me that much more.

As the shuffling sounds grow closer, I have the fleeting thought that maybe I should close my eyes and pray. But as quickly as that thought comes, it goes. God had never intervened before, and even as young as I was, I'd learned that if I wanted to be saved, I'd have to do it myself. Faith was for people who believed in magic, and nothing had sparkled in my world in a long time.

Out of nowhere, a hand whips out of the darkness, grabbing me by the front of my shirt. Letting out a small scream of surprise and fear, I struggle with everything in me to pull in the opposite direction, away from the force that's propelling me forward. It's pointless, though. He's so much stronger than me. Dragging me out from my hiding place with a hand fisted in the front of my ratty t-shirt and into the light spilling from the open doorway at the top of the stairs, he makes sure he can see me clearly before backhanding me across the face. The pain is immediate, and black spots dot my vision, but unfortunately for me, I don't pass out. Maybe if I did, I wouldn't have to feel what I know is coming next.

Exchanging the fist in my shirt for a handful of my hair, he drags me up the stairs and into the bright fluorescent lights of the kitchen. Breaking free and losing what I'm sure is a chunk of hair in the process, I make a beeline for the drawer where we keep the kitchen knives. Before I can get there, however, I'm tackled to the ground from behind. Landing with his full body weight on top of mine, I feel all the air whoosh from my chest, leaving me gasping. Hauling me up, he grips the back of my neck in one meaty hand and shuffles me out of the kitchen and into my bedroom.

We live in a little one-story rundown house so it isn't far from the kitchen to my room. As predicted, as soon as we're inside, he flings me to the floor, slamming the door shut behind him, effectively cutting off any means of escape. I wait for the first lash of the belt, but it doesn't come. Instead, I'm taken totally off guard when a large, booted foot drives into my stomach, where I'm already lying on my side. It happens once, twice, three times before I'm jerked up to a standing position and hit with an uppercut to the chin.

I can feel myself flying, and for a moment, I think maybe God has been watching, and he's finally come for me. I wouldn't mind. At least then, I'd be with Mama. But I soon realized the flying sensation wasn't angels taking me to Heaven; it was simply my body catching air from the powerful force of the hit before landing with a loud thud onto the floor at the opposite side of the room. Feeling the back of my head hit the floor hard, darkness swallows me whole, and I'm glad for it. If history has taught me anything, I know my father is only getting started, and the worst is yet to come.

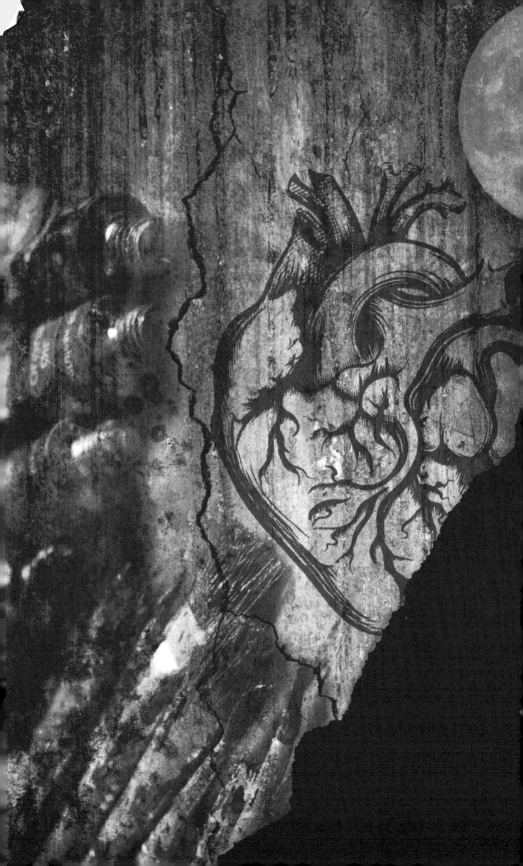

CHAPTER 7

Amelia

My stomach was in knots. Hell, even those knots had knots. Taking a cab to my mother and stepfather's townhouse wasn't ideal, but my nerves had been way too frazzled to brave the streets today. I just knew that if I'd tried to drive my own car here, I would've run over a pedestrian or something. Paying the driver and stepping out of the cab, I stand on the sidewalk for a few minutes to mentally prepare myself for what I know is waiting for me inside. Two bloodthirsty sharks. Even the designer clothing couldn't hide the fact that they had multiple rows of teeth, just waiting to chomp into me.

I wish Merrick was coming today. At least then, I wouldn't have to brave the murky waters alone while wearing a suit made of steak. Well, metaphorically speaking, anyway. In reality, I'd opted to wear one of my favorite pairs of skinny jeans with a flowy blouse. My mother would hate it, which had just solidified the decision in my mind when hunting for something to wear this morning.

Steeling myself, I make my way up the steps to the front door and ring the bell. Barely a second later, an elderly woman, whom I recognize at once, opens the door. Gloria has been the housekeeper here for as long as I can remember. Even before my mother married Peter, Gloria was always there, taking care of me. Her duties ran the gamut as far as housekeepers were concerned. I would even consider her closer to a personal assistant, but she always answered the door when I came over. No way would my mother or Peter deign to do it themselves. I don't mind, though. Gloria was friendly and had always made the house seem a little less cold.

Leaning down slightly, considering that I top her in height by about 5 inches, I give her a gentle hug. "Gloria, it's so good to see you!"

Gloria blusters at the act of impropriety, but I ignore her. She's always been this way. Outwardly stoic, but when I was younger, she'd be the first one to sneak me an extra cookie after dinner. "Miss Amelia! Must you always insist on embracing when you come to visit?"

No matter how many times I've told her that she doesn't need to call me "Miss", she insists that it's the only acceptable way to refer to a lady in a higher station than her own. I called bullshit on that, and I'd told her so. I'd also told her that as long as she continued to call me "Miss", I'd continue to make her uncomfortable with hugs every time I saw her.

Moving into the foyer, I take a quick look around. Absolutely nothing has changed since the last time I was here. The place was like a fucking mausoleum. Which was only fitting, as its two permanent residents were members of the undead. Looking around, I see that every stitch of antique furniture is exactly the same as it was during my childhood. Well, everything except several of the area rugs. Those had been replaced at least once. But I couldn't think about that. Thinking about that would take my mind back to a place I wasn't sure I could handle. Blood ... so much blood.

Shaking myself out of the memory, I quickly look away from the front parlor and further into the rest of the house before staring down at my hands that are shaking with nerves. Gesturing me forward, Gloria says, "Your mother, Mr. Stratford, and Mr. Merrick are waiting for you in the dining room."

I look up quickly from my fidgeting hands. "Merrick is here??"

"Yes, ma'am. He arrived about half an hour ago."

"Thank you, Gloria. I'll be fine from here. No need to announce me," I say, resting my hand on her shoulder for a brief moment.

"Very, well ma'am. It was good to see you as well, Miss Amelia."

Nodding, I slowly make my way down the hallway, with its Persian rugs and expensive paintings forced into the most hideous antique gold frames. I guess being an artist, I'm a bit of a snob when it comes to paintings and the way they're showcased. I believe each one has a story to tell and therefore, the frame should be chosen to match. My mother, however, is content to go with whatever is most expensive and if it shines or glitters, that's just icing on the cake.

As I near the dining room doorway, I can already hear raised voices. Mostly Peter's, which means he's already started drinking. This brunch should be fun. Just as I'm about to enter, I hear a deep baritone cut through the loud ramblings of my stepfather, effectively silencing him. There aren't that many people that have that effect on Peter Stratford. Merrick did, but I knew that hadn't always been the case. For a good number of years, after my mother and Peter got married, I remembered Peter and Merrick coming to blows more times than I could count. From what I gathered, even though Merrick had always been and still was very tight-lipped when it came to his childhood, it used to be much worse. It wasn't until Merrick moved out, well after his 19th birthday, that it seemed like Peter could no longer use him as an outlet for his rage. I still questioned why Merrick hadn't bolted for the door the second he'd been classified as an adult. As much as I'd like to speculate that it had something to do with me, I wasn't that delusional. That particular topic remained a mystery. I thought that after Merrick left, I'd be the one getting the brunt of Peter's violence. I knew my mother got her fair share, but I still expected him to consider me a replacement for Merrick. He'd certainly tried a few times during the handful of years that we all lived under the same roof, but whenever Peter thought to raise a hand to me, Merrick always seemed to be there. Even after he left, Peter made a point to steer clear of me. I had a feeling that was Merrick's doing as well. Perhaps he'd threatened him against touching me? I wasn't sure. But whatever the case, I was grateful. I had enough anxiety and fear swirling around inside me as it was. I didn't need the added insult of bruises.

Finally stepping into the dining room, I find Peter in his usual spot at the head of the table, with my mother and Merrick next to him on alternating sides. I notice there is only one extra place setting, which I assume is for me, and that it's been placed directly next to Merrick. I'm sure that was his doing. He knows I'd rather eat broken glass than sit next to my mother. All gazes swing to me as I enter, and the varying reactions I get are almost comical. Peter looks at me with barely veiled contempt, and my mother plasters on a smile that looks more like a sneer, being sure to showcase teeth I know have been repaired multiple times due to backhands to the face. Merrick barely glances at me before returning his gaze to where he was previously staring out the dining room windows. Making my way over, I air-kiss my mother's cheek, as is expected, silently counting in my head to keep from freaking out. Just being this close to her makes those knots in my stomach tighten painfully. I say an obligatory "hello" to Peter, then take my seat next to Merrick without addressing him at all. My mother is the first to speak, wasting no time in dishing out the insults, in this case, belittling my career of choice, which seems to be her favorite pastime these days.

"So, Amelia, have you given any thought to my idea of joining me as a member-of-the-board for the Gibbes Museum?" I open my mouth to speak, but before I can get a word out, she's already steamrolling over me. "I know you said you didn't think you'd have enough time, what with that little hobby of yours, but I do wish you'd reconsider. Jaqueline Porter's daughter is interning in the Restorations Department, and she doesn't have half of your drive and tenacity, not to mention she completely lacks that killer instinct you need to advance within the ranks of the museum."

I flinch at her use of the phrase "killer instinct". A barely imperceptible flinch, but a flinch nonetheless. I sense Merrick's posture stiffen slightly next to me, but he doesn't remove his gaze from the window, and his expression is one of absolute boredom. Most people would've taken what my mother said as a compliment. She did actually praise me for having drive and being tenacious, and to outward appearances, it seems as though she's actually trying to help me. But I'm no fool. She was just looking for a way to slip in the dig about my "little hobby". To this day, even after several years of being a very successful and well-respected artist, she still refuses to believe my painting is anything more than a phase. A simple act of teenage rebellion that just happens to have lasted over 10 years. If the word "denial" had a picture next to it in the dictionary, it would be her face. I can't even imagine what that face would look like if she ever deigned to take time and actually look past the surface of my art to the darkness beneath.

Taking a deep breath, I say, "Mother, we've talked about this. As much as I love the museum, I have obligations to my patrons. If I don't paint, my agent can't sell. And if my agent can't sell, I don't get paid. If I don't get paid, I can't pay my bills." This concept has always been foreign to my mother because she's always had a man taking care of her. Or at least a man's money.

"I'm surprised you can pay your bills at all. You can't possibly sell that many paintings. I can't imagine who the hell would wanna showcase anything so sick and twisted in their house. Everything you've ever done has been horrifying. I wouldn't want that shit in here," Peter interjects before my mother can respond.

A faint hint of copper floods my mouth from how hard I'm having to bite my tongue. I'm just about to respond, probably to say something that's going to get me in trouble, when Merrick speaks for the first time since I entered the room.

"Don't talk to her that way." It's a simple sentence delivered in a low, menacing tone. I immediately close my mouth and sit back in my seat, looking between Merrick and his father. Peter's face is turning a very disturbing shade of red. Merrick, on the other hand, still appears bored, but his eyes are drilling holes into his father from where he sits next to me. Just then, a maid enters, carrying large trays of eggs, bacon, fresh fruit, and an assortment of pastries. The Stratfords don't have many servants besides Gloria, a single maid that's responsible for cleaning the gargantuan home, and a gardener for the landscaping.

At the distraction, we all lapse into a tense silence as breakfast is served. My mind, however, is still dwelling on Peter and my mother's snide little remarks. I force myself to tamp down the anger that's boiling in my chest and to just focus on my food. The faster I eat, the faster I can get the hell out of here. Just as I'm getting ready to pop a strawberry into my mouth, I feel Merrick's right hand rest on my left knee. Freezing instantly, I glance at him out of the corner of my eye. If it wasn't for the fact that I could feel the pressure of his hand on my leg, I would think I was imagining it. He picks at the food on his plate, completely ignoring me. My first instinct is to believe that he's putting his hand there in a gesture of comfort. To assure me that despite Peter's ire, everything will be fine. But after a moment, that hand moves a few inches higher, his thumb beginning to make small circles at the outside of my thigh, and immediately, my schoolgirl crush for this boy comes roaring to the forefront of my brain, and my imagination is drumming up all kinds of outrageous scenarios, taking something ridiculously small and running with it.

Before I can completely embarrass myself by, I don't know, sticking my hand into the juncture between his legs to gauge whether he's hard or not, I stand up quickly and excuse myself to go to the restroom. Making my way to the bathroom down the hall that's normally reserved for guests during parties, I step inside and head straight to the sink. The bathroom is large, with pale pink marble surrounding the double sinks. Dabbing my face with a cool rag, I stare at my reflection in the mirror. I must be losing my mind. There's no way that touch meant any more than the countless times we've accidentally brushed when standing next to each other at functions or walking down the hallway in opposite directions. It was just a gesture of comfort, nothing more.

Getting a hold of myself, I finish up in the bathroom. With my hand on the doorknob, I brace myself for whatever barbs Peter and my mother still have in store for me. Pulling the door open, I run smack dab into a broad chest, nearly stumbling backwards in my attempt to keep from hitting him. At first, I think it's Peter coming to give me some kind of punishment to make up for the fact that he couldn't light into me during breakfast. But when strongly muscled forearms reach out to steady me, and I lift my gaze, I find Merrick's eyes instead. They don't look bored anymore. In fact, they see a little too much. Taking a hasty step back, I attempt to put some distance between us. That proves to be a massive mistake, as I watch him step further into the bathroom, closing the door behind him.

"Ummm, what are you doing?" I ask shakily.

"Checking on you. Before you left the table, you seemed ... flustered. And more than your usual level of frazzled." His eyes continue to assess me from where he stands, just inside the door. He hasn't moved since coming inside, but suddenly, the room feels infinitely smaller just from having him in it. Looking anywhere but at him, I say, "Oh, yeah, I'm fine. I just really had to pee." Oh. My. God. *I just really had to pee???* What is wrong with me?!

Cocking his head to the side, he takes a step closer. "Why are you so nervous?"

My haywiring brain latches onto the first thing I can think of. "You touched my leg."

"So? It's not like I tried to put my hand down your pants," he replies with a smirk.

Immediately, I feel my spine straighten. Scoffing, I say, "As if I'd let you."

Despite all of Merrick's faults, I know he'd never force a woman into doing something she didn't wanna do. Especially not me. Merrick wasn't privy to many of my secrets, but one that he is was my first foray into sex. It hadn't been pleasant. In fact, it had been one of the worst nights of my life. That aside, I didn't think Merrick lacked physical companionship. Hell, he had probably never met another woman not willing to do literally anything he asked. Just as I feel the beginning pangs of jealousy, a thought occurs to me. Thinking back to all the times we've attended the same charity galas or fundraising parties, it hits me that I don't think I've ever actually seen him with a woman. I file that information away for later.

Taking another step forward, forcing me to retreat until my ass hits the edge of the bathroom counter, he closes the distance until there's barely a foot of space between us. I make the mistake of shifting my body forward slightly to keep the counter from digging into my ass. Meeting Merrick's eyes, I see his pupils are blown wide, the black almost completely replacing the chocolate brown that I'm so used to seeing. The air around us is suddenly thick with ... something.

Picking up on my earlier comment, he makes sure our faces are in line before saying, "Mmmm. You know what I think, Amelia? I think you *would* let me touch you. In fact, I have a feeling you'd let me do a lot more than just touch you." Moving his mouth close to my ear, he whispers, "I bet if I were to put my hand inside those tight little jeans you're wearing, I'd find you soaking wet."

Breaths coming faster, not trusting myself to answer, I give my head a little shake of denial. Suddenly, I feel the ghost of fingertips along the top edge of my jeans, near the button that holds them closed. Those same fingers skim slowly over the waistband of my pants, back and forth, brushing the small patch of skin exposed between the hem of my blouse and the top of my jeans. The touch is teasing and hesitant, almost ... reverent. There seems to be the barest hint of hesitation.

"Should we test that theory?" he asks, with a hint of amusement lacing his voice. I can tell by his smug tone that he thinks I'll balk. I must've imagined the hesitation because it's clear he's playing with me like a cat would a favorite toy.

Annoyed with him and this corner he's backed me into, both physically and metaphorically, I make the split-second decision to call his bluff. Placing my palms on the counter on either side of my hips, I hoist myself up onto the top, slowly letting my legs fall open until there's enough room for a fully grown man, even one of Merrick's size, to stand between. The gesture is a lewd one. It's clearly a challenge and one I'm secretly praying he takes me up on. I'm still half convinced I'm dreaming this entire scenario, and if I am dreaming, then what could it hurt to push the envelope a little? Glancing up at him, the gaze that looks back at me no longer holds any trace of amusement. In fact, I experience a small tendril of fear at the intensity of what I see there. After a second of what looks like indecision, he takes that final step, cradling himself between my spread legs. Looking down, he places both hands on my knees, slowly sliding them up my thighs. I don't miss the way his hands are shaking slightly. From anger ... or excitement?

"Mia, you have no idea what you're doing," he whispers. "Whatever game this is, I don't like it."

"You started it," I reply, leaning forward to say against his ear, "don't you wanna see if your theory is correct?"

He swallows hard and expels a heavy breath. Then, as if he just can't stop himself, he leans down, skimming his nose along the side of my neck, inhaling deeply. At the same time, his hands slide up from my thighs, around to cup my ass, pulling my lower half flush against him. I let out a small gasp at the contact. The sound that comes from the back of his throat is enough to have my thighs trembling. "You smell ..." he begins.

"Good enough to eat?" I ask breathlessly. I don't know what's gotten into me. I'm never this forward with men. And never in a million years would I have entertained the possibility that Merrick would not only say the things he's said, but touch me the way he is right now. Taking my newfound courage and running with it, I skate my hands up his arms, beginning at his wrists before moving up his biceps, which are much bigger than they look under his usual three-piece suit. For a second, I allow myself to just feel him before digging my nails into his muscles, urging him to move his hands again. To grind me against him. To let me feel more of him.

As if snapping out of some trance, he pulls his head back to look into my eyes before saying, "Desperate. You smell desperate." Pushing away from me, he stalks to the bathroom door and exits before I've even had a chance to process what just happened. I sit there on the bathroom counter with my mouth hanging open. Desperate? Desperate?! That asshole!

Hoping down, I take a moment to get my wits about me. Trying to figure out what the fuck just happened, I alternate between pacing and staring off into space, reliving every moment from the second he walked through the bathroom door. Just as I've worked myself up into a good rage, I exit the bathroom and make my way back to the dining room, ready to rip into him. I don't care if our parents see. As I walk into the dining room, however, he's not there. Peter is also missing from the table, leaving only my mother serenely sipping tea. The picture of poise and tranquility. When it sets in that I'm alone in the room, possibly alone in the house with my mother, I can feel my skin start to crawl. A mild sense of panic sets in, but thankfully, my anger overrides it. Forcing my legs to move me in the direction of the table, I demand, "Where is Merrick?"

My mother looks up slowly, meeting my gaze. As my eyes clash with hers, there's nothing there. No love, not even a sense of fondness. Only frigid cold. She must hear the anger in my voice, though, because she answers without question, only a mild sense of interest in her tone. "He said he got an emergency call and had to leave. Your father decided he would go to his office to get some work done. Would you like to stay and chat for a bit?" she asks.

Considering that I'd rather face a guillotine than have a one-on-one conversation with my mother, I decline as politely as possible, not even bothering to correct her on the whole "your father" thing. I need to get to my studio. It's the only thing that's going to help release all of the pent-up frustration, confusion, and, if I'm being totally honest with myself, desire that's currently swirling around inside me. I have a feeling that if I don't pour it all onto the canvas, I'll do something crazy. Like track Merrick down and slap him ... or beg him to sleep with me. Making my way to the front of the house, this time without the assistance of Gloria, my steps involuntarily slow as I near the entryway to the parlor. Without Gloria and the raised voices of my family to distract me, memories from the past hit me like a tidal wave, and my feet falter in the doorway as my gaze unerringly finds the Persian rug that's so similar to the one I knew as a child but that I know can't possibly be the same. That much blood would never come out. Unbidden, the scene begins to play out before my eyes, and as much as I'd like to squeeze my lids together and concentrate on the breathing exercises I read about online, I can't stop myself from reliving that night from so long ago. Though it would take me some time to come to terms with what had happened, it was a night that would forever alter the way I saw my mother.

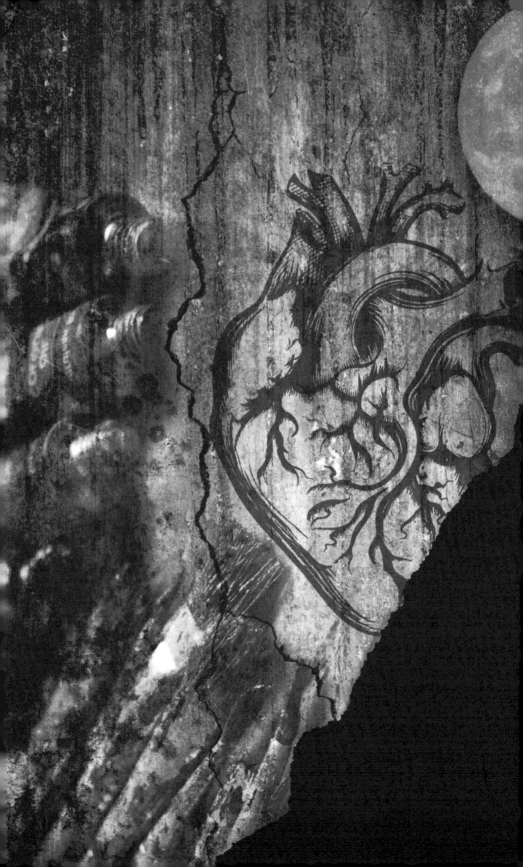

CHAPTER 8

Amelia

5 YEARS OLD

I was five years old. I knew that because my birthday was last week. Mommy and Uncle Remy had thrown a big party in the backyard of our home, with a petting zoo, clowns, lots of games, and a big bounce castle. A lot of kids came, but I didn't know most of them. I wondered if maybe their parents were just friends with mine, and that's why they'd come. None of them really seemed to want to play with me. I wasn't sure why Mommy and Uncle Remy had decided to throw a big party. Mommy had never really cared about my birthdays before; this was the first party I'd ever had. And Uncle Remy didn't seem like the party type. Uncle Remy wasn't really my Uncle. He wasn't my Daddy either. Mommy had married Uncle Remy last year, and he seemed nice, but I didn't really know him that well. He didn't talk to me much. I'd overheard one of the maids saying that he didn't like kids, which was too bad because I felt like a girl needed a Daddy. Mommy had told me that my own Daddy had died when I was three. I didn't really remember him, and Mommy didn't like to talk about him. She got mad every time I brought him up, so after a while, I just stopped. I'd hoped that when Uncle Remy had moved in with us, that we'd be a real family. But they both acted like I was in the way most of the time. It made me feel bad.

I did have Gloria, though. She was our housekeeper but also my nanny. She'd taken care of me for a long time. I loved Gloria. She fed me, gave me bubble baths, and read me stories before bedtime. I wished Gloria lived in the house with us, but she lived with her husband in their own house. I didn't think it was very far away, but I wasn't sure. I just knew she was usually here when I woke up and stayed until after I'd gone to sleep. Tonight had been the same, except she'd forgotten my water. Usually, she'd leave a glass of water on the table beside my bed, but tonight, it wasn't there. I knew I wasn't supposed to get out of bed after Gloria tucked me in. Mommy didn't like it when I wandered around the house alone, especially at night. But tonight, I was really thirsty, and even though I'd tried to make myself go back to sleep, I just couldn't without a drink of water.

So, getting out of bed quietly, I stick my head out of my bedroom doorway and look down the long hall. My bedroom is the last door at the end. Not seeing anyone, I tiptoe the length of the hallway and then down the long staircase that separates the upstairs, where my room is and the downstairs, where the kitchen is. If Gloria had at least left me a cup, I could just fill it from the sink that's in the bathroom down the hall from my room. But since she didn't, I don't have any choice but to go and get one from the kitchen.

Just as I reach the bottom of the stairs and turn to make my way to the kitchen that's at the back of the house, I hear yelling coming from Uncle Remy's office. That wouldn't be unusual normally. Uncle Remy yells a lot in there, especially when he's working. I didn't really like it, though. It made me feel uncomfortable. Gloria had taught me that word. Uncomfortable. It sounded like a grown-up word, so I was trying to use it a lot. Maybe if I was smarter, Mommy would talk to me more. I didn't think it would make much difference with Uncle Remy. It seemed the only time he did talk to me was if he was yelling about something. Like right now. When he yelled, it always made me feel like I was doing something wrong. I always seemed to be doing something wrong. But tonight, it's not just his voice I hear yelling. Mommy was in there, too.

I can't tell what they're saying, but they both sound really mad. Not wanting to get caught and make them even angrier, I get scared and start to turn around and go back to my room. Maybe I don't need that water after all.

Right when I make it to the third step up, I hear the door to Uncle Remy's office crash open. Jumping, I look up toward the top of the stairs. There's no way I'll be able to make it up the stairs before they see me. I'm gonna get caught for sure. With my heart pounding, I run back down the three steps I'd taken and duck down into a tiny space under the stairs, praying no one sees me. Maybe I'd get lucky, and no one would come out of the office, and I'd be able to sneak back upstairs without anyone knowing I was here.

But just as I think that, I hear footsteps coming down the hallway that leads to Uncle Remy's office. They're still arguing, and now that they're closer, I can finally hear what they're saying, though I don't understand some of the words they're using. I just know they're saying a lot of grown-up words and a lot of bad words. Ducking down and making myself as small as possible, I watch as my Mommy comes down the hallway first, with Uncle Remy following behind her.

"Goddammit, Suzanne, do you think money just grows on fucking trees? How do you think this house is paid for, or the Porsche you drive, or all those brunches with that group of socialite bitches you choose to spend time with?" he says.

Stopping for a moment in front of the stairs, Mommy wheels around and says, "Oh please, don't pretend like we can't afford it. It's no different than you going golfing three times a week, your Jaguar, or paying for that little whore you keep down at Edisto Beach."

I don't know what "whore" means, but it doesn't sound very nice. As their yelling gets even louder, I put my hands over my ears to try to muffle the sounds of Uncle Remy using the "whore" word against Mommy and her screaming about some lady that lives at the beach. All of a sudden, I see my Mommy slap Uncle Remy across his cheek. Beginning to shake,

I close my eyes and curl in on myself like the roly polys I play with sometimes when Gloria takes me out to the gardens.

Rocking back and forth with my eyes closed and my ears covered, it isn't until several minutes later that I realize the house is quiet now. I don't hear yelling anymore. Opening my eyes, I don't see Mommy or Uncle Remy at the base of the stairs, where they were before. At first, I think maybe they went outside, but then I hear voices coming from the parlor. They aren't loud any more, though, thank goodness. Maybe now, if I run out really fast, I can make it up the stairs before they come back out. Sliding out from under the staircase, I start to make my way around the banister at the base of the stairs. I'm sweating, even though I haven't been doing any of the things that usually make me sweat, like running, playing, or getting exercise.

Suddenly, I hear Uncle Remy's voice say something about a divorce. I don't really know what the word means, but I've heard it before. They say it sometimes on the shows Gloria likes to watch in the afternoon. I'm not supposed to watch them because they're for grown-ups, but sometimes I sneak into the room and sit on the floor at the end of the couch if Gloria falls asleep. She falls asleep a lot 'cause she's old. After hearing Uncle Remy say the word, I expect Mommy to start yelling back, but she doesn't make any noise. Maybe they're done fighting. Now might be the best time to make a run for it. Just as I reach the bottom step and start up, I hear a noise so loud that it makes me have to cover my ears again, and a small squeak escapes me before I can stop it. I stay like that for a minute or two. I'm too scared to take my hands off my ears. What if I hear the noise again? When I finally do uncover them, I hear nothing.

I'm scared. For my Mommy. For Uncle Remy. What was that noise? Like a loud BANG. I know it came from the parlor, and I wanna go in and check on Mommy, but fear has me frozen on the bottom step of the staircase. Finally, worrying that something bad has happened to my mom, I pad over to the entryway of the parlor. As I get closer, I hear Mommy talking on the phone. I'm not close enough to hear what she's saying, and by the time I get to the doorway, she's already hung up. Stopping in the entryway, what I see doesn't make any sense. Uncle Remy is lying on the floor. There's a big stain that looks like it could either be red or brown all around him. His eyes are open, but he isn't moving. Dragging my gaze away, I see Mommy standing next to the sofa a few feet away. She's holding a gun. I recognize them from some of the cartoons Gloria lets me watch on the weekends. Looking up at Mommy, I see that she's looking down at Uncle Remy, with the gun in one hand and a lit cigarette in the other. I don't know what's happening, but I do know that I don't wanna be here anymore.

Just as I turn to sneak back to the stairs, Mommy's head jerks in my direction, and I see her eyes. They're really red. Like she's been crying. But there aren't any tears on her face. Maybe she cried out all the tears she had inside her, and now she's empty. Putting out the cigarette in the ashtray that sits on the coffee table, she comes over towards me. I don't know why, but I think of the word "uncomfortable" again. Her being close to me makes me uncomfortable now, and I don't know why.

Standing between me and Uncle Remy so I can no longer see him, Mommy crouches down until she's the same tallness as me. She doesn't say anything at first; just looks at me.

Hesitantly, I ask, "Is Uncle Remy okay? Why is he lying on the floor?"

Looking down at me, her expression cold, she says, "No, he's not okay, Amelia. Uncle Remy shot himself. He's gone to heaven now."

I know what heaven is. They teach us about it in Sunday school. I know heaven is God's house, and if Uncle Remy went to live there, he's not coming back. But I don't understand. If Uncle Remy shot himself with the gun, why is Mommy holding it now?

Looking down at the gun still in her hands, I ask, "Why would Uncle Remy wanna leave us to go to heaven? Didn't he love us?"

Mommy glances away before answering. I don't know why, but when she looks back at me, I can tell she's annoyed with me. It's an emotion I recognize because Mommy is annoyed with me a lot. Gripping me by the tops of the arms, she squeezes me too hard. It hurts. I tell her so, and after a minute, she softens her grip but doesn't let go of me.

"Amelia, the police are going to come soon. I need you to tell me why you were out of bed, what you heard, and what you saw."

Knowing that telling the truth is always important, but not wanting to get into trouble, I say, "Gloria forgot my glass of water. I was thirsty, so I came down to the kitchen to get a drink. I didn't see or hear anything until the loud bang sound."

"Good, that's good. Now, I want you to go back upstairs and get back in bed. When the police come, if they ask to speak with you, I want you to tell them exactly what you just told me, ok?"

Glancing around her, I see that the stain around Uncle Remy is much bigger now. It's soaking through all the expensive carpet Mommy had put in a while ago. Suddenly, the tightening around my arms gets harder, and the pain, combined with a sharp "Amelia!" from my mother, has me jerking my gaze back to hers.

Looking into my eyes, she says, "Do you understand?"

"Yes, Mommy."

"Good girl. Now, go back to bed and hurry," she says, just as I hear the sound of police sirens wailing in the distance. Racing back towards the stairs, I nearly run into Gloria as she comes in through the front door. Mommy must've called her, too. Looking at me with a frightened expression, she motions for me to hurry upstairs, so I do. Running down the long hallway to my room, I jump into bed and pull the covers over my head. A few minutes later, I hear more voices coming from downstairs, but no one ever comes up to talk to me. I try my best to go back to sleep, but I can't get the picture of Uncle Remy's eyes staring up at the ceiling or the pool of red liquid all over the carpet out of my head. I stay that way for the rest of the night, with my head buried underneath the blanket.

I didn't know it at the time, but the images of that night would haunt me for the rest of my life. And they wouldn't be the only ones.

CHAPTER 9

Merrick

I feel like I'm losing my fucking mind. This morning had been a mistake. I don't know why I'd felt the need to follow her into the bathroom. I felt like there were two sides to my nature, both locked in a constant battle with each other when it came to Amelia. One half was patient and saw the need to keep a comfortable distance between us while I laid the groundwork for our future. The other half felt the need to look after her. To make sure that she knew she had someone in her corner, ready to defend her whenever her demons reared their ugly heads. Normally, I kept a tight leash on that half. But sometimes I slipped up and, like this morning, I'd show her a little comfort that would then turn into me making an ass of myself. I never should've touched her. Because I knew that when the time came that I fully planted myself into her personal space, she might as well charge me rent because I wouldn't be leaving any time soon. The fact that that time hasn't come yet is eating at me.

Even now, hours later, as I pace back and forth around my empty apartment, I feel like a caged animal, all pent-up rage and sexual frustration. The sounds of my heavy footfalls across the hardwood can't even distract me from the ringing in my ears. It's too fucking quiet in here. Aside from the handful of times Amelia had been here over the years, for some odd reason or another, I'd never had another woman in my apartment.

The act felt too close to what I thought the beginnings of a relationship would be like, so I'd never crossed that line. Since meeting Amelia, I'd tried a handful of times to see other women. Each encounter was more disappointing than the last and further cemented my need for that one special woman in my life. Ugh. I felt like I was on the razor's edge of making some rash decision that would forever alter our future. I had to keep reminding myself that I'd waited nine years. I could wait a little longer.

A good stiff drink, that was what I needed. I'd gotten a text from Deacon a little while ago, letting me know that he was in town for a few days and asking if I wanted to hang out. Usually, we'd just chill at my place, or I'd make the short drive to his house near Savannah, but tonight, I needed to get out of this apartment and out of my own head. Shooting Deacon a message, asking him if he wanted to go for a drink, I'm not surprised when I get a resounding "YES!" literally four seconds later. You would think the son of an alcoholic and a mean drunk would be completely turned off by the sight, sound, and feeling of booze. I knew I had inherited my father's addictive personality. My addiction wasn't to alcohol, though. My addiction came in the form of a woman. I differed from my father in many ways, but the main one was that I was nothing if not controlled. I lived my life in moderation, at least when it came to the booze. In the same way that I was frugal with my money, I didn't imbibe in liquor often. But when I did, I did it with the intention of getting completely shitfaced. I knew that wasn't a good way to deal with my problems; hell, if my father had taught me nothing else, it was that. But sometimes, you just needed to hang out with a good buddy and drown your sorrows in whiskey. However, nowadays, we opt for the more expensive labels. Not only because we had the money to spare but because we weren't as young as we used to be. Something about hitting that 25-year age mark and suddenly, the nights of you staying out, downing shot after shot until 4 or 5 a.m. and waking up the next day without even the tiniest hangover were long gone. I knew if I had more than two drinks, I'd be fucked. I intended to be fucked.

The entire encounter with Amelia in the bathroom was playing on a loop in my head. I kept remembering the way she'd spread her legs and let me run my hands up her thighs and of the way she'd felt pressed tightly against me. I'd never been so close to what I knew would become the center of my world, and I swore, even now, I could still feel the heat radiating off her. I'd been so stupid to follow her into the bathroom. Part of it had been worry for her mental state after the way my father had spoken to her, but another part, a sickly perverse part, wanted to see if she was in any way affected by the way I'd touched her leg under the table. The gesture had been one of comfort at first. I wanted her to know that, even though I seemed cold at times, I was in her corner to back her up whenever she needed me to. But soon, I couldn't resist pushing the envelope, just to see how she would react. I had expected her to shove my hand away or maybe even pop me one, but instead, she'd just sat there, letting me rub circles on her skin before jolting up and running from the room like it was on fire.

So I followed her to the bathroom. I hadn't been prepared for the way the conversation had turned or how she would behave. I'd just been taunting her at first, but she ended up turning the tables on me. Long gone was the little 15-year-old girl with frizzy hair and too bright of a smile. The woman I'd met in the bathroom had been a temptress with a sexy-as-sin voice and the body of a goddess. I wanted to say I hadn't noticed these changes over the years, but truth be told, there wasn't much about Amelia that I didn't notice. I just couldn't make that notice known to her or the rest of the world. At least not yet.

I make my way into the master bathroom. I needed a ridiculously cold shower right now. I fire off another text to Deacon, telling him to meet me at Prohibition at 9 p.m.. I don't wait for a reply but jump straight into the shower and one orgasm later, which I'd like to say I'm ashamed of, but I'm not, I'm getting dressed in a pair of black jeans and button down. I am so sick of the monkey suit I'm forced to wear day in and day out. Having to interact with people in the higher ranks of society seemed to come with the very unwanted side effect of ties. Most days, I walked around feeling like I was choking to death. And while I couldn't wait to get the jacket and tie off most days, I'd become somewhat of a creature of habit when it came to button-down shirts. I didn't feel comfortable in much else, and I definitely didn't think polite Charleston society was ready for me in a t-shirt.

About an hour later, I'm pulling my Bentley into a parking garage downtown. No fucking way would I risk my baby in a metered parking spot on the side of the street. Besides, if all went according to plan, I'd be too plastered to drive myself home tonight anyway. I'd end up taking a cab and leaving my car in the lot until tomorrow. Heading inside, I find Deacon already seated at one of the stools that surround the bar. Judging by the 2 empty glasses in front of him, it's clear that he's already got a significant head start on me. Coming up and taking the stool next to his, I motion for the bartender. When he comes over, I order two fingers of whiskey, making sure to tell him the label I prefer, as well as another drink for Deacon.

Giving Deacon the universal dude greeting of a fist bump, I say, "So, you never said what you're in town for. Not that I'm not grateful for the company, but usually, the only thing that draws you to Charleston is me." I give him a little eyebrow wiggle. It's not a lie, though. Deacon rarely comes to Charleston for anything other than when we have "business". Meaning the handing off of certain pilfered items for future sale. Typically, Deacon steered clear of the city since his father had made his permanent residence here.

At my words, Deacon throws back his head and laughs loudly. It draws stares from several of the ladies further down the bar. Deacon is a good-looking guy, not that I'm looking. But if I were a woman I'm sure I'd find him attractive. With his shoulder-length sandy blonde hair and bright blue eyes, he looks more like a surfer than a fence. I would never tell him this, though. His ego is already big enough. He knows he looks good and takes every opportunity to use it to his advantage.

"I've got a meeting with a prospective client for that little collection you dropped off last night. The meeting isn't until late tomorrow, so I figured, why not have a little fun tonight."

Nodding, I watch as Deacon does a half turn on his stool to survey the area. I know what he's looking for. Deacon is a shameless flirt, and unlike me, he's earned his reputation as a man whore, or as he likes to put it, bringing greatness to the masses. Masses is right. I don't think I've ever seen Deacon with the same woman twice. Just then, our drinks arrive, and clinking glasses, I take a healthy swig. I have a feeling I'm going to need at least five or six more of these just to drown out the feeling of Amelia's skin under my hands or the way her voice got huskier when she practically asked me to eat her out. *Fuck.* Motioning for the bartender again, I order and down two more glasses of the high-priced whiskey. The music is loud in the bar tonight, the same as it's been the handful of times I've been here before, but if I didn't know better, I'd swear I could hear Amelia's husky tone even now. Jesus. I'm hearing her even when she's not near me now. Clearly, this whiskey isn't doing its job.

Just as that thought occurs to me, Deacon nudges my knee with his and casually jerks his head to the side, indicating over to the direction of the booths in the back. Voice sounding slightly awestruck, which definitely isn't like him at all, he says, "Holy shit, I think I'm in love." Being as inconspicuous as possible, I glance over to the area he's looking at, only to have my heart jump somewhere into the vicinity of my throat. Sitting at a booth in the back of the bar alongside a heavily tattooed girl with jet-black hair and eyes that I know are dark brown, I see none other than Amelia. Guess I wasn't imagining that husky tone after all. What the fuck is she doing here?? Judging by her partner in crime for the evening, I'd hazard a guess that it wasn't her idea to come out tonight.

I don't realize I'm sitting there in silence until I see Deacon wave his hand in front of my face in the universal "earth to whoever" signal. Breaking the spell that having Amelia here has put me under, I glance back at him to see him staring at me with a mixture of concern and barely veiled amusement. Giving me a wolfish grin, he says, "So I see you've noticed the hottie in the back booth. Well, I saw her first so I call dibs."

His words have me seeing red for a split second. Gritting my teeth, I reply, "That hottie in the back booth is my stepsister, so don't even fucking think about it."

"No shit?! Well, hell, dude, now you *have* to introduce me."

Before I can even open my mouth to protest, he's out of his seat and weaving through the crowd, heading in that direction. Despite him asking me to make the introductions, he doesn't even wait for me before he walks up to the table, saying something to them that I can't quite hear. Whatever it is, though, has a laugh bubbling up from Amelia's throat while her friend just rolls her eyes. It takes me a moment to remember that this is my best friend, and it's bad form for friends to murder friends. Especially when that friend is your *only* friend. However, the fact that he managed to pull such a genuine laugh from Amelia makes me wanna empty a beer pitcher over his head right in front of them. Coming up behind Deacon and hearing the tail end of the conversation, I know he's just used some cheesy pick-up line on them. Just when I'm about to start throwing punches, I look over to him to see that while he's talking to both of them, his eyes are actually on Siren, not Amelia like I first thought. I've met her several times in the past whenever Amelia would bring her around the house, but in terms of actual conversation, she's a virtual stranger. At least, that's what she thinks. In reality, I knew a fuck ton about the small curvy girl that would look more at home bartending in a place like this than on a stage putting on a concert for hundreds, which she did regularly. So, while I knew a fair bit about her factually, I knew virtually nothing about how her mind worked. Right now, though, her thoughts are coming across loud and clear. She thinks whatever Deacon said was ridiculous and doesn't plan on giving him the time of day. She has no idea what she's done by giving him her best RBF. She's essentially issued him a silent challenge. If I know my friend, he'll be in her panties before closing time. But then again, considering Siren's face at the moment, maybe not, which will only make him that much more determined.

Coming up to stand at my friend's side, Amelia finally notices me for the first time. I watch as those bright emerald eyes darken and form into slits. She's clearly pissed at me for what happened in the bathroom this morning. Good. If she's pissed, it'll make it easier for me to keep my hands off her. However, as I look down and get my first glimpse of what she's wearing, I start rethinking my convictions. Her dress is fucking *green*. Not of the neon variety, which seems to be her go-to apparel whenever she paints. No, the dress she has on tonight is a dark, forest green color and made of some type of body-hugging material that should be recalled by the manufacturer for being potentially hazardous to the health of the entire male population. Yeah that dress is a choking hazard if I've ever seen one. As she crosses her legs, one over the other, the move bares a portion of her thigh that has me biting the inside of my cheek to keep from crawling under this table. Glaring up at me, she crosses her arms in a gesture of irritation, having no idea she's pressing her generous breasts together and putting them on full display for not only me but Deacon as well. Looking over to make sure he's keeping his eyes to himself, I find my friend still staring at Amelia's companion. It's not lost on me that he's missing his trademark smirk. The one he pulls out for all the ladies, even the ones he knows will be a sure thing. There's something else going on here, and as much as I'd like to rag him or even investigate what's happening, my eyes are once again drawn back to the emeralds that haunt me day and night.

Sitting back in the booth, arms still crossed over her chest, I see a hint of mischief in her eyes before she asks, "What are you doing here, Merrick? Following me to make sure I don't find somebody else to finish what you started?"

I know she's needling me, but just the idea of any other man touching her is enough to make me want to lift her out of that booth and throw her over my shoulder like a caveman. I should carry her back to my place and spank that round little ass just for baiting me. Realizing that if I continue with that line of thinking, my boxer briefs are gonna have my dick in a chokehold, I reply, "No, my friend Deacon and I are just having a few drinks. But hey, if the opportunity presents itself, maybe I'll take someone back to my place and let them test out *my* bathroom."

Whatever spell Siren had cast on Deacon seems to be momentarily broken as they're both now watching the exchange between Amelia and I with rapt fascination. After a few minutes of a very intense glare off, Siren finally breaks in by looking over at Amelia and saying, "As much as I'm loving the tension between the two of you, that's so thick I could literally cut it with a knife, I think I wanna dance. Come on, Amelia, let's go."

Deacon and I step back as Amelia and Siren rise gracefully from the booth. When Amelia is standing fully in front of me, I see that not only does the green dress she's wearing hug every curve of her body, but it's also got horizontal slits running the entire length of both sides, showing off the barest hint of the sides of her breasts. I clench my hands at my sides. Anything to keep from touching her. As she and Siren saunter past us, she actually shoulder-checks me. I swear the balls on this girl. Despite the level of unease I feel at seeing her out dressed like this, I can't help the smile that pulls at the corners of my mouth. I know I shouldn't, especially with the bullshit I suffered at my father's hands, but I secretly loved it when Amelia had her little bouts of temper and lashed out at me. It proves that she feels *something* for me, even if that something is rage.

As we watch them make their way to the dance floor, I hear Deacon whisper something that sounds suspiciously like "Jesus Christ Almighty". Deacon, like me, grew up in the bible belt. With his family being from Savannah and his absentee father being in politics, the blasphemy would have anyone else shocked. At the moment, the only thing shocking is my friend's behavior. Before I can rag him about his reaction to the raven-haired viper, my gaze strays back to where the two girls are now dancing in the center of a large crowd of gyrating bodies. They're dancing with each other, thank God, but as I look around the floor, I can see several of the males nearby eyeing them salaciously. I can physically feel my blood pressure rising, and I have a serious concern that if she doesn't cut the shit soon, my head is gonna pop off. I motion Deacon to follow me, then make my way to the edge of the dance floor. By the time we get there, I see that two guys have already moved in closer to the girls.

Amelia's eyes find mine, and I watch as her body moves in a sensual rhythm that has my blood racing. Moving her hands up into her loose curls, she sways her hips back and forth to the beat of the music. With the way her eyes are boring into mine, it takes absolutely no effort to imagine that she's dancing only for me. Over the years, we've goaded each other into crossing that invisible line in the sand a time or two, but never too far and never as blatantly as this morning. Right now I feel like the tide has come in, and that line has completely disappeared. I don't even have it in me to break the contact to see what the hell has happened to Deacon. He could've left the bar entirely, and I wouldn't even notice. Although, considering that Siren is still here, I doubt it.

As I look on, Amelia lets her hands fall from her hair, bringing one back up to crook a finger … at me. She wants me to come dance with her? There's no fucking way. I know the minute I get my hands on her, I'll lose all semblance of control. That thought is overridden, however, when I see another guy, who clearly can't read the room, dance up behind her and put his hand on her hip. *My hip.* Barely containing my rage, making sure she can see my face, I give a small shake of my head and mouth, "Let's go."

Maybe it's the alcohol. Maybe it's nine years of pent-up sexual and emotional frustration. Whatever it is, the second she arches an eyebrow at me in challenge and then presses her hips closer to the other man's, something inside me snaps. Like a bull in a china shop, I shoulder my way through the crowd, people jumping out of the way to give me a wide berth. Maybe the look on my face is making it clear that I'm about to commit a murder in the middle of a crowded dance floor. Reaching Amelia, I waste no time before doing exactly what I envisioned doing back at the booth. I bend slightly, lifting her and throwing her over my shoulder. The guy she was dancing with begins to protest, probably to act the hero, but my growl of "get fucked" and the look in my eyes has him backing down immediately. It can only be attributed to the state of her shock that she doesn't automatically start screeching and beating on my back as I make a beeline to the exit sign at the back of the club.

By the time we reach the door, Amelia seems to have come out of whatever shock-induced stupor she was in because she's throwing every four-letter word in her vocabulary at me, her offenses coming out slightly muffled by her mass of hair and the fact that she's winded from the air being knocked out of her with my every step. Pushing outside, I'm thankful that the parking garage I chose is literally right next door to the bar. I carry her, kicking and screaming, all the way to my Bentley before putting her down.

Getting all up in her face, I point my finger at her, saying, "Don't. Move."

Of course, the second I glance down to locate my keys in the pocket of my jeans, she tries to make a run for it. Lucky for me, she's a walking disaster in heels, so she doesn't make it very far before tripping over her own feet. Catching her with an arm around her waist, I barely save her from face-planting into the asphalt. The only way to compensate for the momentum and both of our body weights pulling in one direction is to jerk her back with so much force that she's slammed into my chest. The motion has my back banging against the side of the car and momentarily knocking the breath out of the both of us.

Once I'm able to take enough air into my lungs to speak, I growl into her hair, "Goddammit, Mia, stop!"

I don't know if it's the use of her nickname or if she's just come to the same realization I have. That every inch of her body is pressed tight to mine. Either way, she finally stills in my arms. I can feel her short, shallow breaths in direct contrast to my harsh pants. Both are loud in the still night air. The parking garage is deserted, except for a few cars near the entrance. I luckily parked at the back of the garage, not wanting to risk anyone getting close enough to my baby to scratch it. I'm not thinking about my car right now, though. At the moment, the only thing I can think about is how good Amelia feels pressed against me. It's like every curve and dip of her body was made to fit every hard ridge and valley of mine.

Knowing she can feel my growing erection against her ass, I lean down to whisper in her ear, "Did you have fun making me jealous? What were you thinking? That you'd go home with him? Did you plan to let him fuck you?" Gripping her hair at the base of her neck, I tug her head to the side as I run my nose along the shell of her ear. "Because I'll tell you right now, I never would've allowed that to happen."

Still sounding out of breath but maybe not entirely from our little tussle, she says, "You've lost your damn mind, Merrick. You have no say in who I do and don't fuck. And I'm getting a little sick of these mixed signals. How about you just pick a direction and stick with it? Either you want me, or I'm an annoyance to you. You can't have it both ways."

Just as I open my mouth to say that I have no idea what mixed signals she's talking about, she must read my mind because she pushes her ass back into me, rubbing herself against said signal, which is hard and aching. I suck in a sharp breath, unable to keep my arm from tightening around her waist, pulling her even tighter against me.

"First of all, there's nothing I can't have. If I see something I want, even if it's not actually in my possession yet, it's already mine. Secondly ..." I let my voice trail off as I move the hand that's not anchoring her against me, running it down from her hip to the bare expanse of thigh exposed by the short hem of her dress. Skimming my palm up, my hand makes its way underneath her skirt until it comes into contact with the scrap of silk covering the juncture of her thighs. Cupping her, I whisper, "...*mine*."

A little gasp leaves her lips before she's jerking away. Turning to face me, she shoves me hard in the chest, my back hitting the side of the car again, and then, before I have a chance to mount any kind of defense, her mouth is on mine. The second our lips touch, I know I'm fucked. There's no preamble whatsoever. No slow brushing of her lips against mine. As soon as my mouth touches hers, I find hers open and waiting for my tongue. Giving up the fight, at least for the moment, I allow myself just a small taste. I've waited so long. There's no one here, no one to see. Dipping my tongue inside, I sweep the inside of her mouth, getting the first hints of flavor that I somehow just know are unique only to her. I can feel a new addiction forming by the second. Quicker than I thought possible, that small taste turns into a feast. Like I said, I'm fucked. Flipping our positions so that she's pressed between the hard car and my even harder body, I plunder her mouth. I'm seconds away from ripping that dress off of her when I hear a throat clear behind us.

Breaking away from Amelia like a little boy whose hand has been caught in the cookie jar, I turn around to see a security guard for the parking garage standing halfway between us and the entrance, almost as if he was afraid to come any closer. I'm just about to tell him to fuck off when Amelia straightens and moves past me. It's then that I notice Siren standing at the entrance, gawking at the two of us. Automatically making a grab for Amelia's wrist, I stop her. Turning, she stares at me, eyes begging me for ... something. Her lips are red and swollen from our kiss. I stare at them as I try to come up with something to say to get her to stay. To get into the car and come home with me. But I can't. So I say nothing. As I slowly let go of her wrist, the hurt that flashes in her eyes is like a punch to the gut. But still, I don't stop her when she turns and makes her way back over to her friend on unsteady legs. Watching her leave the parking garage, I ignore the security guard and get into my car. Something just changed between us. We both felt the shift. And I know, no matter how hard I try, I won't be able to regain my footing after this.

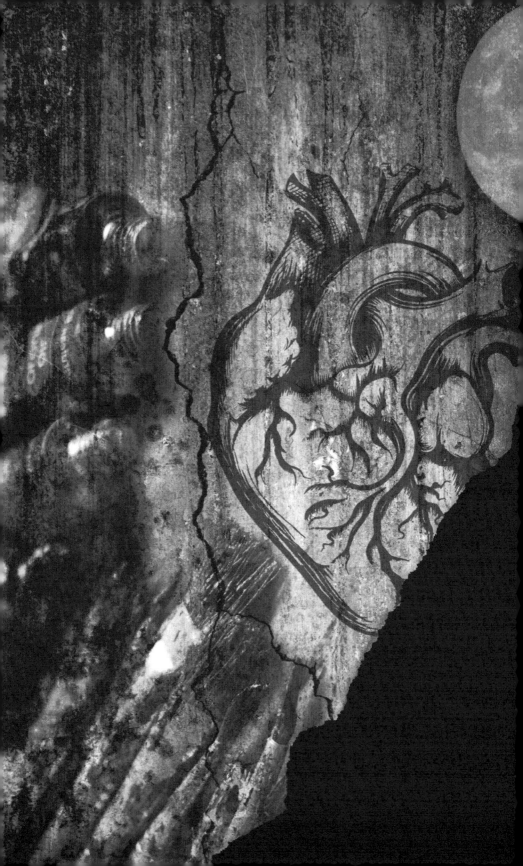

CHAPTER 10

Amelia

Cracking open one bleary eye, I try to figure out if the ringing pervading my senses is coming from inside my own head or from my cell phone, which is God only knows where. Honestly, at this point, it could be either. I blink several times in an attempt to adjust my eyes to the light in the room only serves to remind me that I can currently feel my heartbeat in my brain. I should've closed the curtains before I went to sleep last night. Maybe if I had, I wouldn't feel as close to death as I do right now. Wishing I could just crawl into a hole and hibernate for a year, I pull one of the many extra pillows littering my bed up to cover my face, attempting to block out as much light as possible. And while that does help thwart the sun's attempt at putting me out of my misery, it does little to block out the shrill sound of a phone that's still echoing around the room.

Keeping my eyes tightly closed, I root through the mass of pillows and comforter with my free hand until I find the offending object. I press the power button on the side once to silence the ringing and just hold the phone in my hand for a few seconds while I debate on whether it's even worth the risk of answering, knowing it will most likely cause my head to roll right off my shoulders. Not committing to anything one way or the other, I lift the pillow just enough to allow my squinty eyes to make out the name on the caller ID.

Merrick. Before my hungover brain has a chance to even process what I'm doing, my finger is hovering over the green button, and I'm just about to take the call when the events from last night come flooding back to me. The club, the shots, the dancing. Merrick, carrying me out over his shoulder like a sack of fucking potatoes. I hit the red button because fuck him. My brain clearly doesn't think I'm already suffering enough because it chooses this moment to assault me with the memories of what happened next. Our little tête-à-tête in the parking garage and his subsequent rejection. Groaning, I roll over and bury my head back in the pillows. I made a complete fool out of myself. I practically threw myself at him, and at first, I was sure he felt something, too, but in the end, he chose to let me walk away. So either I read the situation completely wrong, or he's a damn coward.

Whichever the case, he's thoroughly pissed me off, so no, I won't be taking any of his calls. I'm not even sure what he'd be calling me for. I'm sure it's not to apologize. I don't think he even knows how to pronounce the word "sorry". He's probably just calling to rail at me for my behavior last night, and if that's it, he can go to Hell. I'll be damned if I'll answer the phone just so he can slut shame me. Knowing I can't mope in bed all day, I make a loose plan of action. The first thing on the agenda is to find some ibuprofen and chug a gallon of Gatorade, then take a shower hot enough to wash away the remnants of Merrick's kiss and my eternal shame.

Crawling out of bed, I slowly make my way downstairs to the kitchen and take care of the first two things on my list. By the time I'm back upstairs and in the shower, the painkillers are starting to kick in, and I can actually string together coherent thoughts. Although, I'm not so sure that's a good thing because all of those thoughts seem to center around Merrick and the way his mouth felt against mine. I'm not entirely surprised that I kissed him. I've had a crush on him for as long as I can remember, and I did have Jose Cuervo there to back me up. What did surprise me was the fact that he kissed me back, and I don't think he can blame it on the little bit of alcohol he drank before manhandling me off the dance floor.

My mind whirls as I exit the shower, and 10 minutes later, I've donned a t-shirt with a huge sunflower on the front and a pair of cut-off jean shorts. Sliding my feet into a pair of well-worn Vans slip-ons, I reach down to pick up my phone from where I abandoned it on the bed before my shower. Just as I'm leaning down to grab it, the screen lights up, and the ringing begins again. Glaring at the caller ID and the name flashing there, I hit the reject button again, sending Merrick to voicemail. I know he won't leave one, but it still gives me a small measure of satisfaction knowing that he'll hear my voice, basically blowing him off.

Now that I've medicated, hydrated, and washed away last night's humiliation, I make my way outside, and I'm immediately hit with a wave of oppressive heat. I really shouldn't be surprised. We were closing in on May and in the South, that meant it was already hotter than the surface of the sun. Deciding to take the short journey to my favorite coffee place on foot, I daydream about the gigantic iced coffee that will soon be filling me with a much-needed caffeine boost. A few short minutes later, coffee in hand, I wander down to The Battery. At this time of morning, the pier is relatively empty, the tourists choosing to take advantage of the free continental breakfast provided by most of the hotels in the area. Finding an empty swing, I take a seat but don't push the swing into motion. I don't think my stomach, much less my head, would thank me for the unnecessary motion. Taking a healthy sip of my coffee, I gaze out at the marshy land that surrounds the area. There's a distinct smell in the air when you get this close to the water. It's a difficult smell to describe to anyone that isn't from here. It's not necessarily the smell of the ocean or salt water, though those scents are definitely present. It's something else. It's just the smell of ... home. In all honesty, I love it here. A lot of people that I grew up around, especially in school, would talk about their need to get the Hell out of Charleston, sometimes South Carolina, entirely. Not me. Sure, there were places in the city that held a wealth of bad memories for me, but there were other places, like the cemetery, that stood as a refuge when things went bad, and I just needed to be alone for a while so I could try and subdue the dark thoughts running rampant in my head.

The vibration of my phone against my leg, where it rests in my jeans pocket, breaks me out of my reverie and jerks me back into the present. Rolling my eyes, I pull my phone out. Looking down, I see I've got three text messages from Mr. Mixed Signals.

"Why aren't you answering your phone? You know I hate texting. We need to talk about what happened last night."

Merrick

"I know you're ignoring me on purpose. The phone only rang a few times before going to voicemail, so I know you declined my calls. You're acting like a child."

Merrick

"I swear to God if you don't call me back ..."

Merrick

Letting out an incredulous laugh, I tuck my phone back into my pocket without replying. *I'm* acting like a child?? This coming from the man who literally carried me in a fireman's lift out of a club last night because I had the nerve to let a guy get a little too close to me while dancing. I'm still in shock over that little display of machismo. I pray there wasn't anyone there who recognized us. If word of what happened got back to our parents, there'd be Hell to pay. There's nothing that my mother, at least, cares more about than her image. If people were to find out that my stepbrother had all but fucked me against a car in a public parking garage, the gossip blogs would have a field day. Taking a deep breath, I try to reign in the mental spiral I can feel coming on. Right now, I had bigger things to be concerned with, like the possibility of Merrick actually tracking me down and making me *talk* about last night.

Feeling my phone vibrate again, I grind my teeth. Jerking my phone from my pocket, I'm fully prepared to answer and rip him a new asshole, but when I look down at the screen, it isn't Merrick's name I see, but Siren's. Taking a few calming breaths, I do my best to chill and regulate my tone before picking up.

"Hey! What's up?" I say, doing my best to sound nonchalant.

"Well, I was just calling to check up on you. You know, make sure you hadn't done something stupid like murder your stepbrother, or worse, fucked him. But now I'm actually wondering what is up. You sound pissed."

"No, I don't! I'm fine!" I definitely don't sound fine.

"You're breathing into the phone like you've run a marathon. You're also being snippy," she says, though she doesn't sound the least bit offended. She knows me, so she's easily able to recognize my moods.

"I am never snippy."

"Not often but when you are, I can tell. Is this about last night? Because that was definitely … interesting."

I can hear the laughter she's trying so hard to contain. Siren is very rarely serious, or at least that's her public persona. She's the ultimate party girl. Always looking for a good time and rarely lets things bother her. Again, at least that's what she wants everyone to think. I may be the only one who's gotten to see the more damaged side of her. Most people don't know anything about Siren's history, the baggage she carries around, or the many scars that litter her body.

Now is not one of the times she's putting on a facade, however. I know she saw what happened between Merrick and I in the parking garage, or at least the tail end of it, and I know she finds it hilarious. She's been ragging me for years about my little schoolgirl crush on my stepbrother. It's always been a joke up until last night. After we were interrupted by the guard, I was the first to see Siren standing near the entrance to the garage. The look on her face was almost comical. If that tense moment when Merrick let go of my hand hadn't happened, she wouldn't have had time to pick her jaw up off the floor before anyone else saw. Well, it seems she's gotten over her initial shock and is now gonna needle me about it.

"There's nothing to talk about. I made a move on him, and he rejected me. End of story," I say, trying to keep my dejection out of my tone.

"End of story, my ass. I saw that kiss. He was just as into it as you were."

"And yet, he let me walk away. So clearly not as into it as either of us thought."

Siren's silent for a moment before saying in one of the most serious tones I've ever heard her use, "Maybe he's scared. You two have a lot to lose, given who your parents are. Maybe he wants you but doesn't wanna risk the backlash if people find out. Maybe he's protecting you."

Snorting, I give a little shake of my head. "Merrick couldn't care less about my reputation. All he cares about is himself. What *he* wants, what pleases *him*."

But that wasn't entirely true, was it? How many times had Merrick come to my rescue in the few years we'd lived under the same roof? And not just when it came to his father. If I was honest with myself, I'd have to acknowledge all those little moments when he'd intervened to save my ass, even the ones where it'd seemed as though it was done out of a begrudging sense of duty. There'd definitely been more than a few. Merrick had entered my life near the beginning of my "rebellious" stage. I'd done anything and everything to break away from the tight grip my mother had on me, both emotionally and mentally. Some of those acts of rebellion had ended me up in hot water, and more times than not, Merrick was the one to fish me out.

Snapping out of my inner "come to Jesus" moment, my brain catches up with my ears as I realize Siren just said something, but I don't have a clue what it was.

"Sorry, what?" I ask.

"Bitch, would you pay attention?! I said I think you should give it another chance. Throw a little test his way. See if he takes the bait or runs for the hills."

"Hang on. You witnessed my epic failure last night, and you want me to DO IT AGAIN?" I ask incredulously.

"What do you have to lose? He's always treated you like a piece of gum stuck to the bottom of his shoe. It's not like you can get any lower," She says matter of factly.

"You know, you really should consider forgoing your God-given talent with the violin and become a motivational speaker. I think you have a real gift for it."

Her short burst of laughter is followed by an, "I'll think about it." Before we say our goodbyes and hang up. After we've disconnected, my thoughts shift back to the years I spent living with Merrick and our parents. I think back on some of the times that Merrick not only helped me but inserted himself into my life and my business. More than a stepbrother who appears ambivalent should. One memory in particular stands out vividly, like bright splashes of paint against a white canvas. The night I lost my virginity.

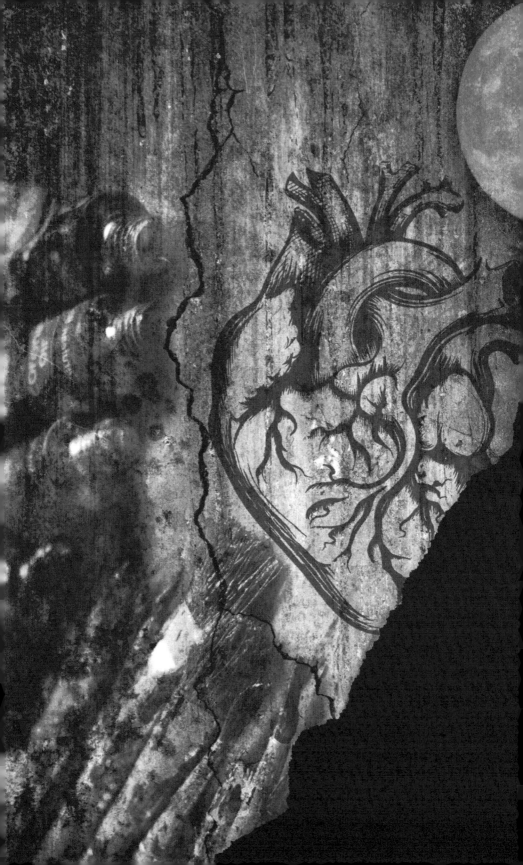

CHAPTER 11

Amelia

16 YEARS OLD

He was late. I should be annoyed, but he was always late, so I was used to it. Jake had called a few hours ago, saying he would be at my house by 7 p.m. to pick me up. Kimberly Walters was having an end-of-summer party at her parent's beach house, and he wanted to go. Deciding to wait for him outside, I go out and sit in one of the wooden rocking chairs that line the front porch. Finally pulling up at 7:30, he takes one look at me in my, if I was being honest with myself, risque two-piece bathing suit and matching cover-up, and lets out a loud wolf whistle that has me simultaneously shushing him and giggling like a schoolgirl. Which I guess I was, although sometimes it felt as though I'd already experienced enough for several lifetimes. I tried not to let my mind wander down that path of thinking because it dredged up memories that had no place on this date. Tonight, I just wanted to feel like a normal 16-year-old girl going to a party with a normal 18-year-old boy.

I'd been so surprised when Jake had asked me out for the first time two months ago. I was a sophomore; he was a senior. At first, I'd been sure I was going to end up the butt of some kind of joke, probably at the behest of my stepbrother Merrick. Even now, a year after our parents had gotten married, I still flip-flopped between crushing on my slightly older step-sibling and wanting to spit in his face, depending on the day and what his attitude was like.

At school, Merrick pretended I didn't exist. Given his good looks and an unending well of charm that seemed to extend to everyone but me, of course, he ran with the popular crowd. So did Jake, though they never seemed to actually speak to each other. They attended the same parties, the same football games, everything. But I never actually saw them interact directly. In fact, Merrick tended to scowl any time Jake tried to insert himself into a conversation my stepbrother was a part of. Even so, when Jake first asked me out, I'd been sure that Merrick had put him up to it. I knew I'd come a long way from the gangly preteen with a flat chest, but I still didn't think I would be what anyone would consider a "classic beauty". Having a guy like Jake actually give me the time of day seemed like a dream come true … or a really bad joke. But after a few dates and a lot of genuine conversation, I'd chalked up my initial misgivings to me just being overly cautious and having a general distrust of everyone. Since that first date, Jake and I have spent a lot of time together. Anywhere I was, so was Jake and vice versa.

So tonight was nothing out of the ordinary. Getting into Jake's topless Jeep was no big feat, but making space for myself in the front passenger's seat amidst all the empty beer cans and fast food wrappers was somewhat of a challenge. This, too, wasn't anything new. Jake drank … a lot. For someone clearly underage, he somehow always managed to have booze on hand. Usually, I could tell his level of intoxication just by the way he walked or spoke. Yes, I was going through a rebellious stage, but I didn't have a death wish. If I thought he was too drunk to get us to the party safely, I wouldn't get into the car with him. I guess that was one good … or bad thing about Jake, depending on how you looked at it. He held his liquor pretty well for someone so young.

Getting to the party doesn't take much time. Folly Beach is only about a 20-minute drive from Downtown Charleston. Walking through the door, we're immediately swallowed up by a huge crowd of people all talking at once. The music is loud, the people are loud, everything is just … loud.

I decide almost immediately that I won't be spending more than a few minutes in the main part of the house. I just need to grab a drink and get out of here before I go deaf. Smiling sweetly and nodding my head absently at everyone while not taking in a word they say, I slowly make my way into the kitchen where there's a keg set up, along with several buckets filled with ice and those premixed cocktails in glass bottles. Grabbing two bottles, I make my way out back to the deck. I knew Jake liked spending time with me, but I also knew that when it wasn't just the two of us, he wouldn't miss me. No one would, for that matter. I didn't have much in common with other kids my age. The heights of their concerns were teenage pregnancies and what adult they were gonna be able to use to buy them alcohol. The only real friend I had was Siren, but she'd recently dropped out of school with literally no warning, then ran off to be with some guy she claimed to be in love with. Apparently, he was older and had "swept her off her feet". Although we'd been best friends for years, I never even got to meet the guy. It was really strange, but every now and then, I'd get a text message or a letter from her, so I knew she was alive.

Even with a closed door between us and music blasting throughout the house, Jake's booming laugh jerks me from my thoughts. Smiling to myself because Jake is always the life of the party, I wander down the stairs, over the sand dunes, and out onto the vast expanse of nearly empty beach.

I loved the beach at night: the darkness, the smell of salt water, and the sound of the waves hitting the sand. I loved it all. But most of all, I loved the moon. On nights like tonight, when the moon was full, you could see it reflected off the water. The light shone like a beacon, casting everything else in shadow. I knew all about shadows. They followed me everywhere I went. They were a part of me in a way that no one else would ever understand. Each one had a face, a name, and a shape. I'd gotten to the age now where I mostly saw them when I closed my eyes. But I'd found that if I painted what I saw, that when I opened my eyes, that particular shadow would never appear to me the same way again.

So when I wasn't in school or with Jake, I was painting. I both anticipated and dreaded the shadows. Sometimes, I wished I was someone else. Someone without so many secrets. But when I tried to picture what that person would be like, it was like looking at a blank canvas. There was nothing there. No shadows *or* light. Because one couldn't exist without the other. So, I just tried to be the most authentic version of myself while still keeping the most ghoulish parts of my past a secret.

The sound of movement behind me tears me out of my inner musings, and I drag my transfixed gaze away from the moon just in time to see Jake fighting his way over the dunes towards me. He's obviously had more to drink since we got here because, while slogging your way through loose sand wasn't easy, he was stumbling a little more than he should have been. I know he sees me, though, because even in the low light, I can make out the little smirk on his face, followed quickly by his eyes traveling the length of my body. I'm not a prude by any means, but something about the way he's looking at me now sets my teeth on edge. Don't get me wrong, Jake and I have kissed and made out a little, but for some reason that I can't quite put my finger on, I've always cut things short before it could get too far.

Plopping down on the sand next to me, Jake grabs my elbow in a rough grip and pulls. Losing my footing in the uneven sand, my flip-flops fall off, and I tumble down next to him. Before I have a chance to sit up, he's already leaning over me, his torso pressing into my chest as his mouth finds mine. Without finesse or preamble, he shoves his tongue inside, nearly making me gag. I can taste the alcohol on him. Smell it on his breath. Knowing that something isn't right, I push at his shoulders until he leans back far enough for me to see that it's not just alcohol that has him acting this way. His pupils are blown wide, and his gaze is unfocused. He's high on something. Someone inside must've brought drugs to the party, and clearly Jake took advantage. I'm used to him wanting to have a good time, and I know that that usually goes hand in hand with beer or shots, but I've never been around Jake when he's high. I don't like it. Not only because he doesn't seem to be registering a thing I say but because it's making him unpredictable, and up to this point, I've been able to set clear boundaries on what I'm willing to do and what I'm not.

Burying his face in my neck, Jake begins to kiss a path down past my collar-bone while his left hand roughly latches onto my breast. Letting out a little squeak of pain and surprise, I do my best to get through to him and gain his attention.

"Jake, stop. I don't want this. Not here," I say in a pleading tone.

Lifting his head, his glazed eyes find mine, and suddenly there's no trace of the boy I've spent so much time with over the last two months. There's something dark in his eyes that has the devil dancing up my spine, and somehow, I know that if I don't get myself out from under him and away from here, something bad is gonna happen. Trying again, I say, "Jake, please. I'm not feeling well. Will you take me home? I wanna go home."

"Come on, Amelia. You've been playing games with me for weeks, and now I finally have you alone, and you wanna go home?"

"Games? What games?" I say in a rush. "I'm just not ready. I've told you that. Soon, I'll be ready soon."

"Always "soon". Well, what if I want "now"?"

Feeling myself begin to tremble, I try to keep my head on straight. Quickly, I try to think of a way out of this that doesn't result in me having to physically fight him off. I hate confrontation, but if he doesn't stop, I'll do what I have to do.

Just as that thought occurs to me, I feel one hand come up around my throat while the other pushes past the waistband of my bathing suit bottoms without warning. My cover-up must've ridden up when I fell. I try to squeeze my legs tightly together to lock him out, but it's no use. He's got about 80 pounds on me. Squirming desperately, I try to call out, but the hand that was bracketing my throat, is suddenly shoved over my mouth.

"Shhh, don't worry. I'll make it good for you, I promise. Just don't fight me," he says in a soothing tone like he's talking to a small child. Feeling my fight or flight responses kick in, I manage to free one of my arms from where they've been trapped between our bodies, and, without thinking, I shove the heel of my palm up into his nose. There's a sickening crunch, followed by a bellow of pain and rage as he rears back, clutching his face. Blood pours from his nose, leaking through the cracks in his fingers as he attempts to assess the damage. His momentary lapse in concentration is just enough to allow me to scramble out from under him. Setting out at a dead run, I push my legs as fast as they'll carry me back towards the house. I have the thought that if I can just make it back to the porch, I'll be fine. He won't want people to see him covered in blood, so I don't think he'll follow me inside. I can catch a ride home with someone else. Hell, I'll even take a cab at this point. Anything to get me the fuck out of here.

Running as fast as possible on the loose sand, I can just make out the lights from the house when a hand grips my hair hard from behind, yanking me backwards. I try to scream, but that hand clamps over my mouth again, and I'm roughly thrown face down onto the ground. I make a muffled sound of pain as the sand scrapes across my face, rubbing the tender flesh raw. I have just enough time to flip over before the full weight of Jake is on top of me. He looks enraged, and suddenly, I know that the drugs can't be blamed for this. The dark look in his eyes tells me that we would've ended up here tonight, with or without the influence of alcohol and narcotics. How did I not see this before? How did I not sense this in him? I'm usually suspicious of everyone, but for some reason, I thought he was different.

I fight as hard as I can, but it's pointless. With one hand covering my mouth and the other alternating between corralling my hands and ripping my swimsuit bottoms down, it wasn't long before he freed himself, forced his hips between my thighs, and pushed his way into me with one hard thrust. Letting out a scream that's muffled by his palm, I cry rivers of tears while he grunts and groans on top of me. His nose is still bleeding, and the drops fall like rain onto my bare chest, each one marking me like a brand. Looking up, my eyes find the moon again, and I know that this moment is destined to become just another shadow, attaching itself to me with claws that dig deep. Staring, transfixed, my watery eyes seek out the light as Jake ruts above me until, blessedly, he finishes with a groan.

I wince as he pulls out of me and flops onto his back in the sand. Glancing over at me, he says in a nonchalant tone, "I told you not to fight me. It didn't have to be like this. Next time will be better."

Standing up, he tucks himself back into his pants before reaching down to help me up. It's a testament to how devoid of emotion I am that I let him pull my bottoms back up and lead me back to the house, going around instead of through, before putting me into his Jeep. I do my best to stay curled into a ball, my body pressed against the passenger door in an attempt to remain as far away from him as possible. The drive from Folly Beach back to Downtown Charleston is quiet. In the silence, my already fractured mind does its best to process what just happened and, in an attempt to preserve what little sanity I have left, compartmentalize it. When darkness gives way to old-fashioned lamp posts, and I realize that we're back in the city, I sit up suddenly and demand, "Let me out! Now! Right now! Stop the fucking car!"

Scoffing, Jake ignores my request. It isn't until I unlock my side and open the door with the intention of jumping out that he slams on the brakes and pulls the car over to the side of the street. He makes a grab for my arm, but before he can grip me, I'm already out of the car and speed walking down the sidewalk. I hear the idle hum of the engine as he sits for a moment, possibly deciding whether he wants to get out and come after me. I pray with everything in me that he doesn't. After another minute, I hear the squeal of tires and see the car speed past me in a blur, leaving me behind. It's at this moment that I let out the breath I didn't know I'd been holding since I jumped from the car. Standing alone on the sidewalk, I stare off into the distance, watching the tail lights from his Jeep grow faint. Glancing around, I try to get my bearings on where I am and realize I'm about four streets down from my house. I grimace from the soreness between my legs with every step. I just want to get inside, take a hot shower, and scrub away the top layer of skin from every part of me that he touched.

Barefoot, walking in a sort of half trance, I don't see the person coming towards me from the opposite direction until I literally bump into them. My nose hits a hard wall of muscle, and it takes me several long blinks before my eyes can focus on the face that's now eye level with mine. It's then that I realize hands are gripping my upper arms. Panic closes around my throat like a vice as remnants of the night return until my emerald eyes meet a set of chocolate brown ones that I would recognize anywhere. It's then that I take stock of the situation and realize the hands on my upper arms probably went there to steady me and keep me from falling onto the pavement when we bumped into each other. However, what was a loose hold is now a tight grip as Merrick takes in my appearance. My hair is a mess, I know my makeup is smeared, and when I realize his gaze is fixated on my chest, I glance down to see that my cover-up has been ripped, and he's staring at the droplets of blood left behind from Jake's broken nose. Rage fills his eyes, and I watch as his jaw tightens to what I imagine must be a painful degree.

"Mia, what the fuck happened?! You're bleeding!" he all but growls.

Unable to speak for fear that I'll have a breakdown and cry right here in the middle of the sidewalk, I shake my head. He must see the anguish in my gaze because, without another word, he leans down and lifts me into his arms. Under any other circumstances, the way he's holding me might seem romantic, and I'd be lying if I said I hadn't dreamed of him swooping me up and holding me against his chest. This is definitely not the way I envisioned it, though. Regardless, I rest my head against his shoulder and allow his scent to permeate my nostrils, washing away the remnants of Jake's beer breath.

Merrick is silent as he carries me through the backdoor of our home and up the stairs to the second floor. It isn't until he's kicking the door shut behind us that I realize we're in his bedroom, not mine. Instead of putting me down, he sits on the edge of the massive four-poster bed, me still cradled against his chest. I can feel his heavy breaths and hear his heart hammering against my ear.

Sounding almost desperate, he says, "Mia, you have to tell me where you're hurt. I can't help you if I don't know what happened. Please, tell me who did this to you."

I'm so unused to hearing concern from him, and for some reason, it strikes a chord in me. I hate the idea of him being distraught, so I say in a low tone, "It's not my blood. It's Jake's. I think I broke his nose."

I immediately feel Merrick's entire body stiffen at the mention of Jake. Reaching down, he gently takes my chin in his hand, lifting my face until I meet his eyes. They're not warm now but dark and a little terrifying. His next words come out very slowly. I'm not sure if it's in an attempt to put me at ease or because he's barely keeping his rage on its leash. "Tell ... me ... what ... happened. Now."

Wincing, I dart my suddenly nervous gaze away. Tightening the grip on my chin, he forces my eyes back to his. Staring up into his eyes, I'm hit with a sudden wave of emotion. I try to blink the tears away, but one spills over, and slips down my cheek. He watches it track down my face with laser focus, and I see his nostrils flare. I have the wayward thought that if he clenches his jaw any tighter, his teeth will crack. In an effort to preserve his pearly whites, I whisper, "He hurt me. I hurt him too, but he hurt me more." Glancing away again, I break eye contact because I can't stand to see the look in his eyes when I say my next words. "He took something I didn't want to give."

An eerie sense of calm seems to come over him at my words. Without warning, Merrick shoots to his feet. I let out a little yelp of surprise and clutch at his neck in an attempt to keep myself from falling to the floor. Sitting me down on the bed and disentangling my arms from around him, he's already halfway to the door before my mind registers what's happening. Jumping up from the bed, I rush over to block his path, putting my hands up in the universal gesture for "STOP".

"No, Merrick, don't! Please. It'll only make things worse," I say as he tries to push past me.

"Worse? How can it get worse?? He hurt you! He took something precious from you! He took ..." he pauses, eyes darting around wildly without focus before clashing with mine. "... something that wasn't meant for him!"

He looks almost crazed. I've never seen Merrick like this. I never would've expected it from him. He usually treats me with such indifference. Like he couldn't care one way or the other about anything I do. This type of response seems completely out of character. But as I look up into his eyes, the small hint of whatever I see there nearly breaks my heart. I'm hit with a sudden sense of urgency. I don't want him to leave. I need him to stay here with me, if only to try to ground him before he goes out and does something crazy.

Reaching up, I place my hands on either side of his face, forcing him to stay focused on me. "Please don't go. I need you." I've never said anything like this to him. That alone is enough to jar him back to the present. To bring him back to this room with me. Instead of halfway across town on the way to Jake's house. After another agonizing moment, he lets out a heavy breath and nods. Taking my hand, he leads me back to the bed. Easing me down to sit, he goes into the adjoining bathroom and comes back a minute later with a wet rag. Crouching down in front of me, he gently begins to wipe away the drops of blood smattering my chest. The cloth is warm and soothing against my skin, and it isn't until he presses the warm rag to the side of my face that I remember the abrasions caused by the sand. The hiss I release is involuntary, and I immediately wish I could take it back because I don't wanna break whatever spell is making him *see* me, possibly for the first time.

He winces at the sound of my pain but doesn't say anything. Going back to the bathroom, he rinses the rag and brings it back to me. One fist clenched, he passes me the rag with the other before turning his back on me. At first, I think he's going to try to leave again, but he doesn't move, just stands stock still. It takes me a second, but then it dawns on me that he's giving me the rag to clean myself ... down there. Using the rag, I grimace as I do my best to wipe myself clean of all traces of Jake. Afterwards, he turns back around and pulls back the comforter, motioning for me to climb in. Not passing up the chance to sleep in his bed, I do. He makes it like he's going to tuck me in, and it's then that I realize that he actually does plan to leave me here. Lightening fast, I reach out my hand and grip his wrist. "Stay with me? I don't wanna be alone."

His gaze is intense as he scans my face, lingering momentarily on the scratches that mar my left cheek before his eyes find mine again. I can see some kind of internal struggle happening, but whatever he sees in my eyes must make the decision for him because he toes off his shoes, pulls back the comforter once more, and climbs in beside me. We lay there for a moment, both of us stiff and unsure what to do. Realizing that my torn cover-up probably has sand all over it, I sit up to remove it, leaving me in just my bathing suit. Glancing over my shoulder, I ask tentatively, "Is this okay?"

At his slow nod, I lay back on the pillow, pulling the blanket up to my chin. We stay like that for another long moment before he turns onto his side, facing me. Tentatively, as though he's worried that I'll be afraid of him, his arm reaches out, circling my waist. He slowly pulls me into him until my back is to his front. He must be drowning in my tangled mass of hair, but he doesn't voice a single complaint. Surrounded by the warmth of his body and his scent on the sheets, the full weight of everything that happened tonight finally hits and whatever lock I'd used to keep my emotions in check breaks wide open. The first tears are silent as they fall onto his pillowcase. When Merrick's arm tightens around me, those silent tears turn to racking sobs. Feather light, I feel him press a soft kiss to my shoulder. He doesn't say anything, only holds me tighter until I've cried out everything. The fear, the hurt, my tears, and any energy I may have had left. I drift off to sleep soon after, pressed firmly against him. When I wake hours later, he's gone. I bring the blanket up to my nose, inhaling deeply. Glancing over at the bedside table, I feel a pang in my chest. He left the bedside lamp on. To keep the shadows away. Looking back, I would mark that night as the first time I fell in love with him.

CHAPTER 12

Merrick

18 YEARS OLD

I don't even know how I got here. Well, let me rephrase. Geographically, I know exactly where I am and the route I must've traveled to get to where my car is currently parked. When I say, "I don't know how I got here," I mean I have no recollection of driving out to Folly Beach. I remember leaving our house with the sole intention of tracking down that motherfucker, Jake, and beating the shit out of him. All I can say is thank God for muscle memory because if it weren't for the fact that I've driven to this beach more times than I can count, I'm not sure how I would've ended up here in one piece.

Leaving Amelia sleeping in my bed has to be one of the hardest things I've ever done in my life. When she'd asked me to stay with her, a part of me literally jumped at the chance to get to hold her the way I'd dreamt of for the last year, while another part of me could barely contain the white-hot rage bubbling inside me at the fact that this little piece of human garbage thought he had the right to take what was mine, and more so than that, to hurt what was mine. Buried somewhere in the recesses of my mind, I knew that this would happen. Not that the woman I was in love with would be sexually assaulted, but that there was the possibility that some other man, who wasn't me, would be the one to initiate her into the world of sex. Never in my wildest dreams would I have thought, however, that it would happen in this way. Against her will, scared and beaten up. Just thinking about it now makes me want to break something.

Which explains why I'm currently sitting outside of the house where the beach party took place. Right after leaving Amelia, I went straight to Jake's house. Of course, I knew where he lived. With Deacon's help, I knew a lot of things about a lot of people. Knowledge was power, and for a boy who'd always had the power taken away from him, the man I'd become now craved it. Unfortunately, when I pulled up in front of Jake's family home in Downtown Charleston, his car hadn't been in the driveway, and all the lights in the house were out. It didn't look like anyone was home. Getting on the phone with Deacon, I gave him Jake's cell number and asked him to use the GPS to ping his cell and find out exactly where the bastard was. A few minutes later, I'd found out that after dumping Amelia in the middle of the street with no fucking shoes, this little shit had gone back to the party that was still going strong, even now.

Getting out of the car, I keep to the cover of shadows, using bushes that could only thrive in sweltering heat like this, using large Palmetto trees as cover. Making my way around the house, I peek into each window, looking for any sign of that rapist piece of shit. Just as I'm about to take the corner of the house that leads to the back, where a large deck overlooking the beach sits, I hear a voice I immediately recognize. Glancing up, I zero in on my target. Jake is on the deck above me, arm slung around a girl's shoulders. With the way he's swaying back and forth, even with the help of the girl, it's clear that he's loaded. I fucking hated alcohol. I rarely drank. It made people stupid and sloppy. The only time I made an exception was when I was with Deacon because I knew no matter what happened, he'd have my back. Standing under the deck, keeping myself pressed to the wall of the house, I watch as Jake and the unknown girl head down the stairs that lead to the sand dunes.

I have a moment where I wonder if he plans to do to her what he did to Amelia. I have a feeling that even if he was so inclined, he wouldn't be able to pull it off, given his current level of intoxication. I follow anyway, knowing I won't get a better opportunity to get Jake on his own. As I watch, he and the girl stumble clumsily over the dunes and down the large expanse of beach. There's no one out on the water at this time of night, and I'm thankful for that. I don't need witnesses to what I'm about to do. If Jake lives to tell the tale, no one will believe him anyway, not as drunk as he is.

I keep a ways back until they've made it far enough from the house that it's safe for me to make my move. Walking up to the pair with purpose in every step, I barely spare the girl a second glance before uttering one word.

"Leave."

Jake turns, probably to ask me where the fuck I get off. The girl, however, takes one look at my face before dropping Jake like a bad habit and bolting back towards the house.

"Hey! Who the fuck are you?" Jake slurs, trying to focus in on my face. If he squints any harder though, his eyes will be completely closed and he won't be seeing shit. It's clear that he doesn't currently possess the mental faculties to engage in a one-on-one fight, but that's fine. I have no qualms about beating the shit out of someone that deserves it, impaired or not. Ever so slowly, I prowl closer to the bastard, deadly menace written all over my face. The rage that I've been tamping down for the last hour has resurfaced with a vengeance. With every step I take closer to him, images of Amelia's scraped face, bloody chest, and torn clothing flash in front of my eyes like a slideshow.

"I think you know exactly who I am, Jake," I say in a taunting tone. "You may be seeing two of me right now, but I promise you, by the time we're done, you're gonna be thanking God that there's only one."

Still squinting, Jake makes the mistake of stepping closer, trying to get a good look at my face. It takes him about three times longer than it would take the average person, but finally, he makes a scoffing sound and says, "Oh, it's you. She sends you to fight her battles for her now? Because I promise you, I didn't give her anything she didn't want."

He's barely finished his last sentence before the tight leash I had on the beast clawing inside me snaps. Lunging for the fucker, I grab his right arm, twisting it behind his back in a hold that I know will only take the slightest bit of pressure, and his shoulder will dislocate. Agonizingly slow, I apply that pressure, hearing the telltale pop of his shoulder coming out of the joint. Within a millisecond, he's squealing like a stuck pig. Pushing him to the ground, I shove him, face first, into the sand. The rough particles fill his open mouth, muffling his cries of pain, but I know that in addition to the agony he's experiencing in his shoulder, his face is going to end up looking like he went 10-rounds with a cheese grater and lost.

Leaning my body over his, pressing his face firmly into the sand, I make sure I'm close enough for him to hear me over the pitiful whimpers coming out of his mouth before saying, "You self-entitled little fuck. Did you really think you could get away with taking something so precious? What was it? Did it finally dawn on you that you were never going to be good enough for her? That she was never going to give it up to you willingly, so you just decided to take it instead?"

He tries to answer but is having a hard time getting words past the mouth full of sand he's currently inhaling. Leaning up enough to flip him onto his back, I give him a minute to choke out the dry sand from his nostrils and mouth. I want to hear what he has to say for himself. I have a feeling this is going to go one of two ways. He'll either pull on the seemingly unending reserve of arrogance he has inside him, and he'll say something smart, at which point I'll beat the shit out of him, or he'll profusely apologize and beg for mercy, at which point I'll beat the shit out of him anyway. The moral? Neither option will save Jake from my wrath.

Just as expected, Jake looks up at me and lets out a raspy laugh, still spitting out bits of sand and seashell. Giving him the benefit of the doubt, I write off his boldness as a side effect from the booze and probably ecstasy he's ingested. That is, until he opens his mouth and says, "I don't know why you give a shit about this, man. She wasn't even that great.

Maybe with some practice, you could turn her into a good little whore. As long as you don't mind my sloppy seconds."

It's at this moment I realize the anger I felt on the way here is nothing compared to what I feel now. A black film covers my vision. I don't even remember lifting my arm, but by the time I look down again, Jake's face is something resembling spaghetti. A mass of blood, broken bones, missing teeth, and torn flesh. The boy is passed out cold, and for some reason, that fact does nothing to lessen my rage. It takes every ounce of strength in me to pull my next punch. Staggering to my feet, I glance around to ensure that no one is nearby. Seeing a child's abandoned sand castle bucket a few feet away, I stagger to my feet, pick it up and head to the water. Filling the bucket, I take the cold salt water, and dump it unceremoniously right into Jake's face. As predicted, he wakes with a sputter, followed by an agonized moan that sounds like a symphony to my ears.

Gripping him by the front of his shirt, I bring my face down close to his. I want to make sure he's conscious enough to understand and process the words I'm going to say next. As I gaze down at his mangled face, I see that both of his eyes are swollen shut. He can't see shit, but I know he can still hear me. Just to make sure, I jostle him, saying, "You still with me, you little fuck? Nod, if you understand me!"

Nodding sluggishly, he starts to babble something, but his lips are busted, and with the way he's spitting out mouthfuls of blood, I can only assume he bit part of his tongue off at some point. Slapping him across the face to silence whatever it was he was trying to get out, I say, "Listen to me very, very carefully. What just happened to you is a small taste of what I'll do if you so much as breathe the same air as her ... ever again. There's a loooot of swamp country out here, Jake. A lot of places someone could dump a body, and it would never be found. Either sunk to the bottom of some marsh or eaten, piece by piece, by a group of hungry gators. Please believe me when I say that there is nothing I wouldn't do for that girl, murder included. I would end your life right now if she askcd mc to, and I wouldn't blink twice. Remember that when you sober up. Because it doesn't matter where you are or who you're with, there's nowhere that I wouldn't be able to find you." Shaking him from where I've got a death grip on the front of his shirt, I yell through gritted teeth, "Say you understand!"

"I ... understand! I understand!" he cries out as best he can. Releasing the front of his shirt, I can't help but draw back my arm, ramming my fist into his face one last time. "Sleep it off," I mumble before standing to my full height and trudging back to my car. I hope Amelia is still asleep by the time I get back home. I'd love nothing more than to slip back into bed behind her, taking warmth from her while providing her the comfort she so desperately needed. I'm tired now, a bone-deep kind of tired. I don't know how much longer I'm going to be able to mask this obsession that's taken root inside me where this girl is concerned. The idea of killing that little fuck never even phased me. I meant what I said to him. If she asked me to snuff out his life, I would. That fact should scare me, but it doesn't. It may scare her, though, and that thought terrifies me. It's only a matter of time before she realizes that the boy she's called "stepbrother" for the last year is now a man possessed, who'll stop at nothing to call her his own.

CHAPTER 13

Merrick

Exiting the little coffee shop on Market Street that I know is Amelia's favorite, I run my hand through my hair in frustration. I don't know why I came here. Realistically, I know she wouldn't be getting coffee at 10 p.m., but after checking a handful of her other favorite spots and finding no trace of her, it was a last-ditch effort. While Amelia is a free spirit in many ways, she's also a creature of habit. For the most part, I could pinpoint where she is at any given time of the day simply because she has a sort of routine about the way she goes through life. I think the structure gives her some sense of control.

But after skulking around the places she would normally go on a Sunday like a goddamn stalker, which, if I'm honest with myself, I am ... she's nowhere to be found. It's clear she's avoiding me. After what happened at the club last night, I'm not sure I can blame her. There was a moment there where I was positive that I was going to blow it, no pun intended. It was scary how close I came to letting myself go and confessing everything just to get her to get in the car and come home with me. She smelled so fucking good that even now, hours later, I feel as though her scent is haunting me. Following me around Charleston, like one of the many ghosts that inhabit this city. Her scent has always been intoxicating, but not in the way that a woman who's spritzed herself with

121

liberal amounts of perfume is. Amelia's favorite scent has always been rosewater. Her soap, her shampoo, her lotions are all rose-scented. I knew this because of the years growing up with her and having to share such close quarters. I may have also snuck into her room a time or two and snooped around. Her favorite scent wasn't the only thing I knew about her. I knew a lot. Probably more than she'd be comfortable with, but ever since that first day, when she'd sauntered up to me in the parlor of her mother's house and proclaimed me to be her new brother, I'd been addicted to that smell. It had wafted off of her and invaded every single one of my senses, to the point where it was now buried so deep beneath my skin that I didn't think I'd ever get it out. Much like the woman herself. Over the years, I'd gone out of my way to seek out that particular fragrance. My apartment was littered with candles that I burned any time I was alone. Which was always. My apartment was my sanctuary. A place of solitude where I could go to escape the prying eyes of the predators I'd chosen to surround myself with, simply to appease my inner child's need for attention and notoriety.

Finally giving up, I check my watch for what must be the hundredth time today, concluding that she must be at home by now. I'll just make a quick pit stop there before heading home myself just to make sure she's safe. I scoff inwardly. I'm such a liar. As if I need an excuse to follow her home. I've done it hundreds of times over the years. You would think by now, I would've stopped making excuses for my behavior and just accepted the fact that I'm fucking obsessed with the woman, and there aren't any lines I wouldn't cross when it comes to her.

It's not a far walk from Market Street to Amelia's townhouse, and even though I stroll down the street like I don't have a care in the world, my insides are scrambling with the need to break out into a run. I just need to see her, to be near her, to make sure that she's home and most importantly, *alone*. Over the years, I know Amelia has had boyfriends if you could even call them that. Pitiful little excuses for men that wouldn't stand a snowball's chance in Hell of making her happy in the long run. They weren't like me. They didn't know everything there was to know about her, and the few that tried to get close enough to learn who she was as a person, I scared off. I'm not sorry about it. Especially after what happened with her first boyfriend. Even now, thinking about that night causes flames to erupt under my skin, and the need to dish out retribution of the eternal variety is nearly unbearable. So, no, I don't have an ounce of regret when it comes to sabotaging some of her other relationships. From the day she walked into that parlor with her squeaky sneakers and paint-smudges on her cheek, she's been mine. No other eventuality existed. I won't allow it.

Coming to the sudden realization that I've made it to her place and that I've been standing in front of the wrought iron gate for God knows how long, I let out the breath I didn't know I was holding when I see the lights on in her little disjointed studio. Filling my burning lungs with air, I fleetingly wonder how long I was holding my breath as I give a shake of my head to clear away all thoughts of anyone else being anywhere near her. As I try in vain to draw in much-needed air, the irony of the situation isn't lost on me. I don't think I've taken a good breath since the day we met, my chest tightening painfully every time she walked into a room or I heard her voice. Making my way around to the back of the property, where I know a small bench sits on the sidewalk outside, I step onto it and hop over the fence surrounding her yard. I've done this enough times to know not to try to enter the property through the front gate. It creaks, and in the still night air, it would be akin to an alarm system. I don't want her to know I'm here. I'm just so keyed up, and I need to know that she's safe, and then I'll be able to go home and take a cold shower to wash away the self-loathing and the smell of her that's still all over my skin.

Keeping to the shadows of the large oak trees littering the property, I slink over to the small studio and my preferred window to watch her from. I've stood here on countless occasions, just watching her paint. It's such a personal process that I almost feel bad for spying on her, but I like seeing her completely at ease with herself, the way she never is when she knows I'm around. Creeping closer to the window, I peer inside. I chose this window to watch from over thc fcw others around the small structure firstly because it gives me an unimpeded view of everything going on inside and secondly because there's only about a four foot gap between this wall of the studio and a tall hedge that runs parallel to the fence on this side of the yard. Because of this, I know there's no chance of the neighbors on the other side of the hedge seeing me.

As I take my first peek through the window, my eyes unerringly zero in on Amelia in the corner near the front door, where a table is set up, covered in cups and jars and canisters of all kinds full of paintbrushes. Another table lines the opposite wall; this one littered with tubes of paint and other odd supplies she uses while creating. Amelia's art isn't conventional by any standards, and she frequently uses odd products and supplies to create a certain effect when painting. As I watch, I see her rummaging through the jars, looking for what I assume is a particular brush. Typically, when she paints, her movements are fluid like water, the brush becoming an extension of her arm with its deft strokes. Tonight, though, she seems on edge, her movements jerky as she prowls around the studio. I wonder if it has anything to do with what happened last night. The very idea that she's still thinking about our encounter in the garage has my cock jerking in my pants.

As I watch, I see her walk over to a fresh canvas that's been set up on her easel. Pallet in hand, she begins. This is also new. From what I've seen while pulling my little peeping Tom acts over the years, she typically sketches out whatever it is she plans to paint before actually beginning. Tonight, however, she must have a clear idea of what she wants seated firmly in her head because she's forgone the use of charcoal and went straight in with the paint. I watch, transfixed, constantly in awe of the raw talent she has inside her. Losing track of the time and how long I stand there, I simply stare, not just at the painting, but at her. I love to watch her work. The way her body moves, the small dips and bends, the tilt of her head, and the curls spilling from her ever-present messy bun all culminate into a sensual dance that has my palms sweating. She's wearing a ridiculously small pair of shorts and what appears to be an oversized sleep shirt that's had the collar cut off so that it's hanging off one shoulder. Too busy staring at her, it takes me a minute to realize what she's bringing to life on the canvas. Unlike her usual style, which is dark and abstract in many ways, this is something else. She's still mainly using shades of black and gray, but this painting isn't abstract in any way. Yes, she's still using those shades to create deep shadows, but this time, those shadows are wrapping around the silhouette of two people so intertwined with each other that it takes me a second to realize they're two separate entities.

Standing stock still, it hits me that it's a portrait. That, in itself, is surprising because Amelia doesn't typically do portraits. But it's not the knowledge that she's stepped outside of her wheelhouse that shocks me to my core. It's the realization that I recognize the two people on the canvas. The ones so wrapped up in each other, they might as well be one person. It's us. Her and me. The faces are as clear as the night of a full moon. Squinting, I take in more of the finer details. We aren't just intertwined but connected. Hands and mouths. Her eyes are closed as I devour her, our tongues dueling with each other. Another shock, like a zing of static electricity, hits me when my real eyes find the matching set on the canvas. They're open, staring at her as we kiss. I huff out a small breath of astonishment. The painting is a perfect metaphor for our relationship. She's lost in the throws of the kiss—living in the moment—while I'm lost just looking at her.

I stand there for a long time, eyes never straying from the painting until I see Amelia straighten from the canvas. Surely she isn't finished already? It's so rare for her to complete a painting in one sitting. It's only when she moves back that even more details come into view. The hand that's possessively cupping one of her breasts while the other is tangled in her hair. My hands aren't the only ones occupied, though. Hers are gripping my bare back, nails digging into my skin. The flesh and bone Amelia stands to her full height. This is the part of the process when she would normally stare at the painting with a critical eye, assessing for any imperfections or anything she'd like to change. But as I finally tear my gaze from the painting, I take her in fully and notice that, if I'm not mistaken, she's breathing heavily. I can see the rapid rise and fall of her shoulders. I'm sure she's exerted herself while painting before, but for some reason, her body language has alarm bells going off in my head.

She's staring at the painting, and while I was transfixed with the image myself only moments ago, now I can't stop staring at her. Slowly, she backs away from the easel, and I have a moment of panic when I realize that she's backing herself into the wall directly next to the window. Before that panic has a chance to fully set in, however, I feel my heart hitch in my chest as I watch her hands move from tucking a stray curl back into her bun down past her neck before skating over her breasts. Pausing there, she cups the full weight of them before lightly grazing a nail over one nipple. I feel that graze like a taser to my system as if she's touched *me* instead of herself. With the overhead lights in the studio and my current vantage point, I can see just how thin that sleep shirt is, her nipples clearly visible through the flimsy material. She isn't wearing a bra. Blinking hard, I give a small shake of my head; surely I'm dreaming all of this. But as I watch her, she seems entranced by the painting, not realizing what she's doing. Or at least, that's what I tell myself until her right-hand leaves her breast and begins to make its way lower. As her hand glides over her abdomen, she takes the last few steps until her back is resting against the wall directly next to the window I'm outside of, just on the opposite side of the glass.

The worry that she'll look over and see me wars with the need to see where that hand is going. Curiosity wins out, and I realize I shouldn't have worried because it appears as though she can't tear her gaze away from the painting. Watching with rapt fascination, I nearly let out a low groan when her hand dips under the hem of the oversized shirt, then into the waistband of those tiny shorts that were going to be the death of me. I know the moment her fingers come into contact with her pussy because she lets out a whimper that I can actually *hear* through the cracks in the windowpane. Her eyes close briefly before reopening to focus back on the canvas.

Knowing that I'm the sickest kind of bastard but unable to stop myself, I reach down and undo the button of my slacks, drawing the zipper down just enough to allow myself access while making sure my pants don't fall to my ankles. Reaching inside and past the opening at the front of my boxer briefs, I pull my cock out, wrapping a hand tightly around it. I don't think I've ever been this hard in my life. Stroking myself from base to tip, I have to bite my lip to keep from letting out a moan that I know she'll be able to hear. Eying her with laser focus, I watch as she touches herself. The combination of the angle and her baggy shirt make it impossible to see what her hand is doing inside those little shorts, but even though I can't see her fingers move across her wet flesh, I *can* see her face and the looks passing over her features are enough to nearly have me spilling into my own palm. Moving my hand up and down my shaft, I spread a bead of pre-cum that's leaked out over the head as I watch her masturbate while staring at our likenesses on the canvas. With every sound that escapes her lips, my breath comes faster and faster, my pace picking up speed until I'm so close to the edge that it won't take much more to push me over. The movement of her hand increases beneath her shorts, and I know she's nearing her climax as well. Just as that thought occurs to me, she whips around, slamming her free hand against the wall of the studio so hard I nearly jump out of my skin. Hanging her head, the movement of her other hand loses its rhythm, becoming more erratic, and the need to hear her come is suddenly a burning fire within me. Giving up the visual of her nearly kills me, but in a split-second decision, I know I'd rather hear her fall. I quickly move to the other side of the window until there's only a thin wall separating us. This close, I can hear more clearly, and as she nears the edge, I stroke my cock faster, squeezing harder, holding myself up with my free hand and resting my forehead against the exterior wall until we're mirror images of each other. Nearly drawing blood from how hard I'm biting the inside of my lips to keep from making any noise as I listen to every sound that escapes her. Every moan, every gasp, every whimper until finally, I hear a sharp intake of breath followed by a split second of silence. The pause is nearly unbearable as I wait with a bated breath of my own, balancing on the razor's edge of sanity. What leaves her mouth next has me coming so hard I see stars bursting behind my eyelids.

My name. She cried out *my* name.

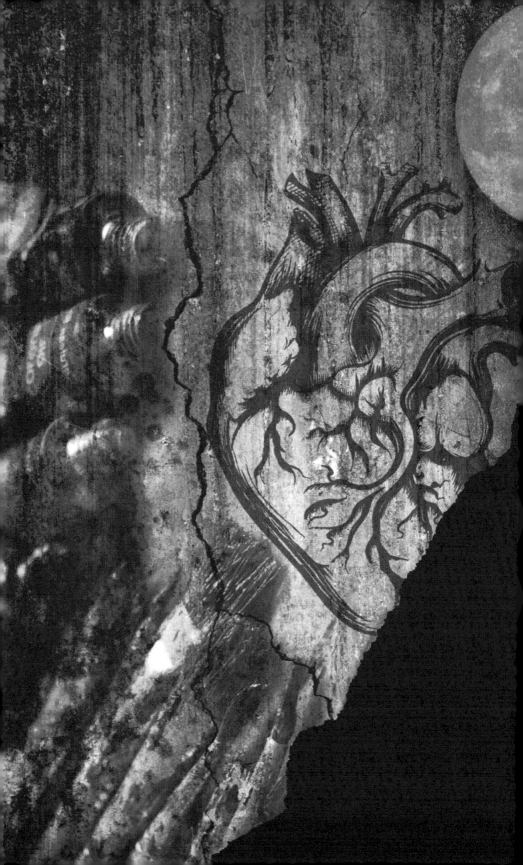

CHAPTER 14

Amelia

Resting my forehead against the wall of the studio, I try to catch my breath. What the actual fuck just happened? Not only had I created a painting that could double as a thumbnail on Pornhub, but then I'd gone and gotten off to the image of me and my stepbrother making out. And worse than that, I'm pretty sure I called out his name when I came. Placing both hands against the wall, I attempt to steady myself so that when I push away to stand upright, I won't just fall over. My legs feel like jelly. Don't get me wrong, I masturbate plenty. I'm not shy about it. But it's been years since I've done it to thoughts of Merrick, and those few times were before I knew what a pain in the ass he was.

Finally getting my breathing under control, I use my palms to push away from the wall until I'm standing up straight. As I shift, I can feel tiny little aftershocks shoot through my core like little zaps of electricity. I can feel my own wetness as well. Turning back around to look at the painting once more, a fresh wave of embarrassment washes over me. I'm not sure why I'm embarrassed. No one is here to see, but just the idea that Merrick has worked his way under my skin enough that not only would I want to paint the two of us together, but the image of the final work was so vivid that I couldn't stop myself from shoving my hand down my shorts and pretending that hand was his, is enough to have my cheeks reddening.

Unbidden, flashes of all the shitty things he's said and done to me, not just last night but over the last few days, run through my head and by the time I've cataloged everything, I've worked myself up to being good and mad. Storming over to the easel, I rip the painting down. I bring my leg up, poised to smash the canvas over my knee and destroy the evidence of my temporary moment of insanity. But as I glance down one last time, my gaze latches onto Merrick's in the painting. I don't know why I painted myself with my eyes closed but left his open. I mean, it's not a normal thing to do, is it? To keep your eyes open during a kiss. A lot of people would interpret it as the person just being bored or not interested in the dueling of tongues taking place, but as I look at those eyes that have been both my saving grace and the bane of my existence since I was a teen, I don't see boredom in their depths. Anything but, in fact. I see connection, desperation, and addiction. Are those things I just infused into the painting based on my own secret fantasies, or did my subconscious bring to life glimpses of something seen in the real Merrick's eyes before that I just didn't pick up on?

Suddenly, I hear a noise outside the window at the back of the studio, causing me to freeze. I quickly lower the painting from the easel, turn it, picture first, and place it against the corner wall where I normally store unfinished or surplus pieces that I couldn't bring myself to sell because of their personal content. Pressing my back to the wall, I slowly slide towards the window, feeling both spooked and absolutely ridiculous. As inconspicuous as I can, I bring my eyes to the glass, squinting to try and make out any shapes in the darkness. The lighting is bright in my studio, and it's pitch black outside. I move my head this way and that, but I can't see a damn thing. Considering no one popped their head up and took the opportunity to give me the biggest jump scare of my life, I'm guessing whatever noise I heard must've been made by some nocturnal critter. I give up on the foolish idea that I could be the plot on an upcoming episode of Forensic Files, and walk back over to where I've buried the painting. Yes, hiding it back here is a much better solution. For some reason, I just can't bear the thought of destroying it. I'll decide what to do with it later. Luckily for me, no one else comes into my studio, so at least I don't have to worry about someone stumbling across it.

Now that my fury over the painting and the irrational fear of impending murder has ebbed, I realize how desperately I need a shower. Leaving the studio, I walk the short little cobblestone path that leads to the house. Letting myself in through the back door, which is almost always unlocked, I make a quick pit stop in the kitchen, opening the fridge and guzzling a large bottle of water. I feel like I've been ridden hard and put away wet. I chuckle at my own pun, but in all honesty, I feel wrung dry. Exhausted and like I could take a 16-hour nap. Considering it's nearly one a.m., I'll settle for a nice hot shower, then bed. I trudge upstairs to the master bedroom and into the attached bathroom. The scent of roses surrounds me immediately. The area is spacious, with a large claw foot tub, a separate standing shower with frosted glass walls, and plenty of counter space surrounding the sink that sits below vanity lights. Perched on the countertop and along the windowsill are several rose-scented candles, while a bowl of potpourri sits atop the back of the toilet. The accent is a little old-fashioned, but I like it just the same. I dim the lights using the dial to my right, muting the harsh glare until it's nothing more than a soft glow. Turning on the shower, I give the water a minute to heat up while I gather all my toiletries from their usual spots on the rack attached to the tub.

Stepping under the scalding hot spray, I allow the water to ease some of the aches in my tight shoulders and even tighter leg muscles. The shoulders I'm used to. I typically suffer in that area whenever I paint for an extended period of time without breaks. My leg muscles are another thing entirely. I'm pretty sure my thighs locked up tighter than Fort Knox when that climax ripped through me earlier, but the hot water soothes some of those twinges before I begin to scrub my body clean and wash my hair with my favorite foaming body wash and shampoo. By the time I finish up and step out of the shower, wrapping a towel around my long curls and another around my body, I'm moving like an extra on The Walking Dead. Dragging myself over to my large queen-size four-poster bed, I pull back the floral comforter and matching Egyptian cotton top sheet, then quite literally, fall in. It's a testament to how tired I am that I don't even remember falling asleep, much less taking my hair out of the towel and putting on an oversized t-shirt. But that's exactly how I find myself when I wake the next morning.

As I crack open my eyelids, that seem to have glued themselves shut overnight, I squint at the bright light pouring in through the bay window that overlooks my small backyard. Sitting up, I stare at it. As I watch, a gentle breeze from outside flutters the deep purple curtain. I didn't leave that window open, did I? I rub my eyes to clear my blurry, sleepy gaze and give my room a closer look, glancing around and taking a quick inventory. Nothing seems to be missing or out of place; still, I can't shake the feeling that something isn't right. Maybe it has something to do with the very vivid, very graphic dreams I had last night. I rub my thighs together under the sheets, and can still feel the evidence of those dreams. Glancing down at my baggy t-shirt, my brows knit in consternation. I *definitely* don't remember putting this on. In fact, I don't think I've ever actually seen this shirt before. When did I buy this? It's almost like a man's white undershirt. I like baggy clothes, but I have no recollection of buying this shirt, much less putting it on last night. As I lift the sheet covering my bottom half, I see the zombie version of me couldn't be bothered to go hunting for underwear, not that I'm upset by that fact. I've recently taken to sleeping naked since the heat and humidity continue to ramp up.

Swinging my legs over the side of the bed, I go over and close the bay window. I'm already paying the electric company a fortune for my air consumption along with the fact that I have to sleep with a fan on every night. Something about the absolute silence of a room, especially when trying to sleep, makes me feel like bugs are crawling under my skin. The ambient noise provided by the fan helps preserve what little sanity I have left.

Speaking of insanity ... as I stand next to the window, I'm suddenly hit with memories of what happened last night. Blushing to the roots of my strawberry blonde curls, which are gloriously disheveled after going to bed wet, I put my head in my hands and let out a groan. As I glance down towards the studio, I remember everything I did there last night. The painting I hadn't planned on. Touching myself, which I definitely hadn't planned on. As my mind starts to run wild, the scenery outside begins to blur as I get lost in the images playing through my head, but not before something strange catches my eye. Squinting against the mid-morning sun, I bring my vision back into focus and see that the door to my studio is slightly ajar. A feeling of unease fills me, and I reach for the first item of clothing I can find to cover my lower half, which in this case, is a pair of leggings. I pull them on quickly, and race out of my room, down the stairs that lead to the first floor, through the kitchen and out the backdoor. I didn't bother with shoes because every second that it takes me to get to the door is another second that I'm internally freaking out. I always lock up the studio at night and would never leave the door unlocked, much less standing open. I remind myself that the neighborhood I live in is affluent and has virtually no crime rate, but somehow that thought doesn't make me feel better as I near the open studio door.

Pausing outside of the door, I briefly wonder if maybe I should call the police and wait for them to arrive before taking a look around, but it would take them God knows how long to get here, and there's a good chance there would be nothing to investigate because everything inside would be fine. At least, that's what I tell myself. It's mostly my own impatience that keeps me from being smart and calling the cops.

Leaning down and picking up a garden hoe, I hoist it up like it's going to actually scare off any unwanted burglars. Gripping the handle, I fling the door wide and let out a short yell that's so high-pitched, I'm pretty sure it'll have dogs barking in the next county over. Rushing in, I brandish the garden tool as if it's a broadsword. My glory is short-lived, however, when I find nothing. There's no one here, and everything seems to be just the way I left it. Putting the hoe down, I take a walk around the room, gaze assessing for any small change in the scenery. I may seem like a scatterbrained mess most of the time, but when it comes to my work, there's order behind my chaos. I know exactly where everything is in this little room. Because I'm so anal about my art, it doesn't take me long to realize that I was wrong in my earlier assessment. There is one hundred percent something missing from my studio. The painting I did last night, the one that was thrown in a corner, hopefully never to see the light of day again ... is gone.

I can't believe it. Retracing my movements, I go over everything I did last night, from the time I entered my studio until this morning, when I woke up. Some of the memories are enough to have me sweating, but for the most part, I just remember being really tired after. Did I forget to lock up the studio? Did someone break in? If so, why? And why take only *that* painting? There are others here that would be worth far more money. As I stand there, stewing in a vat full of questions, a thought suddenly occurs to me. My brain replays the conversation with Adam at the gallery the other day about some of my paintings being stolen after being sold. I can feel goosebumps breaking out along my arms as an idea begins to form. One so outlandish, and yet I'm at a complete loss as to any other explanation. One question keeps repeating itself over and over in my head.

Could that same thief be responsible for stealing this painting, too? I suddenly recall the noise I heard outside of the studio window last night. Oh my God. Could the person who took the painting have been outside my window?? Another thought hits me like a ton of bricks, and I plop down in the old wooden chair next to my paint table. Could that same person have seen me? Been watching me while I touched myself? The idea has me leaning down to put my head between my knees to keep from hyperventilating. I can't shake the idea that someone's been spying on me and that the previous thefts are much more personal than anyone, maybe even me, realizes. Is it possible that I have some kind of stalker?

CHAPTER 15

Merrick

I think most people would be nervous when meeting with a Federal Agent, especially if those people also happened to be high-profile criminals. I'm not one of those people. And it's not because I'm cocky and don't think I'll ever be caught. It's because I know that whenever I pull a job, I've covered every possible track that could be left behind. Nothing can be tied back to me, Deacon, or the little partnership we've created. Between the two of us and our varying skills, we make it a point to only pull jobs that can be handled by the two of us. This way, neither of us ever has to worry about being snitched on. Because of that, as I sit in my car in the parking lot of some little old-fashioned diner, I'm completely at ease. Well ... at least when it comes to meeting with a cop.

Last night was a game-changer. Not even counting the mind-numbing orgasm I had, I now know exactly how Amelia feels about me. She wants me. Yeah, it's possible that she's only sexually attracted to me right now, but that's more than I thought I had a few days ago, so I'll take it. Knowing that she fantasizes about me when she's alone has my blood heating even now. If I'm not careful, I'm gonna walk up to this agent with a tent in my pants, and that wouldn't be a good way to start a handler/informant relationship. But even telling myself this, I can't stop thinking about last night. About that painting. After we'd both gotten off, unbeknownst to the other, I'd seen her toss the painting aside in a fit of anger. I'm not sure what I would've done if she'd decided to destroy it instead. It's not like I could've just barged into the studio, so seeing her simply attempt to hide it from herself, whether out of shame for what she'd done or some other reason, I was thankful. After she'd gone up to the main house, I'd snuck in and taken it. For the time being, I had it hidden away in my apartment. Eventually, I'd move it to its permanent home. Our home. Before leaving for the night, I'd snuck into Amelia's room to find her fast asleep in a tangle of damp towels and nothing else. Not wanting her to get sick, I'd taken off my undershirt and gently put it on her. She must've been even more exhausted than I was from her earlier orgasm because she'd never even stirred. Taking out my phone, I'd snapped a picture of her just as she was. Wearing nothing but my t-shirt, wild curls spread out all around her. Had anything ever looked so beautiful?

As I huff out a deep breath, I glance around the parking lot for the 400th time. When I'd called the Bureau and asked to meet with an investigator, I'd gotten a call back from a deep-voiced, very abrupt agent, instructing me to meet him here at ... 15 minutes ago. The longer I sit waiting, the more annoyed I become. Just as I'm about to call again to curse someone out, I see a sleek silver Aston Martin pull into the parking lot. I thought I was pretentious in my Bentley, but I've got nothing on whoever that guy is. That car is so ridiculously out of place in a parking lot like this that it's almost comical. Letting out a little laugh, I shake my head and bring the phone to my ear. Just as it begins to ring, the Aston Martin pulls up in the parking space next to mine. No way. No fucking way is this the agent. That car is way above an FBI man's pay grade. But, sure enough, as the car is put into park next to mine, a man dressed in a three-piece suit slowly exits the vehicle. Narrowing my gaze, I catalog everything, from his close-cropped dark hair to the shine glaring off his leather shoes. What I see has me questioning everything I know about the Bureau. Professional suit aside, the man looks like a hired killer. Tall, nearly as tall as me, and with probably a good 50 pounds on me, he's big, and the way he rounds the hood of the car makes him appear lethal, each step sure and commanding, exuding power.

Not wanting to be at a disadvantage if he makes it to my car before I'm able to get out, I quickly exit the vehicle and meet him halfway. Up close, I'm able to take in more of his appearance. Dark hair cut short on the sides, longer on top and slicked back in a way that would put any GQ cover model to shame. Paired with aviator sunglasses and a lightly stubbled jaw that looks sharp enough to cut you, I don't even need to see a badge to know there's a gun strapped to his side beneath his suit jacket. Definitely the Fed. But when he removes the glasses, I notice that he's got a rather distinct and unusual facial characteristic. One eye was blue as the sky, the other a moss-colored green. It's a startling contrast, especially as they're both trained on me with piercing intensity. It's after this perusal that I realize he can't be more than a year or two older than me. I reach out my hand, and we meet halfway in a firm handshake. From the looks of him, I'd expect him to attempt to put my hand in a vice-like grip in a bid for dominance—Hell, the guy looks like a boxer, for God's sake—but he doesn't. Just shakes my hand firmly and lets go.

"Mr. Stratford?" His voice is deep and husky, the way someone's would be after they'd screamed themselves horse. And if I'm not mistaken, it holds the barest hint of an accent. It hits me that this may very well be the agent that called me back.

"That's right," I say, slipping my hands into my pants pockets, the picture of nonchalance. "They didn't tell me the name of the agent I'd be meeting, so you are ...?"

"Special Agent Alexi Kapranov," he replies, mimicking my move by shoving his hands into the pockets of his dress pants.

"Russian?" I ask casually, though now that I'm face to face with the guy, it makes what I'm about to do all too real, and I suddenly feel anything but casual.

"Da. Dlya tebya eto problema?" he says with a quirk of a brow. *Yes. Is that a problem for you?* In my line of work, intelligence isn't just for geeks. Sometimes, it helps to know if someone is planning to double-cross you if you speak their native tongue. Does he know that I speak Russian? Why else would he revert to that language? Unless he's not sure and is trying to assess my knowledge of the language. Narrowing my eyes on him, it only takes me a second to realize he's fucking with me. It's clear that he somehow knows I understand what he said. It's also clear that he speaks fluent English, in addition to Russian. That accent also just got a hell of a lot stronger. Seamlessly switching back to English, he says, "The captain said you had some information you wanted to share regarding Peter and Suzanne Stratford?" And now the accent is nearly gone entirely. Interesting. If he can turn it on and off at will, I wonder why he let me hear it in the first place.

"Yes. I'll soon have documented proof showing that my father is embezzling money from a charity he's the chairman of, The Right Path. Have you heard of it?"

"Yes, I'm aware of it. What type of proof are we talking about and more importantly, how do you plan to come by this information? I assume your father isn't just going to hand over confidential data regarding the charity's financials."

Now, the sticky part begins. "I can't say where or how the information will be obtained. If that's gonna be a deal breaker for you, then I'll thank you for your time and be on my way" I say, already turning back towards my driver's side door.

"Wait." It's simply one word but said with such an air of authority that I can tell this man is used to being in command of everything and everyone around him. Turning back, I meet those mismatched eyes head-on, making sure he knows that I won't be bullied or intimidated into doing anything I don't wanna do.

Letting out a little sigh, he says, "Fine. Just provide me with the documentation. I'll have a look at it, and if I deem it worthy of further investigation, I'll contact you. Was there anything else?" Those strange eyes bore into mine as if he's waiting for something else. Why do I suddenly get the feeling that he already knows exactly what I'm going to say next?

Steeling myself because I know that once I've let loose these words, there's no going back. It's not just my life and my personal vendetta against my father. Now I'll be impacting Amelia's life in such a way that I know she'll be angry with me. I reassure myself that everything will work out fine once she realizes the full scope of what I'm doing. For us. For a new life, free of our demons, both metaphorically and physically. I've come too far and sacrificed too much. There's no going back now. I have to see this to the end.

"Yes, there is more. I have information regarding Suzanne Stratford's previous husbands and, more importantly, how they met their untimely demise."

I watch his dual colored eyes narrow a fraction before he says, "What kind of information?"

"Sworn witness statements. Physical evidence from two of the scenes that were preserved without Suzanne's knowledge."

Slowly, he takes a step closer. He doesn't enter my personal space, but he's damn close. His stance indicates more excitement than intimidation, if it's even possible for a man like this to be excited about anything. Even so, he eyes me curiously before saying, "And you're willing to turn this over to the FBI? Why? This is your father and stepmother we're talking about, right? I thought the Stratford family were a bunch of do-gooders that were thicker than thieves."

I don't miss his little comment about "thieves", and for a moment, I wonder if I've made a terrible mistake. Is it possible that he knows who I am? "Yeah, well, public appearances can be deceiving. I'm willing to give up this information because both my father and stepmother belong behind bars. They've hurt a lot of people, and they deserve to rot for it."

Cocking his head to the side, he says, "And your stepsister, Amelia Carrow? Is she a willing participant in any of these crimes?" Clearly, this man has done his research. I'm not entirely comfortable with the sound of Amelia's name in his mouth.

Feeling my face harden, I'm the one who takes a step closer to him this time, definitely entering his personal space. "Amelia is off limits. She will not be involved in this in any way. You won't question her, have her tailed, or do anything else to alert her to the fact that our parents are under investigation. This is non-negotiable. Take it, or I walk right now."

To his credit, he doesn't back down at our close proximity but instead stares into my eyes for a moment. What he's looking for, I have no idea. After another few seconds of tense silence, his mouth tips up at the corners before he says, "Ahh, I see." as if he's just gotten the punchline of a good joke. Finally stepping back, he reaches into his jacket and pulls out a business card. Handing it to me, I see that it has his name and contact numbers, including his cell and email address.

"This intrigues me. And you seem like a man with a plan, so I'll make you a deal. Send me copies of whatever you have. Turn over any and all physical evidence, and I won't divulge to my superiors that my inside man also happens to be wanted by quite a few Federal and International agencies for a number of very high profile-thefts," he says in a matter-of-fact tone. But that hint of a smile still plays around his lips. Far from putting me at ease, I feel my blood run cold as he turns to walk back to his car. Right before getting in, he says, "Oh, and Merrick, you can call me Alexi. I have a feeling we're going to work well together."

I watch him get into his car and leave. Getting back behind the steering wheel of my own car, I sit in the parking lot for a long time. I'm not sure what to make of the Fed. It's clear that he knows who I am, and yet, he didn't arrest me. Could it be that catching a murderer is more important to him than the millions of dollars worth of art, jewels, and antiquities I've stolen? Or does he have other plans for me? I knew from the moment he stepped out of the car that he was more than just some pencil-pushing public servant going through the motions. It's obvious that he has his own agenda. It's also obvious that that agenda isn't exactly on the up and up. But at this point, I have no choice but to ride it out and see what happens. I won't say I trust the guy because he definitely struck me as the type that would bury a knife in your back if crossed, but for now, we both know the status quo, and only time will tell how things will play out. I'll either end up with everything I've ever wanted … or less than nothing.

Thinking back to the information I just told him, I feel like some part of me should feel remorse or guilt over what I've just done. But instead, the only feeling swirling inside of me is ...hope. Hope that this plan will work and that I'll finally be free to go after the one treasure I desire above all else. My emerald.

Tonight's the charity gala at the art museum, where they're honoring Suzanne Stratford for all her *noble philanthropy*. It's a joke, but I know Amelia will be there, so of course I'll be attending. Glancing at my watch, I see I don't have much time to get back home and get ready. Putting my car into reverse, I back out of the space and take off for my apartment, anticipation coursing through my veins in a way no alcohol or drug could ever come close to. Knowing I've set into motion a series of events that will eventually lead me to exactly where I wanna be, I feel a sinister smile forming. Let the games begin.

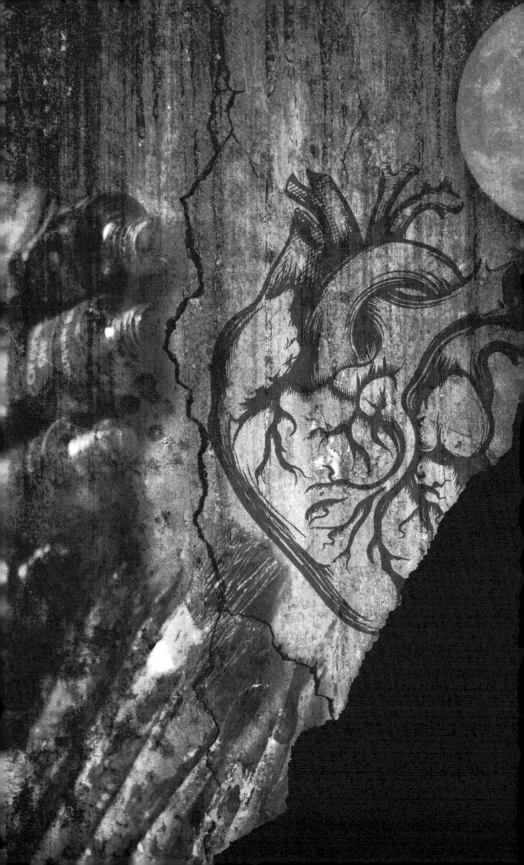

CHAPTER 16

Amelia

The town car pulls to a stop in front of the Gibbes Museum of Art, and the driver quickly exits, rushing around and opening my door before I can do it myself. He's worked for my mother for years and is usually the one to pick me up for functions like this. She refuses to let me be seen exiting my own car. Not with so many cameras at the ready. Even as the driver holds out a hand to assist me from the back seat and onto the red carpet leading up to the entrance, I'm dreading what waits for me inside. Not the art. I love the art. In fact, this is one of my favorite places to be. It's the mask I'll have to don in order to get through the evening. It's the schmoozing and air kisses and polite smile that will be a fixed expression on my face for the next several hours. It's the fact that my mother will be inside, and knowing I'll have to spend more than five minutes in the same room with her. It's enough to have me breaking out in a cold sweat.

Even so, after taking a moment to make sure my facade is in place, I allow myself to be eased out of the car, straightening with all the poise and grace of a princess. As I smooth my clammy palms down the sides of my vintage gown, lights flash before my eyes as a barrage of cameras go off. I knew there would be reporters, of course. Fashion bloggers and paparazzi practically climb over each other as they vie for my attention. Asking me questions or wanting me to pose for a photo in a particular way. Like a good little puppet, I oblige. Not because I'm soaking up the spotlight but because it's expected of me.

My mother sits on the museum's board and has a vested interest in tonight's fundraising gala. Raising money for the arts is definitely a cause I can get behind, but I'm sure the amount of money spent putting on a function like this is taking a serious chunk out of whatever is earned tonight. I'm also sure that, for the majority of the attendees here, this event is just another excuse to mingle, gossip, and blow smoke up each other's asses. If I'm being honest, just the idea of having to be here for the next four hours already has me exhausted. But, seeing as I have no choice after my 15 minutes of fame comes to an end, I move up the short flight of stairs to the entrance of the building, being careful not to trip over the hem of my dress.

I've never been a fan of heels, but I have no doubt my mother would literally bar me from the building if I decided to rock a pair of Vans with this dress. The thought alone has me suppressing a chuckle, and I feel myself relax the tiniest bit. The dress itself is stunning, though. Even I have to admit that. I'm sure my mother would've preferred some poofy ball gown with skirts large enough to make Cinderella jealous, but this dress is way more me. I knew the moment I set eyes on the 1930s vintage Gilbert Adrian gown, with its deep emerald green color and cinched waist, accented with a glittery art deco clasp, that there would be no other dress for me. Paired with a set of strappy silver stilettos and with my unruly curls swept up into an updo, I knew I looked like I'd just stepped off the set of black and white film. Which was *exactly* what I was going for. Few people knew about my love for old Hollywood. The films, the fashion, everything. And if I was going to be made to fake niceties all night, at least I could look decent while doing it. Just knowing I'd chosen this dress myself instead of allowing my mother to bully me into wearing some hideous monstrosity of tulle and lace gave me a burst of confidence that made me feel like I had sheathed myself in at least a thin layer of armor.

As I step inside, I immediately grab a glass of champagne from the tray of a passing waiter. I need liquid courage to get through the bullshit I'm about to have to endure. Making my way into the main room where the party's taking place, I'm immediately enveloped in a cloud of cloying perfume coming off the ladies nearest me. As we peck near each other's cheeks, the varying scents war with each other for dominance, giving me a slight headache and making me just the tiniest bit nauseous. Just when I think I'm going to have to come up with a reason to excuse myself just to breathe, a smooth, deep voice from behind me has goosebumps breaking out onto my skin.

"Amelia."

At the sound of my name and the curt tone, I slowly turn around to face my stepbrother. Merrick's dark chocolate eyes rake my form, holding the smallest hint of ... annoyance? Distaste? I'm not sure, but it immediately puts my back up.

"Merrick," I reply snarkily.

His eyes narrow the slightest bit, and he steps forward. Not too close, but close enough to shoulder the tittering socialites that had surrounded me out of the way. This is the first time I've seen him since that night at the club. The night I humiliated myself. Recounting the events, I feel another wave of embarrassment so strong that it only adds to my defensive attitude.

"Dance with me," he says. Not a request but a demand. Knowing we have numerous pairs of eyes on us, I opt to take his outstretched hand rather than cause a scene. The last thing I need is to add fuel to the fire. These women would already be gossiping behind their hands, most likely seeing something that I knew wasn't there. Merrick had made it clear over the years that I was little more than a nuisance to him, even though I knew that he'd saved me from his father's fists more than once as teenagers. Whatever was going on with us the last few days was probably just some kind of warped test on his part. As much as I wished otherwise, he'd never allow himself to exhibit more for me than brotherly love. He was too tightly controlled for that. Wait. Love? I roll my eyes internally.

Tolerance was a more appropriate word. But it was because of those nights when he'd taken a beating for me or held me as I cried that I tolerated him in return.

Allowing him to lead me out to where other couples dance in the center of the room, I try to quell the butterflies that swirl in my stomach, threatening to burst free. I take a moment to peruse his form since I know he's not looking. Dear God, could this man fill out a tux. A tux, I was sure, was custom-made, just for him. Merrick didn't do "off the rack". Not since he'd made his first million, anyway. It was hard to believe we'd both come so far. Pulling me close, he leans down to whisper in my ear.

"Who the fuck chose that dress for you? I know it wasn't your mother. I'd lay odds that she hasn't even seen you yet, or she would've had a heart attack on the spot."

A burst of annoyance skitters up my spine, causing it to straighten. The act presses us even closer together, my chest nearly brushing his. Looking up, I see his nostrils flare slightly on a sharp inhale.

"I chose it myself. I am grown, in case you hadn't noticed," I say, my voice dripping with sarcasm.

His reply comes with a clench of his jaw, "I noticed."

I don't know why, but his tone and short reply have me glancing up to meet his eyes. They were still annoyed, but there was something else there now. Something that *burned* me. I take a deep breath to steady myself, allowing his scent to invade my senses and cloud my mind. His expensive cologne mixes with a smell that's so naturally *him* to create something spicy with a hint of something citrus. It always reminded me of Christmas. My favorite holiday. It made me want to burrow my nose into his chest and take a big inhale. However, I was sure if I was to act on that impulse, Merrick would drop me so fast that I'd end up a satin-covered heap in the middle of the ballroom floor.

"You need to excuse yourself and go home. Every man in here is looking at you like you're a piece of meat. I don't know what the hell you were thinking, wearing a dress like that."

His words snap me out of my orange and clove-induced haze. Is this guy for real? Clearly, there isn't a feminist bone in his body. I narrow my eyes on him. "What? No."

"No?" he asks, his disbelief at my defiance crystal clear, even in that single syllable.

"You heard me. I said *no*. Maybe I like being looked at. Did that ever occur to you?"

I feel the grip on my hip tighten a fraction, and before I even have time to process what's happening, he's dragging me from the dance floor. I have to grab the skirt of my dress to keep from tripping as he leads me a few feet away to where a pair of balcony doors lay open. He's moving at a crisp pace, and I pray no one notices. I didn't need to be the subject of ladies' room gossip, much less have it get back to my mother that there was even a hint of impropriety between us.

Leading me out onto a thankfully empty balcony, he finally releases my hand to wheel around and face me. He looks ... pissed. *Really* pissed. Not an unfamiliar emotion coming from him, but he was usually much better at containing it.

"What the fuck do you mean, you like being looked at?" he practically growls at me.

Before I have time to answer, however, he's already advancing on me. I experience a momentary flash of fear and take a hasty step back. My bareback, exposed by the dress, where the material dips and pools in ripples just above my tailbone, hits the stone wall behind me. I get a grip on myself, and looking up, I meet his gaze with a stubborn tilt to my chin. He must've seen the hint of fear in my eyes, though, because his ire cools a fraction, and an almost sad look crosses his face.

Bracketing me in with one hand against the wall on either side of my head, he rasps, "Do you really think I'd hurt you?"

I stare straight ahead at his chest because the look in his eyes has mine nearly welling up. I know he's nothing like his father. He'd proven that every time he'd stepped between me and his Dad to take a hit that wasn't meant for him. He removes one hand from the wall. Bringing it down, he uses his index finger to lift my chin, forcing me to meet his eyes again.

"I don't want anyone else looking at you," he says softly. The words sound as if they've had to be pulled from him, and the word "else" hangs heavily in the air between us. The air that's suddenly too thick. I can't breathe. Surely, that came out wrong.

"Were ... *you* looking at me?" I say hesitantly.

"I'm always looking at you," he says, leaning in closer still. For a moment, I think I've imagined the feather-light touch of his lips ghosting over mine. "You're everywhere."

"Merrick ..." I whisper.

And just like that, his hands are in my hair, and his mouth is on mine. I was right earlier when I thought something in him burned. The flames of whatever that was lick at me like a caress, and suddenly, I'm *on fire*. Totally forgetting that we're mere feet away from a gallery full of people, I slant my head, allowing him to deepen the kiss. I can both hear and feel a groan rising up the back of his throat like he's losing a fight with himself, but he takes what I'm offering, running the tip of his tongue along the seam of my lips, demanding I open for him. I do, and before I can even inhale a breath, he's pushing his way inside my mouth. His kiss isn't gentle, but his hands are, as they slowly bunch the material at the side of my dress, allowing his palm to skate along the outside of my thigh. His touch is slow like he's not sure of himself. The way he's handling me, it's almost as if he thinks I'm made of glass. Like I'll break. It's infuriating, to be honest.

"Touch me," I gasp.

"I am touching you. I can't *stop* touching you." He sounds angry with himself. I don't know why. This is every fantasy I've ever had come to life.

Gripping his hand, I guide it beneath my dress, along the small scrap of lace between my thighs. "Touch me here," I rasp against his lips. He squeezes his eyes closed, and for a moment, I think he's going to stop. I think I've taken things too far. That I've embarrassed myself again.

His growled "Fuck it" comes just as I'm on the verge of begging. Feeling his finger hook into the crotch of my panties, he drags them down my legs.

"Step out," he says, lowering to one knee before me.

Doing as he asks, I lift first one heel, then the other, allowing him to remove my underwear. Looking down, he rubs the thin material between his fingers before tucking them into the pocket of his tux. Looking up into my eyes, he says, "These are mine now."

Then he's standing again, and his hand is back under my dress, running along my slick heat before pushing his middle finger inside me. No preamble, no finesse. But I don't need any. I'm already wet for him. I think I have been since he backed me against this wall.

"Fuck, Mia. You shouldn't be letting me do this."

I melt at the use of my nickname. Only when he lets slip the tight reign of his control does he call me that. It happens so rarely that I immediately turn to putty in his hands. He sounds angry at me again, but when I look up to meet his gaze, he rests his forehead against mine for a brief moment before his finger begins to move. Slowly, at first, in and out. Almost as if he's afraid he'll scare me off. He needn't worry. I've wanted this for so long that he could take me right here against this wall, feet away from a ballroom full of people, and I'd probably let him. Arching my hips up to meet his hand, I try to get him to move faster, but he's achingly slow as he withdraws his finger to circle my clit.

Moving his mouth to my ear, he rasps, "Is this what you wanted? Am I touching you enough *now*?"

It's not enough. It'll never be enough. I open my mouth to tell him just that, but he takes that moment to plunge two fingers back inside me while pressing the pad of his thumb against my aching clit, and the only thing that comes out is a strangled cry.

"I've dreamed of you, you know. Dreamed of the sounds you'd make, of the way your body would come alive for me." His hand picks up speed, and then he's thrusting his fingers in and out while his thumb circles me over and over. I'm teetering on the edge of a cliff, terrified to look down.

Afraid I'll fall. Then he whispers, "Of the look on your face when you come."

Taking his other hand off the wall, he shoves it over my mouth just as it opens to scream.

I shouldn't have worried about falling because with just those words alone … I jump.

CHAPTER 17

Merrick

Watching Amelia fall apart in my arms has my entire body practically vibrating. I regret having to cover her mouth with my hand. I want more than anything to hear her scream her pleasure out loud. To hear her cry out my name again, but this time to my face. I have to remind myself, all in good time. I've waited this long; I can wait a little longer. I can't rush things; or I risk losing her and everything else I've worked years for. But, God, my cock is straining against the zipper of my dress pants. For a moment, as she catches her breath, I close my eyes and entertain the idea of freeing myself, gripping the backs of her thighs to hoist her up, and burying myself so deeply inside her, she'd not only see stars but entire galaxies.

Directly after that thought occurs to me, however, I experience a moment of blinding panic. Then what? Regardless of the handful of times I fooled around with girls in my early teenage years, I wouldn't have any idea how to satisfy a woman like Amelia. I wasn't an idiot; I knew the mechanics of sex. But how do you tell the woman you've been in love with since you were 17 that from the moment you laid eyes on her, the idea of touching another woman felt like cheating, and since you couldn't have her, you haven't had anyone? That the only sexual experience you've had since the day you met has been with your right hand? I was fucking 26 years old, for God's sake. She'd laugh in my face.

Letting fear get the better of me for a moment, I gently ease my fingers out of her before she can feel the small tremor in my hand. When I open my eyes, I find hers already on me. She isn't saying anything, just studying my face. I pray that the vulnerability that I know was there when I pushed my fingers inside of her is no longer present. I've gotta get my shit together. I'm running this train completely off the rails. Straightening, I let the skirt of her dress fall back down to cover her. Making sure my expression gives nothing away, I step back and away from her. Instinctively, she takes a small step forward as if to follow me. The move has my hands balling into fists at my sides to keep from taking that step forward again and touching her. But I can't allow myself to go all in with her yet. Not until I've taken care of the issue that is our parents.

I know the rumors that surround Amelia's mother, and for the longest time I thought that's all they were. Rumors. The look in Amelia's eyes, any time she's forced to interact with her, was the first clue that there may have been some truth to those rumors. Recently, new information has come to light that, if true, will make sure she pays for every shadow that ever crossed the emerald eyes I love so much. Then there's my father. That bastard has made my life a living Hell. Both Suzanne and Peter Stratford will get what's coming to them, but until then, I have to keep some semblance of distance between myself and Amelia. If either of them finds out exactly how much she means to me, I have no doubt they'll use her against me. It's been my biggest fear since the day I found out my father had gotten married. From that day on, she'd been my biggest weakness. I had to keep them from finding that out until I was ready for the entire world to know.

With that in mind, I allow the mask of cold indifference that she's so used to to slip back over my face before letting my eyes reconnect with hers.

"That shouldn't have happened," I say coolly.

The hurt that flashes in her eyes has me cringing inside. But I know Amelia. She won't fall apart. She's stronger than that. So I wait for the anger that I know will soon follow. After a second or two, I'm not disappointed, as her eyes narrow on me, and her face twists with a look of complete loathing. It's a look I know well. A look I've evoked from her countless times in the past. A look that I know I've earned each and every time. The knowledge that my rejection of her may somehow cause her to question her own appeal or maybe even make her think she's not good enough causes a twist in my gut. But it can't be helped.

"Then why did it?" she asks, tauntingly.

Thinking quickly, I blurt out the first cruel thought that comes to mind. "Well, it was only a matter of time before someone tried feeling you up in that dress. Figured I'd save you the embarrassment of becoming locker room talk at the country club tomorrow and just do it myself."

Her "Fuck you, Merrick," is the only warning I get before my face is jerked to the side by a surprisingly nasty right hook. I vaguely wonder where she learned to hit like that. I lift a finger to my mouth, and when I pull it back to look down at my fingers, I see they're stained with blood. I allow a little laugh to escape me. She hit me. Not a girly slap across the cheek, but a full-blown right hook. Unlike the times I fell victim to my father's fists, there is no hatred or resentment boiling up inside me. In fact, I've never been prouder of her than I am at this moment. I love the fact that she's standing up for herself. But for both our sakes, I allow my laugh to turn condescending towards the end, if only to mask the fact that I want nothing more than to grab her face and pull her snarling mouth to meet my bloody one, forcing her to taste the evidence of her wrath.

"That was a little immature, don't you think? I thought painting all that dark shit was supposed to help you relieve stress and pent-up anger? Doesn't seem to be working very well."

That's a low blow, and I know it. Because I know why she paints what she does. But at this moment, I need her to be mad at me, not hurt. Her anger will get her through the rest of the night. She still has to feign civility with her mother, and my father will be looking for any chinks in her armor that he can worm his way into. It's one of his favorite forms of torture, finding your vulnerable spots and exploiting them. So, for now, I push down the apology that's clawing its way up my throat and exert every ounce of willpower I possess to keep myself from pulling her into my arms and erasing that look of betrayal from her face.

It's at that moment that I notice the music in the main ballroom has lowered, and I hear the sound of someone introducing Suzanne to everyone before handing the microphone over for her to address the patrons gathered around. I hold my arm out to Amelia, indicating that we should re-enter the ballroom before they notice we're missing. Ignoring my proffered arm, she smooths down the skirt of her gown and slinks past me, entering the double doors back into the building alone.

I wait five more minutes, time in which I use a handkerchief to stem the flow of blood from my slightly busted lip, then follow her inside. I take a spot at the back of the room, my eyes automatically finding her. Even now, grown and having moved out of the family home, she still finds it hard to do anything that will make her mother upset. Especially in a public setting. And since it's expected that she be front and center to support Suzanne, she takes her place near the front of the crowd. I listen half-heartedly as her mother drones on and on about the importance of supporting the arts and digging deep into your wallets. It doesn't escape my notice that, at no point does she mention that her own daughter is an artist whose work sells for tens of thousands of dollars. Suzanne has never been a fan of the macabre work that Amelia produces. I have a feeling that she has at least a small suspicion that she's probably the main source of inspiration for those paintings.

As I stand there, trying not to let my eyes stray to Amelia, I feel some- one approach my side. I know immediately who it is. The malevolence that surrounds him practically oozes from every pore, as does the smell of expensive scotch. I try my best to remain relaxed, not allowing myself to stiffen even the slightest bit. Peter Stratford can sense fear, and I'm sure he'd love nothing more than to know that his presence makes me

THE THIEF AND THE PAINTER

uneasy. But the days of my flinching at his nearness are over. I'm my own man now. I've come a long way from the pathetic little kid who used to beg for his father's love and affection and instead got an empty belly and a belt.

"What are you doing, skulking back here, boy?" he asks casually, but I can hear the disapproval and annoyance in his tone. I don't need to hear the slight slur to his words to know that the expensive glass of Scotch in his hand isn't his first. He's gotten better at appearing sober in public, but only because he believes himself to be elevated to such a status that he has to keep up the appearance of a doting husband and father. He may have everyone else in this room fooled, but I've seen Peter Stratford drunk enough times to know he's got one, maybe two more, before he'll either have to "retire for the evening" or risk causing a scene. Suzanne will ensure it's the former. Over the last five years, she's become a pro at wrangling my father. I know he hits her, but his level of violence with her is nowhere near as bad as it was with me growing up. Maybe he himself buys into some of the rumors about how her former husbands met their untimely ends, and he doesn't wanna be next. I find it very hard to believe that it has anything to do with loving her. I learned a long time ago that he isn't capable of the emotion. It's just not in his DNA.

Recalling that he asked me a question and is expecting an answer, I say, "Can't you tell? I'm trying to remain as close to the door as possible so I can leave at the earliest opportunity. This function is so boring, I'm thinking of stealing something, just to liven things up," I say obnoxiously. I'm not worried about possibly giving away my extracurricular activity, knowing he'll take my comment at face value and assume I'm just being a smartass. He may be a conniving son of a bitch, but he's not the smartest. Sure enough, he doesn't disappoint.

"You have an obligation to this family, you little shit. You should be one of the first to arrive and the last to leave. People will expect you to be here to support your mother."

As hard as I try, I can't stop myself from stiffening at his words. "She's not my mother," I reply, not even bothering to hide the disgust in my

161

tone. My mother was an angel. From what little I still remember of her, she had the biggest heart of anyone on the planet. Her soul was just … pure. What she saw in this mean son of a bitch, I'll never know. Finally looking over at him, I watch his eyes flick down to my lip before returning to mine. I can tell by the look on his face and the grinding of his jaw that he'd love nothing more than to backhand me. And as much as I'd love nothing more than to give him the fight he's so clearly looking for, I've already been hit once tonight, and that was enough. As Suzanne's speech winds to a close, I turn on my heel and make my way towards the exit. I'll wait outside for Amelia to leave before I head home myself. No way would I leave her here alone to deal with the duo of death.

While I lurk out front, in the shadows of a massive oak covered in Spanish moss, my mind drifts back to the balcony and my encounter with Amelia. Bringing my hand up, I inhale. Smelling her on my fingers, I put the middle digit into my mouth and suck, licking away the remnants of her arousal. I repeat the action with the other finger. I feel like a man starved. I can't help remembering how she arched against my hand, trying desperately to get my fingers deeper. Her little whimpers of pleasure and the way her mouth opened as if to scream when she climaxed. I don't know how much longer I can wait to make her mine. I'm desperate to get her into a proper bed and feel her beneath me. To not have to worry about how much noise she makes. To finally show her that she belongs to me and me alone. That she's always been mine. She was just living on borrowed time.

Seeing her exit the front of the Museum, her satin gown floating on the breeze, I make sure she's safely in her car before making my way up to the valet to have him bring my Bentley around. I'll follow her home the way I do most nights. Then, I'll sit outside in my car and wait for the light in her studio to come on, indicating that she's working. That's her usual routine, especially after she's had to do anything involving her mother. Once I know she's safe in her studio, I'll be able to head back to my apartment. I know Amelia's piece of shit agent recently sold the painting she titled "Shades of Shadow," which means I have a job to prep for. There'll soon be a new piece of work hanging on the walls of the home I've bought for us. The home she knows nothing about. I'll steal the painting, collecting her work as though they're pieces of her broken heart that I intend to glue back together. And I guess, in a way, they are. Once I have all the pieces and it's fully functioning again, I'll offer it back to her in the hopes that she'll tell me I can keep it.

The flight from Charleston to LA had been uneventful unless you counted the new flight attendant, Tracy, making excuse after excuse to come over and all but offer to blow me right in the middle of the cabin on my private jet. I bought this plane a little over a year ago after realizing that I needed a more inconspicuous way to travel to and from jobs. Not many people questioned the movements of a multimillionaire and philanthropist, especially when they had their own set of wings. I could say I'd done it solely out of practicality and the additional level of security, considering that most of the time there was something worth several million dollars taking up residence in the cargo hold, but the truth was, while those reasons were totally valid, the immature side of me just thought owning my own plane was pretty fucking cool.

During the long flight, I'd taken the opportunity to go over the diagram Deacon had provided for the layout of the mansion that housed Amelia's latest painting. The Hollywood Hills were home to movie stars and various other celebrities, but it was the palatial estate of one Mr. Eugene Kingsley, located just outside of the city, that I'd be stealing from tonight. After a little research, I'd discovered that he'd purchased Amelia's latest piece via telephone, wiring the money for the painting directly to the gallery. Upon further research, it just so happened that Mr. Kingsley hosted the party to end all parties once a year. As luck would have it, that party happened to be tonight. On the surface, the function appeared to raise money for various causes and charities. In reality it was just an excuse for backroom deals, greasing palms, and to intimidate crooked politicians into cooperating with his booming construction conglomerate. It also held an annual auction of stolen gems, art, and other various stolen goods. Considering we weren't here to purchase anything but instead to steal it, Deacon would be working from behind the scenes, to help me tonight.

Taking the stairs to the front entrance two at a time, I hand over my invitation to the walking T-bone steak stuffed into a tux that's guarding the door. It's a fake, of course, but a very impressive one. Giving me a once over, he hands the invitation back to me and motions me inside with an arm. Breezing into the foyer, I pause just inside to take in the players. I see several faces I recognize. Not that they'd recognize me, but I've done my research. I know the types of people that would attend a function like this, and I normally wouldn't be caught within a 10-mile radius of them. Keeping my head low but staying on alert, I meander through the little groups of people chatting or enjoying a drink off to the sides of the room. Making my way over to the open bar, I order a glass of whiskey that will serve as a prop more than anything else. You didn't need liquid courage when you were as good at your job as I was. Making sure to exude complete relaxation, I meander over to the staircase that leads to the second floor. Taking in its open floor plan and balcony that looks out over the party, I bypass it, heading down the hallway that I know leads to the back of the house and the kitchen.

Ducking into an alcove, I quickly strip off my suit jacket, leaving me in only a white dress shirt and bow tie. Without the jacket of my tux, I now closely resemble just another member of the wait staff. Pushing my way into the kitchen, I move without hesitation to the back, where a door sits off to the side. I know what I'll find inside. A dumbwaiter that's normally used to transport laundry and dishes from the higher floors down to the kitchen and washroom. A dumbwaiter that just so happens to be large enough to hold a fully grown man. Of course, I could've taken the stairs, but that would've left me open to the prospect of running into someone who might question where I was going. This route, while a little more cramped, is safer. I remind myself of that as I climb into the small box, pulling down the grate-style door and pressing the button that will engage the pulleys to take me to the second floor of the house.

I exit into a much quieter room, and take stock of my surroundings. I'm in a small utility room just off the main hallway. Opening the door just a crack, I peek out into the hall, making sure the coast is clear before quickly exiting and sprinting down the walkway to the second door on the left. I know the door will be locked, so I already have my trusty pick set out and at the ready. Making quick work of the lock, I quietly enter what I know is the master of the home's study, and once inside, I take a mental inventory of everything around me. The room is spacious, and if I didn't know better, I'd say welcoming. But as I gaze across the room at the large mahogany desk, I take note of the height difference between Kingsley's chair and the guest chairs sitting opposite it. The chair behind the desk is about four inches higher, and I can only imagine Mr. Kingsley calling people into his study and telling them to have a seat just so he can talk down to them and make them feel less than. I hated people like that. I won't be using a single ounce of what little bit of conscience I have left feeling sorry for this man or what I'm about to do.

I know I have little time, since Kingsley typically makes use of his study during this annual party, for all types of closed-door deals. Tearing my gaze away from the desk, I zero in on the goal for tonight's mission. The painting Amelia titled "Shades of Shadow" hangs on the wall to the right side of the room in a gaudy gold frame that I'm sure weighs 200 pounds. Once I'm directly in front of the painting, I quickly scan the edges of the frame where it meets the wall, checking for any type of alarm system. Not finding anything, I scoff at the lack of security. Sure, Amelia's work doesn't have the notoriety that comes along with names like Van Gogh or Monet, but he still paid a pretty penny for the painting, and the fact that it's just hanging on the wall of his study with no precautions taken makes me wonder how the new owner manages to get anything done with that massively inflated head. Clearly, he's compensating for *something*.

Pausing for a moment, I take in the contents of the painting. To be honest ... it's terrifying. Dark and macabre. The shadows that must've lended to the painting's name are disturbing, to say the least. Taking a step back, I focus hard on the picture, realizing that these aren't just splashes of dark colors across the canvas. The shadows in question don't quite have faces, but they still project a demon-like quality that's unmistakable. Jesus. If this is what Amelia sees when she closes her eyes, how is she not a total basket case? Shaking myself from my thoughts, I make quick work of removing the frame from the wall and then the painting from the frame. This isn't my first rodeo by any means, but I follow a certain set of procedures in order, because I don't ever want to reach the point where I become sloppy at my job. Leaning down, I lift my pants leg to reveal a small tube strapped to my right calf. I don't typically like to carry art this way. It's damaging to the paint, especially the older ones. Rolling it can cause the paint to crack and depreciate the value of the art. Most people don't know that, and they just believe what they see on TV or in movies. Ideally, you wanna keep the art as flat as possible during transport. However, I wasn't worried so much about this piece. It was newly painted, and rolling it wouldn't do too much damage. Sometimes, these things couldn't be helped. Removing the tube, I open it up and, carefully rolling up the painting, slip it inside before strapping it back onto my leg.

As I exit Mr. Kingsley's study, I go back exactly the way I came, exiting the dumbwaiter then the kitchens. Finding my suit jacket right where I left it, I slip it back on and casually walk out the front door. By the time the party ends and Mr. Kingsley returns to his study for a glass of brandy, a cigar, and to congratulate himself on dirty deeds well done, I'll be on my private jet, heading back home.

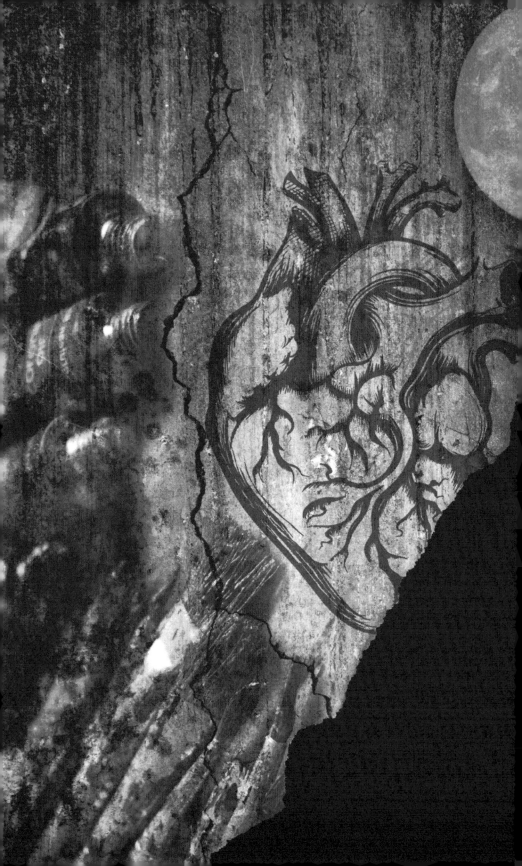

CHAPTER 18

Amelia

7 YEARS OLD

It's been two years since Uncle Remy died. I still have nightmares about it, but I don't tell Mommy. I know she wouldn't like it. I understand what happened a little better now. Being seven and a half means that I'm much smarter than I used to be. The policeman didn't come to talk to me that night like Mommy thought he might. But two of them did come back to the house the next day and wanted to ask me questions. Mommy stayed in the room with me, and I wished she hadn't. I felt like if I said the wrong thing, I'd get in trouble. So I told the policeman and policewoman what I'd told Mommy the night before. I did my best to repeat it back, word for word, like a parrot in one of those pirate movies. I don't think they believed me, but they didn't come back to talk to me again.

Now, two years later, Mommy had gotten married again. This time, I'd gotten a chance to be in the wedding. When Mommy had married Uncle Remy, she didn't want me being a distraction or doing anything that would've embarrassed her, so I'd had to sit in the front row of the church with Gloria and be quiet. This time, though, the man Mommy had married wanted me to be a part of the wedding. I was the flower girl, and I knew I looked cute in my frilly pink dress because everyone said so.

I liked Mommy's new husband. Gloria had told me that's what he was called. I was still confused about how I should address him, though. In the beginning, Mommy had told me to call him Uncle James but when they told me they were getting married, he'd told me I could call him Dad. I didn't think Mommy liked that very much because I saw her make a face behind his back where he couldn't see. Having a Dad had sounded nice and I didn't remember my real daddy so I thought it was okay. So whenever Mommy wasn't around, I called him Dad. When she was around, I tried really hard to think of ways to change my sentences so I didn't have to call him anything. But I liked spending time with my new dad. He actually listened to me when I talked and he wanted to take me places and do nice things for me. I'd listened in on conversations Mommy had on the phone and I'd heard her talking about how my new dad had lots of money, and it seemed like he didn't mind spending some of it on me.

Today, he was taking me to the aquarium. I love the ocean. The Little Mermaid is my favorite Disney movie. I think that's part of why I liked it when we took trips to the beach. Today, though, we're going to the aquarium in Downtown Charleston, and I'm so excited. I really want to see the jellyfish. I like how they come in so many different colors and they're so bright. After getting dressed, with Gloria's help, I go into the bathroom to brush my hair. Mommy doesn't like it when my hair is down. She says I look messy, so I let Gloria French braid it. It's supposed to be really hot today, so maybe it'll be a good thing not to have it on my neck all day.

Gloria says she's gonna look for my sneakers, and usually I wouldn't go downstairs without them on, mostly because Mommy will be annoyed if I'm not totally ready before leaving my room, but I'm just too excited to wait. Practically running down the stairs because Dad doesn't mind when I make noise in the house, I go room by room, looking for him. I only take a quick look into the front parlor before backing out fast. I don't like that room. It makes me feel weird. Like there's a hamster running around in my stomach. After a quick peek and finding no one, I hear voices coming from down the hallway, where the kitchen is. Making my way over there, I walk into the kitchen to see Dad sitting at the kitchen table, drinking a cup of tea, and Mommy standing near the teapot with her back to me. Mommy doesn't like tea unless it's cold and sweet, but Dad was born in England and loves to drink his hot. With milk, not lemon. He says putting lemon in tea is blasphemy. I've heard the word before, but only in church, and I didn't really know what it meant.

Glancing up from his cup, he smiles at me. I smile back. The smile is still on my face when he starts to cough. At first, I don't think anything of it. People cough all the time. I cough sometimes when I'm sick or if one of Mommy's friends comes over who has a cat because I'm allergic. So I'm not too worried ... at first. But even after he coughs several times, he still keeps coughing. Looking up at me, I watch as his face starts to turn different colors. It goes from normal looking to really red, then kinda blueish purple. He starts grabbing at his throat, and I wonder for a second if he's gonna throw up. Maybe he has the flu? I get scared and start to yell for Mommy to help him, but just then Mommy turns around and sees me. For a minute, she just stands there, looking at me. Then she looks at Dad ... but she doesn't help him. Why isn't she helping him?? I don't think he's gonna throw up anymore. It looks like he can't breathe. I start to run forward to try and help him, but Mommy catches my arm and jerks me back. He's not coughing anymore, but I almost wish he was because then I'd know that he was getting some air into his body.

I can't do anything to help him, and I don't understand why Mommy won't let me go. As I watch, Dad's head slowly falls onto the table. He's facing me, and his eyes are open, but he's not breathing anymore, I can tell. His mouth is open, and even though I wanna look away, I can't. I watch as white foamy stuff starts to come out. Just then, the door opens again, and Gloria walks in. She stops just inside the doorway to the kitchen and stares at Dad, then looks at Mommy. Suddenly, Mommy starts crying and screaming and tells Gloria to call an ambulance. I know what an ambulance is because I've seen it in cartoons. An ambulance is supposed to take you to the hospital if you're sick or hurt. I don't think an ambulance is gonna be able to help Dad. While Gloria leaves the room to use the phone, Mommy quickly cleans up Dad's teacup. She takes it to the sink and washes it with soap. Why is she doing dishes right now? She never does dishes. She says that's servant work. And I don't understand why Mommy is acting upset now when she wasn't just a minute ago. But I know if I say anything, I'll just get myself into trouble, so instead, I stay quiet. There's movement all around me, but I can't stop looking at Dad's eyes. They've got red lines all through them. He's looking right at me … but I know he doesn't see me anymore. I know he's dead. As I stand there and stare at him, tears start to spill from my eyes. They fall and they fall, and I can't make them stop. He needed my help, and I couldn't help him, and now he's gone to Heaven, just like Uncle Remy. I wonder what's gonna happen to us now. Will Mommy get married again? What if her next husband doesn't like me? I'm left to wonder about these things long after Mommy tells me to go to my room. I hear the ambulance and police come from where I wait upstairs, but I don't open my door or go out. I just lay on my bed and cry. Why is life like this? Why didn't God want me to have a Daddy? Turning my face into my pillow, I cry harder. After my eyes have run out of tears, I fall asleep and dream of Dad and the white foam and Mommy washing the teacup. In my dream, the police ask me if I saw anything, and I know that even though lying is bad, I have to lie. Because if they take Mommy away, then who will I have left?

More Dads and Uncles would come, but none of them stayed very long. By the time Mommy gets married again, I'm 11 and I know what's happening around me. Most kids are afraid of monsters that lurk in the dark or hide under their beds. But not all monsters look scary on the outside. Sometimes they wear Chanel pants suits, and bright red lipstick. Sometimes they cried on cue and wore dark sunglasses next to closed coffins. Sometimes … they watched you, waiting for you to change from furniture to a liability. Maybe if I remained still and silent, I'd actually make it out of this house alive.

CHAPTER 19

Merrick

I've just made the worst mistake of my life. And that's saying something because I've done a lot of bad things. But this time, I know the consequences will be dire. Staring down at my booted feet, barely visible in the small amount of light cast by the moon, are Mrs. Braden's prize pansies. Prized pansies that have just been trampled by said boots. When this elderly woman wakes tomorrow morning to find that her precious flowers have been crushed, I know she'll do everything short of calling out the National Guard.

There's nothing to be done about it now, though. Stepping over the remainder of the treasured plants, I stealthily cross the short expanse of yard that separates Mrs. Braden's property and the home shared by my father and Suzanne. Keeping to the cover of shadows, I make my way around to the side of the house. I know there are security cameras covering the front and back entrances, and while I could've had Deacon bypass those easily, the purpose of this little visit is personal, and even though I trust my friend with a lot of my secrets, I still don't want to drag him into anything unnecessarily. Based on that reasoning, I've chosen to enter through the window that opens up into the downstairs parlor.

It's currently nearly four a.m. Everyone inside should be asleep. Just to be safe, I take a quick glance through the window. The parlor is dark, and there doesn't seem to be any movement from inside. Gently pushing up the window that I deliberately broke the lock on when I visited the other day, I climb in, dropping to the floor in a crouch. Glancing around, I stay as low to the floor as possible without actually crawling and make my way to the entrance of the parlor. For some reason, the music from Mission Impossible decides now would be the perfect time to play on a loop inside my head. Letting out an inaudible sign, I check to ensure that the coast is clear, then cross the parlor. Bypassing the staircase that leads to the second floor, I head down a hallway that I know leads to my father's study. Not seeing any light spilling from beneath the door helps reassure me that my father is indeed asleep upstairs. Hopefully, it's the black-out sleep of a man who had too many drinks with dinner.

Knowing that this door is always locked, I remove my lock-picking set from the back pocket of my black cargo pants. I make quick work of the lock, and quietly open the door and slip inside. Closing it behind me, I head straight for the massive oak desk and begin my search. As I check each drawer, I'm careful to put everything back the way I found it after I look through everything in and around the desk. Aside from lots of boring paperwork, there's nothing alluding to the crimes I know my father is guilty of. He must have a hidden safe somewhere. Quickly checking behind each of the many paintings lining the walls of the study, I find nothing. I'm just in the process of turning around to give the room one final sweep with my eyes, frustration bubbling up inside me, when the tip of my boot catches on the edge of one of the expensive Persian rugs behind the desk. I crouch down to fix the upturned corner when, out of my periphery, I see the edges of a latch peeking out from beneath the rug. When I pull it back further, I'm hit with the sudden realization that the reason I couldn't find a standard safe, either free-standing in the office or behind a painting, where any normal person would install one, was because it's beneath me. This bastard had a safe installed right into the hardwood flooring.

Letting out a little laugh that borders on maniacal because I was so close to giving up and just walking out, I get down low to inspect the lock.

It's a standard combination lock. I could sit here and attempt to guess the correct combination, but that would be a waste of time. And time isn't my friend right now. If this were a movie, I'd simply press my ear to the safe or use a stethoscope and turn the dial slowly to hear the clicks. But this isn't the movies, and that method, while possible given enough time, rarely works. For speed and efficiency, the best route to go is to drill into the safe. It will leave slight damage, but the hole will be small enough that—given the safe's location—it may be easily overlooked. It's a risk I know I have to take. Reaching into my sling bag, I pull out a small drill and then begin the process of borescoping the safe. This allows me to line up the notches inside by sight.

After several tense moments of splitting my focus between the task at hand and listening for any noise or movement outside of the office, I finally get the latch open. Looking inside, I find exactly what I expected to find. Piles of cash, several manila file folders, and two small black books. Not even giving the cash a second glance, I take a small camera from my bag and begin taking pictures of everything inside the file folders. I have no idea at this point if any of it will be of use, but I don't have time to sift through each page now. Better to have it and not need it than the other way around. Placing all the paperwork back the way I found it, I turn my attention to the two black books. Both are identical in size, but I know the contents will be vastly different. Most modern criminals would keep the proof of their misdeeds on a computer, but no, not my father. He's smart enough to know that computers can be hacked or deleted data can be retrieved by the most advanced police software. Instead, he opts to keep things old-fashioned, and as I open the first book, I see figures that show a mildly profitable 501(c). On paper, everything seems to add up ... until you compare it with the contents of the other book. This one shows vastly different numbers in the donations column, as well as information pertaining to a Swiss bank account.

The smile that crosses my face is everything evil as I take picture after picture of the contents of both books. Did this stupid bastard not learn anything from The Shawshank Redemption? Never keep a second set of books, or you're gonna get fucked. Hopefully, these pictures will be enough to allow Agent Kapranov to obtain a search warrant for the house. Quickly finishing up, I put both books back in place before closing and relocking the safe. Laying the rug back over the spot, I very quietly exit the same way I entered. If this information adds up to what I think it will, it will be the nail in my father's coffin, and I'll be overjoyed to see the look on his face when he sees that I'm the one holding the hammer.

It's been a week since I broke into my father's safe and found all the information pertaining to his potential embezzlement. Well I guess I didn't need to say "potential" anymore. Since that night, I've not only asked Deacon to monitor my father's calls and emails, looking for any signs that he's noticed anything amiss with the safe, but I've also had time to download and examine all of the photos I took. There's no doubt in my mind now, my father is stealing from The Right Path. I can't say I'm surprised. He's always been a piece of shit, jumping from one scam to the next, but you would think that a man in the position he was in now would put aside his penchant for petty crime and try to do better. Although, if these figures are any indication, I wouldn't call what he's doing anywhere near a "petty crime". If these numbers are correct, my father has embezzled nearly four million dollars from the charity he oversees.

I'm due to meet with Agent Kapranov in a few hours to hand over the flash drive with all the information. As a precaution, I've backed up all of the data to an offsite server in the event this guy turns out not to be on the up and up. I take a quick shower, letting the hot water run in rivulets around my face as I hang my head directly under the spray. With both hands braced against the tiles, I just stand under the water and breathe in the steam as it billows around me. I love showers. Growing up, I spent a lot of time outside in the sticky Southern heat. When I'd be brave enough to come back home for clothes or to check in and make sure my old man was still alive, taking a shower wasn't always high on my priority list. Hell, half the time we wouldn't even have running water because my father hadn't paid the bill. I got used to being dirty. Now, as an adult, I cherished the time I got to spend under the spray. I loved the warmth, the quiet solitude, and the feeling of all my sins being washed clean. At least for one day.

Stepping out of the shower, I wrap a towel loosely around my hips before exiting the bathroom. As I step over the threshold into my bedroom, my heart does a stutter step in my chest when I see a man sitting in an armchair on the other side of the room. After years of perfecting the art of showing little to no emotion, it takes nearly everything in me to keep from jumping.

"I'm really glad you weren't jerking off in there because I feel like that would've made this meeting reeeeeally awkward," says Agent Kapranov, his accent barely discernible beneath a heavy layer of amusement.

"Do Federal Agents make a habit of breaking into people's apartments and listening in on them in the shower?" I retort, walking nonchalantly to my closet to search for clothes. Something about this man being in my apartment, fully dressed while I'm standing here half naked, puts me at a disadvantage that I don't care for. "I thought I was supposed to be meeting you at the diner in two hours? Why are you here?"

He shrugs one heavy shoulder as if him being inside my apartment without an invitation is no different than going into the gas station for a candy bar. "I find that people have a tendency to make mistakes, sometimes revealing information they might not otherwise when caught off guard. It's very unnerving to know that someone such as myself could get to you, even in your own home isn't it? I would imagine it would be especially unnerving to someone with your ... extracurricular activities."

"Someone such as yourself? You mean an FBI agent?" I ask, slipping behind the door to my closet to slide on a pair of boxer briefs and worn jeans. I hate the idea of taking my eyes off this guy for even a second. God knows how much snooping he's already done while I was in the shower.

His comment on my "extracurricular activities" has the hairs on the back of my neck rising.

Making a noncommittal noise in the back of his throat, I see when I come out that I was right not to take my eyes off of him. He's now gotten up from his seat and is standing with his hands in his pockets, perusing the items on my bedside table. I realize too late that there's a single solitary picture frame on the nightstand. Glancing at the framed photo of Amelia, he arches a brow before his eyes meet mine again. That stupid fucking smirk is back. Looking at the picture myself before returning my eyes to his, I wonder just how astute this man is. Can he tell just by looking at the photo that it's a candid shot taken without her knowledge? Does he know more about me than I initially thought? What does he know about Amelia? If he's dug into her past and invaded her privacy the way he has mine, I'll put him in the fucking ground. I don't care if it brings the entire US government down upon my head.

Slowly, he makes his way back to the chair and sits again. Leaning forward, the picture of relaxation, with his elbows resting on his knees, he steeples his fingers together. It's only then that I notice that he has tattoos on his knuckles. How did I miss those during our first meeting? Maybe I was too distracted coming to terms with the fact that he knew who I was and the crimes I'd committed. I make a mental note to have Deacon do a little digging on Agent Alexi Kapranov.

"I think we can help each other," he says. "You need your father and stepmother out of the picture. I need someone that can get into tight places undetected and … retrieve something."

"And why do I get the feeling that Uncle Sam won't require me to pay taxes on this employment?" I ask sarcastically.

For the first time, that smirk turns into a full blown-grin. "I like you, Merrick. I've been around a lot of criminals in my life but you're different. You have a sense of humor. And with everything you've lived through, you shouldn't."

Whatever expression I was wearing before his words is replaced by granite. Like a switch flipped, I shut down all emotion. He knows. He knows a lot. A lot more than he should. Going over to the nightstand, I open a drawer and remove the flash drive containing the photos I took in my father's study. Walking over, I toss them in the general direction of his lap. Quick as lightning, his hand flies out and catches it midair.

"I'll have the evidence against Suzanne soon," I say.

Standing again, he nods, putting the flash drive into the inside pocket of his suit jacket and begins to walk out.

"I'll call you soon," is all he says before he leaves right through the front door, which is obviously the way he came in. The front door that had been locked, dead bolted, and alarmed. Not for the first time do I wonder who the hell this guy is. Picking up my phone, I hit Deacon's number in my contacts. I don't like not being the smartest person in the room. Time to do a little digging.

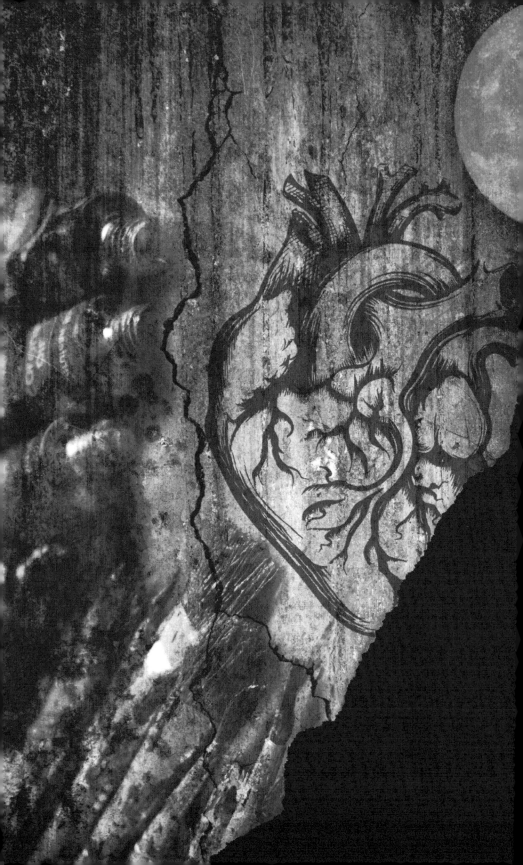

CHAPTER 20

Amelia

"Shit!" I exclaim, nearly dropping the pot full of boiling water and noodles. Catching the pot before it has time for the water to slosh up and burn me again, I carefully dump the contents into a colander. After sitting the pot in the other side of the sink, I turn the faucet to cold and stick my aching hand under the spray. The relief is immediate, though I know it won't last. I'll have to put some aloe on the tender area on the top of my palm that's already starting to turn an angry red color and blister. I don't know how this happened. I cook all the time. Siren and I have had a standing date once a week for dinner for as long as I can remember. The day of the week changes based on both of our schedules, but there hasn't been a week that's gone by without us sitting across a table from each other, catching up over hot food and even hotter gossip. Sometimes, we'd meet at a restaurant, but more times than not, she'd come over to my house, and I'd cook for us. It was easier to talk when you didn't have to worry about some journalist eavesdropping on your conversation and finding a picture of yourself on page six of the local paper the next morning.

I leave the pasta to cool in the sink and make my way down the hallway to the guest bathroom. Rummaging through the medicine cabinet, I locate the bottle of aloe and slather on a thick layer of the cooling gel.

Sighing in relief, I put my hands on either side of the sink and hang my head. I don't know what's wrong with me. Correction. I know exactly what's wrong with me. It was Merrick. He'd gotten under my skin the other night at the gala, and now I felt like I was breaking out in a rash, metaphorically speaking. I both loved and hated the way he made me feel. For the last several weeks, he's had me questioning my sanity repeatedly. One minute he hates me; the next, he's sticking his fingers inside me and making me come on his hand. I couldn't figure him out. That part wasn't a new development, though. Over the years, there had been plenty of times that I'd get a glimpse of an actual human being inside the machine he'd become. In those rare moments, he'd show emotions that I wouldn't have thought him capable of. But to be honest, I was so tired of the back and forth. I knew what I wanted. Why couldn't he figure his shit out? I was starting to think that maybe I'd have to take matters into my own hands.

Just then, I hear a feminine voice echoing down the hallway. "Ok, I'm here. Time to feed me."

Smiling to myself, I leave the bathroom, and as I enter the kitchen again, I'm just in time to see Siren leaning over the sink, inspecting the cooling manicotti shells inside. "I knew this relationship was a sham. You only want me for my food. Well, and my body."

Laughing out loud, she says, "You do have a bangin' body. But yes, it's the food for me. You know I can't resist you when you make Italian." She waggles her eyebrows at me suggestively. Shaking my head and shooing her out the way, I go over to the sink again and begin to rinse the noodles in cold water. I don't wanna have to pay a visit to the burn unit today. Luckily, the ground beef and pork mixture in the bowl next to the stove has come to room temperature. Taking out my baking dish, I begin to stuff the shells with the meat and cheese mixture. Spooning pasta sauce into the bottom of the dish, I lay each stuffed shell side by side in a nice tidy line before adding four more along the sides, completely filling up the dish. Covering the pasta with more sauce, I put the lid on and slip the dish into the oven to bake, all the while listening to Siren chatter on about mundane things and interjecting at various times with an "uh huh" or a "hmmm".

Turning around, I lean back against the kitchen counter and pick up a glass of wine that Siren so graciously poured before I even had a chance to ask. Smiling, I watch my friend. She's so animated when she talks. It doesn't really matter what the subject is. She talks about everything with a level of passion I very rarely feel outside of my studio. Unless I'm with her. She brings me out of my shell, reminding me that there are things out there worth experiencing. Things that don't involve trauma and pain.

I think for her, it was as if she was making up for lost time. Siren and I had known each other since grade school, but there was a period of time, shortly after we turned 16, that she'd simply disappeared. At first, she'd sent letters or called sometimes. But after a while, those just … stopped. I'd tried to reach out to her family for information on where she'd gone, but every time I asked about it, it was almost as if they were afraid to say anything. Then, one day, when I was about 22, I got a call. It was Siren. I was so overjoyed to hear from my friend that the sound of my excitement nearly drowned out the desperation in her tone. Realizing something wasn't right, I'd stopped talking long enough for her to beg me to come get her. When the call first began, I didn't hear the fear, but when I shut up and let her talk, it was plain as day. I didn't waste time asking questions; the only thing I asked was where she was and promised to get there as fast as possible. I'd driven through the night to Louisiana, of all places. When I knocked on the door of the cheap motel, a slit had appeared in the curtains, and a second later, the door creaked open just enough to let me inside. When I saw her … I didn't recognize her. Thin as a rail with bruises all over her beautiful skin. So many questions popped into my head and were on the tip of my tongue, but one look at her and I knew she'd break down if I didn't get her out. So I helped her put her bags in my car, and we drove all the way back to Charleston in silence. I held her hand the entire way, and the way she gripped me was as though

I was the only anchor tying her to this Earth. That if I let go, she would just ... float away.

It was only later, when I'd gotten her to the safety of my home that she'd given me a brief explanation of what had happened to her. After that, it took her nearly a year of living with me and many intense therapy sessions before she was able to go outside without looking for danger around every corner. Over the course of that year, she'd finally divulged some of the things that had led up to that night at the motel. I was no stranger to horror, but the details of some of the things she had had to endure turned my stomach, and it took everything in me not to be sick while she talked. In the end, all she would say was that there had been a man. Someone that she'd loved, who had hurt her. Not just physically, although he did that plenty, but emotionally and mentally as well. Siren wasn't ... right. But then again, neither was I. We had just become very good at faking it. It was lucky for both of us that we had some type of creative outlet for our trauma. I painted. Siren played for the Charleston Symphony. She had the innate ability to make you bawl like a baby simply by playing the violin. As a kid, she'd been a prodigy, composing her own music and playing it without ever putting a single note to paper. She simply played what she felt. For as long as I'd known her, she'd had a violin in her hand. She liked to say that music had saved her. That even when she'd been at her lowest, she'd heard it inside her head. Having gone through what I'd gone through, I knew what she meant. She'd heard music when she dissociated. When reality became too much to bear. Sometimes, I wondered if the "fly by the seat of her pants" Siren was like me. One bad day away from a complete and total breakdown.

Blinking hard, I'm snapped back to reality when a hand waves in front of my face. Glancing over at my friend, I find her staring at me curiously. "Shit. I'm sorry. I zoned out for a minute," I say, trying my best for a light tone. "What were we talking about?"

"I was asking how the gala was. Even with that gorgeous gown you had on, I bet it felt like a meat suit, and you'd gone swimming in a tank full of sharks. I really wish I could've been there. To act as your bodyguard, if nothing else. It sucked that I had a concert scheduled on the same night."

"It was … interesting. I had an encounter … of the sexual variety. With Merrick." Before I can even finish the sentence, I'm physically wincing. Not because I'm ashamed of what happened between us but because Siren looks like a kid who's just found a golden ticket to a real-life Wonka factory. She's practically bouncing on the bar stool she'd taken up residence in next to the kitchen island.

Popping up, she lets out a gleeful, "YES!" that's loud enough to break the sound barrier. Dropping my head into my hands, I can't help but laugh. When I look back up at her, she's wearing a devious grin. "I fuckin knew it! I knew he had the hots for you! What happened? Tell me you let him fuck your brains out in a supply closet while your mother was making her acceptance speech in the next room."

"Jesus Christ, Siren. I did not have sex with him!" I say incredulously before tacking on, "but I would've if he'd asked me." Laughing because the situation is so bizarre that I can't not, I say, "We started arguing, and he dragged me out to the terrace, and then we *weren't* arguing anymore. Next thing I know, he's got me back into a wall with his fingers inside me, and I'm on the verge of screaming the building down."

By the time I finish, her mouth is practically on the floor. Mimicking the gritting teeth emoji, I stand, and wait for her to get her wits about her so she can form a coherent sentence. Finally, she says, "But you didn't have sex with him. What happened??"

"Well, then he reverted back to his normal asshole-ish self. So I kinda … hit him in the face."

Cackling with laughter, she manages to get in enough air to say, "Only you would punch a guy right after he got you off."

Laughing myself now, I down the rest of my wine before refilling the glass. Sobering up, I say, "So what am I gonna do about this? I feel off-kilter like I don't know which way is up anymore. He has to want me, right? I can't just be imagining all this. Unless I'm the butt of some joke, and the punchline just hasn't hit yet."

Staring off into space for a moment, she appears deep in thought. I'm almost afraid to ask what she's thinking. Luckily, I don't have to wait long. "You're gonna have to go over there," she states matter of factly. "Invade his space so he has nowhere to run. Force him to own up to his shit."

Letting out a heavy sigh because I know she's right, I sip my second glass of wine and begin to formulate a plan. If I'm honest with myself, I'm terrified. Taking this step will alter my life drastically, in one way or another. If it doesn't work out, I've embarrassed myself for nothing. My relationship with Merrick will be irrevocably changed. If it does ... the same rules apply. Either way, nothing will ever be the same.

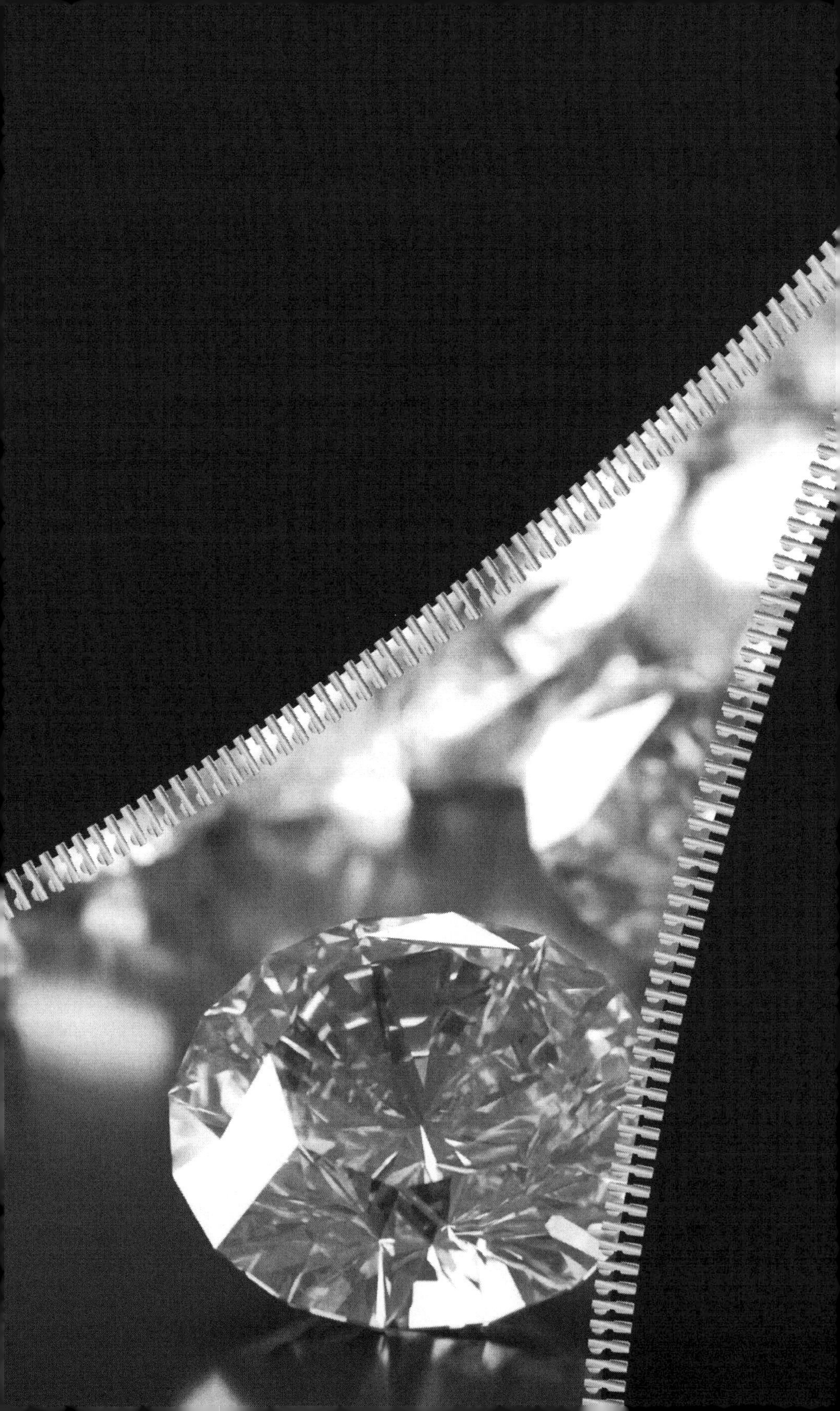

CHAPTER 21

Merrick

I can't sleep. The meeting with Agent Kapranov has been playing on a loop in my head for days. When I'm not overthinking that situation, I'm reliving the night of the gala when I had Amelia writhing on my hand. It's getting harder and harder to maintain control when I'm around her. I'd gotten so good at suppressing my urges over the years. The urge to touch her, to smell her hair, to bury my nose in her neck, to take her in every position known to man and maybe even some I'd just make up myself. But I felt like the wall I'd erected to protect Amelia from my sick little obsession was crumbling. I'd seen the cracks appearing gradually over time. A little one here, a little one there. In the moment, those cracks had been easy to ignore. The other night at the gala, I'd stepped back and taken in the wall in its entirety and come to one conclusion. That wall was about to collapse. I'd waited too long. I could feel myself reaching a breaking point, and God help us both when that time came. It didn't help matters that Amelia was on the other side of that wall, chinking away at all those little cracks, determined to make it to my side. Ideally, I should be ecstatic. This was the response I wanted. To know that underneath all those layers of trauma and paint lay a woman who held some measure of feelings toward me that were more than just familial. Realistically, I was internally freaking out. It was one thing to privately obsess over something that seemed permanently just out of reach. It was another to have that something invade your personal space and essentially dare you to take what you'd previously only dreamed about.

Getting out of bed, I make my way to the living room, and I'm just about to turn on the TV in the hopes that some boring Netflix documentary will knock me out when I hear a loud banging at my door. Not a knock but the sound of someone's fist beating at the door, as if demanding entry rather than asking for it. Narrowing my eyes, I slowly move closer. It's 1:30 a.m. Who the fuck would be banging on my door at this time of night. I swear to God, if it's Agent Kapranov come to "catch me off guard" again, I'll be catching a rap for murdering a federal agent. As I open the panel next to the wall to view the video monitor that shows the camera view from the other side, my eyes widen, and I take an involuntary step back. Reminding myself I'm not a total pussy, I unlock the door and swing it open to find Amelia standing on my welcome mat, looking like something out of one of my late-night fantasies. I may be the only man that wakes up fucking the sheets after dreaming of a woman in a shapeless dress that looks like a rainbow threw up on it. Pushing her way inside, she whirls on me before I've barely even gotten the door closed.

"Okay, enough is enough. I've decided. I'm done with this shit," she says without preamble.

Warily, I ask, "Done with what? What the Hell are you talking about?"

"Oh, cut the bullshit, Merrick. You know exactly what I'm talking about. I'm done with this." She gestures between the two of us. I feel my heart plummet to my feet. I open my mouth to speak, but she quickly cuts me off. "I have one question for you, and so help me God, if you lie to me or feed me some line, I'm gonna knee you right in the balls."

I try my best not to show how her words have the dual effect of scaring the crap out of me and making me want to crack a grin. Considering the fact that she's clearly pissing mad, I opt not to say anything and instead just wait for whatever bomb she's getting ready to drop on me.

"Do you want me?" she asks matter of factly.

Out of all the things I thought she'd say, that definitely wasn't one of them. I honestly don't know how to answer that question. If I reply no, I'd be the biggest liar. If I reply yes, I'd still be a liar because the word "want" is just too simple a term to describe how I feel about her. Maybe "need" is a better word? I needed to own her. To invade every one of her senses, the way she has mine. I needed to fall asleep to the sound of her breathing and wake up to her face every day for the rest of my life. I needed to save her so she could save me. Right now, despite all of the dangers and uncertainty surrounding us, I just needed ... her. So I answer with the same level of simplicity in which she asked me the question.

"Yes," I reply.

She stares at me for a long time. So long that I can feel myself starting to sweat. Our words hang heavy in the air, circling both of us like an invisible cord. Just when I feel like another second will have me cracking under the pressure of her stare, she walks towards me and takes my hand. Wordlessly, Amelia leads me down the hall and up the stairs to my bedroom. She's been here before, so she knows where everything is, but the ease with which she navigates herself through my apartment makes an ache bloom beneath my rib cage. It was as if she belonged here. As if we'd done this a thousand times before. It was just one more reason, added to the millions of others, that reinforced what I already knew. She was it for me. And I was scared shitless.

I was normally a confident man. I knew, even from my limited past experiences, that I was capable of pleasing a woman. But, this wasn't just any woman. This was *the* woman. And I didn't want to just please her. I wanted her to cleave to me. To make her feel so much that she'd become just as wrapped up in me as I was in her. I needed to. Because literally everything was riding on this. Her happiness, my sanity, *our* future.

As we enter my bedroom, my sense of panic increases, and I realize I can't go forward without telling her the truth, at least about this. I owed her that much. She needed to know about my inexperience and the reasons behind it. I had to tell her so she'd understand that whatever was happening between us in this moment was the beginning of something. Something monumental.

Pulling her to a stop just inside the doorway, I tug her hand so she'll turn around to face me. The quizzical look on her face is barely able to conceal the riot of emotions I can see hiding underneath. Insecurity, desire, fear. She's afraid I'm going to stop this, maybe even that I've changed my mind and decided that I don't want her. The very notion is laughable.

I open my mouth to speak, steeling myself for whatever her reaction will be once I tell her that I've never been fully intimate with a woman. I wonder for a second if she'll even believe me. On paper, I know I seem like a playboy, never seen with the same woman twice. Which is true. But what she and the rest of the world don't know is that I've never allowed things to venture beyond the realm of surface-level satisfaction. There were times in the past when I questioned my feelings for Amelia, desperate to be free of this burning obsession I felt day-in and day-out. During those times, I'd tested the depth of my feelings for her by attempting to be with other women. But every time just felt ... wrong. Not morally wrong, just ... not right. Wrong time, wrong scenario, wrong *woman*. Eventually, I just gave up trying to find happiness in the moment, opting to devote my time and energy to securing the forever kind that I knew I'd only have with her.

Forcing the words past my lips is probably one of the hardest things I've ever had to do. And I've been in some pretty precarious fucking positions. Meeting her eyes, making sure she sees that there isn't a single reason on this earth that could possibly make me not want her, I say, "Amelia, I've ... I've never done this."

It takes a second for my words to sink in. I watch as her brain tries to process what I've just said. If it didn't feel like my heart was sitting somewhere in the vicinity of my stomach, I might actually find the entire scenario comical. As it is, I can only stand there, holding my breath and praying to God that she doesn't start laughing.

As I watch her face, I see the moment the puzzle pieces click into place. With a surprised expression, her gaze locked on mine, she replies, "By this, you mean ... sex?"

"Yes. No." Letting out a frustrated sigh, I say, "I mean, yes. I've never had sex. But I need you to understand that I don't consider what we're about to do sex. I wanna make love to you."

She blinks at me. One long blink before I see her eyes become glassy. I wish more than anything that I could be inside her head at this moment. To know what she's thinking, what she's feeling. I open my mouth to tell her why. Why I haven't been with anyone, not fully. To tell her that since the moment I saw her, the idea of being with anyone else seemed abhorrent to me. The words are on the tip of my tongue just waiting to spill out, when she slowly shakes her head at me.

"I don't need to know why. Not right now. Right now, this is enough," she says.

It suddenly occurs to me that she thinks the reason I haven't been with a woman is because something happened to me. Something bad. I wanna tell her that plenty of bad things have happened to me in my short life, but I don't want to burden her with the weight of my trauma. Not now. This moment should be about only her and me. So, when she gives my hand a gentle tug, I let her lead me further into the room.

Stopping next to the bed, she looks up to face me. There's hesitancy in her eyes now. As if she doesn't know where to go from here. Going with my gut, I pinch her chin and lower my mouth to hers. It's a gentle kiss. A barely there ghosting of my lips over hers. Moving the hand holding her chin to the back of her neck, I pull her into me and deepen the kiss, swiping my tongue across the closed seam of her lips until she opens for me. Using her reactions to guide me, I slide my tongue inside. She lets out a small gasp of surprise. Releasing her neck, I coast my hand down over her collarbone, skimming the side of her breast before gripping her hips with both hands to pull her more firmly against me. Finally allowing myself to handle her the way I was dying to on the night of the Gala, I slide both hands down to grip the backs of her thighs, lifting her so she's forced to wrap her legs around my waist. Keeping a tight hold on her, I crawl across the bed on my knees before gently laying her down. I follow, not resting my full body weight on her but propping myself up on my elbows so I can look down at her.

"Are you sure this is what you want?" I begin. "There's no going back after this, and not just because of who we are to each other or who our parents are. But for us. If we do this, you're mine. We have to be careful in public, but in private, I'll own every part of you. Your mind, your heart, and this beautiful little body that's driven me crazy for years."

She looks up at me with such a sense of longing that I already know her answer. Either way, I wait to hear the "I'm sure" before I reply, "Good. Because I wanna fuck you just like this for our first time. Face to face, heart to heart. I wanna feel every inch of your skin touching mine. I wanna see your eyes when you come. I wanna watch your mouth open on a scream that ends in my name."

I can feel the effect my words are having on her. By the time I'm finished, she's squirming beneath me, her breathing labored. Rearing up so that I'm sitting on the balls of my feet, I span her waist with my hands. She's wearing some bohemian style dress that's a riot of colors and patterns. Settling myself between her legs, I place my hands on the sides of her calves, slowly running them up so that the dress is forced to bunch as I expose her creamy thighs and the black lace underwear she's wearing. Telling her to sit up, I lift the dress over her head until she's left in only her panties and a matching bra that only covers the lower half of her breasts. Jesus Christ, I knew her body would be perfect, but the reality is something else entirely.

Just as I go to release the front clasp of her bra, her hand comes up to cover mine, stilling me. Just by looking at her face, I can tell she's nervous. She won't meet my eyes and instead stares somewhere in the vicinity of my throat as she says, "Maybe this is a mistake."

My heart stills in my chest. She's changed her mind. It was too much pressure; I knew it. Her next words, however, surprise me.

"What if I can't do it? What if I can't give you what you need? Maybe you should've chosen someone else to give this gift to."

The fear from a moment ago loosens its grip on my heart. Leaning back down so that we're nearly nose to nose, I force her to meet my gaze because I want her to look at me before the next words leave my mouth.

"There is no one else. There's never been anyone else. My entire world is in this bed." I can hear the desperation in my own voice, but I couldn't care less. I need her to know what this means and the importance of not only my decision, but hers. Nodding in understanding, she removes her hand from atop mine, allowing me to continue. Releasing the clasp on her bra, I lower my head to run my nose down the valley between her breasts, using it to push the cups of her bra aside. Sitting up, I barely give myself a chance to look at her before I reach down and jerk the side seams of her panties hard, ripping them off. She lets out a little hysterical giggle at my show of brute force, but I'm beyond the ability to exercise any finesse. As I sit back on my heels, I stare down at her naked body. After what I'm sure feels like an eternity, I expect her to become self-conscious and try to cover herself. Instead, she lifts her arms, stretching them high over her head. The movement causes her breasts to lift and press together. I read somewhere once that people's pupils dilate when they look at something they like or that makes them happy. If that's true, mine must look like fucking saucers right now.

"I've dreamt about this so many times over the years. In those fantasies, you were everything I wanted and more. Late at night, when I was alone in my bed, I'd stroke myself off to the idea of what your body would look like. My fantasies pale in comparison. I should've known you'd be this perfect."

Turning her face away to hide her shy smile against the side of her arm, she says, "Stop. You're making me blush."

"Good. I plan on following the path of that flushed skin with my tongue," I reply.

Leaning down, I kiss the side of her neck that's exposed to me. I skim my lips down the column of her throat, over the swell of her breast, before swiping my tongue over her pretty pink nipple. It's my first real taste of her skin, and I know without a shadow of a doubt that I'll never get enough. Pulling her nipple into my mouth, I alternate between sucking and swirling my tongue around the peak until it's stiff and begging for my attention. Not wanting any part of her to feel left out, I do the same to the other breast until she's writhing beneath me, her thighs tightening on either side of my hips.

Slowly making my way down her abdomen, I pepper her skin with little kisses, darting my tongue out to fulfill my promise of licking every place that grows flushed under my stare. As I glance up from under my lashes, I can see her head moving side to side on the pillow as though it's impossible for her to remain still. Using my hands to spread both of her thighs wide, I settle onto my stomach, bringing my mouth in line with her gorgeous pussy. Just as I know she can feel the first hints of my breath over her sensitive flesh, she rears up onto her elbows and attempts to clamp her legs shut around my head.

Her next words prove that she's having another moment of self-consciousness. "You don't have to do that. I don't know ... I mean ... what if I don't taste good?" she says, voice shaky with nerves.

A thought occurs to me. "No one's ever done this to you before?" I ask. Slowly, she shakes her head. *Yes.* A wealth of pleasure fills me at the knowledge that I'll be the first person to ever taste her here. To ever bury my tongue inside her. I also take sick gratification knowing that I'll also be the last.

"A night of firsts then. I'll trade you one of mine for one of yours," I say. "Don't be nervous. There isn't an inch of your body that I wouldn't spend the rest of my life feasting on."

After another second of staring at me with uncertainty, she finally gives up the good fight and lets her head flop back down onto the pillow in surrender. I get myself comfortable between her spread thighs, and look up at her, issuing one simple command. "Hold onto the headboard."

She does as she's told and a second later, my mouth is on her. I take one full swipe from entrance to clit then I pull back for a second, to allow her taste to settle fully on my tongue. With heavy breaths, I wonder if this is how addicts feel right after a hit of their favorite drug. I dive back in and spread her open for me allowing unfettered access to her clit, which I lap at lightly for several seconds before sucking her into my mouth. She lets out a strangled cry that I somehow know will haunt me forever, and her back arches off the bed. As I peer up her body from this vantage point, I take a mental photo of how she looks at this exact moment. Free of inhibitions, she lifts her hips to meet my mouth, accepting the ecstasy she knows can only be found with me.

"Merrick, please."

Momentarily releasing her, I say in a teasing tone, "I thought I was pleasing you. Do you need more?"

"Yes, more! Everything. Anything."

And just like that, the gentleness and patience I've been trying so hard to maintain takes a backseat to pure, unadulterated want. Slipping my index finger inside, I curl my finger upward at the same time that my mouth latches onto her clit. Working her into a frenzy, she undulates beneath my mouth for another moment or two before I feel her entire body stiffen, pulling tight as a bowstring. Then she's breaking apart, just for me. Sobbing out my name in an almost incoherent series of cries that shoot straight to my cock. The feeling of her inner walls clenching around my finger is enough to have me grinding my hips into the mattress, desperate to be inside her. Crawling my way up her body, I hover over her. I *need* to feel that tightening around my cock. Now. But still, a moment of insecurity has me hesitating.

As she looks up at me through heavy-lidded eyes, I allow her to see the uncertainty in my face a second before I say, "Mia, I think I'll die if I can't get inside you in the next minute. But I'm afraid I won't know what to do. What you like. Will you show me?"

Her gaze softens, and before I register what's happening, she's pushed me onto my back and is straddling my hips. Reaching for the buttons of my dress shirt, she slowly begins to reveal my chest, one button at a time. As she reaches the last button and pushes the shirt wide, I wait for her reaction to a sight that no one else has ever seen.

"Oh my God," she gasps.

I understand her shock, and I allow her to look her fill. Nearly every inch of my chest is covered in tattoos, and there are barbells running through both of my nipples. As she runs her hands over the artwork, unknowingly setting my skin on fire, I pray she doesn't ask too many questions. Like why I have so many or if it hurt to get this much ink. I don't want to have to tell her that, after having the shit beaten out of you for most of your life, you become somewhat immune to pain. I don't wanna have to explain that sometimes, the pain of getting inked helped distract me from other parts of my body that were suffering far more. Now isn't the time for that type of discussion, so I'm grateful when she remains silent, instead choosing to inspect each image, perhaps trying to guess the meaning behind some. When her fingers reverently glide over a large emerald with a watercolor backsplash that's tattooed directly over my heart, her gaze seeks mine, asking one question I have no problem answering.

"The color matched your eyes perfectly," I say by way of explanation. The look I get in return is so heavy that I know she understands what I'm saying.

Instead of replying, she leans down and presses a gentle kiss over the gem. I can feel my heart kick against her lips and wonder if she feels it, too. Helping me remove my shirt completely, I sit up to take it off, bringing us chest to chest. As I feel her nipples brush my naked chest, it's everything I can do to remain calm and let her keep control of the reins. Scooching her ass back some, she slowly unbuttons my slacks and begins tugging them down my legs, taking my boxer briefs with them. When she has me fully undressed, she crawls back up to me on her hands and knees and, Dear God in Heaven, has a man ever fainted during sex before? Because; fuck masculinity. Trying to get a grip on my emotions, I remind myself that I have to stay conscious if I want to get inside her. With that in mind, I remain perfectly still as she repositions herself over my lap.

She's straddling me again, but this time, I can feel the heat radiating off of her, and I know that I'm now only an inch or two away from the only place I ever wanna be again.

Looking up at her, I ask, "Don't I need to get you ready."

"I've been ready since the day we met," she says.

And without another word, she lifts up onto her knees and positions me at her entrance, slowly lowering herself onto me. Her agonizing pace has me breaking out in a sweat, and instinct is telling me to grab her hips and thrust up into her until I'm as deep as I can get. But I don't wanna hurt her. Besides, I want this experience to last as long as possible. In fact, I'd gladly die in this position.

With patience I didn't even know I possessed, I remain still until she's seated fully on top of me. Giving us both a moment to adjust and just savor the feeling of being connected in a way we never have before, I close my eyes briefly and try to take deep breaths through my nose. That is until she begins to move. Eyes flying open, I watch as she begins to rock her hips back and forth. Jesus, I'm going to last a total of 45 seconds before I spill myself inside her. She torments me with a slow swaying of her hips before she picks up speed, using her hands on my chest to lift herself up my length before lowering herself back down. As she loses herself in pleasure, I watch her eyes drift closed. I watch her hands slowly lift until they're buried in those strawberry blonde curls that I've dreamed of having splayed out across my pillow. The sight has bolts of pleasure shooting through every nerve ending in my body, and I can't take it anymore. Not giving her any opportunity to protest, I rear up, hooking my arm around her waist and flip our positions. Hovering over her and still seated deeply inside her, I lean down and ravage her mouth, our tongues dancing with each other in a rhythm as old as time. I pull back and tug on her bottom lip with my teeth, sucking on it before releasing it with a small *pop*. At the same time, I withdraw my hips until only the tip of my cock remains inside her, then thrust back into the hilt. The motion causes her to cry out, and I commit the sound to memory.

Growling at her ear, I say, "I've been waiting years to hear those sounds. To know that it's my cock that's giving you pleasure. That it's me who's in control of your body."

Her reply is quick and breathy, "Then show me what I've been missing, you stubborn bastard."

I don't know how she has the ability to make me laugh at a time like this, but I can't stop the chuckle that bubbles up my throat. Accepting her challenge, I release the tight hold I've kept on my control, and as I thrust in and out of her, I hook my hand under her right knee, drawing her leg further up and out, allowing me to go impossibly deeper. Our faces are inches apart, and I can feel her exhale of breath every time I grind myself against her. I continue to pump in and out of her, holding her open to my assault. She feels incredible. Everything I imagined and more. But it's her eyes I want now. Her eyes on mine, looking into me, seeing the truth of everything I haven't yet said. Keeping eye contact, I gyrate my hips, grinding against her clit with every downward stroke. The sounds she makes are like vibrant colors, each one unique and breathtaking. Whimper; blue. Moan; yellow. Scream; red.

Never breaking our gaze, I demand, "Tell me you're mine. That you've always been mine." I know I'm using the vulnerability of this moment to put her in an impossible position. Forcing her to admit the truth of her feelings for me.

"I'm yours. Always," she whimpers. I don't know if the "always" is referring to the past tense of the future. For the moment, I'm gonna pretend it's both.

Groaning, I bury my face in her neck, biting down on the soft flesh there. As I latch on with my mouth, I suck until I taste the faint hint of copper on my tongue. As I fuck her wildly, I know she'll wear my bruises tomorrow. Not just the one I've left on her neck, but the impression of my fingertips on her hips and thighs, the bite marks I leave across her breasts. All the while, I continue to rail her tiny little body. Breath catching in her chest, I feel her body start to go rigid beneath me. She's close to coming again. Releasing her leg, I keep my weight braced on one elbow, using the other hand to pin her arms above her head. A few thrusts later, I feel her walls begin to clamp down around me. I know I won't last much longer.

With my eyes locked on hers, I watch as they begin to slide closed, her head tipping back as her body bows beneath me.

"No!" I bark. "Open your eyes." Bright green gaze finding mine again, I say, "I've waited nine years for this," I growl, "I deserve it. Give it to me. Let me hear my name spill from your lips when I push you over the edge."

Just like that, she explodes around me, screaming my name so loudly it'll echo in my head for days. Fucking her through her orgasm, I feel lightning shoot up my spine a split second before my own pleasure begins to take me under. My entire body stiffens, and a look of ecstasy crosses my features. One I know she can see because she's still watching me like a good little girl. As I stare into her eyes, I empty myself inside her. Groaning her name like a prayer, I grind my pelvis against hers in an attempt to get as deep as I possibly can.

Releasing her wrists to brace the brunt of my body weight on my elbows, I do my best to keep from crushing her into the mattress. As our breathing slows, she leans up to pepper soft kisses all over my face. First, the tip of my nose, then my eyelids, which have finally drifted closed in my ecstasy-induced haze, then my cheeks, my chin, and finally my mouth. Lingering there, I kiss her back with as much energy as I can muster. When we break apart, I slip out of her, roll out of bed and pad to the bathroom for a warm cloth. Coming back, I clean her up, then toss the cloth in the general direction of the hamper in the corner. Standing next to the bed, I look down to see her fidgeting with her hands, which I know is a telltale sign that she's nervous. Does she think I'm going to kick her out? With a small smile tugging at my lips, I slip back into bed, wrapping an arm around her waist to pull her back against my chest. Drawing the sheet up over us, I bury my face in the curls I love so much that are now a tangled mess around her head. Feeling her relaxing against me, exhaustion weighs heavy on both of us. Just as I hear her breathing even out, indicating she's fallen asleep, I whisper, "If this is a dream, I don't ever wanna wake up." I stay that way for a long time, just breathing her in, but soon my eyes are growing heavy, and even though I don't want to miss a second of being with her like this, I have no choice but to let sleep take me under.

CHAPTER 22

Merrick

When I woke up this morning, Amelia was gone. I can't say I wasn't pissed off that she'd snuck out like a thief in the night. That was my line, after all. The funny thing was, when I woke to find her gone, I'd had the irrational thought that she had indeed stolen something from me. If only she knew I would freely give her anything she wanted, all she had to do was ask. I'd tried to call her a few times and sent a handful of texts. She hadn't responded, but I wasn't worried. I knew where she was at any given time throughout the day, so I knew where to find her when I was finished with my current meeting. I thought I'd made my position clear enough last night. But it seemed that was only for the duration of time that we spent in a bubble of our own making, cut off from the outside world. Clearly, Amelia still hadn't yet come to terms with the fact that we were inevitable. I was trying not to let it get to me. She'd have her "come to Jesus" moment soon enough. In the meantime, I'd continue laying the groundwork for our future. Laying the next stepping stone along that path, I sit on a park bench at dusk, watching the sun set over the water near The Battery. The irony that so many of the turning points of my life have taken place on this waterfront isn't lost on me. No matter how much money I make, my plans to run as far and as fast as I can have been put on permanent hold. My heart now beat outside of my chest, and if I wanted to truly live, I'd have to follow wherever it went. For now, it called Charleston "home", so I guess I did too.

I wasn't sure how I'd transitioned from a streetwise kid with an unhealthy obsession to a sneak thief so deeply in love that the very idea of being apart from Amelia made me feel crazy. The dangerous kind of crazy. That was why this meeting was so important. The outcome of this conversation could make or break us. Glancing down the shadowy path, I feel my body tense when I see movement.

If I didn't know better, I would be wary of the small, hunched figure coming toward me in the dark. The slow, skulking walk wouldn't be out of place in some heart-racing thriller. I wasn't afraid, though. On the contrary, I had a low buzzing sensation beneath my skin that could only be described as excitement. It had taken me a long time to forge this relationship and convince Gloria to trust me. I didn't believe that she felt any loyalty to Suzanne because if she did, she wouldn't be here right now. She did, however, love Amelia. It was the only reason, I believed, that she'd stayed in that house all these years when any rational person would've run at the first opportunity.

Watching the small woman make her way toward me down one of the paved paths of Riverfront Park, I was thankful for both that fact and the meeting place Gloria had suggested. Shrouded by thick trees and bushes on one side with the ocean on the other, this spot was just discreet enough for a secret meeting. I'd become close to Gloria in the years that followed my moving into the Charleston townhouse. Not as close as Amelia was, but I think after years of watching me watch her, Gloria had come to the realization that while I may be slightly unhinged, there was one thing I'd protect with my life. It seemed that one thing was something we had in common.

When Deacon and I had started digging into Suzanne and my father's backgrounds, in an attempt to uncover any dirt we could find in order to put them away, I had no idea that my secret weapon would wear orthopedic shoes and eat dinner at five p.m. I'm still not sure how Gloria found out that I was investigating Peter and Suzanne, but she'd recently come to me with information that she thought might help. I'd been skeptical at first, not really sure what her motivations were. But it hadn't taken me long to realize that Gloria detested Suzanne and, subsequently, my father. I think if Amelia had had any semblance of a mother figure growing up, Gloria was it. Again, I don't know how, but she somehow knew that one day, all of Suzanne's sins would catch up with her. Or maybe she had just been hoarding information in the event that Suzanne ever became deranged enough to try to murder her own daughter. That was one of the things Deacon and I had uncovered during our extensive search into the seedy underbelly of Suzanne's idea of holy matrimony.

Everyone in the circles of Charleston's elite knew Suzanne had a reputation as a black widow. Knowing and proving were two different things, however. That was where Gloria came in. Once she'd realized that we were on the same side and that I wasn't just some pissant punk looking to strike it rich by conning the next generation of Charleston royalty, she'd revealed to me that she just happened to be in possession of certain items, saved from the scenes where Suzanne's late husbands had met their untimely ends. Turns out—in typical Suzanne fashion—when the police had been knocking on the doorstep, she'd entrusted Gloria to dispose of any items that would surely be deemed suspicious in the eyes of the law. Unbeknownst to her, Gloria had kept these items preserved in secret, in the eventuality that Suzanne decided to turn on Amelia, and Gloria had to step in to protect her.

So when I'd been cornered in a darkened hallway in my parent's home a few weeks ago and told that these items existed, I'd jumped at the chance to take them off her hands. She'd agreed under one condition. That Amelia was not to be hurt or prosecuted for any role she may have unwittingly played in the deaths of at least two of her former stepfathers. I knew I'd have to cut a more concrete deal with Agent Kapranov, but I'd given Gloria my word that I would die before I allowed anything to happen to Amelia. After several moments of scrutiny under eyes that I swear could see straight through to my soul, she'd chosen a meeting place and time to hand over the evidence of Suzanne's past transgressions.

As the old woman approaches, I give her a gentle smile reserved for very few people. Looking down, I see she's carrying a carpet bag very reminiscent of something out of Mary Poppins. Stooping to reach her small, 5'2" frame, I give her a gentle hug. She fusses at me, but even in the dim light from the streetlamps down the path, I can make out the ting of a blush on her weathered cheeks. Handing me the bag, she says, "You better know what you're doing, boy."

I nod solemnly and reply, "Yes, ma'am. Don't you worry, they're gonna get what's coming to them, one way or another." Gesturing to the carpet bag, I ask, "Can you tell me what's inside?"

The older woman walks to a nearby park bench and slowly lowers herself down to sit. I'm struck just then by how frail she seems. For the few short years I lived in the family home, Gloria had been a force to be reckoned with. Her strict rules and stern demeanor had made her seem so strong. It's only now that I truly realize just how tired she must be. She'd spent years watching over Amelia while simultaneously living with so many secrets, the weight of which had to have taken a toll on her. Following her down to the bench, we sit in companionable silence for several moments. I don't want to rush her or pressure her into saying anything she isn't comfortable with, but at the same time, I need to know the contents of this bag and what impact they're going to have on my endgame. Soon, Gloria begins to talk.

"The night Mr. Winston died, I wasn't there. That night went the same as any other night. I put Ms. Amelia to bed, finished up a few final chores, and then went home for the night. I got a call from Ms. Suzanne in the middle of the night. She needed me to come to the house. I immediately thought something had happened to Ms. Amelia, so I rushed over as quickly as I could, not even taking the time to change out of my dressing gown." She gives a little shake of her head and huffs out a breath. I imagine Ms. Gloria out in public in her dressing gown would've been about as shocking as a UFO sighting.

Continuing on, she says, "When I got to the house, I could hear police sirens in the distance, and I swear, I felt my heart drop to my stomach. I was terrified that she'd snapped and done something to harm that girl." Looking over at me she says, "I know what she is. I've suspected for a long time, just like many others have. You know how these hens love to flap their gums any time there's somethin' worth talkin' about? But up to that point, all the rumors about her were just that; rumors. Then she handed me the gun. She told me at the time that it was the gun Mr. Winston had killed himself with. I wondered as to why she was giving it to me instead of the police. I thought, surely they'd want to take it. You know, for evidence. But instead, she handed it to me and told me to get rid of it. She cried, crocodile tears in my opinion, saying that she just couldn't bear to have it in the house, knowing it was the weapon he'd used to end his own life. I didn't find out until much later that the police *had* taken a gun from the house that night. Just not the right gun. The one they took was registered to Mr. Winston and only had his fingerprints on it. The other gun, I suspect, doesn't. It wasn't until the next day that Ms. Amelia told me that she'd gotten out of bed and seen them fighting."

Pausing now, she looks away for a moment before returning her gaze to mine. "The police said it was a suicide. Who was I to nay say the police? Besides … I knew that if I was to come forward with my suspicions, they'd take that baby out of that house, and I'd never see her again. So I did what I was told. Ms. Suzanne never asked me what I did with the gun. For her, once it was out of sight, it was out of mind. It was just another instance of me cleaning up a mess made by the mistress of the house. Cleaning up behind herself would never have occurred to her. It's just the way she was raised. When Mr. Prescott died, I was in the house. I came into the kitchen just as it happened. Ms. Amelia saw everything, although she's never talked about it. But she was there, in the kitchen, when I came in. Again, Ms. Suzanne gave me something to "dispose of". This time, it was a teacup. I knew what had happened, but I just couldn't get the image of Ms. Amelia's stricken face out of my mind. She was already so damaged. I couldn't stand the idea of her being taken by Social Services. So, again, I did what I was told."

Staring at her intently, I say, "But you didn't get rid of them. You saved them. Why?"

Sighing heavily, the old woman leans back against the bench, staring out over the water. "I did my best to protect that girl. When my husband died a year after Mr. Winston, I moved into the house. I thought, if I was there, I could watch out for her. But I couldn't prevent what she saw that day in the kitchen. And at that moment I knew, one day, Ms. Suzanne would get her comeuppance. Evil like that can only exist for so long before it either takes over the house or it's exorcised. I kept the proof so that one day, someone could clean out that house." Giving me a sly side-eye, she tacks on, "Who says you gotta be a priest to perform an exorcism?"

Giving a dark chuckle, I sit back against the bench and gaze out at the water with the older woman. Not being a God-fearing man, I can find the humor in her comment while still appreciating the gravity of everything she's told me. Regardless of my lack of spiritual belief, I send up a silent thank you to whoever is pulling the strings up there. If what's in this bag turns out to be what she's described, I'll be one step closer to my end goal. One step closer to my final heist. One step closer to acquiring the most precious gem I've ever held in my hands. Gloria doesn't know who I am or what I've done. But I think she knows that there's nowhere safer for that jewel than with me, otherwise she wouldn't have met with me tonight. She wouldn't have given her only leverage in a war with the Devil to a boy from the wrong side of the tracks. I won't make her regret it.

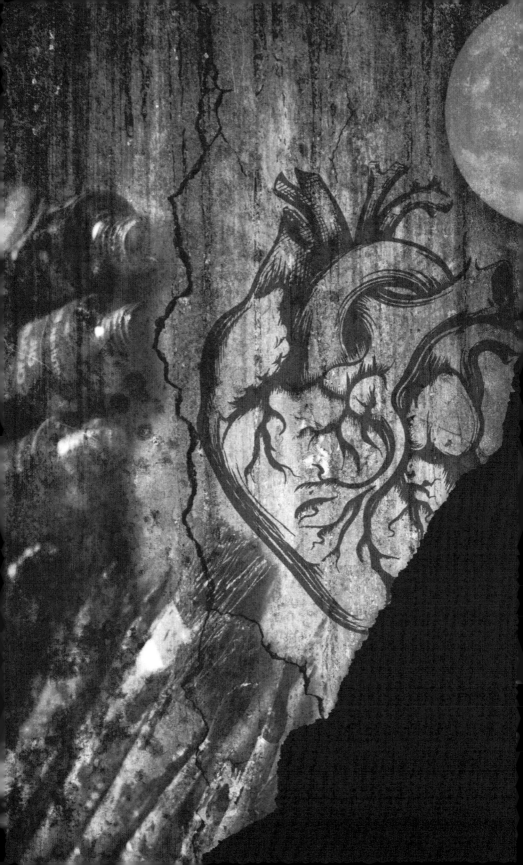

CHAPTER 23

Amelia

I've been sitting in my studio for nearly an hour, staring at the same piece of canvas. There's nothing on it. There should be something on it, but there isn't. This very rarely happens to me. Usually, when I come in here to paint, I have a vision in my head, ready and waiting to burst free. Not this time, though. For some reason, I'm blocked. I feel like a soda bottle that's been shaken to the point of explosion, but the top won't budge to let the pressure out. This is all Merrick's fault.

I can't stop replaying everything that happened last night. It's running on a loop in my head, from beginning to end. Like a horror film, but my favorite, all the same. It shouldn't have happened. I'm both elated and terrified that it did. Elated because it confirmed those little nuggets of suspicion I've had over the years that Merrick always felt something for me, and that there had always been something there, lurking outside of my peripheral vision, metaphorically speaking. Something made of flames and teeth. And oh, how I enjoyed the pain. I didn't expect that. The fact that I was the first person he chose to be with weighs heavy on me. The gravity of that decision isn't something I can take lightly. Whatever the reasoning behind his remaining a virgin up to now, he still chose to be with *me*. That had to mean something. The terror aspect of my feelings was that someone would find out. Well, that and a heavy dose of fear of the unknown and change. If what we did last night were to get out, we'd both be ruined. Not only in the eyes of society, but I'm pretty sure it would place us firmly in the crosshairs of my mother and his father's proverbial guns. Suzanne and Peter have spent their lives breaking us down, so we have no one to turn to except them. The possibility of Merrick and I being together, being able to lean on each other and heal each other, would put them on shaky ground and in turn, make them even more dangerous.

Attempting to run my hands through my hair, then realizing too late that it's pulled up and halfway dislodging the bun, I make a frustrated growl in my throat and fling my charcoal onto the table to my right. Standing quickly, I nearly topple my easel with a burst of nervous energy. I can't do this right now. I need to get out and go for a walk. I need to clear my head. I lock up the studio behind me and jog to the back door of my home to grab my sling bag, then exit the property via the creaky steel gate out front. Wandering aimlessly, I walk block after block, dodging tourists and shoppers. Sometimes, when I'm particularly bothered by something, I'll come out and just walk around the city. The Historical district is so beautiful with its large magnolia trees and cobblestone streets. I watch as the occasional horse-drawn carriage passes by, and a loud voice over a megaphone pointing out important or famous locations on a tour that will take visitors around the city. Even though I can't see it, I can smell the salt water and marsh. A warm breeze blows my disheveled hair over my face, and it's only then that I remember the state of my bun. I quickly take it down, fixing the haphazard mess, then throw it back up again, hoping no one of any importance is out walking the same streets I am. When I finally lift my eyes from my own feet, I realize that they've taken me to The Charleston City Market. The covered but open-air buildings are lined with stalls and tables full of some of Charleston's best artists, crafters, and food vendors. Entering one of the buildings, I can't stop myself from gravitating towards the table of local treats, buying a bag of Benne Wafers and snacking on the thin, crispy cookies packed with toasted sesame seeds. Meandering past the tables, I watch in awe as

216

Gullah women weave sweetgrass baskets. It never fails to amaze me just how rich Charleston is in the varying types of art we produce here. You didn't really have to ever set foot in a museum to find beautiful things made by beautiful hands.

Exiting the market, I cross the street and walk down to The Battery. The closer I get to the pier, the stronger the scent of salt water becomes. The sun is almost gone. Soon, the night market will open and with it will come throngs of people looking for a good meal and a good time. I'm looking more for solitude, so I pass the large fountain where a handful of children still play and manage to find an empty swing at the end of the pier. Looking out over the water, my thoughts unerringly turn back to Merrick. I wonder where he is right now. After sneaking out of his house in the early hours of the morning, I was sure he'd be blowing up my phone as soon as he woke up to find me gone. He didn't disappoint. I've had four missed calls and about 10 texts, all of which I've ignored. Pushing off with my legs, I set the swing to motion in a soft glide. I let out a sigh that's more exhaustion than anything else, and I try to sift through all the thoughts and feelings swirling around inside me. I don't know what to make of this new dynamic between us. Part of me wants nothing more than to grab onto it with both hands and never let go. The other, more rational side of me tells me there's nowhere for this thing to go. Even if it was what we both wanted, there are too many things in the way for us to have anything permanent and growing up the way I grew up doesn't lend much credence to the idea of happily ever after anyway. I let out a little snort of laughter because Merrick is definitely no Prince Charming. Tipping my head back on the swing, I close my eyes and let the cool breeze from the ocean caress my face. I feel calmer now, but I still don't know what to do about Merrick. Maybe it's a good idea to just avoid him for a few days. Give both of us time to come to terms with what happened between us and decide what we wanna do now. I mean, it was only sex. Only one night. Who knows, maybe the next time I see him, he'll be back to his regular dickish self, and this entire inner struggle will be moot.

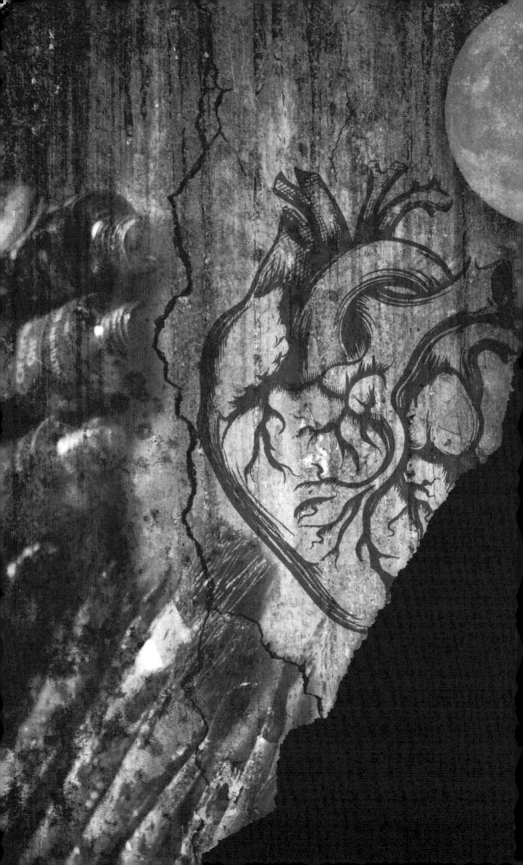

CHAPTER 24

Amelia

Putting my key into the lock on my back door, I push my way inside. Closing the door behind me, I start to make my way across the kitchen when I sense movement to my left. Letting out a little shriek, I reflexively swing my messenger bag towards the intruder. Stepping from the shadows of my living room doorway, Merrick easily blocks the bag, ripping it from my hands and tossing it negligently to the floor. It takes me another second for my brain to register who's in my house. My initial terror dissipates, only to be replaced by another type of fear when I get a good look at Merrick's face. It's only been 24 hours since I saw him last, but he appears to have aged a decade in that time. His eyes are bloodshot, his face drawn. He looks like he hasn't slept in a week. But despite his apparent exhaustion, he's somehow managing to exude both intensity and deadly calm. I'm immediately wary. I know I should question him, ask what he's doing here or how he got into my house, but instead, I stay quiet, waiting for him to make the first move.

Still standing several feet away, he says, in such a quiet tone that I almost have to strain my ears to hear him, "You didn't come over last night." It isn't a question. The accusation is clear. Looking at him, I can't tell if he's angry at that fact or hurt. The guilt I feel is like a punch to the gut. It's on the tip of my tongue to tell him the truth. To apologize and erase that hauntingly lost look from his eyes. But I can't, so instead I go with the next best thing. Evade.

Looking anywhere but at him, I say, "Something came up."

He doesn't reply; just stands there, ensuring that I have no choice but to look back at his face. Slowly shaking his head, he says, "No it didn't." How he knows that I have no idea. Sometimes I get the feeling that he knows me so much better than I think. That maybe he knows me better than I know me. Not for the first time do I wonder just how closely he's watched me over the years when I wasn't looking.

Advancing on me, intensity building with his every step, I'm ashamed of the fact that I feel the need to retreat. Not just physically but emotionally. Matching his steps, I take one backwards for every one he takes towards me until my back hits the closed door I've just come through. He doesn't stop until he's fully in my personal space. Gone is the cold and distant Merrick. The one I've grown so accustomed to over the years. That Merrick, I knew how to navigate. This Merrick is dark and singularly focused, his gaze all-consuming. Gripping my chin in his hand, he forces my face up until my eyes clash with his. "Tell me why you're avoiding me."

"I'm not. I was just busy," I say. It sounds weak, even to my own ears.

Scoffing under his breath, he says, "Bullshit. You're a lot of things, Amelia, but you've never been a coward. You're pulling away from me, I can feel it. Tell me why."

We've never been big on sharing, but we've never really lied to each other either. Realizing that I owe him the truth, I say, "It's just too heavy, okay? I feel too much when I'm with you. I needed space. To think, to regain my composure, to breathe air that didn't smell like you! I don't even know what this is anymore! It's sex, but every time I'm with you, I feel like we're on the verge of something monumental, and I don't know how to handle it!" I'm yelling by the time I finish. How dare he? Who gave him the right to come into my home? To make me feel all of this. To open this door that's been locked for so long that I thought I'd lost the key. Working myself up into a good state of anger, I shove at his chest.

He doesn't budge, so I do it again. He finally allows me a modicum of space by taking a single step back. The reprieve is short-lived, however, because, like flipping a switch, something inside of him seems to snap and the next thing I know, his hand is gripping the hair at the base of my skull, angling my head to the side as he brings his face in so close to mine that our cheeks are practically touching.

He lets out a humorless laugh. The sound has goosebumps breaking out across my skin. "Too heavy? For how long? A week? Two?" Shaking his head in disbelief, sounding angry himself now, he grips my hair in a punishing hold. Running his nose up the length of my neck, he whispers in my ear, "Try years. Endure years of those feelings. Keeping them hidden, repressed. Being in the same house with you day in and day out and every time you got near, it took every ounce of willpower in me not to reach out and touch you. To claim what was mine. What you're feeling right now, I've had bubbling inside me since the day we met. Do you think that by pushing me away, those feelings will just disappear? They won't, trust me. I've tried it. It doesn't work. They only get worse, building and building, until they're eating you from the inside out and eventually you just ... explode."

Not giving me a chance to respond, he uses his hand in my hair to jerk my head back hard, and his mouth captures mine. I don't try to keep him out, so I simply open for him, allowing him to unleash some of that pent-up rage and desire. I'm not sure I could've responded, even if he'd given me the chance. I'm stunned by his words. He's felt this way about me since that first day? And all these years, he's been hiding the fact that he wanted me. Maybe even more than that, needed me. Because what's pouring out of him now definitely feels more like a need than a want. His tongue pushes its way into my mouth, dominating mine. All I can do is allow the assault on my senses. His feelings may have been stronger and present for a longer period of time than mine, but I wasn't exaggerating when I said I felt too much. These emotions he's evoking are all new to me. This is no tepid relationship where two people are just going through the motions. It's not some secret little friends-with-benefits type situation, either. It's not convenient or easy in any way. It's volatile, raw, and desperate. I never allowed myself to believe that there could be anything between us, and now, there's too much. It's as if my head, my heart, and every other emotional receptor in my body is being bombarded by him. I don't know how long my walls will continue to stand against the onslaught.

Releasing my hair, his hands grip both sides of my neck, thumbs on the underside of my jawline. His grip doesn't hurt or scare me. He's simply holding me in place, ensuring that there's nowhere left for me to run. Between his grip on my neck and his body pressing into mine, there's nowhere for me to go. The way he's invading my space and my senses makes it seem as though he's attempting to meld the two of us together, never to be separated again. Just as that thought occurs to me, I realize the hands I'd just used to shove him away are now gripping his shoulders instead, fingers digging into the fabric of his shirt. I guess subconsciously, I was doing the same thing. It's in this moment that I stop fighting him. I'll psychoanalyze later. Right now, I feel like I need him inside me, or I'll die. He must feel the fight drain out of me because as soon as he senses my compliance, the hands he'd been using to hold my head in place fall away and coast down the length of my body, molding my every curve. Breaking the kiss, I glance down at his chest as my hands move to the seam of his button-down shirt. Gripping the edges, I yank as hard as I can. Buttons go flying across the kitchen in all different directions, exposing his beautifully tattooed chest, those barbelled nipples stretched tight across layers of muscle. A chest that's currently heaving, attempting to take in oxygen that was deprived from the both of us during that kiss.

Placing my hand over the emerald tattooed on his chest, I can feel his heart kicking wildly under my palm. Looking up into his eyes, what stares back at me are liquid pools of desire ... longing ... fear. The first two, I understand. The latter, I make a mental note to ask him about later. For now, my focus has shifted from needing space to wanting to be as close to him as I can get. He must feel the same sense of urgency because he

222

seems to have had enough of touching me through my clothes. Just as I did to him, he reaches up to the neckline of my dress and, gripping it in two hands, rips it right down the center. I remind myself to yell at him about that later too. That thought may be the last coherent one in my head because then he's sucking my nipple into his mouth, and I can't even remember my own name.

"Oh, God."

Releasing me, but not before giving my breast a last taunting lick, he replies, "There's no point in crying out for divine intervention, Mia. Not even God could take you someplace I wouldn't follow."

He doesn't give me time to contemplate the deeper meaning of his words before he's coasting his hands along my sides, down to where the thin material of my lacy underwear sits low on my hips. Grabbing the fabric in a tight fist, he jerks hard, ripping them from me. I make another mental note to make him replace my underwear, too. That's the third pair he's either stolen or destroyed. The scrap of lace falls to the floor along with my sanity as I frantically fight the buckle on his belt, then the button of his slacks. As soon as he's free of the confines of his boxer briefs, his hands roughly grip the undersides of my thighs, just behind my knees, lifting my legs and spreading them wide. Clutching onto his neck as my feet suddenly leave the floor, I let out a gasp that quickly turns into a yell, not out of fear but for an entirely different reason, as he shoves inside me to the hilt.

My cry is a mixture of surprise, pleasure, and pain, which mingles with Merricks' grounded out, "Fuck!" Pausing momentarily, he looks down into my face, gauging my reaction. Puffing out great lungfuls of air, he sounds so concerned when he asks, "did I hurt you?"

My expression somber, I nod slowly, replying, "Yes." Then before he has a chance to withdraw or apologize—which I know is coming—I say, "do it again."

His eyes search my face, narrowing slightly as he tries to get a read on my emotions. Whatever he sees in my expression must put him at ease and convey my need for more because the corner of his mouth tips up in a grin right before he withdraws to the tip and slams into me again. Gasping, I let out a little hysterical laugh that's quickly cut off by his mouth as it finds mine again. Then he's setting a punishing rhythm, his upper body pressing mine firmly into the door, his hands press my thighs impossibly wide as he thrusts in and out. I don't know how much more I can take. Every thrust brings me closer and closer to the edge.

Voice-breaking with each slam of his hips, I manage to say, "Merrick ... fuck ... I'm gonna come."

Moving his hands around to the backs of my thighs, he guides my legs around his waist. Bringing our faces close, he says, "That's it, baby. You owe me nine years' worth of sounds. I want them all. Your curses ... your moans ... your screams."

I let out a whimper as his hands move to grip the underside of my ass, dragging me up and down his cock. Voice straining, he says, "I'm not leaving, Amelia. Do you understand? When we're done here, I'm gonna carry you upstairs and spend the rest of the night fucking all the fight out of you. You're done resisting this. Resisting us."

Looking into his eyes, I can see that he means every word. At the moment, there's no part of me that wants to fight him anymore. His words, while meant as both a promise and a threat, don't scare me. I'm too far gone to be afraid. Recognizing that I'm seconds away from orgasm, my inner walls begin to clamp down around him, and I feel one of his hands find its way back into my hair, jerking my head to the side again. He slams his hips forward one last time, grinding them into me at the same moment that I feel his teeth sink into the flesh right over my carotid artery. The combination of his teeth buried in my skin and his pelvis grinding into my clit, have spots swimming at the edge of my vision. Letting out a scream, my walls tighten around him, and I begin to come harder than I ever have in my life. Growling against my neck like some wild animal, I feel him jerk, emptying himself inside me.

It takes several minutes before my senses come back online. When I do, the first thing that registers is Merrick's face buried in the crook of my neck. The second is the feather-light kisses he's placing over the spot he just bit. I have the fleeting thought that here's the prince, soothing the wounds caused by the beast. I can't stop the little smile that crosses my features because never before would I have ever classified Merrick as having any prince-like qualities. Well, aside from ridiculously good looks. It's not lost on me that he hasn't pulled out of me, nor that I can barely breathe from how hard he's pressing me into the back door.

Attempting to break some of the tension that's growing in the midst of our silence, I ask, "You gonna kiss all my boo-boos and make them better?"

Pulling back enough to look down at me, he doesn't laugh or even smile at my attempt at a joke. He just replies in a solemn tone, "Yes, if you'd let me."

Feeling the smile slip from my face, I say, "You can let me down now." I'm acutely aware of how every muscle in my lower body is crying out in protest at our prolonged time in this position.

Slipping out of me but still not letting me go, he shakes his head. "I meant what I said, Amelia. I'm not leaving." Hoisting me up higher, he kicks out of his pants, leaving them right there in the middle of the kitchen floor. Still holding me in his arms, he carries me up the stairs and into the bathroom. Only then does he put me down long enough to start the shower. Turning back to me, he divests us of the remaining scraps that were once our clothes. Taking my hand, he leads me into the shower stall, backing me directly under the hot spray. I close my eyes and sigh in bliss as a small smile touches my lips. I can physically feel my muscles relax and the tension leave my body. When I open them again, I find Merrick staring at me intently. "Do you have any idea how beautiful you are?"

Blushing, I lower my gaze. I'm not some shy wallflower, but I'm also not used to him talking to me like this. Looking at me like this. I think back on his earlier words when he'd let loose the information that he'd wanted me from the first day we met. Whatever's happening between us has been brewing inside him for as long as we've known each other. In the quiet of the shower, images flash through my mind of all the times

225

Merrick was kind to me over the years. All the times he seemed to be there when I needed someone to lean on or risk falling apart. I believed him when he said he'd fix all my problems. Fight all my demons. Thinking back, I realize that's exactly what he's been doing for the past nine years.

Raising my head, I meet Merrick's eyes again and take a single step that feels more monumental than the act of simply putting me a foot closer to him. I stretch myself up onto my tiptoes and place a soft kiss on his mouth. Arms circling my waist, he pulls me closer, releasing an almost inaudible sigh. We stay like that for several minutes before he reluctantly releases me to wash my hair and then my body. I don't miss the way he leans in to smell my skin.

"I love the way you smell. That scent follows me everywhere. I even smell it in my sleep," he murmurs against my skin.

Making quick work of soaping himself up, he reaches behind me and turns off the shower. Stepping out, he gently towels us off before taking my hand and leading me back to the bedroom. As I stand next to the bed, I don't have a chance to feel any type of self-consciousness at the fact that I'm stark naked and in a position that isn't beneath him. Pulling back the comforter and climbing into bed, he pulls me down with him so that I'm half-sprawled across his chest. My small burst of laughter ends with a yawn that I can't seem to contain. Regardless of the threats he made downstairs, he makes no move to touch me in a sexual way, even though I can feel the proof of his desire against my hip. Instead, he turns us until we're facing each other, our mouths only inches apart. Looking up at him, I can tell he's tired too. Not just physically. His face is weary, and I wonder when the last time was that he truly slept peacefully. I watch his eyelids grow heavy as a small smile plays around the corners of his mouth. He called me beautiful in the shower, but lying here, just on the cusp of sleep, I've never seen anything more breathtaking. The sight of him rivals any piece of art I've ever made or seen.

Just as his eyes slide closed, I whisper, "Tell me a secret?"

He's quiet for so long that I start to wonder if he's drifted off to sleep. After another long moment, without opening his eyes, he mumbles, "I don't wanna steal you. I want you to choose me."

I don't know what he means when he talks about stealing me. I'm not even sure he knows what he's saying. He could just be on the verge of a dream, but as I lay there, long after his breathing has grown deep and even, I think to myself that I may have never really had a choice. Some subconscious part of me whispers that my heart chose his long before my head ever recognized a decision had been made.

CHAPTER 25

Merrick

Massive oaks covered in Spanish moss line both sides of the long lane leading up to the house. I usually come here at night, when there's less chance that I'd be spotted or followed. I'd purchased the large plantation house under a fake name with fake documents. That fact didn't make my love of the property any less real. Unfortunately, there were plenty of people within our social circle who wouldn't think twice about hiring someone to trespass with the sole purpose of snooping. There was nothing an aging debutante loved more than gossip, and one of the wealthiest bachelors in the city buying an old, run-down plantation home without anyone knowing would feed those bloodhounds for months.

As I reach the end of the long driveway and the house comes into view, I'm struck again by how beautiful it is. A circular drive leads up to a three-story—if you count the attic space—structure. Large, white pillars accent a wraparound front porch, fully equipped with rocking chairs at one end and a cushioned swing at the other. Internally, the bones of the old house had been fully restored to its former glory, minus the air of racism because, while some Southerners held true to the belief that "the South would rise again", I did not. And I knew Amelia didn't either. I also knew that she loved Charleston and, even if she could pick anywhere in the world to live, she'd choose to stay right here. That was why I'd chosen this house. Not just because of its size and amenities but because it was the embodiment of Southern charm. At least on the outside. The inside was designed to feel like a *home*. My dreams to come of age and get the hell out of this town had been retired the moment I met her. I knew, even then, that wherever she went in life, I wouldn't be far behind. So here I was, building an entire life around a woman who had no idea. If that wasn't insanity, I didn't know what was. Love made people do crazy shit, I guess.

Coming to a stop in front of the house, I get out of my car and, handling my package with care, head to the front door. Using my key, I unlock it and walk inside, closing it shut with a heavy thud behind me. Looking around, what I see is a foyer with a foundation of warm polished hardwood as opposed to cold marble tiles. I'd kept the grand staircase, though. It seemed like sacrilege to tear that part out. I did, however, have it redone in the same beautiful cherry wood that covered the floors. Wandering through the house, I finally end up in the main parlor. This room, like every other room in the house, was devoid of any furniture. Not to say that the house was entirely empty because that wasn't technically true. Leaning down, I carefully open the wooden crate I carried in from the car. There would've been two, but my latest acquisition was currently being framed. I'd make another trip to bring it later. Reaching inside the crate, I lift the heavy frame, and hang Amelia's "Shades of Shadow" on one of the many hooks I'd installed the last time I was here. Stepping back, I admire the piece. I can see why there was such an interest in the painting when it went up for sale at the gallery. It's hauntingly beautiful, like the artist herself. Smiling a little, I look around the room at the other pieces of art lining the walls. Each one an original. Each one different. Each one stolen. There were more scattered throughout the house, along with paintings and sculptures by other artists that I knew Amelia admired.

Making my way through the home, I take in the latest improvements. The hardwood floors have been refinished and waxed to a high shine. The wallpaper in the adjacent sitting room had been chosen by me, specifically because of its color. The deep emerald green was something of an obsession. In fact, every aspect of this house spoke to my obsession with a woman who didn't even know it existed yet. What can I say? I was a romantic. I didn't allow myself to dwell on the possibility that, when finally revealed, she'd hate it. I knew she'd love it as much as I did, especially once she realized that everything about this house was chosen with a specific goal in mind. The eventuality of the two of us building a life together inside of its walls. Of moonlit weddings and vow renewal ceremonies. Of children with my stubborn chin and her gemstone eyes. Of pets and parties and birthdays. Of late nights making love and early mornings making breakfast.

I had to believe that when I finally exposed every flaw hidden beneath my three -piece suits, she'd see past them to the life we could have together. I had to believe it because if I didn't, then everything I'd endured up to this point was meaningless. We were magnets, spaced far apart but pulled towards each other by sheer will. I knew with every fiber of my being that I was put on this earth to find her.

Now, I just had to make *her* believe it.

Locking up the house, I feel my cell vibrate in my pocket as I walk back towards my car. Digging my phone out, I see Deacon's name on the caller ID. I've barely gotten my "hello" out before Deacon is cutting me off.

"Mr. Russia has got some HUGE skeletons in his closet. In fact, he's got a whole fucking graveyard in there. You need to be careful around him, dude."

Stopping in my tracks, I stare out down the oak-lined drive. "Elaborate, please," I say, already not liking how this conversation is going.

"So I've been looking into our new ally. On the surface, he appears on the up and up. Immigrated here when he was 24 and was working for the FBI within a year, despite not having gone through the academy. He spent a few years working sex crimes before taking a position as a profiler and homicide investigator. All in all, the picture of patriotism for his new country."

"Why do I sense a "but" coming?" I ask. I can feel the black cloud forming above me, just waiting to open up and drop the other shoe on my head.

"But ... he's got some anger management problems. He was suspended several times while working in the sex crimes unit for beating the shit out of suspects. After the third incident, he was transferred to homicide. They called it a promotion, but in reality I think they just wanted to get rid of the loose cannon in their midst."

"Well, who hasn't gone into a rage and beaten someone half to death who clearly deserved it?" I say, remembering all those years ago when I'd found Amelia wandering down the street with torn clothes and bare feet.

"That's true. But unfortunately, that's not all," Deacon replies with a heavy pause and an even heavier sense of foreboding.

"For fuck sake Deacon, spit it out before my head pops off!"

"Okay, okay! So I have a flare for the dramatics. I should've gone into theater ..." he says, trailing off as if he's staring into space and truly rethinking his life choices.

I pinch the bridge of my nose and exhale a frustrated sigh before gritting my teeth and saying, "What. Else."

"Right," he says, apparently bringing himself back to the present and our teeth-pulling conversation. "So the way he seemed to worm his way into the Bureau without any prior experience tickled my funny bone a little. Not in a "ha ha" way but in a "how the fuck" kinda way. So, obviously, I needed to know more. But once I got past the surface stuff, there was ... nothing. And I know what you're gonna say. How can there be nothing? That's the thing; there can't just be nothing. Even if he'd been a model citizen back in Russia, there would still be *something*. Birth certificate, immunization records, school records ... something. It was as if the guy materialized out of thin air when he touched down on US soil. So, after finding a nonexistent past, I kept digging and realized that it wasn't so much that there was nothing there. It was as if it had all been locked away behind an impenetrable door. So you know me, I knocked a few times, and no one answered ... so I kicked the door down, then immediately wished I hadn't."

"You gonna tell me what was behind door number 1, Bob?"

Deacon chuckles as though he isn't aware that I'm on the verge of strangling him. Or maybe the chuckle is because he does know. He gets off on making me a nervous wreck.

"Well ... turns out our broody Agent is the son of Ilya Kapranov."

Mouth turning down into a frown, I say, "Why does that name sound familiar?"

"Ohhhh, only because he's one of the leaders of the Bratva and has a reputation of being a particularly sadistic fuck."

"Jesus Christ. Agent Kapranov is the son of a mafia boss?" I ask, though it's more of a statement than a question.

"Mmmhmm. And not just any son, but the eldest legitimate son, and therefore, should be taking his father's place in the organization. Instead, it seems his bastard half-brother is in training for that spot, though from what I've gathered, there's a healthy amount of fear in the underworld as it pertains to our Fed. His half-brother may be getting groomed for leadership, but it appears that it's this guy that's earned the people's respect and terror in equal measure."

"Well, shit," I say, scrubbing a hand down my face.

"Have I ever told you how eloquent you are? You're like a goddamn poet, man."

"Oh, fuck off. Anything else I need to know? Does he kick puppies, too?"

"Not that I've found, but you never know. I'll keep looking," he says.

"Good. I wanna know why he left Russia. He made it clear that he wants me to steal something for him, and we need to know what it is and make sure it's not a set-up before he decides to actually call in that favor."

"Sir, yes, sir!" he replies with fake bravado, and I can just see him actually making a saluting gesture on the other end of the phone.

Hanging up, I stare at the screen for a long time. I've been in a lot of precarious situations, but it's been a long time since I felt this level of unease. Not since the days of hiding from my father's belt. I don't like it one bit. Speaking of my father, it dawns on me that he's hosting a small party at their townhouse tonight for the charity that's currently lining his pockets. Normally, I wouldn't go unless it benefited me in some way, but it'll give me a good excuse to gauge his reaction upon seeing me and allow me to feel out whether he suspects anything after my little break into his study.

The charity he's pilfering from, The Right Path, was started as a program for runaways and wayward youth. Its initial goal was to take kids off the street and give them access to food, basic necessities, a place to stay, and eventually a scholarship. All done in the hopes of helping them make something of themselves and better their lives. The irony of the situation isn't lost on me. The idea of my father, who starved and beat me most of my life, helping kids just like me get off the streets is a joke. Although, I'm sure the original Chairman and founders of the program find it about as funny as I do. You see, Peter Stratford wasn't around for the foundation's creation. He muscled his way in later after he married my stepmother. After he'd transitioned from being a low-level criminal and all-around asshole to being an affluent member of society and ... well, still an asshole. Through means of blackmail, extortion, and intimidation, I'm sure. The fact that he's stealing from a program that was originally started with good intentions will make taking him down all the sweeter.

Checking the time on my watch, I realize that I've gotta hurry if I wanna get back to my apartment and be ready in time to get to Amelia's. I'm sure she's also been pressured by her mother into attending tonight's little circle jerk, and if she's going, she'll be going with me and only me. Now that we've been together, there's no way in Hell I'll let some sniveling playboy grope all over the curves that I can now trace with my eyes closed.

CHAPTER 26

Merrick

Ringing Amelia's doorbell, I wait impatiently for her to answer. I could've gotten in by myself, but I've already scared the shit out of her once, and I don't need her questioning how I managed to get in in the first place. So, I've decided to try the gentlemanly thing and not make a habit out of popping out from the shadowy corners of her house. The only fear I want her to feel from me is in the bedroom. Rationally, I know that's not a natural thought to have, but there's never been anything natural about me. Looking up and down the mostly empty street, I glance at the door with an air of impatience. She better not have left already. If she went to this party without me or, God forbid, with a date, I will drag her into the nearest maid's closet and fuck her so hard she'll forget her own name, not to mention the name of the person she went with. Ringing the bell again, I give a series of sharp knocks directly after. A moment later, I hear her yell from inside, "I'm coming, I'm coming!" I smirk to myself. Before the end of the night, she'll be saying that again. The smirk on my face turns into a full-blown grin when I hear a clatter from inside, followed by a muffled "motherfucker!" She must've knocked something over in her haste to get to the door. I almost feel bad for rushing her, and as she opens the door, it's on the tip of my tongue to apologize. That is, until she opens it fully, and I see what she's wearing. Suddenly, the apology dies on my tongue, along with every ounce of saliva.

The cream-colored dress reaches nearly to the floor and appears to have been poured onto her body. I guess that makes two of us that can't breathe at the moment. The fabric is shimmery, and it looks like there are thousands of little beads sewn into the skirt. The skirt that's sporting a slit straight up the middle and reaches nearly to her crotch. I have the fleeting thought to check to see if she's wearing panties before we leave. If she is, she'll be taking them off. They'll only get in the way. As my gaze moves upwards from the skirt of the dress, I take in the bodice, which is heart-shaped and form-fitting. No straps leave her shoulders and upper back bare, the creamy paleness of her skin is highlighted by the fact that her hair has been swept up into a messy updo of riotous curls, as though they've barely allowed themselves to be contained. Her makeup is minimal, but she doesn't need it anyway. Each and every one of the freckles I've counted while she slept are present and accounted for. The green of her eyes shines brightly from her fresh face, like a front porch light that she's left on for me to find my way home. She's never looked more beautiful.

I open my mouth to tell her so, and at the same time, she opens her mouth and says, "Merrick, what are you doing here?" The confusion is clear in her tone.

Closing my mouth without saying a word, I step into her personal space, forcing her to step back. Slowly, I back her into the house, closing the door behind me. It's clear that it never occurred to her that we'd be going to this party together, and I don't know why that fact annoys me, but it does.

"I'm here to pick you up for the party."

"Pick me up? For the party? The party at our parent's house? No, you're not. I'm going alone."

Stalking towards her, I'm surprised when she stands her ground and doesn't back away. I'm immediately enveloped by that maddening rose-water scent, and the saliva that had evaporated when she'd first opened the door comes flooding back, making my mouth water. Unfortunately, my lust has to fight for dominance over the irritation that her words invoke. Before I have a chance to rein them in, my next words slip out.

"You're never alone."

Fuck. I shouldn't have said that. It's gonna open up a whole line of questioning that I can't answer right now. To my surprise, there's only a moment's pause before she replies, bypassing my comment as if I never said it.

"We can't go together, Merrick. People will talk."

"Let them talk. You know they'll do it anyway. Whether it's about this or something else." Cavalier words for someone who's supposed to be keeping this under wraps until our parents are arrested. But I can't stop myself. Now that I've had her body, the impulses I've wrestled with for the last nine years are beginning to break free, and they're demanding that I make sure she and everyone else knows who she belongs to. I know it's not smart, but I won't change my mind on this. She'll go on my arm or not at all.

"Merrick ..." she begins, but I cut her off.

"You're walking through those doors with me, or I'll throw you over my shoulder again, take you upstairs, and tie you to the bed, where we'll stay for the rest of the night. I'm fine with either outcome. In fact, I'd probably prefer option two."

She glares at me for a moment longer, and I maintain the eye contact because I'd gladly drown in those eyes. After a brief staring match finally breaks, huffing out a breath, I know I've won.

"Let me get my bag," she begins, but I grab her wrist as she moves to turn away. Pulling her closer until the swells of her breasts are brushing my chest, I lean down to run my nose up the side of her neck. As I take a slow inhale, drinking in that scent that's so uniquely hers, I feel her exhale a heavy breath of her own. I breathe in; she breathes out. We're two halves of the same whole. Our parts just don't work properly unless we're together.

Feeling the fight leave her, I move my face from her neck, capturing her mouth in a slow kiss. Immediately, she opens for me, but I take my time, tracing the seam of her lips with my tongue before gliding inside. Careful not to mess up her hair, I use both hands to frame her face, holding her in place while my mouth explores hers. She surprises me by nipping my bottom lip, causing me to pull back. She's got a devilish smile on her face now, as though she's one-upped me in some way. Payback for losing our glare off, I guess. I let her have it. I'll get even with her when we're back here later alone.

Offering her my arm, I wait until she's holding a small clutch from a side table before we make our way outside to my waiting car. Helping her into the passenger's seat, I make sure she's safely inside before sliding into the driver's side and starting the engine. For better or worse, here we go.

As we enter the palatial townhouse, I can feel numerous pairs of eyes burning holes through my $10,000 suit. It doesn't bother me. I've waited nine years to be able to enter a room with Amelia on my arm, and I'm not going to allow a bunch of stuffy old bitches to distract from the fact that she's finally exactly where she's supposed to be. I will, however, keep an eye out for our parents. Because I know that once they see us together, the situation could quickly become like sharks in a feeding frenzy. Both Peter and Suzanne can smell blood from a mile away. It won't take them long to deduce that something isn't right about our relationship if we're not careful. I may be chomping at the bit to display to the world that Amelia is my end-all, but I'm no fool. I know I still have to be careful when it comes to how much we put out to the public. I also know that Amelia and I haven't had our "come to Jesus" moment regarding our relationship. So, while I may be on the cusp of shouting my love from the rooftops, I still have to proceed with caution. The last thing I need to do is scare her away by coming on too strong, too fast. For someone with borderline stalker tendencies, that's a big task.

Making our way into the foyer, I'm hyper-conscious of things like the placement of my hand on her lower back. It takes a will of iron, honed over the course of years, to keep from moving that hand to her hip in a possessive grip and pulling her to me to let everyone here know that she's taken. She's been taken for years. By sheer force of will, I keep my hand where it is as my eyes scope the room for a sign of either of our parents. Not seeing them lingering in the area I usher Amelia toward the front parlor. Right at the threshold of the door, I feel her hesitate. Looking down, I see that her eyes are glassy and unfocused. She's here, but she's not here. I murmur her name, but she doesn't reply. Stepping in front of her, effectively blocking her view of the room. Regardless of who's watching, I put my finger under her chin and lift her gaze to mine.

"Hey. What's wrong?"

It takes a moment and several long blinks before those beautiful eyes finally focus on mine. In a whispered tone, she says, "I can't be in that room."

I can hear the vulnerability in her voice. It makes my heart do a double kick at the knowledge that she's allowing me to see her this way. Open and afraid. It fills me with pride and, at the same time, anger. Whatever happened in this room was bad enough that simply stepping foot on the cream carpet terrifies her. It's then that I remember what Gloria told me about her first stepfather's death. It happened in the parlor.

I rub my thumb lovingly across her chin, saying, "Then we won't go in. Let's mingle around the entryway. I'm sure one of our parents is bound to find us at some point. We'll stay an hour, tops. Then we'll leave, okay?"

Nodding her head, she lets out an audible sigh. I remain where I am, blocking her view of the parlor until she's turned away, and I know it's safe to move. I don't want her to have to see that room again. It bothers me that I don't know the details of what happened there. Soon. Soon she'll tell me all her secrets. And eventually, I'll tell her mine. That thought immediately causes me to break out into a nervous sweat. Knowing that

I can't continue that line of thinking or risk being blindsided when my father finally makes an appearance, I quickly shift back into defensive mode. Minutes that feel like hours tick by while Amelia and I make idle chit-chat with other affluent members of Charleston society. The director of the Gibbes Museum of Art not so subtly tries to pressure Amelia into taking a seat on the Board alongside her mother. Suzanne's doing, no doubt. It's too much of a coincidence that Suzanne mentioned the issue at brunch the other day, and now Mrs. Livingston is all but offering her firstborn, in order to get Amelia to take the spot. Considering that Mrs. Livingston is 73 years old, I don't think her ploy is gonna work. I've met her firstborn, and he's an entitled piece of shit.

Just as I'm about to chalk the entire evening up to a loss and let Amelia know I'm ready to get out of here, I see my father coming down the grand staircase at the back of the foyer. Spotting me, I see him pause, eyes traveling from me to Amelia and back again. Ensuring that there's an appropriate amount of space between us, I wait until my father resumes his walk down the stairs, making his way over to us.

"Ah, Merrick, so nice of you to join us. I didn't expect you tonight. And with your stepsister, no less."

"We just happened to arrive at the same time," I say, trying not to sound too defensive. "I had an important matter to discuss with Senator Hawkins," I reply nonchalantly, throwing out the most believable lie I can think of. I have dealt with Senator Hawkins on several occasions regarding political issues that impact some of the charities I donate to, so it's an easy enough explanation. I disliked the man immensely, though. His treatment of Deacon's mother would've been enough to put him on my short list of enemies, but he was also a little too chummy with my father. Proof positive that the man was as crooked as they came.

"What important matter?" he asks.

"That's none of your concern. It's a private issue. Nothing to worry yourself about." I say back. If looks could kill, I'd be six feet under already. Clutching his glass of what I can only assume is expensive scotch a little too tightly, I watch as his face tinges a lovely shade of red. If we'd been alone and I was a few years younger, he would've already taken a swing at me. As it is, he can do nothing but stew in his own building rage, knowing he has no outlet for it here. Turning to Amelia with a look that's more of a leer, he says, "I don't remember you two wanting anything to do with each other before. Hope you're not trying to get some brotherly love out of him now. Trust me, you don't want it. This one's rotten to the core. Never been good for anything. Never gonna be good for anything. He's too soft. Always has been."

I can feel my hand clench into a fist at Amelia's back, bunching the material of her dress. I know she can feel it too, but she doesn't say anything about me practically mangling her gown, nor does she make any moves to pull away. Keeping eye contact with my father, she finally replies, "How would you know? You've never done anything good in your life. You wouldn't even know what good looks like."

Before she's finished the last sentence, Peter's already taking a menacing step in her direction. Quick as a flash, I'm in front of her, effectively blocking his path. Looking him square in the eye, I say, "Do you really wanna do this in a room full of people? You're not as strong as you used to be, old man, and I'm not nearly as weak. You may wanna think twice before you come anywhere near her again."

Glancing around the room, it's obvious that people are beginning to stare. I can see some of the ladies whispering behind their champagne flutes already. He must see it too, because after another moment he takes a slow step back. Bringing his tumbler to his lips, he tips back the amber liquid, downing it in one gulp. Huffing out a laugh that belies the anger and a not-so-small dose of fear, he walks away without another word. Finally allowing myself to breathe for the first time in what seems like hours, I turn to Amelia. Not meeting her eyes, I ask, "Are you ready to get out of here?"

Nodding, we make our way to the front door, ignoring the few people who call out to us or try to get us to stop to talk. Getting outside into the cool night air, Amelia and I are soon in my car, heading back to her house. I want nothing more than to take her back to my apartment, and even though I know that nothing my father said was true, the years of abuse and degradation are hard to forget. My mind knows that I'm not that scared little boy anymore, but I can't help but feel some degree of inadequacy after his words. I just need to be alone to process the events of the night. Pulling up in front of her home, I put the car in park but don't shut off the engine. On the drive over, I could feel her gaze on me more than once, but I refused to meet her eyes. Maybe my father's right. Maybe I am weak. A coward.

Turning in her seat to face me, she asks, "Walk me inside?"

Staring ahead for a moment, I finally allow that inner voice—the one that's been screaming at me not to leave—to override the doubts clouding my brain. Nodding, I turn the engine off and get out, rounding the car to help her out of the passenger's seat. Walking up the front door, I wait for her to unlock the door and go in. Closing the door behind me, I stand just inside the house. When I don't make any move to come further inside, she turns to look at me. Staring at me for a good, long moment, she seems to finally make up her mind about something and the next thing I know, she's running full steam towards me. In her heels, I fully expect her to trip over her own feet, but at the last second, she places her hands on my shoulders and boosts herself up. Falling back into the door, it's everything I can do to keep my balance and not have both of us end up in a heap on the hardwood floor. She wraps her toned legs around my waist, and my hands move from her hips down to grip her ass. I send up a silent "thank you" to God for that slit in the front of her dress. Pulling her tighter against me, I look up to find her face inches from mine. Her eyes drill holes into me, and as she opens her mouth to speak, I can feel her warm breath against my lips.

"I think we need to have a conversation," she says in a serious tone.

I know what she wants. She wants to talk about what happened tonight. About the things my father said. I know I'm going to have to explain some things to her. Things about myself, my past. But I'm finding it hard to concentrate in our current positions.

Glancing down at her lips, I say, "Later." Before she has a chance to protest, my mouth is on hers, and I'm already starting up the stairs towards her bedroom. Right now, I need to lose myself in her. To forget everything except for the way she feels against me, under me, around me. We can talk after.

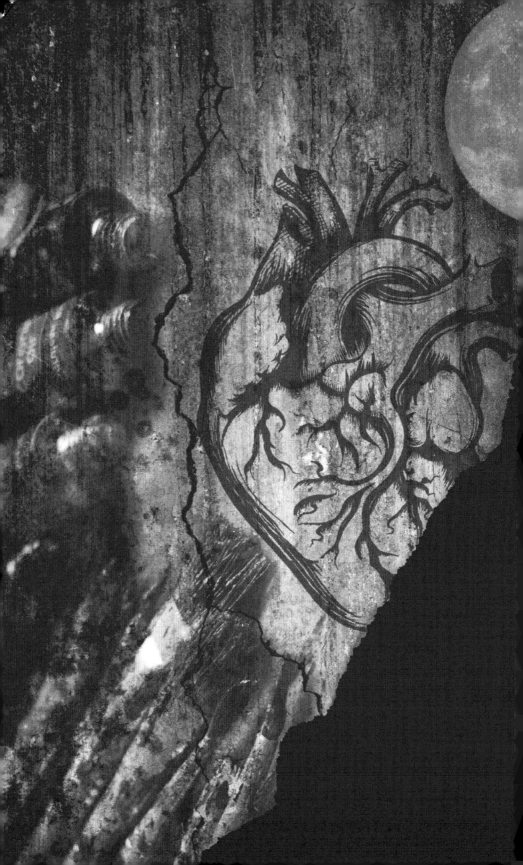

CHAPTER 27

Amelia

I hold on tight to Merrick as he carries us both upstairs. Entering my bedroom, he sits down on the side of my bed, keeping me in his lap. Leaning his head into my chest, he breathes deep before releasing a heavy sigh. Peppering the swells of my breasts with tiny kisses, my breath hitches, and I let my head fall back. Staring up at the all-too-familiar ceiling, it takes me a second to realize the kisses have stopped. Looking back down, I find Merrick staring at me with a look so soft that it nearly has tears springing to my eyes. It's then that I realize he's completely opened himself up to me, displaying a vulnerability that I've rarely ever seen from him. I know his father's words hurt him tonight, even if he won't say it out loud. And as much as I want to break down the final walls between us and reassure him that he's nothing like the person his father described, I don't think he's ready to talk about it. As he said downstairs, it can wait until later. For now, if I can't tell him, I'll show him. I'll show him how valued he is, how special.

Leaning down, I place a soft kiss on his lips. Releasing a groan, his arms go around my back, clutching me to him. We stay that way for several moments, just kissing. Saying everything with our mouths, no words required. Soon, his hands are roaming up my back. Pulling down the zipper on my dress, the material gives, pooling around my waist. As soon as the shimmery fabric falls away, his hands are everywhere. His hands mold my bare breasts, and he slides down the smooth expanse of my stomach before halting where the material bunches at my waist.

Pulling back, he says, "I need to see something."

Moving his hands to the outsides of my thighs, where they're spread wide over his lap, he slowly skates them upward until his right hand disappears into the slit at the top of my skirt. Pushing his hand between us, I feel his fingers dance over my bare center.

Growling low in his throat, he says, "I fucking knew it. I knew you weren't wearing panties. Did you do this for me?"

My nod is interrupted when I feel one of his fingers brush softly over my clit. Jerking in his hold, I feel his other hand tighten on my thigh. As I wait for his next move with bated breath, I'm taken off guard when he says abruptly, "Stand up."

Climbing off his lap, I stand in front of him. The move causes my dress to drop to the floor in a heap. Standing there in nothing but a pair of strappy stilettos while he's completely dressed has me a little off-kilter. It makes me feel vulnerable, and the imbalance of power is clear. Taking his time perusing my body, his hands come up to touch all the places his eyes have just skimmed. As he molds my curves, his hands move the way mine do when I paint. Fluid and sure. He knows exactly what he's doing and what he wants the outcome to be. Standing suddenly, the move forces me to take a step back or risk tripping over my dress. Walking around until he's standing behind me, I feel his palm press firmly into the center of my back, bending me at the waist over the side of the bed. I'm not sure what he's doing, but I allow my upper half to lower to the bed, burying my fingers in my hair to keep my hands from fidgeting.

"Spread your legs," he commands.

Doing as he says, I widen my stance, turning my face to the side to try to see exactly what he's doing. The added height of my heels puts me at the perfect angle over the bed, and I have a feeling that somehow he knew that would be the case. Running his hands up the backs of my thighs, I try to concentrate on his face and not what those clever hands are doing. His eyes track the progress of his hands, and with a look of rapt fascination, I feel him press a thumb into me. Biting back a moan, I bury my face in the comforter. Taking my eyes off of him for even a second was a mistake. I realize that too late as I look back to find him on his knees behind me. Before I have time to blink, his tongue is making a sweep from my clit to my opening. Gasping, I involuntarily jerk forward. Not allowing me an inch of leeway, his hands grip my hips in a punishing hold, pulling me back to his waiting mouth. Latching onto my clit, he applies a gentle suction that soon has my legs trembling where I stand. Just as my knees are about to buckle out from under me, he stops.

His voice comes from high above me as he stands again. There's a slight tremble in his tone as he says, "Don't move."

A second later, he's gone, and I hear the sound of a zipper being pulled down. Before I have a chance to look back at him, I feel the press of his cock at my opening. Gripping my hips to hold me in place, he pushes roughly into me in one hard thrust. Letting out a cry, my hands leave my hair to grip the comforter in some desperate bid to ground myself against the onslaught of feelings hitting me all at once. Holding my hips steady, he slides out of me until only the tip remains inside. I look back to find him staring intently at the place where we're joined. Pausing for a fraction of a second, he holds himself there before slowly pushing back into the hilt. Then he's setting the pace for the climb up to my inevitable downfall. My current position ensures that he has total control over what's happening between us. I'm his to move, his to command.

Thrusting in and out in a punishing rhythm, he leans his still-clothed upper body over mine. I can feel his tie glide up the length of my spine, and it only adds to the already overwhelming sensations he's invoking in me. Reaching his hands up to where mine are clutching at the blanket for purchase, he pries my fingers apart until his are tightly intertwined with mine. Curling our now joined fingers around the comforter, he thrusts hard, grinding his hips against my ass as though he can't get deep enough.

Gravelly words whisper in my ear as my breathing becomes choppy.

"You're mine." Thrust. "This body is mine." Thrust. "This pussy is mine." Thrust.

"Merrick ... I can't ..."

"You can. You will. Give me what I want."

I don't know what he wants from me. My brain can't process anything except his movements inside me and the building tension low in my belly. He's fucking me relentlessly now, his motions erratic. He seems ... crazed. Disentangling one hand from mine to grip the hair at the base of my neck, he rears up slightly, forcing my back to arch as he whispers in my ear.

"I'm gonna come inside you, Mia. And then I'm gonna watch my cum run out of you before I use my fingers to push it back inside where it belongs. By the time I'm done with you, you're gonna wake up tomorrow wondering if my baby is already growing inside you."

My "oh my God" is barely discernible through the moan that breaks free from my throat.

His words are like a match to an unlit fuse. Sparks fly, and suddenly, I'm going up in flames. Spasming around him, I cry out his name as my body ignites. Fucking me through my orgasm, he releases my hair, allowing me to collapse against the mattress in a boneless heap. Feeling his back press hard into mine, he pushes in one last time before emptying himself inside me, just as he promised. I'm not big on religion, but the way he groans out my name in return makes it sound like a prayer. I have one last coherent thought before all sense leaves me, and that's that maybe Heaven is real, and it just so happens to be wherever he is.

CHAPTER 28

Merrick

The smell of flowers pervades my senses, and for a split second, I'm a little boy again, and I think it's my mother. That thought doesn't last though, because I know in my heart that she's no longer here with me. She hasn't been for a long time. My second thought is that even if my mother was still around, the scent currently surrounding me is the wrong flower. My mother used to smell like lavender blooming in bright sunlight. The fragrance I smell now is both new and not new. Tonight wouldn't be the first time I've woken up to that smell, but it was always accompanied by an empty room when I opened my eyes. This time, the scent is warm and soft. It has smooth skin and long legs intertwined with mine. Feeling something tickle my nose, I slowly crack open my lids to find my face buried in a mass of wild curls. So that's why the smell of roses is so strong.

Mia's small body is pressed into mine, her back to my front. Her breathing is deep and even, and she seems so peaceful right now. I know she suffers from nightmares. I've seen her fitfully sleep and heard her cry out during some of the times that I snuck into her house in the middle of the night just to be near her. Right now, however, she seems to be resting easier than I've ever seen her, despite the fact that I've got one arm slung around her middle and a hand cupping one of her breasts possessively. I suppose even in my sleep, I wanted to make sure she couldn't go far from me.

As I lie there, feeling her heartbeat steady against my palm, I realize that my heart is beating in time with hers. If anyone else had said that to me, I'd say that idea was ridiculously romantic and highly improbable, but I'm experiencing it for myself. I stay that way for several long moments, simply feeling the thump thump thump of our heartbeats. It isn't long, however, before I feel my cock begin to stir. Having Mia's naked ass pressed into my groin is not conducive to an easy night's sleep.

After making love to her earlier, I'd gently pulled out of her, being sure to keep her in her bent-over position long enough for me to watch my cum run down the insides of her thighs. After using a finger to collect the creamy liquid, I'd made good on my promise and pushed that finger deep inside, eliciting a halfhearted moan from her. Satisfied that I'd wrung every ounce of pleasure ... and energy from her, I'd picked her up and carried her into the bathroom. After divesting myself of the clothes I'd never even removed during the entire time I was fucking her, I put us both in the shower. Allowing the hot water to run over my sore muscles, I made quick work of washing both of us down before toweling Mia first, then myself off. Then I picked her up and carried her back into her bedroom. By the time I reached the bed she was already asleep in my arms. Gently laying her down, I'd curled myself in behind her, pulling her body flush against mine before sleep finally took me under as well.

Now, I'm slightly regretting that decision. Having her soft curves pressed against me is the very definition of torture. I feel my cock harden painfully against her ass, and I can't stop myself from using the hand that had been just gently cupping her breast to give her nipple a light pinch. She stirs within my arms but doesn't wake. Leaning up, I try to look down at her face, but it's still dark out, and what little moonlight is shining through the bedroom windows is too busy playing shadows over her naked body to worry about illuminating her face.

As my hands roam over her soft skin, I keep expecting her to wake up at any moment and tell me to fuck off and let her go back to sleep. I know

I wore her out earlier, but I can't help the flex of my hips against her ass. I guess you could say I'm making up for lost time. Nine years worth of lost time. I feel her mumble something incoherent and press her ass more firmly into my now aching cock. Suddenly, an idea occurs to me. My gut instinct is to reject it, but the more I think about it, the harder it becomes to breathe. I know I'm the sickest kind of bastard, but I wonder what Mia would do if I were to just slide my way between her thighs and she woke up to the feeling of my cock moving deep inside her. I'm both leery and excited by the thought. Not giving myself a chance to second guess, I move my hand down between her thighs, testing her wetness with my fingers. I don't know if it's residual cum from our earlier round of sex or if, even in her sleep, her body knows to be ready for me. Whichever is the case, I use it to my advantage, bringing that same hand down to grip the back of her thigh and raise it higher, effectively opening her up to me. Gripping my cock in my hand, I move it to her entrance, using the wetness already accumulated there to rub the head back and forth several times before slowly easing myself inside of her. It's so hard to see her face in the darkness but as far as I can tell, she's still sleeping soundly. A dark part of me wonders how long I can fuck her before she wakes up and realizes what's happening. The last thing I wanna do is scare her, but I also don't want to suppress my darker desires when I'm with her. There are already so many secrets between us. I need to be able to show her at least some facets of my true nature and have her want me anyway.

Holding her in place with one hand gripping her hip firmly, I slowly withdraw before easing back inside. As I do, I lean down to bury my face in her hair, placing gentle kisses along the back of her neck, then the tops of her shoulders. Even through all of this, she doesn't do anything more than sigh in her sleep and squirm against me as though she knows something isn't right, but she can't seem to wake herself up enough to investigate what that is. Regardless, the more she squirms, the more turned on I get. Soon, my thrusts are coming faster and harder. With each thrust of my hips, I apply more and more pressure against her. The feeling of never being deep enough is like a sickness inside me. She needs to wake up now. I need her willing participation before I explode. Wrapping an arm around her middle again, I squeeze the same breast I had my hand on earlier while simultaneously nipping her hard on the back of her shoulder. As if struck by lightning, her head turns, and I can make out the whites of her eyes in the dark as they flash open. At the same time, a moan leaves her mouth before she whispers, "What ... what are you doing?"

Keeping my mouth pressed to her ear, I say, "Fucking you." I punctuate my words with a hard thrust of my hips, deeper and deeper. "I plan to spend so much time inside you that your body just won't feel right when I'm not."

To her credit, she doesn't freak out or try to give me some lecture on consent. I'm well aware that fucking her while she's asleep isn't right. But neither am I, and I make no apologies for that. She'll get used to it. Considering I'm the last man that'll ever be inside her, she'll have to.

Pressing herself back into me, meeting my thrusts, she grips the pillow beneath her head, bringing the corner to her mouth. Biting it to keep from crying out, she releases a little yelp of surprise when I reach up and jerk the pillow away, tossing it across the room where it hits the wall before falling to the floor. Face a mask of annoyance, I remind her, "Uh uh, Mia. Every sound from your pretty little mouth belongs to me. I wanna hear what my cock is doing to you. Tell me what you feel. Paint me a picture, baby."

Groaning, she lets her head fall down to the now flat surface of the mattress. Not allowing her an ounce of reprieve, I abruptly pull out of her, quickly turning her body around so that she's facing me instead of away. Side by side, chest to chest, I grip the back of her thigh and bring it up until it's resting high on my hip. Reaching underneath her leg, I find my cock again, pushing it back inside her in one swift thrust. As I grip her ass in one hand, I maneuver her lower body to accommodate each thrust of my hips. In this position, there's nowhere for her to go. Nowhere to hide. Our faces are inches apart, and I can feel her breath coming in harsh pants. I know mine are the same. As my hips pick up speed, her panting breaths turn to moans of pleasure. Thrusting harder now, it's hard to keep a steady rhythm, and my hips move frantically.

Just as I near the edge, Amelia suddenly grips both sides of my face. The move surprises me enough to have my gaze flying up to meet hers. Refusing to break eye contact, she says in a strained voice, "You're not rotten. You're not soft. You're not good for nothing." Each sentence is punctuated with a stroke of my cock. Pausing, she adds, "You're everything." I can hear the utter conviction in her voice. She believes it, and she wants me to believe it, too. I don't know how she knew. She knew that my father's words had dug their way under my skin, but the way she's looking at me now is like being washed clean.

Body trembling, I crush my mouth to hers, and grip her ass to pull her tighter against me as I push myself into her as far as our positions will allow. Through our open-mouthed kiss, Amelia lets out a cry just as I feel her inner walls spasm around me. Holding her as she comes apart in my arms, I'm helpless to do anything but follow her. Because when all's said and done, I'd allow her to walk me straight through the gates of Hell, as long as she was holding my hand.

CHAPTER 29

Merrick

As our breathing evens out, I slip out of her body but keep a tight hold on her so she can't create even an inch worth of space between us. Letting my eyes roam over her face, I'm reminded of all the times I've watched her sleep without her being aware that I was there. As I stare at her in the soft early morning light that's just beginning to invade our dark little bubble, I know that I'll never get tired of looking at her. I could watch her face and the way she moves every day for the rest of my life. I don't know why but I suddenly have the overwhelming urge to talk to her. *Really* talk to her. We've gone through so many years where I had no choice but to act as ships passing in the night. But now, now that I have her in this bed with me, like this ... I need to talk to her. To really start the process of purging my sins and letting her see the real me. I also just wanna hear her voice. Hear her voluntarily tell me about the darkest parts of herself. Her hopes ... her dreams. Her voice is another thing I don't think I could ever get tired of.

Brushing the hair back from her face, I say, "Did you know I used to listen to you sing in the shower? When you'd get under the spray and start belting out 90's pop hits, I'd slide down the wall outside the bathroom door and just sit on the floor and listen to you sing."

I don't tell her that I still do that. That I know that she still sings those same songs in the shower of her own house now. That I grin like a fool every time she tries to hit a high note and fails. I don't allow myself to divulge that much because that would provoke questions I don't think she's ready to hear the answers to just yet.

Staring back at me with squinted eyes that cause them to crease slightly in the corners, she says, "Well, at least that's all you were doing outside my bathroom door while I showered."

For a moment, I'm stunned. Blown away by the fact that she didn't immediately cringe at the revelation of me skulking around without her knowledge. The fact lights a small match of hope inside me that maybe she won't bolt for the door the second I tell her my darkest secrets. Letting out a little laugh, I press my forehead to hers. The accompanying silence isn't tense or awkward in any way. It's just ... easy. I'm perfectly content to lay here with her just like this for as long as she'll let me. Just the two of us, tangled up in each other, simply enjoying the moment. Not five minutes go by before the silence is broken again, however, this time by her.

"I could hear you, you know. Late at night, through the wall that separated our bedrooms. I know you were old enough by then to put up a fight, but I also know sometimes you didn't win. I cried for you every single time." she says. It takes me a minute to connect the dots, but when I do, I can't help the way my body stiffens against hers. It's an automatic defense mechanism and something I can't control. I've been conditioned over the years to clam up or deflect whenever someone wanted to broach the topic of my father's abusive nature. But this is Amelia. If there's anyone who should be allowed to see that facet of my life, it's her. And maybe she's already seen a lot more than I gave her credit for. Forcing my muscles to relax, I take a deep breath before replying.

"So are we gonna trade secrets now?" I say, fake humor lacing my voice.

"Don't do that. Don't minimize your pain, your trauma. You don't have to pretend with me." she says.

Pulling my face back from hers, I lower my gaze before saying, "I'm sorry you had to hear that."

"I'm not. When you and your father first moved into our house, I thought you hated me. You always seemed to have this icy exterior that was impossible to penetrate. Every time we ran into each other, it was like you couldn't even stand to look at me. Then, when I started to hear things at night ... him yelling ... I realized you were dealing with your own demons. You didn't have time to entertain a young girl with problems of her own. I thought for sure the second you turned 18, you'd be gone, and I'd never see you again. But you stayed well past your 19th birthday. Why did you stay when I know it must've been Hell for you?"

I remain silent for a moment, debating whether or not to tell her the truth. Staring at a spot on the wall, just past her left shoulder I don't say anything for a long while. I'm sure she thinks I'm not going to answer. I can tell by the way she starts to pull back, creating a small gap between our bodies. Tightening my arm around her waist, I pull her flush against me again. Tipping her chin up with my finger, I stare into her eyes, allowing her to see the answer written all over my face. Then, leaning down, I place feather-light kisses on each eyelid, and then the tip of her little nose, then one cheek after the other.

Just as I'm leaning over to brush my lips across her forehead, I hear a whispered, "Oh." Her tone is one of revelation, and I'm unsure how she's able to pack so much emotion into a single-syllable word. But underneath the outermost layer of surprise is something akin to awe. It gives me hope. Hope that maybe the imbalance of feelings between us over the years may be starting to even out.

"You should've gone. It would've saved you so much pain. Pain that I'm the cause of."

Shaking my head, I say, "That type of pain is fleeting. I've had that pain, off and on, all my life. That pain, I can tolerate. If I'd left, a piece of me would've been left behind. I would've been out there in the world, going through the motions. But my heart ... my heart would've still been sitting outside that bathroom door, listening to the sound of the shower and waiting for Britney Spears to start."

From the look on her face, I can't tell if she wants to laugh or cry. Not giving her a chance to do either, I roll onto my back, bringing her with me until she's nestled in the crook of my arm, her hand resting over the large emerald tattooed over my heart. Flattening her hand over the spot, she holds her breath for a moment. A moment in which I know she's trying to detect the rhythm of my heart. Once she locates the spot where it comes through the strongest, she lifts her head to place it on my chest, pressing her ear against it. The move puts her mass of curls directly in my face, but I don't mind. Breathing in that scent that's so uniquely her, I let out a sigh, and with it goes nine years of longing for something that's finally within reach. That's the last thought I have before I fall asleep. The world won't want us to be together, but they don't matter. The only thing that matters is me and her and this heartbeat.

As I sit in my apartment waiting for Agent Kapranov to show up, I've never felt like more of a sitting duck. I didn't want to leave Amelia this morning, but when I'd gotten a cryptic text from an unknown number telling me to be at my apartment by noon, I'd had a suspicion that it was the mysterious Fed. He was the only person that I knew had the access and skills to get my private number, and after having Deacon run a check and being unable to trace the text, my suspicions that the sneaky Russian was behind the cloak and dagger routine had only gotten stronger. Especially when I'd gotten a series of follow-up texts about an hour later, asking if I was looking to secure a high-priced escort or if I was in the market for discreet "herbal enhancers". I knew by this time that the Fed was fucking with me again.

Honestly, I was having a hard time getting a read on this guy. To the outward appearance, he wouldn't be out of place at some underground cage fight, nor would anyone photographing for GQ magazine turn down the chance to put him on the cover. He was a walking menace in a three-piece suit. A hired killer's worst nightmare … until he opened his mouth. I got the impression that Agent Kapranov was highly intelligent, clearly had a very distinctive sense of humor, and was someone you'd never want to turn your back on. Though I had a feeling, whether you were facing away or looking directly into the man's eyes, you'd still never seen the bullet coming. The fact that Deacon was able to dig up so much dirt on the Fed didn't sit right with me. Normally, I'd write that off as part of Deacon's impressive resume of skills, but something about the ease with which he'd uncovered Alexi's past set my teeth on edge. Why would a man with such a tainted background, now working for the US Federal Government, not put more safeguards in place to conceal his origins? My personal take? Somehow, the Fed had allowed us access to information he wanted us to have. Nothing more, nothing less. Why was the biggest question? I knew he wanted me to steal something for him, but what? And to what end?

These were the types of situations I hated. I was a man used to being in control. Outside of my relationship with Amelia, I took pride in the fact that nothing happened to me that I didn't want to happen. I had gotten out from under my father's thumb and made not one but two names for myself. The idea that there was someone out there setting me up so they could pull my strings like some kind of puppet rankled. It made me edgy and irritable. Until I knew what the Agent's endgame was, my future balanced on a tightrope.

Glancing at my watch, I get up from the living room chair to pace. I've done some version of this on repeat for the last hour. Up, down, up, down. It was 10 minutes past noon, and I was tempted to text the unknown number back and tell him to go fuck himself, but I'd bet money that that number was for a burner phone that had already been tossed. In addition to the iffy situation with the Fed, I think part of my irritation was having to leave Amelia behind this morning. I would've been perfectly content to stay in bed with her all day, but she'd also had to meet her mother for lunch to discuss something having to do with the museum. It was most likely another ploy to try and convince her to join her mother on the board of trustees, which I knew Amelia had no interest in doing, but when Suzanne Stratford called, you came. That wouldn't always be the case. Depending on the outcome of today's meeting, if the bastard even decided to show up, Suzanne and Peter would soon be locked away where they couldn't hurt anyone else.

Just as I'm getting annoyed enough to attempt calling the unknown number, there's a knock at the door. Striding over, I open it to see Agent Kapranov standing on the other side, oozing charm and menace in equal measure. A lesser man would cower. A lesser man would slam the door in his face and make a run for it. I was in no way lesser.

"Oh, so we actually knock now? I was sure you would've shimmied up the balcony," I say in a snarky tone.

Walking past me as if I've already invited him in, he says, "I could've. My climbing skills are legendary. Probably not as good as yours, though." He has the audacity to *wink* at me.

"I don't like you. I just want you to know that," I reply—my tone sounds pissy, even to my ears.

Nodding solemnly, he says, "That's understandable. You don't know me."

"Oh, trust me, I know plenty," I say. Fuck. Knowing I may have just tipped my hand, I scowl at him. Goading me into saying things I shouldn't is probably number 13 in the FBI's guidebook on interrogation. Or maybe he just knows how to get under my skin.

Tipping his head to the side, he studies me for a moment before saying, "It's okay if you don't like me, Merrick. I still like you. We have more in common than you think."

"Such as?" I ask, not really expecting him to answer.

"Well, as I'm sure your friend Deacon has already told you, neither of us comes from the best stock. Grekhi ottsa. The sins of the father and all that."

I don't even bother asking how he knows about Deacon. Clearly, he's a step ahead of both of us. Staring back at him, I again wonder why he's telling me this. Why he's allowing me information on his back story?

Sick of the bullshit, I say, "Let's just cut to the chase Agent Kapranov. What is it exactly that you want me to steal for you? And what could be so well protected that a member of the FBI has to resort to using a thief to get it?"

I stare in awe as the mask falls from his face. The smirk is gone, as are all traces of levity. In a hollow voice, he says, "I lost something five years ago, and I need your help to get it back."

Interesting. It may be a ruse, but something in my gut tells me that this man standing before me now is the real Alexi Kapranov. He's dead inside. I can hear it in his voice. I recognize it because I know the feeling all too well. Acting on instinct, I decide then and there to give him a modicum of trust.

"What did you lose? And where is it now?"

Shaking his head, he says, "No. I will tell you, but first, I want your word that we have an understanding. You help me, and in exchange, I'll take down your parents and offer you my protection."

Studying him, I ask, "What makes you think you can trust me? For that matter, why should I trust you?"

"Call it intuition. I meant it when I said we had more in common than you think. We've both been broken and whittled down by life, the pieces scattered to the wind. The person who could fix you is right here in this city, nearly within your grasp. I need to find mine. And you're gonna help me. Do we have a deal?"

Sappy metaphors aside, I understand exactly what he's after now. A woman. Whatever he needs me to steal, he thinks it will lead him to her.

Letting out a heavy sigh because I really don't want this to come back to bite me in the ass, I walk forward, hand outstretched. Grasping his in a firm shake, I simply say, "Deal."

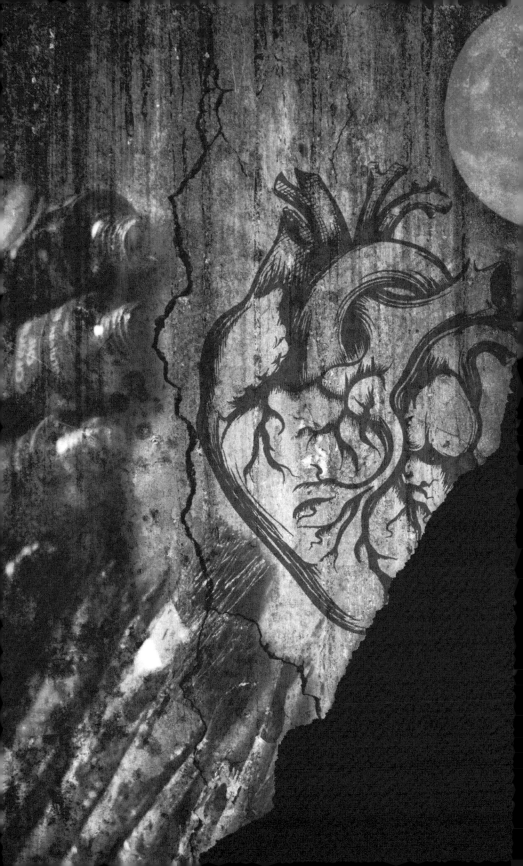

CHAPTER 30

Amelia

Wandering around the museum, I take time to stop at each painting or sculpture and simply absorb the love and care that went into making each piece. Most people, when they view art, whether it be classic or modern, see the price tag and base the piece's worth on that alone. More discerning eyes will look at a painting and critique the methods used, brush strokes, and use of color. My system for assessing the worth of any type of art is simply how it makes me feel. What emotions does it invoke? What memories does it pull from my mind that make it more relatable to me? Some pieces cause pain, while others imbue you with joy. The emotions felt are different for everyone, and that's why art is so subjective. It speaks to each person differently. As I wander the rooms, I allow time for myself and the piece in front of me to have a conversation. I know my mother is waiting for me upstairs, probably glancing at her watch impatiently. I could've gone straight up to the conference room where she requested I meet her, but from the moment my feet hit the floor this morning, I've been a nervous wreck. Knowing I had to meet my mother for what I was sure was another discussion as to why I didn't want to join the museum board made leaving the cocoon of Merrick's body wrapped around mine that much harder. I don't know how many times I have to turn her down before she realizes that I'm perfectly content to create my own art and sell it for a fraction of the cost of most of the ones hanging around me right now.

When I hear the click of heels on the marble floor behind me, I didn't need psychic powers to know that it's her. I can practically feel the temperature in the room drop by 10 degrees. Feeling a knot form in the pit of my stomach, I pretend not to hear her as the aggressive sound of her shoes grows closer and closer. Finally, she steps up beside me, where I'm standing in front of a painting of a young woman with a red ribbon cascading down from her raven hair. Tugging on the end of the ribbon is a small child.

Under her breath, because God forbid anyone should overhear and find out how successful she was at raising an unwillful child, she says, "Amelia, you're half an hour late. You know I don't like waiting."

My mother doesn't like a lot of things. But I keep that thought to myself as I reply, "I got caught up. Is this piece new?" I gesture to the young woman and little girl. For some reason, the painting causes my mind to flash back to Merrick's words from last night. As I stare at the little girl tugging the ribbon, I feel an answering tug in me.

She looks at the painting, but based on her dismissive answer, I know she doesn't actually *see*, much less feel anything. "How should I know? I'm not the curator."

You would think that someone who sat on the board of trustees would have some knowledge as to what was actually being displayed in the museum. But this type of attitude is par for the course where Suzanne is concerned. If it doesn't have a big dick and an even bigger checking account, she wasn't interested.

Shaking my head slightly, I ask, "Why am I here, Mother? Why did you need to see me?"

She lets out an exasperated sigh as though she's dealing with a small child and she's run out of patience. "Amelia, I'm not going to discuss private matters in a public setting. Anyone could overhear. I swear, sometimes I wonder if all that paint thinner has damaged your brain."

It's on the tip of my tongue to tell her that my brain was damaged be-yond repair long before I started painting—thanks to her. That however, would simply prolong this encounter, and I can already feel the jitters beginning to stir under my skin. Steeling myself, I say, "I'm ready to go upstairs if you are."

Without a word, she turns on her heels and begins a brisk pace towards the elevator that will take us upstairs to the conference and meeting rooms. Jogging a little to keep up with her, we make it to the elevator, and I thank God for small favors when the doors open as soon as she presses the button. The quicker I get upstairs, the faster I can get the Hell out of here. As we reach the second floor, I follow her into a small meeting room just off the hallway near the elevator. I wait for her to close the door before turning back to see her taking a seat at one end of the large rectangular conference table. Pulling out the chair next to her, I make sure to casually slide it a few inches further away as I sit down, trying to be as inconspicuous as possible so she doesn't realize that I'd rather put my hand over an open flame than be within arms reach of her.

"Amelia, how long has it been since you moved out of the family home?" she asks.

Not expecting that question, I reply, "Uhhhh ... roughly six years?"

"Is that a statement or a question?" she says in a sarcastic tone.

Biting my tongue to keep the retort that's bubbling up my throat inside, I don't say anything. Not that it would have mattered anyway. She continues without even really waiting for an answer.

"Six years of fiddling with paints and brushes and barely scraping by. Meanwhile, you have no man to speak of, no children, and you ignore 90% of the invitations for the social gatherings put on by our friends."

It takes me a minute to fully digest what she's saying. My brain latches onto the part about "no man to speak of", and the first thing that pops into my head is waking up in the dark early morning hours to the feeling of Merrick at my back as he slid inside my body. Feeling the tips of my ears burning, I know my face is red. It's moments like these that have me cursing my pale skin.

Fidgeting under my mother's stare, I ask, "What's your point, Mother?"

"My point, Amelia, is that you're not getting any younger. When you wake up and finally come to the realization that you've wasted the last six years puttering around that little studio of yours, you're going to find that no man is going to want you because your best years will have been thrown away on some little hobby that barely puts food on your table. It's way past time that you start thinking about your future. Who's going to support you when your paintings stop selling? You need to start looking for a husband and find fulfillment like I have."

Fuming now, I close my eyes and count backwards from 10. Taking deep breaths through my nose, I try my best to formulate an articulate response instead of simply scratching my nails down her overly made-up face like I really want to. "I don't need a husband to feel fulfilled, Mother. I'm quite happy with my life as it is right now."

We sit staring at each other for several minutes. Minutes that feel like hours. I refuse to break the eye contact because I'm getting tired of running scared when it comes to her. Huffing out a breath, she says, "Well, I can see this entire meeting was a waste of time. You need to go home and think about what I've said. We can discuss it further over dinner one night this week. Send your schedule to my assistant so he can let the cook know what to make."

Confusion evident on my face, I say, "Why can't I just call Gloria and let her know what to cook?" Gloria always handled things like that, and I'd much rather talk to her than my mother's assistant.

Not bothering to look up, she gathers up a file folder she'd sat on the table when we first entered the room. As she straightens from her chair, she replies, "Gloria left, and I haven't found another suitable candidate to take her place yet."

Taken aback, I lean forward in my seat and say, "What do you mean she left??" I can barely formulate the sentence through my shock. I wouldn't say that Gloria and I were extremely close, but we were close enough that I don't think she'd have just up and quit without telling me.

Pinching the bridge of her nose, she exhales a heavy breath before saying, "Lord have mercy, Amelia. I mean, she left. She never showed up for work a few days ago, and I don't know where she went. But it's clear she's abandoned her job, so, naturally, she's fired."

She continues talking, but my brain doesn't register the words. Something isn't right. Gloria wouldn't have just left without saying goodbye. She's been working for my family since I was a baby. Hell, she was more of a mother to me than the woman standing before me. For her to just up and leave doesn't sit right with me. I make a mental note to ask some of the other staff the next time I go to the house. As I sit contemplating everything my mother's said, it takes me a minute to realize that I'm now alone in the room. She's left without a backward glance. That's fine with me. I didn't want to carry on the conversation anyway. The only thing I wanna do right now is try to call Gloria, and if I can't get in touch with her before the end of the day, I'm going to the police to file a missing person's report. I can't help the dark thoughts that invade my mind. Growing up with my mother, I know exactly what she's capable of. If she did something to Gloria, I have to wonder why. Why, after so many years of faithful service, would my mother want to harm the housekeeper?

By nine o'clock that night, I was sitting in the police station, waiting to be interviewed by a detective. After trying Gloria's number about 12 times and the calls going immediately to voicemail, I'd been so anxious that my hands would barely open the travel bottle of pills that I carry in my purse. As I clutch my phone in a death grip, I peer at the screen for the thousandth time, willing it to ring and for me to see Gloria's name pop up on the caller ID. It doesn't, though.

At the sound of my name, I look up to see Merrick coming into the station, closely followed by a man I've never seen before. He's big and hulking and kinda scary. I can't find the energy to worry about that, though, because within seconds, Merrick is across the room and pulling me out of my chair and into his arms. Looking past him to the man standing at his back, I see him watch us with a penetrating gaze. He's intimidating despite his casual stance and his hands loosely resting in his pants pockets.

Pulling away, I create a little distance between myself and Merrick. I know it's a police station, but even cops talk, and I don't want any gossip getting back to my mother or Peter. As I look into Merrick's face, I see the slight flexing of his jaw. He's not happy. Attempting to gloss over the slight, I pull him a few feet away from the other man.

Despite the eyes on us—or maybe because of them—Merrick takes my face in his hands and, leaning down to capture my gaze with his, he says, "Are you okay? What happened? Did someone hurt you?"

I can hear the panic in his voice, but underneath that panic is a thick layer of rage. He thinks someone's done something to me, and if I confirmed that, I know there's nothing that would stop him from avenging me. For a split second, my mind jumps back to a late night so many years ago when he held me as I cried in his arms. I saw Jake not long after that night. I know what he did to him, even if I've never confronted him about it. Coming back to the present, wanting to alleviate his fear, I say, "I'm okay, don't worry. I'm here about Gloria. She's missing."

If I didn't know him as well as I do and if I wasn't as in tune with him as I am now, I might miss the flash of trepidation in his eyes. But I do know him, so I ask straight out, "Do you know where she is? Tell me, Merrick. What's happening?"

Shaking his head, he takes a step back before answering, "I don't know. You tell me. How do you know she's missing?"

"I've tried calling her a dozen times and it goes straight to voicemail. I went by the townhouse, but the maid said she hadn't seen her in several days. Her things are still there, Merrick. She wouldn't just ... leave." My voice breaks on the last word.

Taking me in his arms, prying eyes be damned, I allow him to hold me as I bury my face in the material of the black button-down covering his chest and simply breathe him in. As the citrus and clove scent fills my nostrils, I feel myself come down, and the Earth steadies itself under my feet again. When I pull away, the man from before is standing directly next to us. Startled, I rear back. If it wasn't for Merrick's steadying hands on my upper arms, I probably would've fallen over.

"Um, excuse me. Who are you?" I ask. My gaze shifts back and forth between Merrick and the other man as they have some type of silent exchange. It only lasts a second, but I catch it nonetheless. Not replying to my question, he looks to Merrick and says, "Let's take this outside."

I'm already shaking my head before he's even finished the sentence. We can't leave. I haven't gotten to file the missing person's report on Gloria. Her husband is gone, and she has no other family. Clearly, my mother doesn't care. If I don't pursue this, no one will.

Taking my hand in his, Merrick leans down close to my ear and simply says, "Trust me?"

I'm torn. I want to trust him. I mean, I do trust him. But this is important, and I feel like there's something bigger at play here than just a missing housekeeper. Like there's a thread dangling just out of my reach, and if I could just grab it, everything would unwind ... but I can't. Allowing me a minute to make my own decision, which I appreciate, I finally relent and let Merrick walk me out of the station by the hand. The strange man follows, not too far behind us. As we exit the station, I notice that the air outside is still muggy and humid, even at night. Summer truly is on its way.

Rounding the corner of the building, we enter an open parking lot filled with police vehicles. Merrick pauses, causing me to fumble my steps a little as I nearly run straight into his back. Turning, he steadies me and then looks to the other man. Motioning for us to follow, he leads us to the very back of the lot, where a sleek Aston Martin is parked. I quirk one eyebrow and let out a low whistle. The sound has the hulking man turning back to face me with a small smile on his lips.

Looking from me to Merrick, he says, "I don't blame you one bit, Merrick. She's a cute little thing."

Voice lowered to nearly a growl, Merrick replies, "Keep your fucking eyes to yourself, Kapranov."

Completely lost as to what's going on here; I'm getting increasingly annoyed by the second. I need to go back inside and speak with the detective. They need to be out looking for Gloria. They need to be talking to witnesses, or whatever it is they do. They need to do *something*.

Losing the last shred of patience left in me, I turn back to the stranger and say, "Can someone explain to me what the fuck is going on?"

The strange man finally steps forward and—after a quick glance at Merrick—holds out his hand to shake. "I apologize, Miss Carrow. My name is Alexi Kapranov. I understand that you wanted to file a missing person's report on someone. I'm an agent with the FBI. I can take your statement.

Looking back to Merrick, who nods, giving me the go-ahead, I begin to tell Agent Kapranov everything I know. When I get to the part about how I found out that Gloria was gone, I see another one of those cryptic side-eye exchanges between the Agent and Merrick. Something is going on here, but I don't know what. Even so, I give Agent Kapranov every bit of information I can think of. All of Gloria's personal info, or at least what I know of it. He writes down all the pertinent information in a little notebook as I talk.

Nodding, he reaches into his suit jacket pocket and pulls out a business card. "Here's my contact info. If you think of anything else, don't hesitate to give me a call. I'll do some digging and see what I can find. In the meantime..."

He trails off as he glances back to Merrick.

"I think it would be a good idea if you took her home. There's not much that can be done tonight, but if the housekeeper hasn't surfaced by the morning, I'll start an official investigation."

Shaking the Agent's hand one final time, Merrick puts his arm around my shoulder and guides me over to the passenger's side door of his car, which I'm just now noticing was parked directly next to Agent Kapranov's.

He eases me into the passenger's seat, and I wait for him to come around the car and slide into the driver's side. As he buckles himself in, he rests a hand on my thigh as he puts the car into drive and takes off. After a few minutes, I find my eyes growing heavy. It doesn't take any pressure from Merrick for me to lean my head over and rest it on his shoulder. Turning his head to the side, he lowers it in close and places a soft kiss on the top of my head.

"Get some rest, baby. I'll take care of you," he says.

Groggy and already half asleep, I reply, "No, I'm not tired." My words are belied by the yawn that creeps in after my sentence. "I'm just gonna close my eyes for a minute."

As he chuckles under his breath, he says, "Of course you're not. You just rest your eyes and let me worry about everything else."

I know he's humoring me. Even in my drowsy state, I recognize that. But honestly, I'm too tired to call him on it. Despite my protests to the contrary, I'm out in a minute flat. When I wake up again, I'm in a bedroom that's not my own. In a bed that's not my own. Turning my head to the side, I look at Merrick's face. It's relaxed and exhibiting a kind of peace that I've come to realize only surfaces during times like this when he's asleep. Gently turning onto my side so our bodies are facing each other, I scooch over until my face is mere inches from his. Sliding my right hand under his left one, that's resting on the pillow near his chin, I interlock our fingers, closing our hands into a single solitary loose fist. Bringing it to my mouth, I lightly kiss the warm skin on the top of his hand before lowering our joined fists back to the pillow. At moments like this, all of my previous fears and reservations about getting into a relationship with my stepbrother don't seem nearly as important as the feeling of whatever this is that's happening between us. This feeling is what poets write about. It's what nearly every person on Earth spends their life searching for. It's the beginning and the ending of everything. Despite all the reasons we shouldn't be together, the one reason we should seems to outweigh everything else. I let out a sigh that ends on a little laugh. This entire time, I've been trying so hard not to fall in love with him that I couldn't see what was already there. What's probably always been there. I just wasn't ready to acknowledge it.

I don't know how long I lay like that before I fall back to sleep, but one thing I do know is that his face is the last thing I see before I close my eyes. As I drift out of conscious thought and into the realm of dreams, I can only hope I wake up to the same thing.

CHAPTER 31

Merrick

I wake before Amelia. As much as I want to stay in this bed and never leave, I need to call Deacon. Glancing down, I see our hands are joined together on the pillow between us. I wonder who initiated the contact. Probably me because, even in my sleep, I have the overwhelming need to keep her near me. Easing my hand from hers, I execute a very graceful, if I do say so myself, tuck and roll out of bed. Standing, I stare down at Amelia's sleeping form for just a minute longer. She looks exhausted. There are dark circles under her eyes, and her hair is in disarray from where I took the hair tie out before putting her to bed. I'm sure she won't thank me for the tangles when she wakes up, but I'd rather her have bedhead than a headache.

Leaving her to rest, I gently close the bedroom door behind me and make my way to the kitchen to fix a cup of coffee. While I wait, I grab my phone from the kitchen island where I left it last night. Looking at the screen for the first time in several hours, I see that I've already got three missed calls and a handful of texts from Deacon. I've also got a text from Alexi. Opting to deal with Alexi first, I read the message. He has indeed initiated an investigation into Gloria's disappearance. According to him, a run of Gloria's financials and cell phone logs shows that there's been no activity for three days. No withdrawals from her checking account, no use on her debit card or any of her credit cards and her phone has been fully powered down for three days. In this day and age, no one on Earth goes three days without using their phone for *something*. I just know Suzanne has something to do with this. It's too coincidental that Gloria meets with me to hand over the evidence against Suzanne and then a few days later, disappears. Texting Alexi back, I thank him for updating me and confirm that I'll continue to look into things on my end. He responds within a minute of my text, saying he should know more by this afternoon and asking if I'd be able to meet to discuss what's going on. I confirm with him, then switch over to my contacts and dial Deacon's number. He answers on the second ring.

"Dude, I was getting ready to send a search party out. Don't ever leave me hanging like that again."

Rolling my eyes, I move over to the coffee pot to pour a cup of much-needed caffeine into a mug. "I was sleeping, dickhead. It's been a long few days."

"You were sleeping ... alone?" I can hear the laughter in his voice. Leave it to Deacon to inject humor during a time when everything seems to be going to shit. To be honest, I'm not the least bit surprised. This is Deacon's personality. I learned a long time ago that humor is his defense mechanism. He seems to think that if he laughs about it on the outside, no one will be able to see how much it bothers him on the inside. Having been friends with him since my early teens, I've also seen the realer side of him. He's damaged, just like me. Just like Amelia and Siren. As I'm starting to learn, just like Alexi. Someone should go ahead and name us the island of misfit toys because we'd somehow found solidarity with each other when life wanted nothing more than to see us break down.

Pulling myself back to the present conversation, I reply, "Amelia is sleeping in my bed, but something tells me you already knew that."

Chuckling under his breath, he says, "I did. I've got alerts set up to ping me whenever someone's name that I've flagged shows up anywhere online. I got an alert in the wee hours of the morning that she'd been at the police station filing a missing person's report. I pulled the footage from the cameras at the station and traced you both back to your car and then through traffic cams to your apartment. Was that our mysterious mafia man? Fed? Which came first, the chicken or the egg?"

"For fuck sake, Deacon, at least let me drink my cup of coffee before making me deal with your shit. I'm barely awake. Yes, that was Alexi. I wanna ask if you've managed to get your hands on any more info regarding him, but I worry that we've got bigger issues at play right now. As you saw, Gloria is missing. Did it occur to you to do some digging while you were cyber-stalking me home?"

"We're gonna circle back around to that "Alexi" thing. Since when are we on a first-name basis with someone who could put you in prison for the rest of your life? As for Gloria, yes, I did do some digging. What the Fed said in his text was true. There's been no movement on any of her financials and no digital footprint for the last several days. However, I did pull the last known location for her cell phone. Give you one guess where it was when it powered down for the last time."

I don't ask how he knows what Alexi said in his text messages because this is Deacon, and after years of being his best friend, I don't question how he comes by information anymore. The man is a digital savant. If it connects to the internet, he can access it. I've also long given up the fight over establishing personal boundaries. It is what it is. If anything bad ever happened to me, I'd rather have him know how many times a day I take a piss than for him to not be able to find me.

The information about Gloria is troubling, though. I know exactly where her phone lost service. Taking a deep breath I say, "It was the townhouse, wasn't it?"

"Ding, ding, ding!! Tell him what he's won, Johnny!" he says like an overly exaggerated gameshow host.

"Fuck!" Running my hand over my face, I feel the weight of the world pressing down upon my shoulders. I'm so close. So close to the end of this nightmare. I can see the light at the end of the tunnel, and she's got big green eyes and freckles across her delicate nose. The brightest light in my otherwise dark world. I vow here and now that if Gloria is dead and the case against Suzanne falls through, I'll kill her myself. I won't allow one more day to go by where Amelia feels like she has to constantly look over her shoulder to see if a knife's been planted in her back. Even if it costs me everything, I'll free her of these demons. Even at the cost of losing that light at the end of the tunnel. There's no reason for both of us to live in the dark. Having resolved myself, I feel a type of calm overtake me. I think once you've made the decision to take a life, you're setting yourself on a course that can't be reversed, and with that comes a type of peace. Especially when you know you're doing it for the right reasons and that those reasons are justified.

"Don't worry, bro, I'll find her. Wherever she is, there's gotta be a trail. Whether it was left by her or by whoever took her."

"Try to track Suzanne's movements over the last week. Any video footage you find, send to Alexi. In fact, I think you should come by tonight. He's going to be here, and it's probably time for you two to meet. He already knows who you are anyway," I cut him off before he can say anything about wanting to remain anonymous.

"Ewww. An FBI agent? Come on, man. That's like asking a pig to jump into a swamp full of gators. I know I'm a tasty ass snack, but I don't wanna get eaten."

Shaking my head, I let out a laugh because, with Deacon, you can't not laugh. "Just be here at eight, you dick. I promise no one will take a bite out of your ass."

In the ensuing silence, I know he's vacillating with himself. I also know that in the end, he'll come. Because he's always had my back. Now is no different.

"Fine. But if he locks me up, you're breaking me out," he says finally.

"Of course, I would. With that pretty face, you'd never survive in prison," I reply. Laughing out loud, he hangs up in my face. Even with everything that's going on and everything that's still yet to come, I can't help smiling a little. He just has that effect on people.

Opening the front door, I come face to face with a glowering Deacon. He's 20 minutes early, which is a good indicator of his nerves over this meeting. Deacon isn't usually the type to be early to anything. He arrives exactly when he means to. No earlier, no later. I've always known that that's how he operates, so him getting here 20 minutes early is a clear sign that he's not happy with me for mandating his attendance tonight. Unfortunately, it can't be helped. Sure, I could've probably bullshitted Alexi on where and how I got most of the information I came by, but there was something about Alexi that mirrored something in me. I won't go so far as to say we bonded when we had our little talk about his missing "piece", but I also recognized something simmering just beneath the surface of his cool yet intense exterior. It was longing. Longing that bordered on desperation. People did crazy things when they got desperate. I don't know why I care or why I'm making it my concern, but my gut was usually right about these types of things. I'd had similar feelings about Deacon. When we'd met, neither of us was the trusting type. Hell, we still aren't. But despite our surface differences, it had been like looking in a mirror. Same boy, different trauma. It made it easy to befriend him and subsequently trust him in a way that I hadn't ever trusted anyone else.

I was relying on that trust to flow evenly both ways tonight. I knew he didn't wanna be here, and yet, he'd still come. And that said it all. Trying to ease some of the tension I could feel coming off of him in waves, I say, "What? No flowers or chocolates? Well, you brought me a corsage, at least?" Holding my hands up as if waiting for a small arrangement of flowers and ribbons to appear, I laugh a little at the pissy look he gives me as he pushes past me into the apartment.

Making himself comfortable on the living room couch, he kicks his booted feet onto the coffee table, the picture of nonchalance. I don't buy it for a second. My instincts are confirmed when, not 30 seconds later, he springs up from his sitting position to pace around the room. The normally laid-back man is now a ball of nervous energy.

"I swear to God, if this Fed walks in here and cuffs me, I'm gonna use every weapon at my disposal on you, including my teeth, if he drags me out of here," he says.

Snorting, I reply, "He's not like that. He's ... different."

"And you would know this, based on the two times you've met him, which equated to what ... 20 minutes total? I mean, the guy is the son of a Bratva boss, for God's sake."

"I think you and I both know that oftentimes, fathers and sons differ greatly," I say, giving him a knowing look. I'm not only talking about my father but his as well. We're nothing like the men that sired us. I don't think Alexi is either.

Huffing out a breath, he concedes defeat, but not before making one final point. "You know he has a nickname in Russia, right? They call him *Prizrak*. The Ghost," he says with a cocked eyebrow. "Because, and I quote, "If you see him, you're already dead.""

Raising brows of my own, I process this new information. While a nickname like that doesn't jive with the idea of a cool and collected Federal Agent, it isn't such a stretch to believe that the man I've met several times now is capable of earning that kind of moniker. Opening my mouth to respond, I'm cut off by the sound of three sharp raps on the door at my back. Mouthing the word "Behave" at Deacon, I turn and look at the surveillance screen mounted inside of a panel in the wall. Speak of the Devil, or should I say, Ghost, and he shall appear.

Opening the door, I usher Alexi inside. With a handshake, I gesture to the now-empty living room. Where the fuck did Deacon go? As if summoned by magic, he waltzes back into the room holding a beer in one hand and, as I feel my eyes narrow in on the spot, Amelia's hand in the other. Grinning at me because he knows exactly what he's doing, his gaze shifts from me to Alexi. I watch the smile practically melt off his face as Amelia releases his hand to come up and hold it out to Alexi. Shaking her hand as well, he gives Amelia a warm smile that I have a feeling, not many people are on the receiving end of. Walking up to stand between Alexi and Deacon, I make the introductions. Alexi holds out a hand, and for a second, I think I'm going to have to slap Deacon in the back of the head to get him to comply, but after another second of silent appraisal, he finally extends his own.

"So you're the Fed, huh? Question. Is it true that the Kennedys had Marilyn murdered?" Deacon says, by way of greeting.

Jesus Christ. I am gonna end up having to smack him in the back of the head. Just as I'm lifting my arm to do just that, Alexi smirks and says, "Shouldn't someone with your skill set be able to find that out on their own?"

Welp. Cat's outta the bag now. No putting it back in. Looking past the two of them, I see Amelia glancing back and forth between them as they exchange barbs. She looks adorably confused. She met Deacon at the bar that night, but prior to that, I've never allowed her close enough to know anything about my personal life. She has no idea who or what he is, the same way she doesn't know any of the information we found on Alexi. I need to keep it that way. At least as far as Alexi is concerned. My skin prickles with unease. I don't want to lie or hide things from her, but considering how deep I've dug my own grave, what are a few more omissions in the grand scheme of things?

Moving past Alexi, Deacon takes up his previously abandoned perch on the couch, gesturing to Amelia with a waving hand. "Come sit next to me, dollface."

Glancing over at me, she seems to make a split-second internal decision before moving to stand next to my place on the other side of the coffee table.

That's my girl.

Putting my arm around her shoulders, I gesture to Alexi with my free hand, indicating the empty armchair to the left of the couch. Taking a seat, he leans forward with his forearms resting on his knees, and once again, I take notice of the tattoos adorning the knuckles of both hands, though now that I know more about his past, they make total sense.

Suddenly, the doorbell rings. Stiffening because all the visitors I've been expecting are already here, I quietly move back over to the door camera. Looking at the live video of the person on the other side of the door has me rolling my eyes and gritting my teeth in frustration. Glancing back at Amelia, she stares straight ahead, the picture of innocence. I don't buy it for a fucking second. Unlocking and opening the door, I swing it wide to allow the short, curvaceous little demon into my home. I don't bother asking why she's here. Siren barely spares me a glance as she makes a beeline straight for Amelia. Watching them embrace, some of my previous irritation dwindles away. The girl has proven herself to be a good friend to Amelia, and for that I'm grateful. I suppose the least I can do is be civil. Just as I close the door behind her, I see Deacon sit forward on the couch, eyes tracking the girl's every move. If she feels his eyes on her, she doesn't acknowledge that fact as she introduces herself to Alexi. As if Deacon doesn't exist, she takes a seat at the opposite end of the couch, folding her hands over her lap and tucking her bare feet beneath her. Somewhere between Amelia and the sofa she's rid herself of her shoes. I rub a hand over my mouth to hide the grin trying to break free as I have an internal debate on how long it'll take before Deacon tries to stealthily move in closer to her. Glancing over at Alexi, a silent conversation ensues. Me, asking with my eyes if it's okay for Siren to be here. I take him not standing up and leaving as his agreement that he's okay with it.

Leaving Amelia's side for a moment, I pull two dining room chairs over so that, once seated, the five of us form a circle around the coffee table. Prefacing the discussion, because I know the girls will have questions otherwise, I say, "Amelia and Siren, you've both met Deacon before. I've asked him to be here because Deacon has a very special set of skills. Skills used for many things, including getting information where others can't. He's great at research and has the ability to access databases that aren't available to the average person." Looking at Deacon, I say, "Go ahead."

As he sighs heavily, I know I've got him. He's giving in and trusting that I know what the fuck I'm doing. Listening intently, I subconsciously reach out and pull Amelia's chair closer to mine. I'm sure what we're about to hear will be hard on her.

"Well, there's not much more to report than what we knew last night. Like the Fed here, I've run down all of Gloria's financials, and there hasn't been any activity. The car she owes outright has been parked around the block from the townhouse since the day she disappeared. In preparation for this little soiree, I traced Suzanne's movements over the last week via her cell phone." He winces a bit as he says that last part, glancing apologetically at Amelia. I move my hand over to cover hers, where it's formed into a tight ball on top of her thigh. Looking up at me, then down at my hand, she slowly unclenches her fist, turning it over to link her fingers with mine. If it was Christmas time, I swear I would've lit up like a goddamn tree. Knowing that she finds comfort in me being here makes me all the more protective of her. She's strong but also so breakable. I just wanna shield her from all the ugliness of the world. From anyone that would even think of harming her. The very thought sets off a chain reaction of so many strong emotions within me, and suddenly, I know I'm capable of murder if killing someone meant saving her life. Taking a deep breath, I tune back into what Deacon is saying.

"... she's been moving, but hasn't gone anywhere unusual or overly suspicious. Mostly boring ass lunches and getting her hair done." He rolls his eyes at this. "Her actions aren't the type I'd classify as normal for someone that may be responsible for a kidnapping ... or worse." Again, he glances at Amelia with a sympathetic gaze.

"I've been to the townhouse," Alexi speaks up for the first time since we sat down. Looking over at him in surprise, I reign in the questions, wanting to burst free from me and wait for him to continue. "I've placed bugs inside the front parlor and the master bedroom. It was the best I could do, given the circumstances."

I'm guessing the "circumstances" he's referring to are the fact that he didn't obtain a warrant to bug the house. Knowing he's breaking the law to help us is both shocking and not, all at once. I would imagine the Federal Agent in him wasn't too keen on going in without the proper paperwork. But if his roots are any indication, he's probably also had plenty of practice at breaking the law.

"That was a big risk. Thank you," I say, meaning every word.

He nods once but says nothing more. In the ensuing silence, Amelia finally speaks, "I don't understand why my mother would wanna harm Gloria. She's worked for my family nearly my entire life and has been living with us for years. What motivation would my mother have to hurt her?"

Covertly, I glance at Alexi, giving the most imperceptible shake of my head. He must understand my meaning, though, because he doesn't answer. He simply waits to see if myself or Deacon are going to respond. When neither of us does, Amelia lets out a sigh of frustration. I'm not sure if it's because of the situation or because she feels like we're holding something back from her. I hope it's not the latter. Rubbing my thumb in slow circles on the inside of her palm, I try to ease some of her stress.

"I've started an official missing person's case on the housekeeper, but it's been nearly a week since she was last seen or spoken to by anyone and, as even the most novice of true crime addicts will tell you, after the first 48 hours, the chances of her being found unharmed dwindle significantly," Alexi says. "In the meantime, I know a few men that I've asked to tail Suzanne and see if they notice anything unusual."

I have to wonder if these "few men" are members of the bureau or if they're criminals, but I don't ask, nor do I care. I'll take all the help I can get at this point.

"What makes you all think that Suzanne even has anything to do with this?" Siren pipes up. Her distrust of all the men in the room, including me, is clearly palpable. Not sure why. It's not as though any of us have given her any reason to fear us. Well, besides me manhandling Amelia on the night of the club outing.

Making another subtle gesture for both Alexi and Deacon's sake this time, I give the most plausible answer I can think of right off the top of my head. "Well, Gloria's lived at the townhouse for quite a few years, and we all know it wasn't always the safest of environments." I pause there because I'm not sure how much Amelia has told Siren about her past, and I'm not sure what she'd be comfortable with me sharing, even if she knew that Gloria had told me of some of the horrors she'd witnessed as a child. Siren must know or suspect at least the bare bones of Amelia's home life growing up because she only nods slowly without saying anything more. We talk amongst ourselves for several more moments before breaking up. As each person leaves, we agree to update the rest of the group if any of us get any new information.

As I close the door behind Siren—who's the last to leave—I turn to the room that now contains only Amelia and myself. Walking up to her, I frame her face in my hands, tilting her head up until she meets my eyes. "You okay?" I ask.

Nodding, she says, "Merrick, we need to talk."

Feeling a knot form in the pit of my stomach because no one ever uttered those words and then followed it up with something good, I pull her down onto the couch with me. She looks nervous, which makes me nervous. Gripping her hand again, I blurt out the scariest of all the thoughts swirling around my head.

"You're not leaving me," I say, trying desperately to tamp down the panic I can already feel stirring to life.

Cocking her head to the side, she studies me with a puzzled expression as though trying to figure out some great mystery. For some reason, it both puts me at ease and raises some kind of silent alarm inside of me. Taking pity on me, she finally says, "Merrick, I'm not leaving. For better or worse, it's us against them now."

I'm not sure who "them" is. Our parents, who have no idea the shitstorm I'm about to rain down on their heads? Society, who would surely have us practically stoned as heathens when they find out we're together? The world that's even now trying to yank the rug out from under us after having put us both through so much already? I'm not sure who she speaks of, but they all apply.

Continuing on, completely ignorant of the push and tug of my internal thoughts, she says, "There are … things. About my past. Things that I didn't wanna talk about with the group before I'd had a chance to talk to you. Bad things that happened long before you and your father came along." Pausing, her eyes lower until she's staring at her lap. I know some of the bad things she's talking about, but I hate the way she won't look at me. As though she's ashamed when she has absolutely no reason to be. She's a survivor. A warrior, fighting battles both internal and external and still living to tell the tale. She's so much stronger than she gives herself credit for.

Not wanting to let on that I know some of what she's alluding to, I bring my fist up under her chin, raising her face until she's forced to meet my eyes again. "What kind of things?" I ask.

Emerald eyes bounce back and forth between my chocolate brown ones. For a moment, I feel as though she could read my mind. Not that she'd need to bother. Everything I wanna convey to her at this moment is written all over my face. I don't care about her past. Whatever she's seen, whatever she's lived through, it's only made her into the woman sitting in front of me right now. The woman who made me feel something other than pain for the first time since my mother died. The woman I'm desperately in love with.

Seeming to make her decision, she straightens her spine before saying, "I'm sure you've heard the rumors about my mother. About her killing her previous husbands. Well, I think … no … I know they're true. When I was five, I walked into the front parlor only seconds after she shot Remy Winston. I was also there, in the kitchen, when she poisoned James Prescott. I was seven that time. To this day, I don't know why she hasn't found a creative way to get rid of me. I've thought about it every day since. Lived with that cloud over my head. I'm the only living witness to two murders, and I've been terrified my entire life that she'll wake up one morning and decide I'm next. I'm still terrified. I have crippling anxiety, panic attacks, and night terrors. I'm … fucked up."

To say I'm shocked would be an understatement. Gloria had alluded to the fact that Amelia had some knowledge of what her mother was capable of, but I never would've guessed at the horrors she's seen. I can't imagine seeing shit like that every time I closed my eyes. Now I better understand why she paints what she does. She's trying to rid herself of her demons. But the way she talks makes it sound like she believes that having lived through these things makes her somehow damaged. Maybe even unloveable. God, she couldn't be farther from the truth.

"Mia. None of what you just said changes a damn thing between us. You're still you. And if you can see past all the beatings I took and all the days I didn't get to eat, and still want me, then there's nothing you can tell me that would make me feel any differently about you than I did 10 minutes ago."

Picking up her hand, I place it over my heart before saying, "Kiss me." Looking confused, she does what I ask nonetheless. Leaning in, she presses her lips to mine in a gentle but firm kiss. Jerking back with a gasp, she looks down at where my hand covers hers over my now racing heart.

Remembering the other night, when we lay in bed together, and she put her ear over my chest to listen to my heart, I catch her eye again before saying, "It's just you, me, and this heartbeat."

We stay that way for another long moment before she climbs into my lap, wrapping her strong legs around my waist and arms around my neck. Burying my hands in her hair, I hold her in place while I ravage her mouth. Unlike the kiss from moments ago, this one is wild and hungry. Pulling back, I look at her face. Her eyes are still closed, her lips red and puffy, still slightly pursed, as though she hasn't finished savoring the moment. After everything she's said and the way she's opened up to me tonight, it's on the tip of my tongue to tell her everything. All my fears, flaws, and insecurities. To confess all my crimes and throw myself at the mercy of her court, to be judged how she sees fit because she deserves the truth.

Then she opens her eyes, and in the dim lamplight of the living room, there's an emotion there that I haven't seen before. Was it always there, and I was just too stupid to see it? In this moment, there's no way I could miss it. It shines so brightly, and I don't even think she's aware of it. But

I see it nonetheless. And I can't stand the thought of snuffing it out. So when she looks at me and says, "Take me to bed." I do.

Tomorrow's another day. Maybe I'll confess tomorrow.

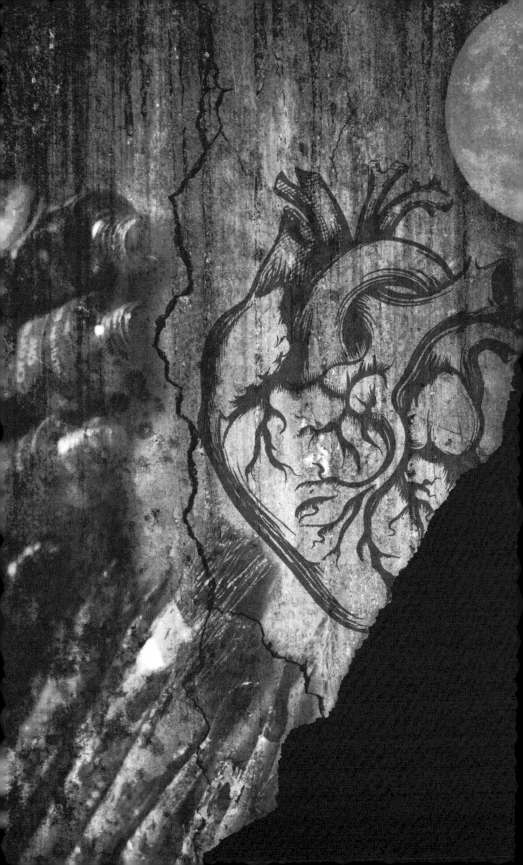

CHAPTER 32

Amelia

Something isn't right. I can feel it. Easing out of bed, I do my best not to wake Merrick. When I first opened my eyes, our faces were nearly nose-to-nose. With an arm slung around my waist, effectively trapping me against him, I'd taken a moment to appreciate how peaceful he looked when he slept. I didn't want him to wake up and find me staring at him like a creep, but as I lay there, taking in every curve and angle of his face, I couldn't help wondering if he dreamed. I didn't think he was like me. Over the nights we'd spent together, he hadn't jerked or shaken in his sleep. He hadn't whimpered or cried out. And he hadn't woken up screaming. So I wondered if he'd always slept like the dead or if this was a new development, perhaps something he only did with me. Inwardly scoffing at myself, I'd taken one last long look at his sleeping face before extracting myself from beneath his heavy arm and sliding out of bed.

I slip into one of his oversized t-shirts, and pad out of the bedroom and to the kitchen. It takes me a few minutes to figure out how to make coffee. Not that I'm an idiot, but his machine has too many fucking buttons. You shouldn't have to have a PhD in engineering to make a cup of coffee. After several minutes of cursing under my breath and cleaning up more than one spill, I finally get it to start brewing a cup of espresso. While I wait for the coffee to finish brewing, I steam some milk and, after finding some bottles in his cabinet, add a few pumps of white mocha syrup to a cup. Combining the mixture, I end up with something resembling a latte. It'll do.

Stepping out of the kitchen, I go into the living room and take a seat on the couch, crossing my legs beneath me. Looking at the time on my phone, I see that it's still early, so I hope Merrick stays asleep for a bit longer. I need to call Siren. We didn't get a chance to talk last night after she showed up for the group meeting. Dialing her number, I wait for her to pick up. Five rings later, and I'm still waiting. On the sixth ring, right before I know the voicemail will kick on, she answers. I hear scuffling and a whispered "hold on", followed by what sounds like her fumbling the phone several times. What the hell is going on?

"Okay, sorry. Go ahead," she finally says a minute or two later, still in a hushed tone.

"Ummm ... where are you? What's going on? And why are you whispering?"

"I'm, uh ... nowhere. Here. Talk. Why the hell are you calling me so early?"

A thought occurs to me. It seems so far-fetched, but at the same time, it wouldn't surprise me one bit.

"Siren? Are you doing a walk of shame?" I ask, barely containing the laughter that wants to bubble up out of my chest.

"Oh, shut up. You don't know me!"

I do know her, which is why it's so funny. This isn't her first walk. It's not even her 10th. Siren doesn't do commitment. Because of her intimacy issues she's become a pro at slipping out before the faceless man wakes up. Though, this time, I don't think he's so faceless.

"Tell Deacon I said hi," I reply, this time unable to hold back a giggle.

"Oh my God, I hate you. Why are you calling me??" she asks. She sounds so exasperated, but I can tell she's smiling.

Turning serious now, I say, "I have a weird feeling."

"Maybe it's indigestion. Take an anti-gas pill."

"Bitch. No, it's not indigestion." Glancing nervously towards the stairs that lead up to the bedroom, I say, "I think Merrick is hiding something from me."

Voice deadly serious now, she asks, "Like what? I saw him last night. The way he looked at you ... he's in it for the long haul. I don't see what could be so important that he'd risk losing you as opposed to just telling you."

Her words strike a chord in me. I hope beyond hope that she's right because I've moved past the point of worrying about what our parents or society will think of us being together. Something changed last night. It was like a lightbulb turned on in my head, except it didn't just turn on. It exploded, the sparks flying in every direction, all at once. I think my heart has felt that way for a long time. It's just taken my head a while to catch up.

"I hope you're right. But even if that's true, there was something ... off, during the meeting. There was a moment when he made eye contact with Agent Kapranov, and it was like they were speaking telepathically. I got the feeling that he was warning him against saying something. I got the same feeling the other night at the police station. I can't explain it."

"I didn't see that exchange. Probably because I was too busy wiping Deacon's drool off my shoulder. But I'm sure it was nothing. It's just your anxiety talking. You two being a thing comes with a lot of pressure, mostly from outside sources. It would be enough to make anyone anxious."

"You're probably right, and yeah, my anxiety gets the best of me all the time. But have you ever had that feeling of impending doom? Like, you can't put your finger on the root cause, but you just feel like something bad is gonna happen?"

"All the time," she says. And immediately, I wish I could take back my question. I know she doesn't like to talk about those years that she wasn't in Charleston, but I'd bet money that that's what she's thinking about now. Whoever hurt her during that time is still there in her head. The same way that the events of my childhood are always there. I don't like reminding her of that time or bringing up topics that could trigger her to remember what happened during those lost years. Sometimes, though, like now, it's like walking into a dark room, and because you can't see, you run face-first into a wall. It can't be helped because you don't foresee it. Still, I cringe at the knowledge that I've dredged up feelings she'd rather keep buried.

"I'm sorry," I say. There isn't much else I *can* say. I don't know all the details, and until she's ready to share those with me, I can't find any way to help her other than to just be here.

"It's okay. It's not your fault," she says. I can hear the monotone enter her voice. Like she's reciting a script that she's concocted to defend herself against unwanted thoughts. I wonder, not for the first time, if she should get into more extensive therapy. I'm not sure how to bring it up, though. The few times I've suggested it before, I felt like I was walking into a minefield. It didn't end well. There was a lot of crying.

Glossing over the subject, she goes back to what we were talking about before, her voice becoming animated once again.

"Did you spend the night there?" she asks.

"Yeah ...?" I reply, unsure where she's going with this.

"So you need to go home to shower and change then. Pretend like that's what you're doing, then follow him and see where he goes. If nothing comes of it, then I'd put it out of your mind," she says, tacking on, "I'm sure nothing will come of it."

"Yeah, I'm sure you're right," I say. Maybe if I tell myself that enough, it'll be true. Saying our goodbyes, I remind myself to bring up this thing with Deacon again the next time we're face to face. I can't just let that slide. It's either gonna be very interesting or absolutely disastrous. Then again, that could be said for a lot of things, including this newly concocted plan.

Finishing the last of my coffee, I head back upstairs to find Merrick still sleeping. Going into his bathroom, I make use of his toothbrush to get rid of my coffee and morning breath. Somehow, I don't think he'll mind. Padding back into the bedroom, I climb back into bed beside him. As he begins to move, I curse myself inwardly for waking him up. But his eyes never open. He simply throws that heavy arm back around my waist and draws me closer. Our noses are nearly touching again now, and I feel so stupid staring at him while he sleeps, especially this close. I swear, if he opens his eyes suddenly, I'm gonna give those horror movie scream queens a run for their money.

But he doesn't. Not even when I brush the hair back from his forehead. Nor when I lean down to gently kiss his lips. Running my hand gently over his muscled chest, I marvel at all the artwork he's put on himself over the years. I still don't know how the Hell I didn't suspect there was this much ink under all those straitlaced button-downs. And if finding his torso, back, and arms heavily tattooed was a shock, I can only imagine the look he saw on my face when I discovered the barbells running through his nipples. I'm sure it was a look worth remembering, even if it is to needle me with later. No pun intended.

As I move my hand over the patterns, tracing each one, I start to see things I recognize. A paintbrush, splashes of watercolor here and there, and quotes from some of the poems I took inspiration from when naming each of my pieces. In my awe and fascination, I run my fingers over the images. Realizing my mistake, it's already too late when I accidentally graze my hand over one of his piercings. Eyes flashing open, he focuses on me immediately. No grogginess, no needing caffeine before coming fully away. No. He's instantaneously alert, as if he had been the one waiting for me to wake up, not the other way around. To my credit, I don't shriek or make any other typical horror movie girl moves.

A lascivious grin forms around his sexy mouth. In a movement so fluid you'd swear we'd been doing it for years, he rolls on top of me, effectively pinning me to the mattress. Sitting back on his haunches, he looks me up and down before saying in an awestruck tone, "You're wearing my t-shirt."

"All my clothes are dirty," I retort.

"Mmmm ... well, by the time I'm done with you, those clothes won't be the only things that are dirty."

His words are like a zap of electricity. I can feel the shock waves throughout my entire body. Hunching over slightly, he places both hands on the outsides of my thighs, just below the hem of the t-shirt. Achingly slow, he slides those hands up the smooth expanse of skin. I can feel goosebumps breaking out over all the areas he's touched. With a look that's part concentration and part fascination, his gaze stays riveted to each and every inch of skin he uncovers. When he reaches the juncture of my thighs, and I'm seconds away from spreading my legs and telling him to do with me what he will, he instead changes course, bypassing my center in favor of moving his hands up and under the shirt to circle the expanse of my waist. Gripping my waist in a firm hold, he subtly pulls my lower half closer to his. Once he's done that, those sneaky hands continue their upward glide until his fingertips are brushing the undersides of my breasts. Shivering at the way he touches my body, I let loose a little whimper, biting my lip to keep from begging.

As he looks down at me, he says, "You're gonna smell like me now. My scent will be all over you. Everywhere you go today, you'll get a whiff of my cologne or deodorant or laundry detergent, and you'll think of me. Of the ways your body comes alive only for me." Brushing a thumb over one nipple while the other hand moves up to fully cup my other breast, he leans in close and says, "You'll let me do anything I want to this pretty little body, won't you, baby?"

I'm losing focus, and my brain can't seem to latch onto anything he's saying. All I can do is nod my head and let out a little, "Mmmhmm, anything."

Smile full of praise and eyes full of hunger, he says, "Touch yourself for me."

Wait, what? I know my brain is addled and not fully online at the moment, but surely he didn't just ask what I think he did. "What?" Really eloquent, Mia. Jesus.

Removing his hands from under the shirt where they'd been systematically tormenting both nipples in turn, he sits back up to his full height and says, "You heard me. Touch yourself. I wanna see what you do to yourself when you're alone and thinking about me."

Arrogant man. The audacity! He wasn't wrong, though. Over the years, there have been times when I'd be unable to sleep at night and for whatever reason, his face would pop into my mind. On those quiet nights, I'd touch myself, pretending it was his hands instead of my own. The act, combined with the knowledge that he was the catalyst, was so forbidden it only ramped up my desire. Just like the night that I painted the two of us together. I'm not shy by any standards, but I can't say I ever expected this man to ask me to get myself off in front of him.

Taking a deep breath, I put my hand down between my thighs, underneath the shirt that's fallen back down to cover me. Grazing my fingers along my core, I'm surprised at how wet I already am. I mean, I shouldn't really be shocked. This man looks in my direction, and I might as well be the spokesperson for adult diapers.

Watching my hand move under the shirt doesn't seem to work for him. Leaning down slightly, he reaches for the hem of the shirt and pushes it up past the apex of my thighs, exposing me all the way to the middle of my abdomen. In this position, I can't move my legs, which are currently draped over his thighs, effectively spreading me wide and opening me up to his ravenous gaze. The look in his eyes is dangerous and a little bit terrifying. I can't say I don't like it.

As my hand moves back between my legs, I reach down to gather some of my own wetness, bringing it back up before using it to make slow circles around my clit. The act causes an involuntary reaction, and my hips rise from the bed, back bowing a little before settling back down. All the while, Merrick stares at the area between my spread thighs in rapt fascination.

Finally tearing his gaze away from that sensitive spot, his eyes travel up the length of my body. Once again, his hands slide beneath the shirt, bunching it up until he's exposed both breasts to the cool air now. Leaning down to whisper near my ear, he says, "You've never looked sexier than you do right now, wearing nothing but my t-shirt, and I'll let you put it back on later, but for now, I want it *off*." Sliding an arm under me at the center of my back, he lifts my upper body off the mattress while using his other hand to rip the shirt away. Laying me back down, he leans back once more, taking in all the creamy new skin he's just uncovered.

"Much better. Continue," he says. It's not a request, it's a command. At this moment, he's the one in control, and he knows it.

Taking a steadying breath, I continue to make slow glides over and around my clit before dipping down again, pushing one finger inside. The move rips a gasp from my lips, and I can't help but close my eyes at the pleasure. Merrick's next words jerk me out of that happy place I go to whenever I'm alone and thinking about him.

"How's that finger feel, baby? Is it enough, or do you need more?" he asks.

"I need more."

"Here, let me help you," he says, and in the next second, he's buried two fingers deep inside me, curling them upward so that they hit a spot that I didn't even know existed before I met him.

Crying out, my hand automatically falls away to allow him to take the reins while I brace myself for whatever he's about to do to me. Fingers stilling, he says, "I never said you could stop. Keep going."

Growling in frustration, my hand returns to my aching clit, circling the tiny bud until I'm squirming on his fingers, desperate to come. All the while, he watches me. The way my body moves, the expressions lighting my features, the slide of his rough fingers in and out of me.

"That's my girl," he says, voice laden with satisfaction, making me feel so special. Like I'm the only one he's ever looked at like this. The only one he'll *ever* look at like this.

Desperate with need, I moan, "Merrick, please."

"You wanna come, baby?" At my affirmative nod, he says, "move your hand."

I do as I'm told and remove my fingers. As he takes control of my pleasure, I have the sudden thought that although I technically took his v card, the training wheels on his bicycle fell right off, and now he's making up for lost time.

He keeps two fingers buried deep inside me and uses the pad of his thumb to move in tight circles around my clit. Then he begins to move his fingers, thrusting them in and out, all while maintaining that agonizing rhythm on that bundle of nerves that are sending tiny lightning bolts shooting throughout my entire body. Soon, I can feel a tightening sensation in my lower belly, and I know I'm close to coming. He must sense it too, because he stops the torturous circles and chooses instead to use his thumb to press down hard onto my clit while I wantonly ride his fingers. My hips rock up and down on his hand, and the change in sensations is enough to send me over the edge. Walls spasming around his thick fingers, my back bows off the bed, and a scream leaves my lips seconds before he leans down and captures the sound with his mouth.

Within the next second, he's slamming into me, eliciting another cry. Whether for pleasure or mercy, I'm not sure. Fucking me through my orgasm, our lips and tongues meld as he breathes into my mouth, "I can feel you coming around my cock. Clamping down on me like you want me to stay here forever. Don't worry; I'm not going anywhere. I'm gonna start off fucking you nice and slow, then ride you so hard that you'll feel me for hours after we're done." His words are punctuated with a slow withdrawal followed by another hard thrust of his hips. Finally breaking the kiss, his back straightens again so that he's looking down at my body, completely exposed to his predatory gaze. His eyes are darker than I've ever seen them, the pupils blown wide. Fingers dig into the flesh at my hips, and in addition to the soreness he promised, I know I'll also find bruises that match the same pattern as his fingertips when I look in the mirror tomorrow. Using the grip on my hips, he holds me firmly in place as he pulls out nearly to the tip before easing back in again. He repeats this motion again and again, taking his time with me, all the while staring transfixed at the place where his body and mine are joined. Each thrust forward, combined with the pressure he's exerting on my hips, pushes him deeper and deeper. I clench my jaw to keep from crying out at the pleasure, but I can't stop myself from glancing down to where he's disappearing into me. When my eyes return to his, it's to find that his focus has shifted from between my legs to my breasts, which are bouncing with every hard thrust. Leaning back down, he braces a hand on the headboard so that he can capture one nipple in his mouth. Sucking hard, then swirling his tongue around the tip, he alternates the motion for several seconds before giving the opposite breast the same treatment. He releases my nipple with an audible pop, and his face travels upward until I feel the wet glide of his tongue on my collarbone. Tracking the movement, I feel him lick from my collarbone up the side of my neck, tasting the sweat that's begun to dot my skin. I don't know how it's possible that he's putting in all the work, yet I feel like I'm getting the best cardio of my life.

Sinful tongue reaching my ear, he licks the shell before saying in a husky tone, "Are you ready?"

Voice gone breathless, I ask, "Ready for what?"

Without replying, he braces his other hand on the headboard, using it for leverage as he withdraws his cock to the tip before slamming into me so hard I practically feel my teeth rattle. Gasping out his name, I grip his powerful forearms to brace myself for what I know is coming. He's going to make good on his promise. I have no doubt that I'll barely be able to walk tomorrow. Gripping the headboard with iron control, his hips slam into me over and over—each thrust threatening to shatter me into a million pieces. A drop of sweat falls from somewhere above, landing on my cheek and causing my eyes to rake over his body the way his did over mine when we first began. He's always been handsome, but right now, he's fucking beautiful. Muscled skin slicked with sweat; I watch as his abs clench and unclench with every push and pull of his hips. The perspiration on his chest makes the colorful tattoos even brighter than before. As my eyes track up to his face, I find his penetrating stare already on mine. His hair is a wet mess, plastered to his forehead, as I'm sure mine is. As his powerful thrusts inch me further and further up the bed, I release his biceps in favor of winding my arms beneath his to dig my nails into the backs of his shoulders. The growl that rumbles up his throat is all male and has my insides trembling. Pushing the boundaries of my luck—because I don't want to fall over the cliff without him—I rear my head up and flick my tongue across one of the barbells piercing his flesh. Throwing his head back and releasing a long groan, I can feel him begin to swell inside me. Releasing the headboard, he lowers himself until we're torso to torso, and his grip on me mimics my own. Hands gripping the tops of my shoulders from underneath, his thrusts losing their rhythm in his frenzy to finish us both. Capturing my mouth with his, he sinks his teeth into the flesh of my bottom lip and murmurs, "Come. Now." As though my body has been trained to recognize his commands, my stomach tightens again, back bowing until, for a moment in time, I'm suspended in space. Eyes locked on his, I see entire galaxies in their dark depths. For that brief moment, I'm lost in the void, surrounded by stars. Then I'm crashing back down to Earth in time to hear the word, "*Mine!*" leave his lips in a broken cry as he thrusts one final time, emptying himself inside me.

As I lay there, sucking in lungfuls of air, I recognize that he was right. He owns me, body and soul. And I can't be mad about it because I never really put up much of a fight, did I?

CHAPTER 33

Merrick

Closing the door behind me as I leave Amelia's home, I breathe a small sigh of relief. On the one hand, I wanted to keep her with me. After the most intense orgasm I've ever experienced, we both fell back to sleep, limbs tangled and exhausted. When I'd woken up the second time, only to find myself alone, I'd had a split second of panic. Jumping out of bed and throwing on a pair of loose sweatpants, I'd nearly fallen down the stairs in my haste to find her, forgetting that my legs were little more than jelly at that point. Then I smelled the coffee. Immediately, I felt my stomach settle, and it no longer felt like I was on an out-of-control roller coaster. That is, until I found her in the living room, and she'd voiced her intention to go back to her house to shower and change clothes. This business with Gloria made me extremely uneasy, so I have to admit, my knee-jerk reaction had been "fuck no, you're not". Immediately, I recognized my mistake. Amelia wasn't a completely unreasonable person. There were times when I took charge, even outside of the bedroom, and after an initial period of obstinance, she would see the reason in my argument and concede. Then, there were times that I knew beyond a shadow of a doubt that she'd fight me to the death on something. This had been one of those times.

Despite the fact that Gloria was missing, neither Suzanne nor Peter had been brought in for questioning yet. I wasn't sure if that was because Alexi was putting some kind of plan in place or because there was no definitive proof that Suzanne was in any way involved with her disappearance. As Amelia saw it, our lives didn't just stop based on suspicion. She'd argued with me that she still needed to be in her own home, needed access to her studio, and still had to visit the gallery on occasion. Regardless of how hard I pushed, she refused to be cloistered in my apartment for the foreseeable future. At the height of the argument, I'd had the slightly unhinged thought of carrying her back upstairs and tying her to my bed until she saw reason. Knowing that wasn't an option, I'd made the critical mistake of trying to dictate that she wasn't going anywhere. It was at that point that she threw a glass candle at my head.

Taking a moment to breathe deeply—because I could feel myself bordering on irrationality—I'd offered a compromise. She could go home to shower and change, then paint for a few hours, as long as I was the one to take her there and back, and she allowed me to search her house before leaving. I didn't think it was a good idea to tell her that I would've followed her regardless, but that was the truth nonetheless. After a few minutes of mumbling under her breath something about "pigheaded men", she'd agreed. Sometimes, I swore, it was only my absolute adoration for every facet of this woman that kept me from putting a gag in her mouth. Which brought me to my current position outside of her door. Despite my reservations about leaving her here alone, I knew it was for the best. I had to make a trip out to the plantation house, and I wasn't ready to take her there yet. So I'd dropped her off and told her I needed to take care of a few things myself and that I'd be back to pick her up tonight because, whether she liked it or not, she was sleeping in my bed tonight and every night in the future.

Heading back to my car, my thoughts are consumed with the missing housekeeper. While I was grateful that, at the very least, I'd gotten the physical evidence to put Suzanne away for murder two times over, I still needed Gloria as a witness when the trial began. As I drive, distracted by this newest development, I don't notice the car that's trailing me a few cars back. Nor do I notice it when I turn off the main road and onto the oak-lined driveway leading to the plantation house. Pulling up to the front of the house, I get out of my Bentley and unload a new wooden crate from the trunk. Jogging up to the front door, I know I'm pressed for time, so I quickly let myself into the house, completely forgetting to lock the door behind me.

Taking the grand staircase two steps at a time, I heft the wooden crate in my arms and make my way to the master bedroom. This room—like all the others—is empty, but for the paintings lining the walls and a few other random pieces of art scattered throughout. Opening the crate, I pull out the painting of myself and Amelia that she did that night I watched her in her studio. The night I saw her get herself off to the image of us kissing, pulled from her own mind. The night I stood outside with my forehead pressed to hers, only a thin wall separating us, and stroked myself off to the sound of her crying out my name.

Hanging the newly framed painting on the wall, I straighten it and step back to admire the placement. I chose this spot, right above the fireplace of the master bedroom, for a reason. When all of this is over, and we've made this house our home, I want this painting to be the second thing I see when I wake up in the morning and the second thing I see before I close my eyes every night. The first is Amelia's beautiful face. I'm not sure how long I stand there staring at the painting, committing every inch to memory, but so wrapped up am I in the details that I don't recognize that someone else has entered the room until I hear a floorboard creak behind me. Movement out of the corner of my eye catches my attention, and I whirl around to find a pair of shocked emerald eyes moving between me and the painting, then back again. Eyes set in the same face I'd just been staring at on the canvas. A face that holds so many emotions in this moment, ranging from confusion to awareness. Betrayal to anger. Feeling my lungs seize up, I open my mouth to speak, but before I can get any air in to offer some sort of explanation, she spins and bolts for the stairs. Blind panic has my feet moving before I've even realized what

I'm doing. I have no idea what I'm going to say when I catch her; I just know I *have* to catch her. If she leaves before I have a chance to explain myself, I'll lose her forever. Taking the curve at the top of the staircase at a dead run, I leap down the stairs, catching her just as she reaches the landing. Gripping her shoulders, I turn her around to face me.

Breathing heavily, I start to say her name, but I'm quickly cut off when she jerks out of my hold, shoving me hard in the chest with both hands. Stumbling back a step, I brace myself for her to make a run for the door, knowing I'll give chase. But she doesn't. She just stands there, staring at me.

Holding my hands up in a gesture of peace, I say, "Mia, please. Just let me explain."

She flinches as though the sound of my voice alone hurts her. I hate it.

"I don't need an explanation. I walked through this house. I've seen everything. You're a thief, aren't you? You stole from me." It's an accusation, not a question, and for a brief moment, I wonder if she's talking about more than just the paintings. If she's accusing me of stealing something far more precious.

Shaking my head, I move forward again, thinking that if I can just hold her, she'll remember what we have, and it'll be enough to make her stay and hear me out. Wrapping my arms around her, I say, "No, it's not like that. I didn't steal *from* you. I stole *for* you."

A sob breaks free from her throat. "Liar!" Fighting to free herself, she pushes and shoves, beating her small fists against my chest. Fearing she'll hurt herself, I reluctantly let her go but stay close enough to stop her if she makes a move for the door. I can't let her leave this house.

As I step away I don't take my eyes off her face. A face that's now cast down, as though she can't stand to look at me. Breathing heavily, she wraps both arms around herself as if to guard herself against me. Finally lifting her head, she lets me see her eyes. They're twin pools of glass. Opening her mouth to speak, she says in a shaky voice, "I have no idea ... who you are." Her voice cracks halfway through, and when her chin begins to tremble, it's almost my undoing. As I watch a tear spill over and down her cheek, it feels like a knife in my gut. Each one that falls is another plunge of the dagger. She may be the one that's been wronged in this situation, but I'm the one that's gonna end up bleeding out right here in our house.

Face a mask of desperation, I plead with her. "Don't say that. You do know me. You know me better than anyone else. If you just give me some time, I can explain everything. I can make you understand."

"Make me understand? Understand what? That you stole my paintings? That you've been watching me without my knowledge? I'm not a fucking idiot, Merrick. After seeing you and Agent Kapranov last night, I knew there was something you were keeping from me. I just never expected it to be something like this. I've gotta hand it to you, though. You played your part really well. I actually thought you cared about me. The way you touched me, it almost felt like you lo-..." Cutting herself off, she makes a scoffing sound as though she was about to say something so improbable that it would've been ridiculous.

A bitter laugh escaping, she says, "I let you touch me. Fuck me. Sleep in my bed."

The way she throws out the words "Fuck me" makes the act sound seedy and distasteful. But it's the way she says, "Sleep in my bed" that makes me pause. As though that part hurts her more than allowing me inside of her body. That alone proves to me that she does actually feel something more for me. That it wasn't just sex to her. That we were destined to save each other.

I need her to hear me out because I know if I can just explain the reasoning behind what I've done, she won't leave. Right now, she thinks I used her just to steal from her. She has to know that everything I did was for her—for us. But just as I take another step to bring myself within arms reach of her again, her hand flies up and cracks hard across my face. Within the single solitary moment that it takes me to recover from the shock, she turns and flings the door wide, running for her car. Before I can get outside, she's already in the driver's seat, and I'm a split second away from throwing myself in front of the car. Anything to stop her from leaving me. But I'm too late. Tires spinning, gravel goes flying in every direction, and when the dust clears, the only thing left of her are her tail lights. Standing in the driveway of our empty house, I don't know what will be left of me. Whatever it is, without her, it won't be enough.

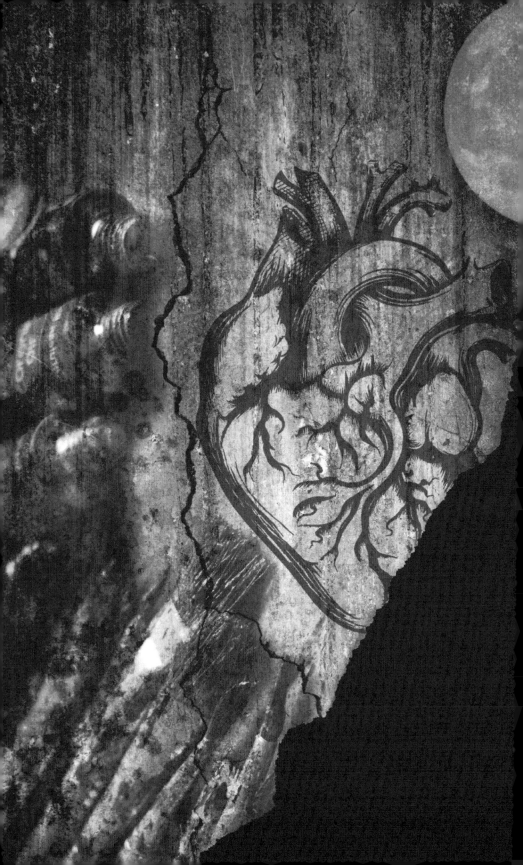

CHAPTER 34

Amelia

My hands shake uncontrollably as I turn the knob on the door to my studio. This happens whenever I allow my emotions to pile up on themselves without finding an outlet for them. Usually, that outlet is painting, and it always seems to be the place I return to anytime I'm feeling overwhelmed. Although lately, Merrick has served as an outlet for some of that pent-up emotion. Right now, though, he's the cause of it. There's an ache in the center of my chest. Rubbing at the spot, I'm suddenly hyper-focused on my breathing and heart rate. Bringing two fingers from one hand up to my other wrist, I check my pulse to see how fast my heart is beating. In the recesses of my mind, I know that I'm probably just on the verge of a panic attack, and I'm most likely not about to die from a heart attack, but that's the funny thing about the human mind. I can know I'm fine and still believe I'm not fine. Unfortunately, the body follows suit to whatever the mind believes.

I read somewhere once that there was such a thing as "Broken Heart Syndrome". That the tendons inside the heart can snap or break with severe emotional trauma, causing the heart to lose form, resulting in a lack of blood flow. That it's not just in stories but that it is actually possible to die of a broken heart, and for some reason, that otherwise useless tidbit of information comes back to me now. Making my way over to the rows of blank canvas, I suddenly know exactly what type of piece I want to paint today. If I don't keel over first.

Picking up a 24x36 inch canvas and placing it on my easel, I'm thankful that I've already pre-treated all of these with Gesso because I really can't wait for it to dry. I need to get this out now. I'm afraid if I don't, my chest may literally cave in on itself. Putting my AirPods in, I decide to deviate from my usual painting playlists and instead choose something that I know will speak to the turmoil roiling through me. The deep and melodic voice of Vessel fills my ears as I pick up a piece of charcoal and begin to sketch out shapes. My strokes are feather light over the fabric, and by the time I'm done, I have the basic outlines of what I want. Picking up my oil paints, I disperse them evenly onto my pallet and begin to work. Unlike with the charcoal—this time—my strokes are bold and deliberate. Deciding to do this piece alla prima, I mix colors, not only on the pallet but on the canvas as well. The differing shades of black and gray blend with the bold red to create something that's at once dark and also lighter than my usual work. I'm not sure how long I stand there, hunched over. All I know is that I'm lost to my process, my emotions being wrung from me and pouring themselves onto the fabric. When I finally step back from the canvas, my entire body feels achy, stiff, and exhausted in a way I've come to recognize and appreciate.

Sitting my pallet down, I cock my head to the side and observe what I've created with a critical eye. I do this after each piece, sometimes going back to correct something or make a change where I see one's needed. Not this time, though. This time, I leave the painting as is. As Vessel would say, if there are mistakes, they're perfectly misaligned. I wouldn't change a thing about it. It's raw and real, possibly one of the most gripping things I've ever created. As I sit and stare at what will be a finished piece once I've glazed it, what stares back at me is my own heart. Not some cheesy cartoon thing but an anatomically correct heart. And it's broken, the tendons inside easily visible through the layers. There they sit, snapped and disintegrated, taking what should've been a normal, beating thing and replacing it with something that's withered away and damaged. It takes me several moments of staring transfixed at the broken threads to realize that I'm crying. Tears stream down my face, and if the wetness on my paint-splattered apron is any indication, I must've been crying for a good portion of the time I was working. This has happened once or twice before, but this time feels different. Sometimes, I'm so overwhelmed by what I'm feeling that when I'm finally finished with a piece, the release of emotions is almost cathartic, and I'm left blissfully empty. Unlike those times, however, this time, I still feel *everything*. Why can't I just feel nothing? Surely feeling empty is better than whatever this is? This is *agony*.

Pressing my palm to my chest, I sit down on the floor and sob like a baby. How is it possible to feel so much pain over an organ that isn't even really mine anymore? Like a ton of bricks hitting me in the face, I realize that what's on that canvas is an accurate representation of what currently resides within me, and if it beats at all anymore, it no longer beats for me. Maybe it never did. Once I've applied the glaze and the painting dries fully, I'll pack it up and have it sent to Merrick's apartment. It's only fitting that the copy be delivered to the thief who stole the original.

Three days later, as I'm preparing the broken heart painting to be packed up, the doorbell rings. For a moment, I have this irrational thought that it's Merrick. That he's come to confront me in the hopes that he can convince me that, despite the fact that he's a criminal by nature, I should trust him and his feelings for me. But even as I walk to answer the door, I know it won't be him. Not that he hasn't tried numerous times to contact me over the last three days. First, he called my phone repeatedly, to the point that I had to block his number, then sent me emails full of apologies and pleas to just "hear him out." They've all gone unanswered. He hasn't come to my house, though. I have a feeling that he wants to put the ball in my court and allow me to come to terms with everything. That doesn't stop him from tossing the ball at me repeatedly every time I ignore it.

Walking to the backdoor, where the chime sounded, I lift the curtain to look through the window, seeing Siren on the other side. Opening the door, I leave her to let herself in while I go back to crating up the giant painting that I ended up naming "Flatline". I'll be glad once I get it inside the crate and out of this house. Every time I see it, I can't stop the tears that seem unending at this point. Hunting in my storage closet, I've just found the bubble wrap when I enter the kitchen to find Siren staring at the painting.

"Amelia ... Jesus. What is that?" she asks. I hear no disgust in her voice. Siren has never disparaged anything I've painted. She's always understood that my art is a reflection of things from my subconscious. There may have been times when she would ask me about the details of a certain piece, but other times she simply understood that once it had been poured out onto the canvas, I didn't want to relive it. Her voice now holds notes of anger and hurt. To some extent, she understands what brought this piece to life, so I don't bother to answer her rhetorical question. Instead, I begin to wrap the finished and framed painting in bubble wrap.

Coming up behind me, Siren places her hand over one of my own. It's only then that I realize my hands are shaking. Using her hand on mine, she gently turns me around to face her, then pulls me in for a tight hug. As though some invisible dam has broken, I practically collapse into her. Sobbing like a small child, I pour out every residual drop of emotion that seems to have just redoubled since finishing that painting.

"Oh, babe. What did he do to you?" she says. Uncaring of how my tears are soaking her shirt, she holds me tighter. It's a good thing, too, because I worry that without her support, I'd simply break apart and crumble to the floor.

Between sobs, I manage to get out, "He's a liar and a thief."

She doesn't say anything else. She just holds me and lets me cry until I feel blessedly rung dry. She pulls me into the living room, and lowers us both to the couch. I have a suspicion that she wants me as far away from the painting as possible. She recognizes that the emotions behind its creation are still there, incorporated into every brush stroke. She doesn't want me to be triggered again. Reaching over to the nearby coffee table, she grabs a box of tissues and hands me one. I blow my nose loudly, and take another to wipe the remaining tears from my face. Waiting patiently, she does nothing more than stare at me, allowing me to take my time in explaining. I'm not even sure where to begin. A part of me still feels loyal to him, even after all the lies he's told. If I'm honest with myself, I don't want him to go to jail. I don't hate him that much. So, I hesitate before remembering that this is Siren. She's always had my back and even been my spine when I couldn't stand straight. She would never tell anyone my secrets. So, taking a deep breath, I force the words past my lips.

"Do you remember a few weeks ago, I told you that someone was stealing my paintings after they'd been sold?" I ask.

Nodding, she looks confused for a split second, and then a look of total disbelief transforms her features. If her eyes got any wider, they'd fall out and roll to the floor.

"Wait. You don't mean to say that Merrick is the one that stole them, do you?" I can hear the incredulity in her tone. I understand the sentiment. It's almost too fantastical to believe. If it wasn't for the proof I saw a few days ago and the fact that I know Merrick is extremely intelligent and capable, I wouldn't believe it myself.

"He did. I saw them a few days ago. Set up in some house halfway between here and Edisto."

Face pinched, she says, "Okay, hang on. What house? You found this out after we talked about you following him the other day?"

Dropping my face into my hands, I take a moment to compose myself. I'm gonna have to explain this from the beginning so she understands the context and the full scope of what happened. Taking several calming breaths, I lift my head again and begin. I explain to her how I told him that I needed to go home for clean clothes, just like we had discussed. About how I'd gotten in my own car and followed him after he dropped me off. I describe the large plantation home in detail to her, including the fact that as I'd wandered the rooms of the house, I'd seen not only several precious works that had been missing for years but also my own paintings. Finally, I tell her about finding Merrick in an upstairs bedroom, hanging the painting I'd created of the two of us. The one that I'd found missing from my studio the morning after. By the time I'm finished, her mouth is hanging so far open it would be comical if I actually had it in me to laugh.

Several long moments pass as she processes everything I said. Finally, she breaks her silence by saying, "So he's clearly been doing this for a long time. No novice would be able to pull off thefts like that."

That's something I've thought about extensively over the last three days. When I think back to the artwork I saw in the house, I recognize several that were reported stolen years ago. Unless they're forgeries, the fact that he has them in his possession can only mean that he's been stealing for years. This better explained all the times he'd disappear for several days during the brief years we'd lived together at the townhouse. It also explained how he'd amassed the wealth that now kept him living in the lap of luxury. The wealth that paid for his fancy car and designer suits. The wealth ... that he gave to charity. Fuck! Dropping my head back into my hands, another sob, this time softer, leaves me. He's lied, and he's hurt me, but at the same time, I have to recognize that he's not actually a bad person. He's just done bad things.

Siren leans over and puts an arm around me. As though she can read my mind, she says, "I've met bad people. I've known bad people." There's a heavy pause before she finishes. "I've ... loved bad people." Shaking her head, she looks at me with a kind of wonder in her eyes. "Not even the ones I loved looked at me the way he looks at you. He may have lied and hidden things from you, but I know what that look means because I used to see it shining from my eyes whenever I looked in a mirror at the reflection of the bad person standing behind me. Merrick is in love with you. Now you have to figure out if you love him back and if you can forgive him for believing that the end justifies the means."

Staring off into space, I don't have to do much thinking to answer the first part. I am in love with him. If I didn't love him, this wouldn't hurt so much. But I don't know if that love applies to all of him or just the parts he let me see. To the person that I thought he was. The truth is, I won't be able to answer that second part unless I speak to him. Unless I give him the chance to explain—what he so desperately begged for—and I don't think I'm ready for that. The truth is, I was a coward. I was afraid to hear that everything had been a sham. That every soft touch, every whispered word, every longing look was a lie. And that in reality, he was a criminal, and I was just a job to him. But even more so than that fear, I was deathly afraid that it wasn't just some sick joke. That every intimate moment we shared and every insight into his soul that he let me see was real. That terrified me. Because if that were true, that means that he felt that way about me ... and still did this. And I wasn't sure I could live with that.

Like a ray of bright light cutting through my inner turmoil, Siren says, "Okay, here's what we're gonna do. We're gonna open a bottle of wine ... or three ... and get completely shit-faced. Then we're gonna order some pizza and eat until we feel sick. If you're gonna wallow in misery, you might as well do it with a full stomach and a nice buzz."

Letting out a little laugh, I bump my shoulder against hers. I honestly don't know what I'd do without her. She's always been my rock. An immovable object in a sea of chaos. Even during the years that she wasn't here, I channeled her energy to get me through some pretty horrific times. When she came back, she was ... changed. But somehow, still the same.

Looking over at her, I give her a small smile before saying, "Thank you. For everything. And ... I'll take that wine now."

I had a lot to think about, and if I knew Merrick, which I wasn't even sure at this point that I did, he wouldn't be giving me a lot of time to get that thinking done. Even knowing what lay ahead of me, I was taking tonight for myself. I was going to try and put all of this ugly business out of my mind, at least for tonight.

After I got rid of that damn painting.

CHAPTER 35

Merrick

Looking around my apartment, I survey the wasteland I've created. The entire living room looks like a bomb went off. Was I robbed? While that would've been a sick bit of irony, no. Unfortunately, the upended tables, broken glass, and debris weren't the result of a break-in or even an accident. All the damage that lay before me now was self-inflicted. I couldn't even look at the area to my right, where the large wooden crate lay in splinters. I knew if I did, it would only set me off again. I wasn't mad at the crate or even its contents. The truth was, I had trashed my apartment in the hopes that it would keep me from hurting the person that I was really angry with. Myself.

It's been five days since Amelia ran from me. Five days that I've spent in Hell. To say I've been mentally unstable would be an understatement. I've gone from the highest of highs to the lowest of lows. Or so I thought. Then, the crate arrived. It didn't take a genius to figure out what was inside. A painting, obviously. And with the return address on the shipping label showing Amelia's home, I knew whatever was inside that crate was going to hurt like a son of bitch. Even knowing that and bracing myself, I wasn't prepared for the impact. The explosion that had obliterated my already damaged and tattered soul. There was nothing left of me but ash. In a fit of rage and despair I'd destroyed anything within reach. I didn't care that the furniture was expensive or that some of the decor was irreplaceable. All I wanted to do was purge myself of this pain. This pain that felt like thousands of knives were stabbing me all over. How could someone survive through this kind of pain?

It was hard to explain all of the emotions that had hit me at once when I opened the crate and pulled out the contents. The first thing that struck me was the color. Unlike the majority of her work, this painting had vibrant strokes of red throughout. Propping it up against the wall of the living room, I'd taken in every detail of the anatomical heart. That's when I saw the broken tendons. The strands that held the heart together had been severed. That was the moment that I realized the full extent of the damage I'd done. The little index card stuck in the bottom left corner of the frame that read *Flatline* was just the nail in my coffin. After breaking everything within arms reach, I'd sunken to the floor in the middle of my living room and buried my face in my hands. That's exactly where I'm sitting when Deacon finds me. I don't ask how he got in, and to be honest, I don't really care. I just want him to leave. But as he enters the living room and surveys the damage, he very eloquently says, "Holy fuck, bro. Now, where the hell am I supposed to sit?"

"You're not supposed to sit anywhere because you're not staying. Leave." I say through the hands still covering my face. I know my tone is curt, and he's done nothing to deserve my attitude, but I've gone beyond the realm of caring. Losing his friendship would just be shit-icing on my already shit-filled cake.

I don't realize he's moved until he's hunkered down right in front of me. The giveaway is the fact that his voice sounds mere inches from where my head rests in my hands.

"Look at me, man."

As I lift my head, I stare at him in the hopes that it'll intimidate him into leaving me alone. I should know better. Placing his hand on my shoulder he asks, "How long have you been like this?"

I'm not entirely sure what he means by "like this", but I answer in the context of what I think he's referring to. "I was fine. I've been fine. Until that was delivered." I indicate the painting. Glancing over at it, he stands up and goes over to inspect the piece of art. He turns back to face me, and the look of pity on his face makes me wanna throw up.

"You're such a fuckin' liar," he says. "Your clothes are wrinkled, your eyes are bloodshot, and you look like you've lost 10 pounds. That means you haven't been eating or sleeping. I think you deciding to go all HGTV on this place means you're anything but fine."

"She won't answer my calls or respond to my messages. I've lost count of the number of times I've apologized to her voicemail or email. The only reason I haven't gone to her house is because I know that I've already taken so many things for granted. She'll never forgive me if I invade her space again without permission."

"So when I've pinged your cell, and it's shown me that you've been standing across the street from her house, the data must've been corrupted?" he asks, a hint of sarcasm in his tone.

Looking him straight in the eye, I say, "I said I was sorry, not that I was reformed. Anyway, why are you spying on me? And why are you here now?"

Turning serious now, he says, "There's been some unusual activity with your father's bank accounts. He's started making regular transfers to an offshore account. Individually, the transfers aren't enough to raise any red flags with the bank or IRS, but he's been making them every other day for the last two weeks. We've been so busy worrying about the evidence against Suzanne that I wasn't keeping a close enough eye on your father. I'm sorry, man. That's my fault."

I take in everything he's telling me, processing it slowly. I don't like it, but at the same time, I'm grateful for the distraction.

"Do me a favor. Can you turn the painting around to face the wall? I can't think straight with it sitting like that," I ask. I know it makes me a coward, but I can't stop my eyes from straying to it every few seconds, and the more I see it, the more I'll think about it.

Moving to the painting, he does as I ask. Going into the kitchen, he pulls up a chair from the dining room table. "I'm not sitting on the damn floor."

I pick myself up off the floor, follow his lead, and pull a chair over. Sitting down heavily, I rest my forearms on my knees, leaning down slightly. "He's getting ready to run. There's no other explanation as to why he'd be moving money."

"Is it possible that he found out about your little nighttime excursion into his safe?" Deacon asks.

Shaking my head, I say, "I don't think so. I've broken into places with far superior security and not left any traces behind. Something else must have him spooked. Keep a close eye on him for now. I'll contact Alexi and see where we are with the warrants. In the meantime, keep an eye on Amelia for me. For her own protection. If she doesn't want me near her, that's fine. But that doesn't mean I won't have eyes on her, even if they aren't my own."

Nodding, he stands up. "Will do. Now, how about you throw on some real clothes and let's go out and get something to eat? I know you probably haven't eaten anything all day. While I was in the kitchen getting a chair, I snooped in your fridge. The only shit in there is a bottle of mustard, a small pack of lunch meat, and a stick of butter."

I'm not entirely sure I have it in me to go outside and socialize with the general population. But I also know Deacon, and he's worse than a nagging wife. If I blow him off, he'll just order takeout and stay here annoying me for the next several hours. Standing up without a word, I go into my bedroom and grab a pair of jogging pants and a T-shirt. The only person I've ever set out to impress wants nothing to do with me. I don't really give a fuck what anyone else thinks. Slipping my feet into some sneakers, I head back out of the bedroom to find Deacon peeking at the painting again. He jumps like his hand's been caught in the cookie jar, gives me a sheepish grin, and moves to the door. I promise myself that I'll go out and grab some food to satisfy Deacon, then come back to wallow in my own misery a bit more. I know Amelia's radio silence is a form of punishment, but there's no amount of hatred that she could hurl in my direction that would come anywhere close to the disgust I feel for myself. For a brief moment in time, I held the world in the palm of my hand. Now, both hands are empty, and I'm left alone. Always alone.

As we walk into Husk on Queen Street, I can feel the eyes on me. Looking around the half-empty restaurant, I cringe inwardly at some of the faces I see. I recognize many of them. They're from our same social class, and while the majority of the patrons are just your average middle-class diners, the ones that know my face are staring daggers in my direction. I don't get it. I mean, I know I look like something a cat choked up, but you can't tell me these people have never seen someone in a pair of sweatpants before. As we make our way through the restaurant, their eyes continue to follow me. I can even hear whispers. I can't quite make out what they're saying, but something isn't right. I suddenly have a really weird feeling.

I follow Deacon to a table in the courtyard, and I'm grateful that this area of the popular Charleston eatery hasn't packed in yet for lunch yet. Sitting down opposite Deacon, I can't help but look back at the more crowded part of the restaurant. Even now, I can see people looking at me through the windows that overlook the courtyard. Face pinched, I stare down at the empty table setting in front of me. As a server comes by to take our drink order, I have the thought to order something much stronger than iced tea. But I've never liked alcohol much. While it may temporarily numb the pain, the problems will still be there when it wears off. It also just reminded me too much of my father, and I never wanted to be anything like him. In fact, the last time I took a drink was the night we ran into Amelia and Siren at the bar. Shaking my head to try to clear it, I do my best to think about anything else.

Ordering a glass of tea, I sit and wait while Deacon orders a soda. I know Deacon drinks, so I wonder if he's refraining on my account. I open my mouth to say something but then close it again. It is still early. Maybe that's why he's not having a drink. I listen with only one ear as Deacon also asks the server for today's copy of The Post and Courier. I don't say anything. I already know why Deacon asked for the paper. He plans to scan it for any mention of his father. Senator Hawkins was just as much of a piece of shit as my own father. The only difference was, where my father was stuck with me and therefore beat me because of it, Deacon's father refused to acknowledge his existence. Don't get me wrong, he knew Deacon was his son. But from the day that Deacon's mother, Anne, had told her married lover that she was pregnant, the two had ceased to exist to him. He'd thrown her and his unborn son away like garbage. Like mine, Deacon's life hadn't been all flowers and rainbows, either.

I'm broken from my inner musings when the server comes back to drop off our drinks and Deacon's paper. As I take a sip of my tea, I can't help but continue to glance back over my shoulder to the inside of the restaurant. They were still staring. What the fuck is going on? Hearing a choking sound from the other side of the table, I jerk my head around just in time to see Deacon spit tea all over the table.

"Jesus, Deacon! What's wrong with you?" I say, using my napkin to wipe drops of tea and spit from my cheek.

Clearing his throat, I watch as his face turns from an oxygen-deprived red to ghostly white. "Uhhhh, bro, you need to see this."

Gingerly, taking the half-soaked paper from his hands, I turn it around to face me and almost choke myself, only in my case, I'd be choking on my own tongue because my mouth has gone completely devoid of saliva. The headline at the top of the page reads, "Keeping It All In The Family?" Below the headline is a picture of Mia and I leaving my apartment a few days ago. The day my world exploded. This picture was taken before she followed me to the plantation house. In the photo, Mia and I are holding hands, clearly looking as though we both just rolled out of bed. Feeling my chest tighten, I stare at the picture for a long time. We looked happy.

Seeing the reminder of what was is nearly too much to take. Tearing my gaze from the photo, I skim the accompanying article. As my eyes rove over line after line of salacious claims and accusations, I can feel my blood beginning to boil.

I mean, the majority of it is true, but aside from the picture, the writer of this piece doesn't actually know that. It's a massive liberty, and one that's going to put an already hurting Mia into a tailspin. Pulling out my phone, I dial her number for the hundredth time in the last few days. Just like all the times before, I get a message saying, "the number I've dialed cannot be reached."

"Fuck!" I say, hanging up before it has a chance to disconnect me.

Deacon winces. "I don't know how I missed this. It's my fault. I should've gotten an alert when your names appeared in the online version of the article. I could try to get onto the net and scrub it, but that won't do anything for the copies that have already been printed and shipped. I'm sorry, man. I'm just fucking up all over today."

Rubbing a hand over my tired face, I say, "It's not your fault. It was bound to happen eventually. I just wish we could weather the storm together. But she won't fucking talk to me." I'm yelling by the time I finish the last sentence. Looking over my shoulder, I catch those same eyes on me.

"WHAT?!" I say. Immediately, heads turn away as they titter amongst themselves. Gossip-mongering old biddies.

"What are you gonna do? You know your dad and stepmom are bound to see this at some point today. You gonna try to head it off?"

"I don't fuckin know. This is just ..." I gesture at the paper in front of me. "I don't have the energy for this bullshit. It's only gonna make the situation between Amelia and I worse."

"Well, let's just get something to go, and we'll head back to your place to try to formulate a plan. Hopefully, we'll beat the photographers there," Deacon says, signaling to the server who's been standing off to the side, afraid to approach since my outburst.

I nod, then sit stoically, staring off into space while he orders some-thing for the both of us. I don't know why I can't catch a damn break. I know Amelia is gonna be freaking out when she sees the article. Knowing her mother, she'll have her on the phone already. Looking down at my own silent phone, I can only hope that this provokes her to reach out to me. Even if it's just to bite my head off, I'll take whatever I can get.

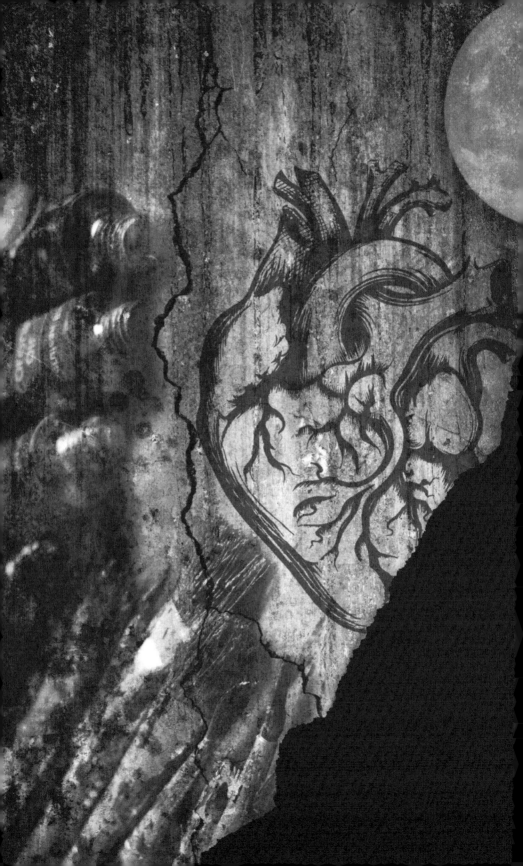

CHAPTER 36

Amelia

Oh my God, that terrible sound is going off again. Feeling blindly for my phone, I crack one eye open to try to make out the name on the screen. Expecting it to be Merrick, I'm surprised when I see my mother's name instead. And just like that, I'm wide awake. Blind terror has that effect on people. Why would she be calling me this early? Glancing at the time on the phone screen, I see that it's not actually that early. She will have already had breakfast and coffee, pouring over the page six gossip columns in the hopes that she'll see someone she knows and can get on the phone with her socialite friends to discuss whatever it is at nauseam.

Not in the mood to deal with her shit right now—I hit the button to send the call to voicemail. Sitting up, I do my best to stifle a yawn as I recall the reason for my fatigue. I'd spent another night alternating between rage, fear, and pain. Rage at all the lies Merrick fed me. Fear at the prospect of him being arrested—because, for some reason—my stupid brain still felt a sense of loyalty to the bastard. Then there was the pain. Not of the physical variety, exactly. Although, it did feel like someone had carved their way into the center of my chest with a rusty spoon and scooped out my bleeding heart. I finally cried myself to sleep ... again ... in the wee hours of the morning. I knew Merrick was sorry. I didn't even have to talk to him to know that. The more I thought back to the day I'd found him in that house, the more details I remembered that I'd either forgotten or chosen not to acknowledge. I saw the look on his face when I told him that I had no idea who he was. The pain I'd seen there couldn't be faked. Neither could all of the good deeds he'd done for me over the years. So yeah, I knew he was sorry. I guess I just needed time to process everything and decide if I was going to allow that to be enough. If I could trust that what I'd seen was the extent of his lies. That I could trust that he wouldn't lie to me again. If I couldn't, there was no way forward for us.

Speaking of Merrick, my phone lights up again and again, that irritating noise almost deafening in the still silence of my bedroom. I really needed to change my ringtone. This one was way too obnoxious. Glancing at the display, I do indeed see Merrick's name this time. Taking a deep breath to steady myself, my finger hovers over the green button that will accept the call. At the last minute, though, nerves get the better of me, and I send that call, too, to voicemail. Not 60 seconds later, the phone goes off again. I swear, I was gonna stick it in the toilet bowl. Well ... after I peed, which I really need to do right now. Looking down at the annoying little device, I pause just as I've gotten to my feet at the side of the bed. It's my mother again. Weird. Usually, she would just send me a snarky text and be done with it. Getting a funny feeling in my stomach, I answer the call.

"Good Morning, Mother," I say, ever the polite and dutiful daughter.

"Do you have any idea what you've done?! Amelia, how could you?! I'll be a laughing stock for the rest of my life!" she screeches from the other end of the line, so loud that I have to briefly hold the phone away from my ear. What on Earth is she talking about?

"Mother, I have no clue what you're yelling about," I say in my best, smooth, placating tone. I don't know what she thinks I've done, but my mother has always had a flair for the dramatics, so I'm sure it can't be that bad. I just need to talk her down from whatever ledge she's on at the moment.

"It's everywhere! Oh my God, EVERYWHERE! The Post and Courier, The Chronicle, online, everywhere!"

"What is?" I ask, perplexed.

"Check your phone! I can't ... I can't deal with this right now ..." she says, sounding close to hysterics before the line goes dead. Great. She's hung up on me.

My face is a mask of confusion as I pull up the internet browser on my phone and go to the website for The Post and Courier. Flicking through the headlines and the contents of today's paper, I do a double-take when I see my name. Hands shaking, I click on the headline that reads, "Keeping It All In The Family?"

Once the article loads, there's no missing the photo that takes up nearly the entire page, just below the headline. It's Merrick and me. Holding hands. Feeling the room start to tilt, I collapse back down to the bed I just vacated. My hands are trembling so badly that I can barely read the words on the screen. With every sentence, the anxiety builds and builds until a panic attack has me fully by the throat. Gasping for breath, I root around in my bedside table drawer for my pills.

Oh my God. Oh my God. Oh my God. This ... can't ... be ... happening.

Dry swallowing a pill, I stare transfixed at my phone. Keywords jump out at me like creepy clowns at a circus. Stepbrother. Forbidden. Taboo. *Incest.*

The last one is ridiculous. We're not even blood-related. Regardless, this is bad. So bad. I don't know if I'm strong enough, especially now, to weather the storm that's gonna come along with an article like this. This is probably why Merrick was calling earlier. Maybe to warn me? And if not, I wonder if he's seen this. I wonder what his feelings will be. Will he still wanna be with me? Wait. Forget whether or not he would still wanna be with me! Do I even wanna be with him?!

... Yes. Yes, I did. There are still things he needs to atone for. Questions he needs to answer. Things he needs to explain. I pull up his contact in my phone, and I'm seconds away from hitting the call button when I pause, thinking. Yes, I do wanna be with him, but for once, I don't want him to swoop in and save me. Even though we created this mess together, I need to prove to myself that I can deal with this on my own. That I'm strong enough to do it on my own.

Hearing a commotion outside, I get up and, on shaky legs, go to the bedroom window to look outside. Immediately withdrawing my head, I back myself flat against the wall. There's an entire gaggle of photographers and journalists outside my front gate. Thank God that my entire yard is gated because I have no doubt that if it wasn't, any one of those photographers would risk life and limb to peep their cameras through one of my windows.

"Shit, shit, shit." I chant to myself over and over. I know, of course, that that won't help. Taking a few deep breaths, I feel myself relax somewhat. I can tell that my medication is kicking in because the sheer number of people lurking outside my property doesn't seem that big of a deal now. My mother, on the other hand … that's gonna be a big deal. I'm going to have to either call her back or go see her later today. I opt for the phone call, the lesser of two evils.

I drop my head back against the wall, and take a deep breath. Looks like I'm on house arrest for the time being. Might as well make a pot of coffee and queue up some Netflix.

I'm sitting cross-legged on the couch in a pair of sleep shorts that have little rats on them and a t-shirt that reads "Morally Gray Is My Favorite Color". With a bowl of popcorn in my lap and reruns of Frasier on TV, I hear the back door open and close and know it's Siren. I don't jump when she uses her key to get inside without knocking or ringing the bell. With the amount of Xanax I've taken, I don't think I'd jump if an ax murderer decided to use the hide-a-key. I hated that I had to resort to medication to calm my nerves, but I also wasn't ashamed of it. Sometimes, people need help, just to get through life. I was one of those people.

After taking a shower, I'd come downstairs to put on some coffee, then called Siren while it was brewing. She hadn't had any idea what was going on either. I'd had to point her in the direction of the article, to which she'd simply replied, "Well, it was bound to happen." I didn't think that was very helpful, and I'd told her as much. After a good long talk, she'd promised to come over and keep me company until the gossip mongers dispersed. Warning her that the front gate was swarmed, she'd snuck in through the back by, very gracefully, I'm sure, climbing up on a bench that sat on the sidewalk just outside my side gate, then hopped over.

Coming into the living room, she looks at the half-empty bottle of wine on the table and, without saying another word, goes back into the kitchen, returning with a second bottle as well as an empty glass for herself. Sitting on the couch next to me, she reaches over, and takes the popcorn from my lap just as I've got a handful raised to stuff my face. Pausing, I turn to her, cheeks bulging like a squirrel storing up food for winter. I put on my best *what the fuck* face. In return, she bursts out laughing. Laughing myself, I try my best not to choke on a kernel of corn. I don't want my last moments to be spent choking on popcorn because I was eating my feelings.

The entire situation I currently find myself in isn't the least bit funny, but it somehow seems less pressing after medication and half a bottle of wine. I know I shouldn't be mixing the two, but desperate times call for desperate measures. Siren and I take turns with the popcorn bowl, and not much is said until an episode or two has gone by.

"So, you gonna call him?" she asks. I don't need to ask who the "*him*" is.

Sighing heavily, I say, "I don't know. I just feel so overwhelmed; Gloria still being missing, the Merrick situation, and don't even get me started on my mother. I tried to call her back a little while ago, and she wouldn't answer. She's probably in a drug-induced coma right now."

She nods slowly, as though processing everything I said, and then turns back to the TV without saying anything else. I don't tell her that it's my mother that worries me the most. Growing up, I got used to watching my back around her. I never was and still aren't sure why she didn't get rid of me after Uncle Remy died. And if not then, then why not after Dad ... I mean, James died? It never really made sense to me why she didn't just rid herself of her burden as it was clear that she knew how. And it's not as if she ever really loved me. I came to recognize that years ago. It's something I've made peace with, but I wonder if she somehow thought that if she kept me around and I grew up to be a carbon copy of her, that somehow her legacy would live on. Or maybe she just wanted to get me old enough to take out a life insurance policy on me. Who knew?

This thing with Merrick, though. I had a bad feeling that there would be serious repercussions from this. Not just in the society pages or with the various influential families that ran this city, but from my mother and Peter. Fuck. I'd forgotten all about Peter. I wonder if, even now, Merrick was dealing with backlash from his father. Sighing inwardly, I resign myself to the fact that I'm going to have to call him soon. We need to clear the air. He owes me an explanation, and maybe it's the wine talking, but I think I might be close to ready to hear it now.

A few hours later, as mid-afternoon comes around, Siren stands from the couch, stretching her arms over her head. The move pushes her ample cleavage up and into full view. I honestly didn't know how she wasn't having to beat the guys off with a stick. My friend was a stunner. To this day, I still wonder from time to time what happened to her to make her the way she is now. Commitment phobic and carefree. I know someone hurt her; that much is obvious. I've seen the scars on her back. The ones she's tried her best to hide by getting them covered by tattoos. I could only hope that the person who did that to her was currently rotting in Hell.

Arms lowering, she looks over at me and says, "I've gotta go, babe. We've got rehearsals tonight, and if I'm late again, the conductor will have a full-blown meltdown."

"No worries. I'll just be here, waiting for Daphne and Niles to get together and stuffing my face with junk food," I say.

Laughing, she leans down and kisses the top of my head. Walking back towards the door she came in through, she pauses halfway there. Turning around, she says, "You should call him. I bet he's miserable."

"Good," I grumble, though halfheartedly.

Chuckling under her breath again, she says, "It's too late for both of you. You're already too far gone."

As she leaves me with those parting words, I hear the back door open and then close again. I'm still sitting on the couch about 20 minutes later, when my text chime goes off. Looking down, I see it's from my mother. I inwardly cringe. She hates texting, so she must really be in a state.

Mother - You need to come to the house today. We need to discuss what's happened and what we're going to do for damage control.

Me - There are journalists camped out outside my house.

Mother - Well, you tell them you have no comment, then get over here!

Face pinched in annoyance, I stare at the texts for several long minutes. Realizing that she'll only keep nagging if I don't deal with her, I text her back.

Me - Give me an hour or two, and I'll be over.

Tossing my phone onto the couch, I lean my head back with a groan. I am so not up for this today. But I get up and head upstairs to change anyway. I just hoped I could find a way through that group of vultures outside without getting picked apart.

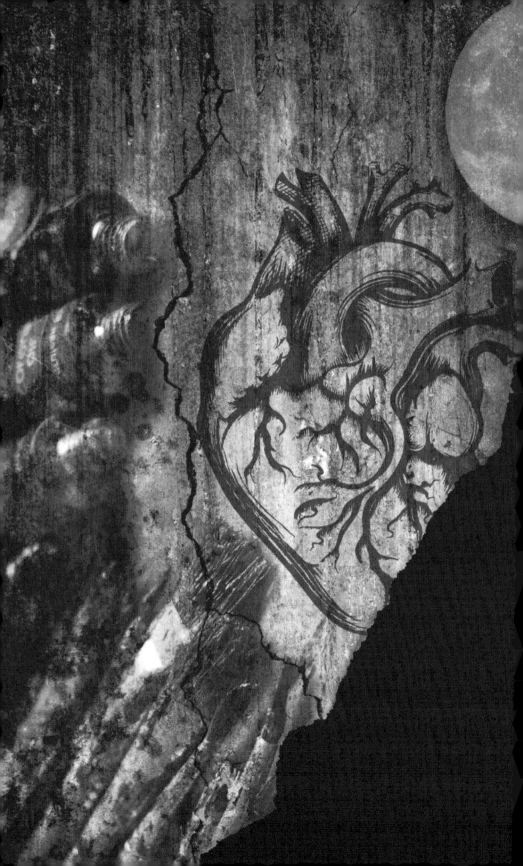

CHAPTER 37

Amelia

Standing on the front porch of the townhouse, I ring the doorbell and wait. It takes me a minute to remember that Gloria isn't here. That I won't see her face when the door finally opens. I'm suddenly overcome with a wave of sadness so strong it has tears springing to my eyes. Sniffling, I do my best to keep them from spilling over. I doubt my mother will be the one to answer the door because it would be beneath her, but just in case, I don't want her to see me with tears in my eyes. Not only would she love the opportunity to rip into me about something so stupid as how splotchy my face looks or how bloodshot my eyes are, but she would use my pain as an open wound to get under my skin. Like a starving gator, Suzanne can sense a wounded animal—or, in this case, a person—a mile away. She's already going to be irate enough with the current situation I've found myself in.

As one minute turns into two, then two turns into three, I look around the porch and surrounding sidewalk nervously. I find it weird that there aren't any reporters stalking my mother's door. Maybe because they know I don't live here anymore? Looking back at the still-closed door, my face turns down in a frown. Someone should've answered by now. If not my mother, then surely the maid. I do still have a key to the house, so I could always let myself in, but I'm not sure if I should. This house hasn't felt like my home in a very long time. Even when I was actively living here, there were just too many nasty memories for me to consider it a "home". Still, as I stand there, I get the feeling that something isn't right. Debating whether to just go in, I curse myself for not calling Merrick before deciding to come here. Even after everything that happened, I should've told him, but I know he wouldn't have wanted me to come. I know he would've actively tried to stop me. He's never trusted my mother any more than I trusted his father and with good reason. I'm sure at this point, they're both vultures circling overhead, waiting to hear of the death of our relationship so that they can swoop down and pick our bones clean. Today should be like Thanksgiving dinner for them.

This is stupid. Pulling my key ring from my sling bag, I quickly find the large ornate skeleton key that I know matches the lock to the front door. Unlocking it, I slowly push open the door. Doing so with caution, I stand on the porch for a second longer, looking into the dimly lit foyer. I can't get my feet to move. I have the hysterical thought that maybe they know something my brain doesn't. Leaning my head into the entryway, I peek around. All the rooms are dark, and I don't see anyone inside. Looking behind me, I glance back out to the sidewalk, then left and right, to see if any of the neighbors are out. I know it sounds stupid, but I would feel a lot better if someone saw me go inside the house. Looking back inside, I feel both wary and foolish, acting like a scared little girl who's afraid something's going to jump out of a dark corner and eat me alive. Well ... considering the nightmares I've witnessed in this house, it's not such a far-fetched idea.

Steeling myself, I make a decision. Stepping into the foyer, I slowly close the door behind me, and I immediately regret my decision as what little light there was spilling in through the open door is now gone. Reflexively, I reach behind me to flip the light switch near the door, hoping to illuminate the foyer. Flicking the switch back and forth, the terror building inside me starts to boil over when nothing happens. The lights don't come on. Stupidly, my shaking hand continues to move the switch up and down in the hopes that the chandelier above me will suddenly fill the darkened room with light. When my brain truly registers that what I'm doing isn't accomplishing anything, I glance to the left, where the front parlor is. It's completely dark in that room, no light spilling in from open curtains, no end table lamps turned on, nothing. Staring into that room, I can feel the rest of my insides begin to tremble. I start to shake my head back and forth as I make a move to turn around. I've seen enough horror movies to know this is exactly how the main female character dies. Useless pop culture knowledge aside, the idea of walking into that room is the very definition of nightmare fuel. No fucking way. As I turn to face the front door again, my hand barely touches the knob when I feel it. A sharp pinching pain in the side of my neck. I don't have time to wonder what caused the pain. I don't even have time to brace myself for the impact of my body hitting the floor. Before my legs even have a chance to give out from under me, my vision goes black and then … nothing.

Someone's calling my name. I can hear it, but it seems so far away. Distorted, like I'm at the bottom of a deep hole and the voice is overhead. All of a sudden, I'm jarred fully awake by a hard slap across my face. Crying out, the taste of copper fills my mouth, and I know my lip has been busted by whoever it was that just hit me. When my brain comes completely back online, other pain starts to register. There's a throbbing in my head, unlike any headache or migraine I've ever experienced before. In addition to the feeling of my brain doing somersaults in my skull, even the blood pooling in my mouth can't distract from how dry it feels. If I didn't know any better, I'd think it was packed with cotton balls. Still, without opening my eyes, I try to lift my hands to clutch my aching head, but for some reason, I can't. I tug, but I'm met with resistance. As the last remnants of fogginess dissipate, I realize that the reason I can't move my hands is because they're tired behind my back. My first instinct is blind panic. The need to thrash around in an effort to free myself is nearly overwhelming, but instead, I attempt to steady my breathing as the voice that seemed so distant and unintelligible, begins to come through clearer. I recognize it. It's Peter.

"Wake up, you stupid bitch! I know you can hear me!" He sounds enraged, but I don't miss the slight slurring at the end of some of his words. I lived with the man long enough to know when he was drunk.

I don't reply immediately, debating on the best course of action. If I open my eyes, I'll be better able to assess the situation, and maybe I can try to find a way out of this. But on the other hand, the sooner I appear fully conscious, the next phase of whatever this bastard has planned will begin. In the silence that follows, I hear a tap tap tapping sound. I don't know what's causing the noise, and I'm not sure I even wanna know. I feel so fucking stupid. I should've suspected something like this was going to happen. Though I am surprised that it was Peter who drugged me instead of my mother. I thought for sure, with Gloria's disappearance, that my mother had something to do with it and that it was only a matter of time before she decided I was too much of a liability to keep around. I guess Peter beat her to the punch, literally.

Tap Tap Tap.

There it is again.

Squinting my eyes open just a fraction, I try to take stock of the room. Peter is standing near the fireplace, his back to the flames roaring in the grate. I have the wayward thought that I must've been out for a while. I know that fire wasn't there before. As I follow the tapping sound to its source, I see he's got a gun in his hand. Oh my God. I watch as he taps the barrel of the gun against the marble top of the mantle. That's what was making that sound. Trying not to hyperventilate, I make another desperate attempt to free my hands where they've been zip-tied together behind my back. Considering my position in the room and the soft cushion underneath me, I realize I'm sitting on one of the sofas in the parlor. As if being in this room didn't already make me wanna throw up, and if I live through this, I'll never be able to set foot in this house, much less this room, ever again. I dart my eyes around the room, and see that besides Peter and myself, it's otherwise empty, and I wonder where my mother is. The texts I received earlier came from her phone, so I wonder if he's finally had one drink too many and done something to her. The normal emotions one should feel at the thought of something terrible happening to their mother are unsuspiciously absent. I don't feel anything. Well, besides foolishness at coming here in the first place and terror. Lots of terror. Strangely, not at the thought of dying. I've seen so much death in my life that I don't fear it the way I used to. What actually scares me is the idea of never seeing Merrick again, of him having to go on without me. Grief is a funny thing. If I've learned anything over the years, it's that grief never truly leaves you. You just learn to walk beside it. I've had to walk hand in hand with grief for so long. I don't want that kind of life for him. I wonder if—after everything that's happened—he regrets wasting so much time on me. I know I regret not telling him that I love him. I regret the last words I said to him. They play on a loop in my still-ringing head.

I have no idea who you are. I have no idea who you are. I have no idea who you are.

The eerie voice of my stepfather breaks through my inner turmoil. "Ah, so you *are* awake. Fucking finally. Do you know what a pain in the ass you've been? You're lucky I need to keep you alive to make this trade; otherwise, I would've put a bullet in your head, just like your psycho mother did to Remy Winston."

Knowing I have no choice now that he knows I'm awake, I open my eyes fully, but remain slumped on the couch so he won't be able to see my hands as I stealthily attempt to get out of the zip-ties that bind them together. I can feel the hard plastic of the restraints cutting into my skin. I can feel the chafing begin and know it won't be long before my wrists are a bloody mess. None of that matters now, though. Pausing for a moment as I process his words, I stare stunned. He knows? For how long? And why not confront my mother about it? He had to know he was in danger. But then again, he's no boy scout himself.

347

CANDICE CLARK

For years, I've secretly wondered if I was crazy for the things I saw in my head. Were they memories or the delusions of someone with mental illnesses they didn't even know they had? To hear Peter confirm one of those cases really brings home the fact that my mother was indeed the monster I've always thought her to be. And if I didn't make up Uncle Remy's death, then that means that I didn't imagine James Prescott's either. She poisoned him right in front of me. Even though, deep down, some part of me always knew these events were real, I feel sick to my stomach. Trying to concentrate on not throwing up, I take slow, deep breaths.

In through the nose, out through the mouth. In through the nose, out through the mouth.

Suddenly, something else Peter just said registers, and my breathing hitches. He said something about a trade. Oh God, I pray that Merrick isn't, even now, on his way here. If that's the trade Peter's talking about, then Merrick is in danger. There's no way Peter's gonna let either of us leave this house alive. It would be too detrimental to him. Merrick has to know that.

If the roles were reversed, would that stop you? No, it wouldn't.

Fighting the zip-ties with renewed purpose, I keep one eye trained on the gun in Peter's right hand. Seeing where my gaze is focused, he looks from me to the gun and back again.

"What? You wanna try to take this from me?" He gestures wildly with the gun, arms flailing. My flinch is reflexive and something I can't control, even though I know he gets off on fear. Peter sober is scary enough. Add booze and a firearm, and I wanna sink as far into the couch and away from that gun as possible. Seeming to regain his focus, he says, "You think you got you in you? That *killer* instinct? Does it run in the blood?" He's baiting me. I know he is. In addition to fear, he loves to taunt his victims. I remember the way he'd needle Merrick when we were younger, trying to break him down mentally before trying to take him apart with his fists. He used to say the most horrible things, about how worthless he was, about how his mom got cancer and didn't love him enough to

348

fight to stay alive. Peter's always been good at making you feel less than. It's one of the tricks in any good con man's arsenal. I know this, but I also know that if I can keep him talking, it may buy me precious minutes in order to get out of these restraints and ... do what? I have no idea. Try and find a weapon and fight him off? Make a run for it? Who the fuck knows. All I know is that I've gotta get loose before Merrick walks right into a trap.

Taking a steadying breath, I say, "You knew she was a killer, and you married her anyway? Why?"

He gives a dark chuckle. One completely devoid of real humor. "I heard the rumors. I didn't know in the beginning if they were true or not, but I also heard that she'd racked up from the last few husbands in their wills and from life insurance, so I figured I'd make her think I was the rich one, she'd marry me, then I'd off her before she had a chance to off me. Little did I know that the bitch was nearly broke. So, I had to stick it out for a while to let the new life insurance policies I took out on her ripen. In the meantime, I had to find another source of income while pretending to be the doting husband to one of the snobbiest cunts in this city."

"If all you needed to do was wait a bit for the heat of the life insurance policies to die down, why'd you stay for so long? And what other source of income?" I ask, trying not to let my face betray my elation as I manage to get one thumb out of the zip tie at my back.

"You're a nosy little bitch, aren't you? Why are you asking so many questions? You tryin' to get a taped confession?" This time, his laugh is full of humor as he glances to the side of the room. I follow his gaze, and see my bag lying on the plush cream carpet. Next to it is my cell phone. He knows I'm not recording him. He's just fucking with me.

Coming closer to me, he leans down until he's close enough for me to smell the scotch on his breath. Getting close to my ear, he says, "Maybe I'll answer your stupid questions if you give me a little something in return." Palming my breast with his free hand, he pinches my nipple hard. On instinct, I jerk back, but there's nowhere to go. Laughing, he says, "Tell you what. I promised you'd be alive, but I didn't necessarily say you'd be in one piece. Come on, give Daddy a little taste. Show me how tight that young pussy is, and maybe …" He trails off, building the suspense. I feel like my insides are coming apart. The way his hands touch me, it's Jake all over again. Only this time, I don't want Merrick to come to my rescue.

"… maybe I'll tell you where Gloria is." he finishes.

My breath catches in my lungs. Of all the things I expected him to say … that wasn't even in the ballpark. I'm so confused. Up to now, I'd been convinced beyond a shadow of a doubt that my mother was the one responsible for Gloria's disappearance. But, now … is it possible that Peter's the one that took her? Knowing what I have to do, I lower my gaze, biting my bottom lip between my teeth. Doing my best to project a picture of both innocence and carnality.

Gaze trained on my mouth, he says, "Yeah, look at you, pretty girl. You want it, don't you, you little slut. What happened? My boy couldn't satisfy you? You took a test drive in the newer model, but I bet you really wanted to take a ride in a classic, didn't you?" Licking his lips, he rubs the front of his pants, palming his erection. I do my best to hold down the bile, trying to climb its way up my throat.

As I fight the nausea down, I put on my best husky tone that I pray belies the fear and loathing I feel inside and say, "Maybe. I might be persuaded to see what you've got under the hood. If you tell me what happened to Gloria." I have no idea where I'm getting this car banter from. So many late nights of watching restoration show reruns, I guess. I thank God for it now, though.

Grinning, he takes a step back and automatically, I let out the breath I didn't know I'd been holding. Continuing his walk backward, he keeps his eyes trained on me, raking his gaze down my body as if he can already see me naked. The look is just another violation to add to my long list. I begin to wonder where he's going until he says, "You wanna know where Gloria is?" Disappearing down the hallway, I hear a door open and then close. Within a few seconds, he's back. "Here you go," he says, dragging a bound and gagged Gloria behind him. My first instinct is to jump up and help her. But I know I can't. I'm useless right now. I can only watch with wide eyes as he leads her over to one of the armchairs nearby, shoving her down hard into the seat.

"See? She's here and alive. I found out your mommy dearest planned to off me just like she did to her other husbands. See, she's been putting arsenic in my scotch bottles. Not much to start, but gradually increasing the dosage. She's actually stupid enough to believe that the cops would think I'd died of complications from the booze instead of what she put in them. I kept wondering why I was feeling sick off and on. Didn't take a genius to figure out something was off. So, I had several things in this house tested for poison. Turns out, I was right. So, naturally, I knew I needed some kinda leverage over Suzanne. That's where old Gloria came in. I overheard her on the phone with that piece of shit son of mine. One of the two only living witnesses to some of Suzanne's horrible misdeeds. I knew if I took Gloria, people would suspect her, not me. I also knew it was only a matter of time before they took her down. Since I have Gloria now, Suzanne will fork over every dime in her account and let me leave, or I give Gloria straight to the feds. I mean, I have some money put away, but that's nothing compared to what your mother will give me to keep me quiet. Every last penny she has left from husband number four ... or prison. Sounds like a good deal to me. As for you ... I don't think it'll take that worthless boy of mine to realize you're gone and come looking for you. I'll make sure to get rid of him too, before I go. Little shit's always been a liability."

As he finishes his little speech, I watch him walk over to the sidebar, setting the gun down long enough to pour himself another drink. I can't figure out if he's brilliant or absolutely insane. Just as I have that thought, I manage to wriggle my right hand out of the zip tie behind my back. Keeping my hands where they are for the time being, I still keep my eyes on Peter and the gun he hasn't picked up again yet.

Movement out of the corner of my eye has me darting my gaze to the right. Seeing a shadow in the hallway outside of the parlor, I watch as my mother peeks around the corner. Putting her finger to her lips, she silently tells me not to give away the fact that she's here. I'm not sure which one of them I'd rather have to face off with, but I decide to stay put and see how this plays out. I just pray whatever's gonna happen happens before Merrick shows up.

Taking advantage of Peter's lapse in judgment by setting the gun down in favor of booze, my mother decides now's the time to make her move. Coming around the corner, a gun of her own drawn, she says, "Oh, Peter. What a mess you've made of everything."

Spinning around, glass still in hand, scotch goes sloshing as he makes a move toward his own gun. As she raises hers higher, Suzanne takes several quick steps into the room, bringing the gun into closer proximity to Peter, making her target much bigger and lessening the chance of a near miss. He knows it, too. Putting his hands into the air, he takes a few steps away from the gun.

"Suzanne, baby, there you are. I've been looking all over for you," he lies.

Not buying it for a second, Suzanne makes a tsking sound before saying, "Don't bullshit me, Peter. I heard everything you just said, and now that I know your little plan, it makes it so much easier to justify killing you."

Peter scoffs, but I can see the sweat starting to bead up on his forehead. Darting my eyes from my mother to Peter, then to the gun not three feet from me, I debate how I'm going to do this. If I make a move for the gun, I know I can get to it before Peter, but then there's nothing to stop my mother from shooting me. I doubt she'd even blink twice. Then she'd kill Peter and probably Gloria too, just for good measure. If I make a run at my mother, there's a good chance I'll be shot in the scuffle, and then there's nothing to stop Peter from going for the other gun and killing all three of us. The moral? Either way, I'm fucked. The only thing I have in my favor is the element of surprise. They don't know my hands are undone, so whatever I decide to do has to be quick. I suddenly have the thought that if I can distract my mother long enough for Peter to wrestle the gun from her, I can go for the other gun myself and possibly have enough time to shoot Peter before he can get to us.

Decision made, and I address my mother for the first time since she entered the room, "Mom, help me, please," I plead. Taking her eyes off Peter for a moment, she looks at me with a cold stare.

"Amelia, this is all your fault, you know. If you hadn't decided to go and fuck your stepbrother, none of this would be happening. Now, there's no way to get rid of this mess except by wiping the entire board clean."

Wiping the entire board clean? Is she saying she plans to kill all of us? Again, I'm not the least bit surprised. The only concern I have at the moment is trying to prevent as much bloodshed as possible. Before I have a chance to respond, however, Peter takes advantage of my mother's momentary lapse in focus. Darting towards her as though he plans to physically take the gun from her, I flinch at the deafening sound of the gun in her hand discharging. Watching, I see a dark red stain start to bleed through the front of Peter's shirt. When he looks down, he almost seems surprised at the gaping wound in his chest. The look of shock is frozen on his face as he falls hard to the floor. As I look on in horror, a dark pool begins to seep out from underneath him, leaching into the plush carpet. My breath catches in my throat, and I have the thought that it's Uncle Remy all over again. Except this time, my mother has no intention of calling the police. She now has two witnesses to get rid of.

"Son of a bitch!" she screeches. Whirling on Gloria and I, she points the gun in our direction. I know I'm only going to get one shot at this, and learning from Peter's mistakes, I quickly roll off the couch, diving down low to take my mother's legs out from under her. Not expecting the move, or at the very least, not expecting me to go for her lower half as opposed to the gun itself, there's a split second where time seems to stand still. Then everything is happening all at once. Knocking my mother's legs out from under her, she falls to the floor, losing her grip on the gun. We both watch as it tumbles across the carpet, landing several feet away. I can hear Gloria trying to cry out past the gag in her mouth. There's also a loud bang from somewhere else in the house, but I can't allow myself to become distracted. Grappling for purchase, gripping handfuls of the plush carpet, I attempt to pull myself towards the gun. I'm nearly there when I feel a brutal tug at my hair, and I'm suddenly pulled backward. I let out a yell of pain and surprise and fall, giving my mother time to reach the gun first. Gripping it tightly in her hands, she leaps on top of me, pointing the gun directly at my chest. Using both hands, I grip the barrel of the gun, trying to wrestle it away. We're in such close proximity now that the gun is pressed between our bodies as we both fight for dominance. Suddenly, there's another explosion of sound as the gun goes off. Loose hands fall from the barrel, and as I peer down at the space between my mother's body and my own, a bright red stain begins to form on my upper chest. Two for two. The entire scenario seems to play out in slow motion, though some rational part of my brain knows that the battle couldn't have taken more than a minute or so from start to finish. Dark spots begin to swim in my vision, effectively blocking out my mother as he hovers over me, frozen in place. I wanna reach up and shove her off me. I wanna try to get the gun away from her again so she can't do any more harm. But I can't. My limbs feel heavy, and I just can't seem to drum up the energy to do anything more than turn my head towards the doorway to the parlor, where there seems to be a big commotion. Warm chocolate eyes find mine as they begin to slide closed.

The last sound I hear before I pass out is a masculine roar of utter agony. Then blackness.

CHAPTER 38

Merrick

I feel like my brain just stopped functioning. When I'd gotten the call from Alexi earlier, saying that the lab had confirmed the evidence I'd given him to be legitimate and that the FBI would be raiding the townhouse today, with the intention of arresting Suzanne for murder and my father for embezzlement, fraud, and money laundering, among other things, I'd been elated. Then Siren's name popped up on my caller ID, and I knew, even before answering, that something was wrong. I could count on one hand how many times Siren has ever reached out to me over the years, and every single one of those times, had been an emergency. Normally, it had to be a matter of life or death in order for her to wanna talk to me. So the instant I saw her name, I felt a ball of lead drop in my stomach.

Picking up, I'd decided to forgo the bullshit pleasantries and instead just said, "What's wrong?"

That's when she'd told me. Told me that Amelia had gotten a text from Suzanne saying she had to come over to figure out the best PR angle to play "preserve the family name". Then she tells me that she hasn't heard from her since and that that was hours ago. She had a gut feeling that something was terribly wrong, and now so did I. Trying to think past the sudden buzzing in my ears, I'd somehow managed to dial Alexi and ask him if the team would be ready to move in now, as opposed to later. If not, I was going alone. I didn't give a shit about the law or protocols. The woman I loved was in danger, and if there was even a remote possibility that I could get there before something catastrophic happened, I was going. That's when Alexi told me that the bugs in the house picked up intel that Amelia might be inside. He was already mobilizing the team, and by the time I sped through Charleston traffic, nearly killing several tourists in the process, and arrived at the townhouse, they were already there and getting ready to move in.

Waiting while each agent moves into position around the house is literal torture. They're taking too long. I've got to get inside. Suzanne could be doing God knows what to Amelia, and there was no one in the world better equipped to save and avenge her than I was. Just as I'm on the verge of losing my shit, strapping up with borrowed weapons and blasting my way in, the men out front signal that they're ready to break the door down.

Walking up to me, Alexi hands me a bulletproof vest. He can tell by the look on my face that there's no way in fuck I'm sitting this one out. I appreciate the fact that he doesn't try to talk me out of going inside with them. I remind myself to thank him later if we make it out alive. Handing me a gun that's surprisingly heavy for its size, we cautiously make our way up the front steps and to the door. Just as my feet hit the welcome mat, there's a loud pop from somewhere inside the house, followed by an incoherent shriek and then the sounds of a struggle. I can hear feminine cries of pain and the sound of glass and furniture breaking. My heart freezes in my chest, and my lungs stop working properly. It takes me several seconds to remember how to breathe, and then one of the SWAT team is breaking the door in, and agents are spilling into the house like a plague.

As I step in behind Alexi, gun drawn, I see an empty foyer. Just as I'm about to call out for Amelia, the sound of a second gunshot splits the air. Pinpointing the area of origin as the front parlor, I quickly sprint across the foyer and enter the room, gun pointing directly at a back that

I recognize as Suzanne's. She's crouched on the floor, straddling another body that's lying prone underneath her, partially covered by her hunched form. I can tell immediately, based on the tie-dyed pants, that it's Amelia she's got pinned down. Peering around Suzanne's body, I can just make out Amelia's face as I enter the room. Our eyes meet briefly, before I round Suzanne, who finally looks up to see my gun pointed directly at her face. Putting her hands in the air, she drops the weapon she was holding, stands and stumbles back, right into Alexi's chest. Leaving him to deal with that bitch, I turn back to Amelia to help her up off the floor and into my arms. Whatever our issues, we'll work them out. We've come too far for me to just give up and let her go.

The area is clear now that Suzanne is being cuffed and read her rights, and I finally get my first good look at Amelia. It's then that I notice the large patch of red blooming on her chest, soaking the white material of her top. The contrast between the bright red and white fabric is stark. My eyes fly up to meet hers again, only to find them closed. Letting out an inhuman roar laced with rage and agony, I crouch down next to my woman.

"No, no, no," I say, pressing my bare hands over what I can now see is a bullet wound in the upper part of her chest.

"Wake up, baby. You can't go to sleep. Open your eyes for me, please!" I know I sound desperate, my voice pleading, but I don't care. Nothing matters except stopping the flow of blood and getting her to a hospital.

"Someone fucking call 9-1-1!!" I shout. There's movement all around us, and I vaguely hear someone talking into a radio—requesting an ambulance—but I can't focus on anything except for the fact that Amelia's eyes are still closed. Keeping pressure on the wound with one hand, I take the other and lightly smack the side of her face.

"Mia, baby, open your eyes! Stay with me!" I plead, still lightly tapping her cheek. I can't breathe. I feel as though every drop of blood leaking from her takes an equal piece of me with it. If she goes, I go. If she dies, there won't be anything powerful enough to keep me here.

Lashes lifting, her eyes suddenly flutter open. Blinking rapidly, as though she can't focus on anything, her gaze swings around the room until it lands on my face.

"Merrick?" she croaks out.

"Yes, baby. It's me. I'm here. You're gonna be okay. Help is coming. Just stay with me."

"It's okay. It doesn't hurt. I'm just ... cold. Can you get me a blanket?"

Panic flaring, I apply more pressure to her wound with my right hand, slipping my left under her neck to lift her head slightly, raising her face closer to mine so all she can see are my eyes.

"Do you remember what I told you?" I ask, gaze boring into hers. The beautiful green that I love so much appears dull and unfocused now. "I told you, there's no place God could take you that I wouldn't follow. Do you understand? If your heart stops, so will mine. It's just you, me, and this heartbeat, remember? There's nothing in the world more important right now than keeping that heartbeat going."

A small smile touches her lips, but her eyes start to flutter closed again. Desperately, I lift one of her tiny hands, placing her palm right over my heart. Over the emerald tattoo that she knows is underneath my shirt. Eyes focusing on mine again, I feel her nails dig into my shirt. For a split second, I'm encouraged to believe that she's gonna be fine. The paramedics will get here, and they'll get her to the hospital and fix whatever needs fixing.

That is, until the hand that had just been gripping my shirt releases, falling limply to the floor. The sound that bubbles up my throat is one of unimaginable pain. "Where the fuck is the ambulance?!" I scream behind me in the general direction of the foyer.

Leaning down, I stroke the side of Amelia's face. She feels so clammy, and the color has drained from her cheeks. I kiss lips that have gone pale along with the rest of her face.

"You can't leave me now. You never told me you love me. If I'm everything, then so are you. You're supposed to give me a lifetime to show you that." Remembering the painting, I say, "If I have your heart and it beats for me, then I say when it stops. And that day isn't today. Do you hear me??"

I get no response. The rise and fall of her chest is slower now, barely discernible through her blood-soaked shirt. Feeling wetness run down my face, I know I'm crying. I don't care who sees. Every single tear I let fall holds a hope, or a dream, or a plan that I had for us. A drop for every child we're never gonna have. A drop for the wedding dress I won't get to see her in. A drop for the plantation home that will sit empty now. Releasing a sob, I cover my face with my free hand.

"Sir! Excuse me, sir! I need you to move out of the way!" a man's voice says behind me. Dropping my hand, I look up to see two paramedics rushing in. Stumbling back, all I can do is stand there as I watch them work at saving Amelia's life. At saving my life.

Hours later, or maybe it was minutes? Days? I don't know anymore. All I know, as I sit in the hospital waiting room, is that I've never felt more alone. Even when I was younger and I'd have to hide in the cellar to escape my father, I had memories and plans to keep me company. My mind was always working. Whether to dissociate from the situation by remembering my mother or dreaming up what I'd be when I got older. Of places I'd travel to, money I'd have, people I'd meet. Right now, though, the thought of reliving memories is terrifying. I don't want to have to rely on memories of Amelia to keep my company. To keep me warm. Why is it always so fucking cold in hospitals? Putting my head in my hands, I tug at the ends of my hair. Maybe if I pull hard enough, I'll open my eyes, and this will all have been a bad dream. When I lower my hands, however, the nightmare remains. As I look down, I notice for the first time that my hands are covered in dried blood. Amelia's blood.

They wouldn't let me ride in the ambulance with her. Once they'd shoved me out of the way, I'd had to watch while they put her on oxygen and tried to stem the flow of blood. I vaguely heard the paramedics throwing out terms like "hypovolemic shock" and "25% blood loss". I didn't know what any of that meant. I just knew she wasn't waking up. As I stared at her lying on the floor of that parlor, I just wanted her eyes to open again. Five men. Paramedics and firemen. Worked together to get her onto a gurney and out into the waiting ambulance. Even through my shock, I'd tried to convince them to let me go with her, but they said there wouldn't be enough room and they needed the space to work. As much as I hated watching those doors close in my face, I knew the smart thing to do was to let them do their jobs. I'm not sure how long I stood in the street. I guess I should be thankful that I wasn't hit by a car, but I wasn't thankful. I wasn't thankful at all. I still wasn't sure that I wouldn't walk back into traffic by the end of the night. No one would tell me anything. They just kept saying she was in surgery and that someone would be out to speak with me. I both wished for that and dreaded it.

Scrubbing my blood-soaked hands down the legs of my pants, I stand up and begin to pace the room. I've been alternating between this and staring blankly at the wall for God knows how long. Earlier, as I'd stood in the street staring at the place where the ambulance tail lights had disappeared, someone had stepped into my line of vision and wrapped their arms around me. It took me a minute to realize it was Deacon. I had no idea when he'd come or how he even knew to come. Maybe Alexi called him? I wasn't sure about that either. I wasn't sure about a lot of things. Like what had ultimately happened to Suzanne. I knew my father was dead. I'd seen him lying on the floor, his blood pooling around him, and as I'd watched the paramedics work on Amelia, I'd had the irrational thought that I didn't want his blood touching her. Crime scene or not, if that puddle had spread too close, I was going to push it back by whatever means necessary. He'd done enough damage already. But Suzanne though? Her actions may have cost me everything, and if that ends up being the case, I'll make her pay with her life. An eye for an eye. Revenge may be the only thing that kept me alive. At least for a while.

As I turn on my heels to retrace my steps back to the other side of the room, I nearly run headlong into Deacon. He's holding two coffee cups, and if my reflexes were better, I might've been able to save him from the burn caused by the hot liquid sloshing over the rim of the cup. As it is, all I can do is mutter an apology as I watch him grit his teeth in pain. Taking one of the cups from him, I bring it to my lips but then lower it down again without even taking a sip.

"Did you see any doctors on your way in? Did anyone say anything?" I ask. I don't even try to disguise the hint of desperation in my tone. He's seen me at my worst, just like I've seen him the same.

Shaking his head, he gives me a sad smile. That face people make when they expect the worst but don't want to say it out loud. I guess that was good because I didn't wanna hear it. I refuse to accept the possibility. It just didn't seem possible that the world could go on without her. The fact that she'd still been alive when she reached the hospital had to mean something, right? If anyone knew how strong she was, it was me. She hadn't lived through so much just to die before we had a chance to enjoy life. Hell, so had I. Didn't I deserve some happiness? Hadn't I earned her?? Not for the first time tonight, I send up a silent curse at God. *You've never done anything for me. You owe me this.*

Deacon's voice breaks into my blasphemous thoughts. Placing his hand on my shoulder, he says, "Hey man, you should go home and shower. Maybe change your clothes? I can stay here in case there's any change."

Shrugging off his hold, I say, "I'm not leaving. I have to be here when she comes out."

Staring at me for a long moment, he nods. "I'll go to your place and get you some clothes then. You can wash up in the bathroom and change."

Sitting back down in the chair, I stare vacantly at him. Or maybe through him would be a more accurate statement. I know he's only trying to help, but I can't find it in me to fake niceties right now. Standing there for another moment, he lets out a heavy sigh and then leaves. More time passes. No one comes.

Suddenly, a pair of legs encased in black enter my line of vision. Glancing up, I see Alexi standing in front of me. Sitting down in the seat next to me, he stares off in the same direction I do, at the double doors that lead to the operating rooms.

A few minutes pass before he finally speaks, saying, "She's gonna make it."

Hearing someone else say it out loud somehow holds more weight than all the times I've repeated it to myself. Looking over at him, I ask, "How can you be sure?"

"Linii sud'by perepleteny syurprizami." *Fate lines are twisted with surprises.*

I open my mouth to respond—I'm not sure with what—when the double doors ahead of us open. A man, wearing scrubs and a cap covering dark hair flooded with silver, walks towards us. Standing up sharply, I feel myself wobble a little on my feet. A strong hand grips the back of my elbow to steady me. Looking over at Alexi, I give him a nod in thanks, then turn back to the doctor who's been sent to deliver my fate.

"Mr. Stratford?" he asks, glancing between myself and Alexi as though unsure who is who.

"I'm Mr. Stratford," I say. My voice sounds hoarse like I've been screaming out loud for the last several hours, instead of just inside my own head.

Glancing over at Alexi, the doctor appears uncomfortable for a moment, as if he isn't sure if I want him to speak in front of others. Giving him a nod of encouragement, I wait with bated breath for him to start talking.

The doctor takes in a large gulp of air and then releases a heavy sigh. I feel my heart sink to my feet, and the urge to simply melt into the floor hits like a ton of bricks. She's dead. Feeling my insides begin to tremble, I suddenly can't get in a good breath of air. It's only when the doctor begins to talk I realize it's because I've been holding my breath this entire time.

"She's alive," he says. I have the urge to stop him simply to make him repeat what he just said. As though I need to have it reaffirmed in order for it to be true. Before I can do that, however, he continues, "We lost her twice on the table but got her back. It was touch and go for a while after that. She'd lost a lot of blood. She had to have several transfusions during surgery. The bullet entered through the area just above her heart, making a clear exit through the area between her shoulder blades. If the bullet had been three centimeters lower, she would've died almost instantly. The fact that pressure was applied to the wound right away and that no one tried to move her kept her from losing even more blood than she did. I'm not gonna say that she's totally out of the woods because the next 24-48 hours is critical, but she's young and strong. I think the chances are good that she'll make a full recovery, given time."

As he finishes speaking, I slowly sink back down into the chair, burying my face in my hands. The flood of emotions is so strong that I can't stop the sobs from escaping. Neither the doctor nor Alexi says anything. Hell, I don't even know if they're still here. I can't focus on anything except the fact that she's alive, and despite Suzanne's best efforts, she's still here with me. I stay that way for several minutes. Feeling a hand on my shoulder, I look up to meet Alexi's mismatched eyes again. Glancing around, I see that the doctor is gone. I would imagine he sees shit like this all the time. He doesn't wanna stick around for the theatrics.

"The doctor said she's still heavily sedated, and after a period of a few hours to monitor her, they'll be moving her to a room. He said you'll be able to go in and see her then."

I didn't hear any of this, so wrapped up in my own elation and the emotions taking me over. I silently thank Alexi for being here. If it wasn't for him and the rest of the FBI storming the house, Amelia would most certainly be dead. For some reason, I don't think the way he's behaved towards us is typical FBI protocol, but either way, I'm grateful for everything he's done. Opening my mouth to tell him so, he simply gives a shake of his head and offers me a small smile. I'm not sure why but the smile reminds me of what he said before, about fate lines being twisted with surprises. If I wasn't a person who believed in fate before, I am now. It was fate that brought Amelia into my life when I needed her most. It was fate for me to fall in love with her before I even really knew what love was. It was fate that saved her life and subsequently, mine. I'm not sure what condition she'll be in when I'm able to go in and see her or if she'll even want to see me after all the lies I've told. All the secrets I've kept. Regardless, the second I'm allowed, I have to at least see for myself that she's okay to reassure myself that everything the doctor said was true. Resolving myself, I make the decision to do something that I never thought I'd be capable of doing. I'm going to give her the space and time she needs to heal and hope that during that process, she realizes that our fate lines were destined to intersect, that those lines run deep throughout the body and straight to our hearts. My line to her heart and her line to mine, and I have to give her time to figure that out on her own so that when she's ready, she can reach out and tug on those lines to bring me back to her.

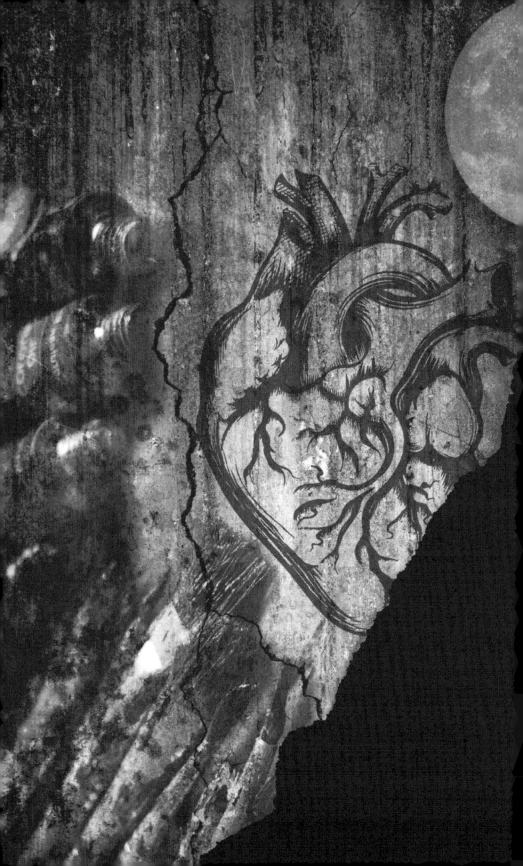

CHAPTER 39

Amelia

Beep. Beep. Beep.

The unknown noise breaks through my consciousness first. Right after that comes the pain. *Fuck!* Everything hurts. My chest feels like it's on fire, and out of reflex, I try to bring my hand up to see what's causing that pain, but it feels like my arm weighs a thousand pounds. Somewhere between the incessant beeping and the pain, I have the thought that if I just open my eyes, I'll be able to see what's wrong with me. That seems to be a monstrous task. By sheer force of will, I crack my eyelids open, but everything appears blurry for several long minutes. Blinking hard, I dart my eyes around the room, trying to take in the details of where I am. It looks like a hospital. Tilting my head towards the beeping sound, I see that it's coming from a monitor showing my blood pressure, oxygen saturation, and heart rate, the last of which appears to be the cause of the beeps. I'm definitely in a hospital.

Rolling my head in the opposite direction, I see a figure curled up on a chair that sits on the right side of my bed. It doesn't look like the chair was meant to be this close, but as if whoever the figure belongs to pulled it from its designated spot near the window. Squinting my eyes, the person's features begin to come into better focus. It's Siren. She has her head resting on a pillow that's propped up on the arm of the chair, and she's covered in a thin hospital blanket. She must be freezing. I can feel the weight of several blankets covering me, and I'm still cold. I've always hated how cold hospitals are. I wonder how long I've been here. Based on the dark circles under Siren's closed lids, I'm guessing for a while. Laying there, I try to wrack my brain, attempting to piece together the events that brought me here. At first, there's nothing. I know the memories are there, but it's as though they're floating in my peripheral vision, just out of reach. Closing my eyes again, I concentrate hard on reaching those floating bubbles. One minute, I'm reaching out, then without warning ... POP. Suddenly, the bubbles around me are popping all at once and I'm bombarded by images. Peter with a gun. Gloria tied up and gagged. My mother shooting Peter. My mother shooting me. Then Merrick ... oh my God, where is Merrick?? Opening my mouth, I let out a small cry. A cry full of fear, pain, and regret. The noise must alert Siren because when I open my eyes again, I can see her form hovering over me through the tears spilling over.

"Amelia? Are you okay? What hurts?? I'll go get the doctor!" She sounds panicked. Yes, everything hurts, but the pain that's causing these tears isn't the type that can be eased with the push of a syringe. Well ... maybe that's not entirely true, but at the moment I don't want to numb away this hurt. I want to know if Merrick is alright. And I just want to cry everything out and purge my system of the misery surrounding what happened.

Licking my dry lips, I say, "No, don't. I'm okay."

Easing back down into the chair, she grips my hand in a tight hold. Giving her a reassuring squeeze, I say, "How long have I been out?"

"Well, you've woken up a few times, but you were so doped up and groggy that I don't think you knew what was going on around you. This is the first time you've been conscious enough to speak. All in all, you've been unconscious for four days."

Four days?? Again, my thoughts turn to *where is Merrick?* Looking around the room, my brows pinch together when I don't see anyone else there. No hulking figure standing over me, demanding that I live. That

I tell him how much I love him. No. Maybe I imagined that? It's so difficult to tell what's real and what isn't. Looking back to Siren, I give her a questioning look at the same time that another tear rolls down my cheek.

"He's alright. He was here. For the first two days, he wouldn't leave. He showered and changed in the bathroom there." She indicates a closed door on the wall opposite my bed. "It was only after the first 48 hours, when the doctors told us you were out of the woods, that he finally went home. He told me to tell you that he was giving you some time and space to think about things, whatever that means. Oh, and he said to follow the beat? Which I'm guessing is an inside thing, seeing as it makes zero sense for you to be dancing right now."

Staring off into space, I think about her words. She doesn't understand. I can tell by the way her forehead wrinkled with confusion when she said it. How could she possibly understand? I've barely had time to come to terms with the reality of who Merrick is, much less actually process my feelings on the subject and decide whether this is something I can live with or not. *Live with.* I remind myself that I almost didn't get the chance to even make that choice.

Follow the beat.

Letting out a heavy sigh, I close my eyes. I really want to talk to Siren. To tell her everything that happened at the townhouse. Unfortunately, that's my last conscious thought before the darkness of exhausted sleep drags me back under.

It's been a week since I was shot. In all that time, I haven't seen Merrick once. Siren has been the most constant by my side, but I've also gotten several visits from Alexi, both in Agent mode and on a friendly basis. I think it was a little bit of both that pushed him into telling me about Merrick's alter ego. *The Black Knight.* After assuring me that he was the only one within the FBI who had made the connection and that that knowledge of that connection would stop with him, I felt slightly better knowing that Merrick wouldn't be getting himself arrested. Gloria has also come a few times, the first of which she spent crying and apologizing for everything that happened. After explaining her role in how things unfolded, I know she feels an immense measure of guilt. I don't fault her, and I told her that. The more I've thought about things, the more I've made my peace with the idea that everything happened the way it was supposed to happen. Peter was a plague on this Earth, and many lives will be made better by the fact that he's no longer here. For his treatment of Merrick alone, I hope he's currently rotting in Hell. My mother is another matter. Her penance will be paid in half measures. Part of it will be doled out during her remaining years alive, which she'll spend sitting in prison. The other part will be whatever happens after death. Either way, I know her darkened soul will never make it to Heaven. I've come to terms with that fact as well, and I've stopped the "what ifs" that have followed me throughout my life. What if I'd been a better daughter? What if she'd never remarried? What if I'd gotten her help ... therapy, medication, whatever? *What if.*

The truth is, I don't care anymore. The days of inner persecution are over. It was never my responsibility to save her or to prevent all the terrible things she did. She chose that path. All I can do is choose my own and hope that the choices I make are the right ones. I have to start thinking with my heart rather than my head.

Follow the beat.

I know where the beats lead. They lead straight to a man who's lied to me consistently, hidden things from me, and only shown me half of who he really is. They also lead to a man who held me while I cried, protected me when I was in danger and stared into my eyes while we made love. Most importantly, they lead to a man whose chest kicks wildly, only for me. I've done a lot of thinking over the last week, and the conclusion I've come up with? I'm in love with a thief. Not only one that steals art and gems, but a thief that's stolen sacred moments and kisses, and any alternative ideas about who I'd choose to grow old with. He's taken from me, but he's also given. He's given so much of himself. He's let me burrow my way beneath his skin, occupy all of his waking thoughts, and taken life-threatening risks to secure my happiness. The truth is, if I'm honest with myself, I'm not mad at Merrick anymore. While his actions may be somewhat questionable, his motives aren't. They're sweet and honorable and bursting at the seams with love.

I'm getting released from the hospital today. The doctors said that I've made wonderful progress, and with some more rest and maybe some physical therapy down the line, I'm well on my way to a full recovery. Pausing in the act of changing from the dreadful hospital gown into a pair of yoga pants and a t-shirt, I stare at my naked chest and the now very visible scar near the area where my heart lies. Placing my hand over the scar, I can feel the thump, thump, thump of my heartbeat. Smiling to myself, I know exactly where I'll end up. It was a foregone conclusion, really. Despite the things we had to hash out and the tough conversation we were going to have to have, there was no place I'd rather be and no one else I'd rather make a life with. My heart beat in time with his. Maybe it always had, and it took almost losing that beat entirely for me to realize that.

Gingerly pulling the t-shirt over my head, I slip my feet into a pair of ballet flats and exit the bathroom. I could hear it ... the beats. Wherever they led, I would follow.

CHAPTER 40

Merrick

My fucking can opener was broken. Throwing the thing across the wide expanse of marble countertop, I glare at the half-opened can of soup in front of me. I swear to God, if it wasn't for the fact that I'd literally die if I didn't eat, I'd throw my hands up in the air and say, "What's the damn point?"

I thought the period of time following the day that Amelia found me at the plantation house was bad. Turns out, I didn't even know what bad was. For a week now, I've lived in Hell. Granted, a Hell of my own making, but Hell nonetheless. I get no sleep, have barely eaten, showered every other day at best, and resembled something close to a caveman at this point. Did I give a shit? No. In truth, I was miserable. It's taken every ounce of willpower I possess not to go up to the hospital. I've been getting regular updates from Alexi, Deacon, and even Siren. The curvy little brunette had paid me a visit three days ago when I was only halfway through my transformation into the epic representation of the Neanderthal I am today. The moment I opened the door to my apartment, I knew. I could tell by her face that she knew everything. Then she'd taken one look at my pitiful state, and she'd spared me what I was sure was a tongue lashing the likes of which this world has never seen. Sighing and shaking her head, she'd pushed her way inside and made herself busy cleaning up the mess that was my apartment. While she did that, she barked orders at me to go shower, shave, and change my clothes because she could "smell the despair from a mile away". I could've fought her, but I knew it would've been futile and really, who had the fucking energy? Not me. So I'd cranked the shower to hotter than Hell and put on fresh clothes after. I hadn't bothered to shave, and she made no mention of it when I finally exited my bedroom, entering a now clean living room and kitchen. Granted, a living room devoid of furniture, which still hadn't been replaced since my painting-induced rampage. After forcing me to eat something, she'd made herself comfortable on the one remaining couch, and I knew, whether I liked it or not, I was going to have to have a conversation with her and convince her that my intentions were good even if my actions weren't. We'd talked it out, and she'd actually given me an encouraging smile before leaving.

Now, two days later, I was nearly back where I started. Granted, I'd been putting my dirty clothes in the hamper instead of just dropping them on the floor, and I'd been putting my dishes in the dishwasher instead of leaving them lying on every available surface. But in terms of appearance, I still behaved and looked ridiculously feral. I knew it. My beard was no longer a five o'clock shadow but had turned into full-blown scruff. My eyes were bloodshot from lack of sleep, and all I wanted to do in this moment was eat a damn can of Campbell's Chunky, yet it seemed that the world was conspiring to put me out of my misery.

At the sound of my doorbell, I hang my head and actually groan out loud. If that was Siren again, I was going to call the cops and have her arrested. The woman was too bossy for her own good. Making my way over to the door, I open the panel on the wall to view the camera and the image of who was standing on my doorstep. Feeling all the moisture in my mouth suddenly dry up, I stare at the little monitor, sure I'm imagining what I see on the screen. It's Amelia. Here, at my door. Shaking myself out of my shock-induced stupor, I quickly unlock the door and deadbolt before she has a chance to change her mind and leave. Opening the door wide, I stand there, effectively blocking the door because I can't take my eyes off her. She looks so fucking good. Even as I'm filled with fear at the idea of what she has to say to me, the fact that she's up and walking around, looking so much like the version of her that existed before that terrible day, makes me want to drop to my knees and thank whoever is upstairs for saving her.

After a few moments of silence, she pushes past me into the apartment. Closing and locking the door behind her, I turn to find her staring at me.

She looks me straight in the eyes and says, "So you're a thief." It's a statement, not a question.

The room is so quiet, I wonder if she can hear how hard my heart's beating. This is the moment of truth. I knew eventually I'd have to do this. Come clean to her about everything. Explain myself and my actions over the last nine years. Longer than that, if you counted what I had to do to survive before I met her.

Even though I'm terrified of her response, I can't lie to her anymore. Staring back at her, I reply, "Yes, but I can explain."

Her eyes, those eyes that first ensnared me all those years ago, look back at me with piercing intensity. "How long?"

"As long as you've known me. Longer." Glancing down, I give a small shake of my head. I'm not ashamed of *most* of the things I've done. But I know that I'm only going to get one chance at this, and I need her to understand what brought me here. To understand what made me this way. So far, she hasn't turned around and walked back out the door she just came through. I think she wants to hear me out, thank God. So I take a deep breath and begin to talk.

"Growing up, all I ever knew was fear. I was afraid of everything. It was both my worst enemy and my best friend. I had nothing else. Fear of my father, for the pain I knew at his hands. Fear of the unknowns in my life. How and when was I going to eat next? Were the authorities gonna find out what was going on in my house and take me out, only to put me someplace worse? Every day, I lived in fear."

Meeting her eyes again, I continue, "I got tired of being a scared little boy. Of allowing other people to control my feelings and dictate how I lived my life. I knew if I wanted to better myself, I'd need money. You never really know how important it is unless you've had to live without it. I saw the way my father operated and the knack he had for manipulating people. But he always thought too small. Each con only got him so far. I knew I had to be better, to think bigger. First, I'd figure out how to feed myself, and then I'd teach myself everything I needed to know to be a higher class of criminal. In the beginning, it was just a matter of survival. Over time, that morphed into greed. I had a visceral need to have what others had and to have everything my father neglected to give me. So I stole." I give a small shrug. "And I was good at it. As I got older, my skills got better, and my scores became bigger. When people started asking questions about the mastermind behind these jobs, someone gave me the moniker. To this day, I still don't know who. I met Deacon, and for the first time in my life, I had someone I could trust at my back. We looked out for each other. I was content with that. I thought I was happy. Then I met you."

Pausing, swallowing past the lump that's suddenly formed in my throat, I take a step closer to her, encouraged when she doesn't take a step back in response. Reaching her, I bring my hands up to frame her face, saying, "You walked into that room and looked at me with these eyes." I run my thumb over her cheek beneath one of the eyes in question. "They were so bright when they met mine, but I could see a darkness beneath that called to my own. Then your mother said something to you, and with one blink, the darkness nearly snuffed out the light. I knew that if manipulated in just the right way, that light would shine brighter than any jewel I'd ever stolen. I wanted to be the reason behind that light, but the timing wasn't right. You were young, and aside from a sizable nest egg, I had nothing to offer you. Family drama and emotional baggage. I knew, no matter how much I wanted it to be otherwise, that I couldn't just reach out and take you like I did with everything else. So I waited."

Expression inscrutable, she finally says, "Nine years. You waited nine years. What took you so long? Why not when I turned 18? I wanted you;

you had to know that. Was it the money? Because you know I don't care about that."

"It wasn't just the money. Yes, that was part of it, but that wasn't everything. When our parents got married, I knew that if either of them ever got wind of my feelings for you, they'd use you against me. Especially my father. I couldn't risk you becoming collateral damage in a war that began years before I ever even met you. We had to be free of them, before I could take that step." Scoffing at myself, I say, "I hate that you ended up getting stuck in the crosshairs anyway. I tried so hard, for nine years, I held you at arm's length while I gathered as much evidence as I could against both of them. I had no intention of touching you until they were put away for good. I didn't want the blood that covered their hands to stain any part of the new life I had planned for us."

"Planned for us? How could you make plans for us without even asking me if it was what I wanted?" she asks incredulously. Pulling away from me, she begins to pace back and forth. This isn't going at all how I planned. I can feel the panic bubbling up inside me, threatening to spill over. "What if I'd said no? Better yet, what if someone had come along, swept me off my feet, and I fell in love with *them*? Would you have just *taken* me then?"

I can feel the dark mask of possession overtaking my face. I know she can see it in my eyes. "Yes. You were mine. You've always been mine."

"And I'm just supposed to be okay with all of this? With you being a fucking cat burglar? Sneaking into people's homes and stealing their valuables??"

I let out a little laugh at her use of the term "cat burglar". Jerking her head toward me, the look she gives me would burn another man alive. I can feel her gearing up for what I'm sure will be a glorious tirade, but before she can go off on me, I reach out and still her pacing with my hands on her shoulders. Looking down at her with a grin still playing at the corners of my mouth, I say, "God, you're so beautiful."

Glaring at me, she replies, "Don't even think about kissing me."

The hint of a grin turns into a full-blown smile. Shaking my head, remembering her nasty right hook and not wanting to get hit in the face again, or worse, have her hurt herself while trying to knock me out, I don't try to kiss her just yet. Instead, my expression turning somber, I tell her, "It's true. I've lied to you about a lot of things. But please believe me when I tell you that I love you. From the moment you walked into that parlor all those years ago, in your scuffed Converse and your face smudged with paint, I've been in love with you. At the time, I didn't recognize the emotion for what it was because I'd never experienced it before. I was too young when my mother died to really remember that feeling. In the beginning, I thought what I felt for you was just an obsession, and in many ways, it was. You haunted me, day in and day out. I ate, slept, and breathed you. That obsession only grew stronger over the years, to the point that I knew it would be you or it would be no one. So, I began to slowly curate a life for us, one piece at a time. Not once did I entertain a reality where you and I didn't end up together. You're it for me. You always have been. So yes, I'm a thief. But for once, there's something that I want to own without having to steal it. Your heart. The real one. I need you to give it to me freely."

By the time I'm finished, tears are spilling from her eyes. I honestly can't tell if she's moved by what I said or if what I'm seeing are tears of regret; and she's going to walk out of that door any minute and out of my life for good. Looking up at me, she whispers, "I can't give you something that's already yours. You didn't need to steal it; it always belonged to you. I love you so much. You may have seen yourself as a black knight, but you've always been my savior. I don't care that you're a thief. I don't care about the sins of your past. I just want your future."

Letting out a laugh that sounds slightly maniacal, I try my best to be gentle as I pull her into my arms, burying my face in her neck and just breathing her in. Pulling back slightly, I ask, "Will you come somewhere with me? I wanna show you something the way it was meant to be seen."

As we drive down the dirt road, towering oaks covered with Spanish moss close us in from both sides. I see Amelia fidget in the seat beside me. Reaching out with the hand that isn't in control of the steering wheel, I take her left hand and thread our fingers together, resting them on my thigh.

"Don't be nervous. I promise you, it won't feel the same as last time," I say, giving her an apologetic smile.

Nodding, she doesn't say anything until we reach the end of the drive-way, and the large house comes into view. Within the last few weeks, while I was wallowing in a pool of my own misery, landscapers have been out to the house. The lawn and gardens have been transformed. Large weeping willows have been planted around the house, creating the perfect amount of shade for a family picnic ... when the time comes. Pulling up the circular drive, I stop in front of the house. Releasing Amelia's hand, I step out and go around the car to help her out. I don't want her hurting herself in any way.

Capturing her hand in mine again, I gently tug her up the short flight of stairs to the wrap-around front porch. She glances left and right, up and down, taking in the details she missed the first time. A small smile touches her lips when her eyes land on the two wooden rocking chairs facing out into the yard. Taking my keys from my pocket, I unlock the front door, pushing it wide. She walks up to the door but sticks only her head in. Looking around, she brings her head back out, then hesitates on the doorstep, almost as though she's afraid to go in. I feel a sharp pang in my chest. I wish I could see into her head. I can't tell if she doesn't want to enter because what happened here before somehow tainted it for her or if she has lingering PTSD from what my father did to her the last time she stepped into a dark and empty house.

Not wanting to rush her, I step inside first, leaving the door open and letting her take her time in deciding whether she wants to come in or not. Eventually, she gingerly steps inside. Sunlight spills in from the open door behind her, creating almost a halo effect. Standing there in awe, it's at this exact moment that I have the epiphany that this woman saved my life. There isn't a single doubt in my mind that without the obsession she provoked in me years ago, I'd be dead now. She gave me something to live for. Proved to me that there was true good in the world, not just pain. I can never repay her for what she's done. The best I can do is try to be a light for her, leading her out of the darkness whenever its sneaky hands tug at the hem of her consciousness. Standing there in the foyer of *our* home, I'm struck dumb at the realization that this is the first day of the rest of our lives. The first day that she's truly mine with nothing more standing in the way of our future. Holding my hand out for hers, I wait until I see the moment she makes up her mind to trust me in this. Slipping her hand in mine, she lets me lead her through the first room. As we walk, she stops frequently to look at individual pieces of art. Sometimes her own, sometimes pieces I've taken over the years that reminded me of her or that I thought she'd like. Not to say that this entire house is only a representation of her. There were also paintings and sculptures that I just greedily wanted for myself. She inspects each one, marveling at the fact that they're here, in front of her, instead of hanging on the walls of some stuffy museum. As we make our way through the house, eventually, we reach the bedroom where she found me the first time. I meant what I said to her before. It doesn't feel the same as last time. This time, I know she's in this room with me. This time, I have nothing left to hide. The weight of my secrets has been lifted, and as she looks at the painting she did in her studio all those weeks ago, of the two of us wrapped up in each other, I can tell that she's seeing it through fresh eyes as well.

As much as I wanna stay in this room with her and recreate what's happening in that painting, it's the next room I want her to see the most. The last time she was here, she found me in our bedroom, so she never got to go down the hall and open the door next to ours.

"Let me show you the next room. I think it will be your favorite," I say, nerves making my voice waver slightly.

She gives me a quizzical look but doesn't argue as she follows me back out of the bedroom and down the hallway to the closed door a little ways down. Stepping back, I gesture for her to open the door. She looks wary but reaches for the handle anyway. Pushing the door open, she stands in the doorway, her beautiful mouth forming a perfect O. I laugh under my breath because her reaction is almost comical. Suddenly, all the nerves that I'd built up leading to this room melt away. I knew she would love it. Slowly walking inside, she takes in the scene. Unlike the rest of the house, which sits mostly empty, this room is fully furnished. Walking over, she runs her hand along the top rung of the cherry-wood crib before moving over to the rocking chair that sits in the corner with a stuffed rabbit in its seat. Picking up the plush little toy, she sits in the chair, gliding back and forth, clutching the rabbit to her chest. For a split second, I blink, and the rabbit is a baby, and I'm watching my wife nurse our child. The imaginary scene causes a knot to form in the back of my throat. While I try to compose myself, Amelia stands and, still carrying the rabbit, looks around the room and at the shelves already filled with children's books and little nick-nacks.

Looking at me, she asks, "Did you hire someone to decorate this room?"

Shaking my head, I say, "No. I chose everything in this room myself. Spanning the course of years, I picked out every item here." Nerves returning, I say, "But if there's something you wanna change, you can. We can get rid of everything if you want and start fresh."

Shaking her head, she does another quick sweep of the room before returning her eyes to me. When they meet mine, I see that hers have turned glassy with unshed tears.

"How could you love me this much?" she asks, her voice filled with wonder.

"How could I not?" I reply simply.

Laughing, even as tears track down her cheeks, she throws her arms around my neck, pulling me close. We stand there for a long time, her still holding onto the rabbit in one hand. Pulling up an invisible calendar in my mind, I mark the date.

Day 1 of forever.

EPILOGUE

Merrick

5 MONTHS LATER

Amelia was anxious. She kept twisting the large emerald on the ring finger of her left hand. It was a nervous tell. One that I'd come to recognize. Since the day I'd slipped the ring onto her finger and made her my wife, she'd spin it around and around anytime anxiety got the better of her. I guess it was good, in a way. If she was spinning it, there was little chance of it falling off or being lost and her not noticing. At the same time, I hated that she felt the need to spin it as much as she did. The ring in question had been quite difficult to come by. Before becoming the tie used to bind us together, it hadn't been seen for a good number of years. It and its six accompanying pieces had once belonged to Elizabeth Taylor and had last sold at auction for $23,000,000 to a private collector. The majority of the collection was rather ostentatious. Not something a good little Southern girl would wear to small friend and family gatherings. But the ring was a different matter. I knew Amelia loved old black-and-white films. She loved everything to do with the golden age of Hollywood. So even before we were officially a couple, I'd "acquired" the set. After I'd shown her some of the other items tucked safely away in the home we now shared, I came to find that Amelia actually had a very good eye for gems. When I'd proposed, and she'd seen the ring, her first reaction had been reverence. At its beauty, its history. She'd insisted that she couldn't possibly wear it out in public, but she'd still let me put it on her finger and for the rest of the night, she couldn't stop glancing down at where it set heavy on her left hand. Despite her protests to the contrary, she'd never taken it off again. Seeing it on her hand had caused a very similar reaction in me. Reverence. Even now, I still sat back and marveled at how lucky I was. I'd been a poor boy from a broken home who'd done unimaginable things to claw my way out, and this woman still wanted to be with me. Looking over at her now, I watch as she spins the ring around her finger a few more times. Reaching my hand over, I capture hers in mine, effectively stilling her movements.

"Everything's gonna be fine. Don't worry. Whatever happens, we'll deal with it. Together," I say, my tone conveying a confidence I don't entirely feel. But I also don't want her to worry over problems that aren't really problems yet.

She chews on her bottom lip. Another nervous tell. "But what if something goes wrong? What if they check it and there's nothing there? What if we made a mistake?"

Bordering on hysteria now, I take her other hand and turn her to face me in the seats lining the walls. "Mia, calm down. Nothing is gonna go wrong. We know why we're here, and that's simply to confirm what we already know to be true."

She nods, though I'm not entirely sure she's even listening to the words coming out of my mouth, so I open it again, not actually sure what I'm going to say next. My words, however, are cut off when an elderly lady wearing purple scrubs and carrying a clipboard enters the room.

Glancing around, she says, "Mrs. Stratford? Amelia Stratford?"

I have to close my eyes briefly because I honestly don't think I'll ever get tired of the way that sounds. Opening them again, I help Amelia gather her sling bag, and we follow the nurse to a small room where the lights have been dimmed to almost pitch black. The only light available is coming from several screens and monitors on rolling carts. The equipment looks complicated and if I'm honest, a little scary. As the nurse hands Amelia a paper gown and gives her instructions, I try to make myself as unobtrusive as possible. The last thing I needed was for them to try to have me thrown out for being in the way. And if it came to that, they'd have a hell of a fight on their hands because there was no fucking way I was leaving. Where my wife goes, I follow.

As the nurse exits, thankfully ignoring my presence in the corner, I move over to a chair near the bed. Amelia is lying on the table with my hand in hers when the doctor walks in. After a few pleasantries and the answering of some questions Amelia and I had, he gets to work. Rolling up the paper gown, the doctor exposes her abdomen. Squirting some blue-tinted goop onto the end of what looks like the tool you'd use to find studs in drywall, he places it on Amelia's stomach.

At first, nothing happens, and for a split second, I have the terrible fear that Amelia was right. We did make a mistake. But then ... a sound comes over the monitor.

Thump, thump, thump. It's fast but steady and strong. Looking over at Amelia, I watch the way she looks at the monitor, transfixed.

"Would you like a few pictures and a sound recording to take home with you?" the doctor asks.

"YES!" we both say in unison. Amelia laughs, but it's the type of watery laugh you let out when you're also on the verge of crying. Watching the doctor finish up, he hands me a few printed pictures and says he'll have the audio file sent to us via a download link in an email. When he leaves, telling Amelia that she can clean up and get dressed now, he also leaves the monitor on, whether by accident or on purpose; I don't know. But as Amelia looks over at me with those beautiful green eyes full of wonder and a deep abiding love for something that's barely even in existence yet, I listen to the audio loop playing on the monitor.

Thump, thump, thump.

"Some things change, while others stay the same," I say, leaning up to place a kiss on her belly.

Giving me a puzzled expression, she says, "What do you mean?"

"It's still you, me, and this heartbeat, except now, it's *this* heartbeat," I say.

Catching a tear that rolls down her cheek, she laughs a watery laugh. I smile back in return and open my mental calendar.

Day 153 of forever.

Want more?

TURN THE PAGE FOR A
SNEAK PEEK INTO THE
NEXT BOOK IN THE *THICK
AS THIEVES* SERIES.

PROLOGUE

Siren

Somewhere in my foggy brain, I register the sound of music. That, in itself, isn't unusual. I hear music in my head all the time. Music has been an integral part of my life for as long as I can remember. Being the daughter of affluent—albeit neglectful—parents meant being exposed to many of the finer things in life. But in terms of music, I think I felt the beauty of it long before I came to recognize the part it played in cultural status. It didn't matter if it was classics played to a packed house by a full orchestra or a street performer playing blues music for three or four people on the corner; If it was done well, music of any kind could be transcendent. It was that connection to instruments, lyrics, and composition that led me to my chosen profession as a violinist with the Charleston Symphony. So it would be safe to say that music has always been a part of who I am. I, like most people, had my favorite pieces. Each one evoked different emotions within me, which was why I loved music so much.

As I try to open my bleary eyes and bring my consciousness back online from whatever is causing the confusion clouding my mind, the first emotion I feel is fear. As my brain clears and the music begins to register, I realize that I recognize the piece. It's Bach's Chaconne. A hauntingly beautiful work of art that I used to adore. Now, the sound of it causes absolute terror to coarse through my veins like battery acid. I haven't heard this piece in years. I haven't wanted to. This particular song was associated with the best and worst years of my life. Years that I wished I could wipe from my memory, but, unfortunately, you couldn't do that when the scars of the past weren't only figurative but literal.

I feel so confused. I don't know why I would've put this song on. And I don't know why I'm having such a hard time focusing on anything other than the panic associated with the music. This has happened a few times in the past. In the early days, I'd unerringly hear the song and immediately dissolve into a full-blown panic attack. It's taken me a long time to come to terms with the horrors of my past, and a lot of that came only with the knowledge that I'd survived.

Fighting to shake myself awake, I wonder if I'm stuck in another nightmare. They've plagued me off and on for years. Ever since I escaped from that Hell on Earth, that had once been a fantasy come to life. Forcing my eyes open, I blink hard to adjust my vision to the darkness that surrounds me. The music is loud now. Maybe it's been loud this entire time, and I was just too out of it to notice. The piece seems to swell in time with my anxiety as my vision clears, and I'm able to take in more details of the room around me. It's difficult to see, even with the blurry film gone from my eyes, because the light is dim. Some things register immediately, however.

I'm in a bed, but it's not my own. In a room that's not my own. In a house that's not my own. I don't recognize anything in this room, but whoever owns it clearly has money. Every piece of furniture is ornate and ostentatious. It reminds me of the furniture I lived with growing up. Lifting my arm, I bring my hand up to rub my eyes, but I feel like my entire body is working on a delay. Fighting to sit up, I feel like I'm underwater, struggling to kick my way to the surface. The pressure on my chest is immense, but that's probably the oncoming panic attack. I feel as though my heart is beating a mile a minute. Racking my brain, I try to recall what I was doing before this. The last thing I remember was texting Amelia before going to sleep, but that was in my own bed. I have no idea how I got to wherever I am now, and the unknowns are causing all sorts of crazy scenarios to run rampant in my mind. Squinting, I wish I could locate a lamp or light switch somewhere so I could take in more of the room surrounding me. Maybe I could get a better idea of where I am and how I got here.

"Hello, mia Sirena."

Feeling the blood in my veins freeze, every other part of my body immediately follows suit. That voice. It's a voice from my nightmares. A voice that I never thought I'd have to hear in real life ever again. No, no, no, no. It's not possible. He's dead. I killed him. I watched the blood drain from his body. Gaze tracking the voice, I see a large figure sitting in an armchair in the corner of the room. It's only now that my senses register something else. Something they hadn't before. The smell of cigar smoke. A very distinct cigar. As I watch, the figure brings the cigar to his mouth, the bright orange glow on the end momentarily illuminating a face that haunts me, but one that I thought was dead and buried. Feeling my insides begin to tremble, those tremors soon turn to full body shakes.

"You don't look happy to see me, Bella." the voice croons. "Did you think I'd let you go that easily? You should know me better than that."

Pulling my knees to my chest, I blink past the tears now streaming down my face. If I'm here and that voice is real, no one will know where to find me. By the time they even realize I'm gone, there'll be no saving me. I won't be lucky enough to make it out alive twice. Once was a fluke, but twice would be defying fate. That voice once told me that he was my destiny. Has anyone ever spit in the face of destiny and lived to tell the tale? I thought I did—once. I guess I was wrong. It looks like destiny has caught up with me. I want so badly to dissociate. To revert to the coping mechanism that used to get me through moments, hours, and days of misery. But my flight or fight responses are on full alert. Without moving a muscle, my eyes track the distance of the door relative to where I am and where he is. If I'm fast enough, I might make it. I wasn't always fast enough before. Those nights were among many where I wished I was dead. If I don't make it to the door before he catches me, I know how quickly I can be back there. After nearly three years of waiting, I can only imagine the pain he has in store for me. I have to run, to get as far away from here as I can. To hide, until I can figure out how any of this is possible and how I can fix it. I can't afford to fall apart right now, as much as I'd like to.

The voice from the corner comes again. "I don't like the pictures you've put all over your body, Sirena. It's almost as though you were trying to cover my art. My signature, painstakingly written over and over in your flesh. How are people going to know who you belong to now?" Making a tsking sound, he says, "I can't have people thinking they can touch what's mine. I suppose I'll just have to redo all my hard work. It will hurt me ... and you ... but you brought this on yourself."

Releasing a sob, I bury my face in my hands. I shouldn't cry. I know he likes it. But I can't stop myself. The iron grip that this man has had over my life reaches far beyond the six years I spent with him in Hell. The only thing that kept me alive was when my pain turned to rage. The fear was always there, but, at that point, I'd had nothing to live for and, therefore, nothing to lose. I would either get away or die in the process. I'd gotten away. I remind myself now that I'd gotten away. I could do it again. Making a split-second decision, I spring from the bed, thanking God that the man was arrogant enough not to believe that I should be tied down. Sprinting in the direction of the door, I hear movement behind me. Knowing he's coming, I race the handful of feet to the door, blessedly reaching it first. Blindly gripping the knob, I turn it quickly, jerking the door open only a few inches before an impossibly large palm slaps against the door directly next to my face, effectively slamming it closed again. At the same time, a hand roughly grips my hair in a punishing fist, pushing my face hard against the wood as a massive body presses into me from behind.

Mouth close to my ear, I feel his breath a second before the tip of his tongue darts out, running along the length of the shell. Hissing through gritted teeth, he grinds himself into me from behind, and I can feel the hardness that he's not even attempting to disguise. I meant it when I said he liked to hear me cry. He liked to hear me scream, too. Even knowing that, terror has my mouth opening on a high-pitched wail that's abruptly cut off when my head is jerked back sharply and then slammed into the hardwood of the door. As I see spots swim before my eyes and feel my body begin to slump downward, I hear a deep chuckle followed by a whisper.

"Haven't you learned by now, Bella? You'll never escape me. Even when you thought you were free, you were just on a longer leash. We'll have to start back at the beginning of our training, I see."

As another louder and more sinister laugh escapes him, he eases back enough to allow me to fall to the floor in a heap. That laugh is the last thing I hear before blackness takes me. Not for the first time, I pray that I don't ever wake up.

About the Author

Candice Clark is an avid romance reader-turned-writer who lives in South Carolina with her man-child husband and small daughter, who her mother always warned would be just like her. She was right.

In addition to writing, she works full-time, owns an Etsy bakery, and has a thousand other hobbies that allow her to complain about how stressed out and stretched thin she is.

She's a down-to-earth, middle-aged woman who feels 97 most days and suffers from chronic pain and massive anxiety. She hopes to use these challenges to write relatable characters with relatable personalities in an effort to help improve the real-life perception of mental health struggles.

Beginning her reading journey as an early teen with titan authors like Nora Roberts and Johanna Lindsey, she is excited about combining classic writing styles and plotting with the more edgy subject matter commonly found in today's Indie Author Community.

Made in the USA
Columbia, SC
15 September 2024

011135f0-0ab4-4217-91b6-f3a15e6a8e50R01